Other books by Kirt Hickman

Worlds Asunder

Worlds Asunder
Venus Rain
Mercury Sun

Age of Prophecy

Fabler's Legend
Assassins' Prey
Host of Evil

Nonfiction

Revising Fiction: Making Sense of the Madness

For Children

I Will Eat Anything

FABLER'S LEGEND

AGE OF PROPHECY: BOOK 1

All is legal in the fight against evil. . .

Kirt Hickman

QP Quillrunner
Publishing

Published in the U.S.A. by
Quillrunner Publishing LLC
Albuquerque, NM

Printed in the U.S.A.

Cover art by Don Dyer

Book design by Janice Phelps Williams
Typeset in: Iowan Old 11/15, Mrs Eaves Italic 13/14, Vahalla

Cataloging-in-Publications Data is on file with the Library of Congress.
Library of Congress Control Number: 2011925076

ISBN 978-0-9796330-6-5

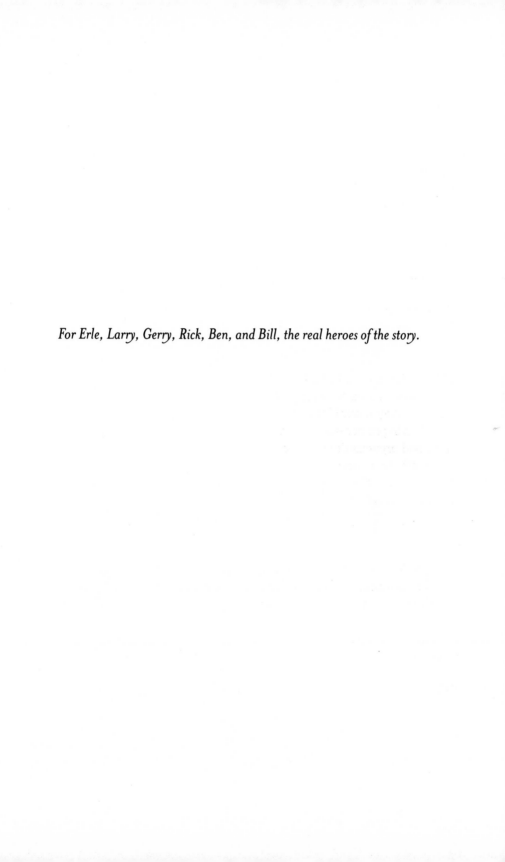

For Erle, Larry, Gerry, Rick, Ben, and Bill, the real heroes of the story.

ACKNOWLEDGMENTS

A book like this can't be created by one person alone. It took the tireless effort of many people to make *Fabler's Legend* a reality. My thanks go out to all of you.

To Erle Guillermo, Gerry Raban, Ben Valerine, Larry Koch, Rick McLaughlin, and Bill Birchler for your assistance in developing such a dynamic plot.

To my network of critiquers and test readers: Erle Guillermo, Gerry Raban, Laura Beltemacchi, Lisa Hickman, Ben Valerine, Larry Koch, and others. Special thanks to Nancy Varian for catching the things that the rest of us didn't.

To my editor, Susan Grossman, for ensuring that *Fabler's Legend* is the best that it can be.

To all my peers at SouthWest Writers, for your constant moral and technical support. I've learned so much.

To Don Dyer and Janice Phelps Williams, for exceeding all my expectations for book and cover design.

To my wife, Lisa, for giving me the time and encouragement to begin, to endure, and to finally complete *Fabler's Legend*. I couldn't have done it without you.

And most of all, to God for blessing me with the necessary time and talents.

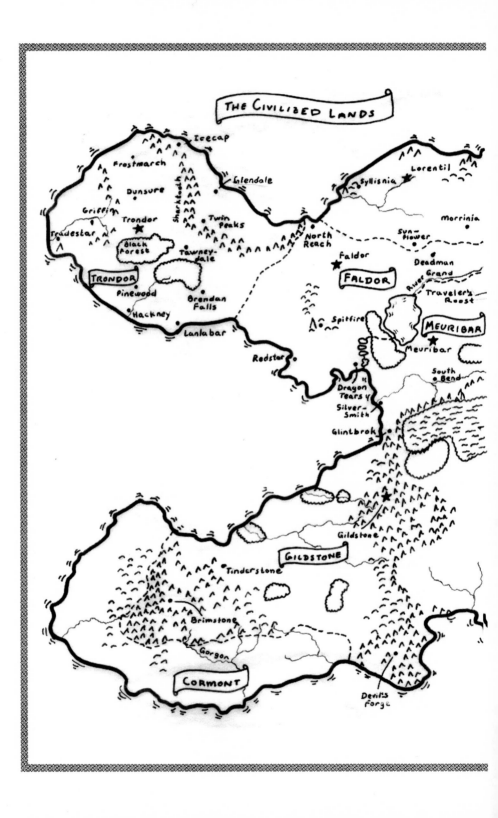

PROLOGUE

Allushen the Taleweaver sat cross-legged, onstage, in the smoky taproom of the Wicked Sailor alehouse after having refilled the incense burners smoldering at the front corners of the stage. The mixture filled the barroom with a thick pall of fragrant smoke, stifling the usual odors of stale mead, vomit, and unwashed bodies. Within minutes, the haze became so thick he could no longer see the far wall, but that didn't matter. His audience wouldn't be watching him during his performance anyway.

The customary clamor of rowdy drunks was absent from the Wicked Sailor that night. Oh, the patrons had consumed their fill of alcohol, to be sure. Their sedate mood was an effect of the peculiar blend of scullcap, salvia, chamomile, and other herbs burning in the incense bowls, a mixture that also encouraged the loosening of purse strings and contributed markedly to the collection of coins littering the stage.

He surveyed the crowd before beginning his final tale of the evening, a prophecy of darkness, the ominous future foreseen by the great seer Mortaan at the beginning of the current age. The legend, known now as the Last Prophecy of Mortaan, foretold the end of the Age of Prophecy and entered the nightmares of every civilized person who believed in the power of divination.

He began his narrative in a clear, resonant voice. As he spoke, an image formed in his mind.

A black-haired peasant, a mere boy, progressed in age through scene after unremarkable scene until he reached the age of maybe seven harvests. Then the immortal Vexetan, a god of immense form, with six tusks protruding from a fang-laden face the color of rotten cheese, appeared to the boy as he wandered alone in the woods.

Vexetan spoke to him in low, murmuring tones, and bestowed upon him a headband—or perhaps a crown—woven from human sinew. As he did so, the tip of the god's finger touched the back of the boy's head, causing a patch of his hair to wither and whiten. The medallion that adorned the front of the crown began to glow, brighter and brighter, until the entire scene became an intense, brilliant white.

When the image cleared, the boy was much older, nearing adulthood. The white lock of hair remained at his nape, but the crown and medallion were either gone or just hidden away.

The anointed man, as he moved through life, beguiled everyone he spoke to, bringing himself personal power and significant wealth. He didn't flaunt his riches, however, but hoarded them away for sometime in the future. Finally, his ability to charm intensified until none could refuse his will.

Then he gave back to those he favored, awarding medallions of onyx and gold to the ones he chose to use, medallions that matched the one given him by the dark lord Vexetan. When his time came, he donned once again the sinew crown and began to exert his will over those he had subverted.

The scene changed and Allushen described what he saw. These were not precognitive visions, however. Allushen was no prophet. He simply knew the story so well that his mind preceded his voice in the telling, and the hallucinogen burning in the bowls enabled him to bring it to life in the weave around him. This was his secret, the reason he had become a legend in the art of legends. He coaxed each scene into vivid realism for his audience. His voice delivered it vibrantly to their ears and the incense produced the illusion in their minds.

A goblin slave, toiling in a field of barley under a blazing sun, rose from the stalks with a sword in his hand. He turned it upon his warder and ran whooping through the field. Weapons appeared in the hands of his fellows as well. Together, they stormed their master's home, murdering everyone inside and burning the structure to its clay foundation. The scene replayed itself in a multitude of settings, with subtle variations of detail but always the same result.

Pastures, forests, and mountains flew past as Allushen swept his audience northward to a kingdom in chaos, where an army of men gathered near a hill under a baron's banner.

All at once, a horn's blast split the crisp morning air, followed by the roar of ten thousand men as they raised their weapons and stormed the hill, engaging the enemy who waited. The battle raged on as the sun set and rose and set again. Seasons changed, and still the struggle continued. At last, the screams of the dying faded and the dust of battle settled to the ground. The baron stood over the body of the enemy he'd defeated, an enemy whose face might have been his own.

The image dissolved into a scene of sweltering sunlight, palpable and sticky. Vexetan himself sat upon a moving sea of sand with a steaming pot the size of a tinker's wagon nestled in his immense lap. The ground around him began to boil and a host of demons poured forth from the cauldron into the unsuspecting world of men.

The peasant boy appeared now as a man who'd come into his full power. He stood upon a mountain, cloaked in black, with his arms spread wide and his head thrown back, the medallion blazing upon his forehead. Three armies flowed down from the mountain and engulfed the surrounding countryside, sweeping away the civilized masses who stood to oppose them.

Out of the setting sun flew a mighty dragon who, in a single breath, consumed the entire nightmare in flame.

"So will begin the Age of Darkness," Allushen intoned, "as it has been foretold."

CHAPTER 1

Nicklan Mirrin frowned at the old woman. It was late in the day and her wagon was still laden with wares. "Three." He held the copper coins in his open palm. Seeing them would make her want them all the more. A half-pound jug of raw honey sat on a barrel between them.

"Four." She thrust out her chin and her eyes hardened in her wrinkled face.

"You sold me the same size jug for three last month."

"Long winter. You pay four."

"I can't afford four. I still have things to buy."

"I tell you what," the old woman said after a moment's hesitation. "You buy full pound. I give you for six."

Nick guffawed. "I don't have four. What makes you think I can pay six?"

But the old woman stood firm. She might have been a statue carved from a tree stump. Nick knew the type, and he'd been on the opposite end of the sale often enough to know she wasn't as needy as she claimed to be.

He glanced again at her brimming wagon. "Ah, forget it. Like you said, it's been a long winter. Honey's a luxury we can't afford." After pocketing his coins, he walked across the packed-earth aisle of the Cedar Falls weekend market and examined the cooking utensils in the tent there, utensils he had no intention of buying.

When he emerged a few minutes later, the old woman held up the honey and waved Nick back to her. "You buy something every week. I tell you what. Today I give you half pound for three."

"Free?" Nick said, playing the game.

"Three! Three!" She poked three bony digits into the air. "You pay three."

Nick scrubbed his chin. He'd already told her he didn't need the honey. He could probably talk her down to two, but that wouldn't leave her much coin to live on. "All right." He surrendered the copper and stuffed the jug into his bulging pack.

"Next time four," she shouted as he walked away.

Nick was no longer listening. In front of him, a trio of young boys, playing swords, waved sticks at one another until a man wearing the green vest of the village watch started making shooing motions at them.

"Out of the aisle before you hurt someone," the watchman said.

The boys raised their sticks as if to challenge him. He gripped the pommel of his own sword and ran at them, growling, his face contorted in mock rage.

Laughing, the children fluttered between the booths and ran off.

They'd grow up and learn to play swords for real someday. Their innocence would fade quickly then. They wouldn't laugh so easily.

And maybe someday Nick would have kids of his own, whom he could play stick-swords with, growl at, and chase around, laughing. For now, though, he was content to just help his folks work the family farm.

He perused the remaining tables and booths, threading his way through the throng of villagers, merchants, gypsies, and roughnecks. The majority of the crowd wore homespun tunics and trousers much like Nick's own. Only the great sword he wore across his back set him apart. Though nearly everyone carried some kind of weapon, most preferred smaller, more discrete arms.

Finally, Nick came to the colorful tent that anchored the row of merchants: Madam Grenda, the fortuneteller. By then he'd purchased everything on his list with a few silver coins to spare.

"Nick!" his friend Zen, whom he'd met at the market several months before, called from a few aisles over. The mage waved his staff, a gnarled branch of walnut polished near the top by the oils from Zen's hand over years, perhaps decades, of use. His cloak of fine blue-gray fabric shimmered in the sunlight.

Nick waved the mage over. Though Zen's elven blood made his age difficult to determine, he must have seen at least ten harvests beyond Nick's twenty—if for no other reason than the extent of Zen's travels, assuming all of his stories were true. At times, though, his lack of maturity made him seem like he was barely out of adolescence.

Not that this bothered Nick. He just figured it was part of the maturity cycle of Zen's longer-lived elven half. Besides, Zen was the only friend he had who'd traveled enough to relate to Nick's own stories of adventure.

Zen, his mustache and beard trimmed to nothing more than a fashionable frame for his delicate features, greeted Nick with a bounce in his step. "I made my first construct yesterday."

"Construct?"

"A being of pure ice. It was small, no bigger than this." He waved one hand over the other and, with a spark of clear blue light, produced a chunk of ice the size of his fist. "But it moved and everything."

"I've seen you create whole animals of ice."

"Yeah, but for those I borrowed the life force of other living things.

This was different: a creature created wholly from the magic of the weave, and from the realm where ice itself lives." He moved his hand as though the ice in it was hopping toward Nick's face and emitted a ghostly sound. "*Oo-oo-oo-oo.*"

Nick knocked the ice away. "All right. I get it." He pointed to the fortuneteller's tent. "Let's go in."

"You go ahead. I'm out of coin."

"I'll buy." Nick grabbed a fistful of Zen's sleeve and pulled him inside.

Madam Grenda, a large woman with a long mane of curly red hair, mature features, and an ample bosom, sat alone at a small table, twirling a jeweled dagger in her hands. Her tight-fitting, red-and-gold blouse exposed significant cleavage in the sunlight that filtered through the colorful fabric of the roof.

"Come, gentlemen. Sit down." Grenda collected two silver coins and stowed them with the blade somewhere beneath the table. She plucked a deck of fortune cards from near her elbow and shuffled them. "Silence, please."

The woman spent several minutes chanting and manipulating the deck ceremoniously before laying out several cards, one at a time, and issuing her first prediction. "Determination is your path to success," she told Nick.

It was a typical fortune and just about what he'd expected. One could accomplish almost anything with little more than prudence, practicality, and hard work. He was hoping for something more specific. "What about girls? Do you see any girls in my future?"

She smiled, placed her hands on her breasts, and jiggled them. "If you want the girls, they'll cost you extra."

Nick looked at his boots and mumbled a polite rejection.

"Don't you worry, Nick Mirrin. Handsome boy like you, built like you are. Especially with your blond hair, rare as it is in these parts." She patted his cheek. "You'll do fine."

"And you, my magely friend." She chanted over her cards once again and drew several out onto the table. "Oh." She looked up at Zen's face, then back down at the cards.

"What is it?" Zen asked.

Madam Grenda hesitated. "This says your heart is dark and empty, that you will know joy, but only after you've faced the specter of deeds gone wrong." With that, she fell into silence.

Nick thanked her. He rose and followed Zen from the tent. "That was ominous."

Zen shrugged. "She's a charlatan."

"Maybe. But a dark and empty heart?" Nick thought about the time he and Zen had spent together. The mage seemed childish at times, but dark and empty? He shook the idea aside. Zen was anything but dark and empty.

As the two stepped into the crowded plaza, a rude villager shoved Nick against the corner of Grenda's pavilion. The ox of a man stood a head taller than Nick's own height of six feet, with matted black hair and filthy clothes that stank of the man inside them. The whole thing might have been an accident until he placed a hand against Nick's chest to hold him there. A heavy work hammer swung like a pendulum in his hand.

Zen kept walking, apparently unaware that he and Nick had become separated. Within moments, the crowd enveloped him.

"What's your problem?" Nick asked the brute.

The man brandished his fist, upon which metal studs protruded from the knuckles of a fingerless leather glove.

Nick tried to move. His sword had become wedged between his backpack and the corner pole of Grenda's tent, where he couldn't easily draw it. Even if he could, he had no intention of swinging a sword that size in the crowded market. "I'm out of coin, if that's what you're after."

The man moved his face closer, his breath foul in Nick's nostrils, and said nothing.

Several villagers stopped to see if the confrontation would develop into something worth watching, until one women stepped forward with a cutlass in her hand. She was older than Nick by at least half a dozen harvests and had a severe aspect to her features that hinted at a hard life. Her black hair was pulled up behind her head, but strands stuck out at odd angles, as though they hated the confinement. "Hey, you. Tough guy. Why don't you go pick on somebody who's as ugly and foul-smelling as you are?"

The ox looked her up and down, scowling. He glanced at her cutlass and at Nick, then sulked away to join a group of men loitering nearby. Each carried a makeshift weapon, one of which appeared to be the handle from a gardening hoe, broken off and whittled to a point at one end. Another held a pitchfork, while the third sported a small, battered shield that looked as though it had been discarded by a dwarf during the Age of Dragons and salvaged from the midden by its current wielder.

"You okay?" The woman asked Nick.

"Sure," he replied, more than a little embarrassed to have been rescued by a woman. "You know that guy?"

"I know the type. They back down as soon as somebody stands up to them. Name's Jade." She stuck out her hand, which he shook.

"Nick Mirrin."

"Really?" Jade gestured with her chin toward Madam Grenda's tent. "You believe in that sort of thing? Fortunes and such?"

"I don't know. I guess."

"I do. That's why I came here today. Just last week, Grenda told me I'd meet you here. Said we'd get along." Jade nudged him playfully, then became serious. "Actually, she said you could help me with a business venture."

"I don't know. I—"

"Walk with me." She squeezed past Grenda's tent and beckoned Nick to follow.

Zen had returned. He maintained a respectful distance, keeping an eye on the ox and his friends. Nick nodded once to him, then followed Jade into the sloped field beyond the market.

They walked in silence for a minute before Jade said, "You keep a journal, Nick?"

"No. Why?" He stopped. "What did Madam Grenda tell you, exactly?"

She shrugged. "How about your father or grandfather?"

"What?"

"You are Gaddy Mirrin's grandson. Aren't you?"

"Yeah, but..." Nick shook his head to clear it. The whole conversation seemed disconnected—unreal. "What do you know about my grandfather?"

Jade gave him a smile and started walking again. "He was a scholar, wasn't he?"

"Of sorts." Nick caught up to her. "He studied the prophecies of Mortaan. Why?"

"Well then, he must have kept notes."

"I guess. But that was a long time ago."

At the bottom of the hill, Jade stopped on the bank of Cedar Creek, little more than an ambling brook. "Does he still have it?"

Nick eyed her for a long moment before answering. "He's dead. I doubt my father—"

"Oh come on, Nick. A study of the end of civilization. You expect me to believe your family would lose such an important collection of knowledge?"

Nick hesitated. "What do you want with it? You offering to buy it?"

"No, but my employer..." She gave him a sly look. "We play this right, it could work out well for both of us."

Nick's eyes narrowed. The fog of hope that had clouded his perception since Jade had mentioned Madam Grenda was now gone. "Who are you?"

Just then, a short distance downstream, three men stepped from the trees, including the ox with the work hammer and two of his friends, those with the spear and the beat-up shield.

Before Nick could reach for his sword, Jade cut the thongs with her dagger and the sword fell, sheath and all, to the ground. Her cutlass rang clear of its own sheath. "You gullible child. If you haven't got that journal on you, you'd better think real hard about where it is, 'cause we're not leaving without it."

Nick stared, open-mouthed and weaponless. "You've got to be—"

"I have no desire to hurt you," Jade said. "But most of the time, Sledge couldn't care less about what I want." She inclined her head toward the ox with the hammer.

"I don't have any journal," Nick said. "I don't know anything about it."

A minute later, the trio of thugs surrounded him. He spun slowly, trying to keep them all in sight at once. Yet they didn't attack.

"Throw me your backpack," Jade demanded from outside the circle.

Nick worked the straps off his shoulders with sweaty hands and tossed the pack to her.

As soon as she had it, she upended it, scattering his purchases all over the ground. To her thugs, she said, "Keep him busy."

The man with the shield slammed Nick from behind and he stumbled forward. Before he could recover, the hoe-handle spear raked his side, leaving a tear in his shirt and a searing scrape across his flesh. Nick ignored these. Sledge was the real threat.

The ox swung his huge hammer in a wide, lumbering arc.

Nick sidestepped and the shield slammed him again. He swatted aside a jab from the wooden spear and elbowed the man who held it. After that, the attacks came in too fast and the pounding began to take its toll.

"Don't kill him yet," Jade shouted. "The journal's not here."

But it was too late. Sledge was out of control and the other two men were following his lead.

Zen used his staff to club the fourth thug, who had trailed Nick and the woman from the market. With a grunt, the man crumpled to the ground and lay still at Zen's feet.

"You there," Zen shouted from a short distance up the hill. "Hold fast!" He pointed the tip of his staff, he hoped threateningly, at Nick's attackers.

All three stopped, allowing Nick time to regain his footing and step away. The man with the spear decided to call Zen's bluff. He rushed up the hill, leaving his cohorts behind.

The woman gave Nick a long, measuring look and then pointed at Zen. "Don't just stand there. Kill him!" She raised her cutlass at Nick. "Last chance. Where's the journal?"

With three men charging him, Zen jabbed the butt of his staff into the ground to make it stand upright beside him and began chanting. Threads of the ever-present weave coalesced around him. He gathered them into his hands and formed them into something substantial, something real and physical. By the time the spear-wielder had traversed half the distance, Zen had conjured in his hand a razor-sharp sliver of ice the size and shape of a horseshoe nail. He spoke a command word in an ancient tongue the elves had used during the Age of Magic, and the shard lifted from his palm. It hovered for a moment, twirling slowly, as though suspended by a single thread of the weave, seeking its target as a loadstone seeks true north. Then it hurtled forth and buried itself into the spear-wielder's eye. The man dropped his weapon and grabbed his bleeding face as the force of the shard's impact threw him back. He sprawled, motionless, in the wild grass.

The other men continued their charge. Zen didn't have enough strength for two more weavings, so he attacked their leader. A second ice shard formed in his palm and hovered briefly before he launched it into the woman's lower back.

She grabbed the wound and staggered. "Bloody Vexetan."

In that instant, Nick swept her feet from beneath her and scooped up his own sword. Gripping it by the hilt, he flung the sheath away. The woman crab-walked backward, trying to gain the distance she needed to stand, but Nick kept pace. He batted her cutlass aside when she tried to raise it, and then pressed the tip of his blade against her chest.

She dropped her sword and lay back, her arms spread in surrender. The two men charging Zen quickly assessed their chances and fled into the nearby woods.

"You all right?" Zen asked, walking the rest of the way down the hill.

"Yeah." Nick took a slow breath. "Thanks to you."

Zen dismissed his contribution with a wave of his hand. "What was that all about anyway?"

"Who knows? Something about a journal of my grandfather's." Without moving his blade, Nick inclined his chin toward two village watchmen who were jogging down the hill from the bright booths of the market.

"It's okay," one of the men said between heaving breaths. "We saw what happened. We just weren't close enough to intervene." He retrieved the woman's cutlass, and the two watchman heaved her to her feet.

The man Zen had clubbed was still alive, so the guards secured both him and the woman as prisoners.

"We'll send someone back for that." The watchman indicated the remaining body, dead beside the makeshift spear. He took Nick's name and Zen's, in case he needed to question them later. "You guys go on home. We'll hold these two until the watch captain can properly investigate the matter."

Zen helped Nick gather his belongings and the two set off, Nick carrying his great sword in his hand until he could replace the cut thongs that had secured it to his pack. It was just as well that Nick keep the weapon handy, for the same reason that Zen walked him home—two of the criminals were still out there somewhere.

By the time Zen and Nick neared the Mirrin farmstead, it was late in the evening. Nick stopped suddenly and grabbed Zen's shoulder. He sniffed the air. "Smell that?"

"Smoke."

Above the nearest screen of trees, a thick black column rose toward the darkening sky. "Oh, no." Nick bolted ahead. They'd been walking into the wind, and his home was the only structure for at least a mile in that direction.

The two sprinted around the last bend just in time to see Nick's farmhouse collapse upon itself, the ruins ablaze from the ground up.

CHAPTER 2

ick's father sat against a fencepost a short distance from the smoldering structure, his face buried in his hands. Several of the neighbors had rushed over to help stem the blaze, but they were too few and too late to mitigate the damage. Everything was gone.

Nick dropped his pack and sprinted forward. "Pa!"

His father looked up, squinted in the dying light, and climbed unsteadily to his feet. He wrapped his son in an embrace.

Nick hugged him for a long moment, then stepped away to arm's length. "What happened? Where's Ma? Is she all right?"

Stricken, his father looked at the ground and shook his head.

A neighbor placed a hand on Nick's shoulder. "She was inside. I'm sorry. There was nothing anybody could do."

Nick's gaze shifted to the house. The stone hearth stood, the chimney a solitary, blackened spire in the orange glow of the flames. A few stalwart neighbors continued to sling bucket after bucket of water from the pump house onto the embers.

Fists clenched, Nick marched over, snatched a bucket from one of the men, and shoved him aside. He heaved the whole bucket, water and all, into the middle of the ruins and screamed, "It's gone already! Can't you see that? It's all gone." Tears welled in his burning eyes. "Go home!"

Some turned quietly and left. Most stayed until well past midnight, when the moon—always stationary in the night sky—reached its fullest, brightest illumination. Finally, the uncomfortable silence drove them away as well, with promises to return on the morrow. After that, only Nick, his father, and Zen remained.

Nick sat down as close to the house as the heat would allow and wept silently until his entire body felt spent. By then, much of the house had cooled and the sun was beginning to brighten the horizon.

He plodded through the ruins, avoiding numerous hot spots where embers continued to glow, until he found his mother. When he did, his heart felt as though it had dropped out of his chest. Half her flesh burned off the bone, she lay crumpled in a corner of the kitchen with her back on the floor and her legs splayed up the wall as if she was a broken doll tossed there by a careless child.

"Oh, Ma." He should have found the sight sickening, but nausea didn't rise in him. Rather, the roof of his mouth ached and he choked back a sob as he sank to the floor, cross-legged, beside her. He closed his eyes and held her blackened hand, no longer seeing her as she was but as she had been the morning before—smiling and singing a song with which she'd lulled Nick to sleep as a child. While she sang, she sealed a jar of sourdough she was saving for biscuits the next morning. The jar sat nearby now, its clay shattered and blackened. The family would probably be eating those biscuits at that very moment if his mother had been alive to bake them.

Nick sat for a long time before his father placed a weather-worn hand on his shoulder. "Come on. Let's get her out of the house. We'll bury her somewhere proper."

Nick thought for a moment. "How about under that old oak at the south end?" It was the most picturesque corner of the property.

His father nodded. "I think that would be fitting."

Together, they found a canvas tarp in the work shed, wrapped his mother's body in it, and tied it around her, gently but snugly, with a few pieces of rope.

He and his father spent most of the morning digging her grave. Finally, they lowered her in and began replacing the dirt. Neither spoke. They would have time later to recount their memories. Right now, for Nick at least, the loss hurt too much for him to speak.

Zen, to his credit, seemed to realize that they needed to do this alone. Rather than disturbing them, he stepped through the rubble, conjuring a cold fog over each of the hot spots, making the ruins safer to pick through when the time came to do so.

All the while, Nick's mind flitted through memories too numerous to recount, most from a time when the whole family had been together—before his brother Marik, and then Nick himself, had gone off to apprentice with their uncle Harimon's merchant caravan. Several of the memories reoccurred in endless variations, like the ones from nights when the four of them played flip-chip or bones around the kitchen table by lantern light until the wee hours. They all knew their chores would get them up early the next morning, but they were having too much fun to care.

As Nick and his father placed the last shovelfuls of dirt onto the grave, Zen joined them. He stood near Nick, his silent presence as steadfast and comforting as that of Nick's father. Eventually, they all returned to the house. It was time to see what they had left from which to rebuild their life.

The three of them heaved away the pieces of roofing that covered large sections of the floor, and then began picking through the debris.

"The fire came out of nowhere," Nick's father explained. "One minute everything was fine. The next, flames roared over the rooftop.

I never seen anything like it."

"Where were you when it started?" Nick asked.

His father made a tired motion toward the east. "In the field." He paused and sighed. Tears began to show in his eyes once more. "I couldn't get to her, Nick. I tried."

"I know, Pa. Go on. What happened next? Did you see anyone near the house?"

"There was nobody. I would have seen them." His father paused. "It was weird, though. There was no more than a gentle breeze in the air, but the flames inside whipped around something fierce, like they was caught in a whirlwind or something, blowing first one way, then another. It was unnatural. They burned higher and hotter with each gust. When I tried to get to your mother, I was struck back by a blast of air so strong it nearly knocked me out." He grunted. "I never seen anything like it."

The image of his mother's body, looking as though it had been thrown into the corner, returned to Nick's mind. A mounting rage began to overshadow his grief as he told his father about Jade, Sledge, and the others who'd attacked him the day before. "I think the two events are related."

His father said nothing, so Nick asked, "You know anything about a journal of Grandpa's? The woman said she was looking for his journal."

"Yeah." His father pulled a cooking pot from the ash and placed it on the meager pile of salvageable possessions. "He spent most of his life researching the Prophecy."

"I know. He used to tell us stories when we were kids. Is that what the journal was about?"

His father nodded weakly. "It contained a lifetime of notes. Everything he'd learned about the Prophecy. He was so determined to find a way to stop it. Though I thought it was a fool's purpose, I respected his determination."

"Where is it now?"

"Your grandfather asked me to keep it safe when he died. He had this notion that someone would come looking for it someday."

"His journal? Why?"

"I'm not sure. I guess he must have found something in the Prophecy that suggested it... at least to him."

"Really? Grandpa's journal is mentioned in the Prophecy?"

"At the time, I didn't believe it, but that was his dying wish. So I hid his notes under the hearth." His father picked up an iron poker, chipped the mortar from around one of the stones that skirted the fireplace, and scooped a pile of parchment and ash from beneath it.

Nick picked carefully through the handful of page fragments that had survived the flames. They contained no mention of the Prophecy, just vague references to a few supposedly enchanted relics.

That evening, Zen offered them both temporary lodging at the home of his master, Jarret Grannock, a mage of moderate means and respectable reputation. Nick accepted.

His father, on the other hand, declined. "I'll borrow a room in town for a couple of days," he said, "and make arrangements to begin rebuilding." After all, the farm had been the family home for six generations. "If I don't keep busy..." A strangled sob choked off the rest of his words. "Come with me," he said when he recovered.

"I can't." Tears formed again is Nick's eyes. He willed them not to spill down his cheeks. "Ma didn't just die last night. She was murdered. For this." He pulled the scraps of parchment from his pack and brandished them before his father. "Somehow I'm going to find out why."

When Nick arrived, Zen introduced Jarret Grannock's manservant, Beltrann, who greeted them at the door wearing a plain shirt with brown leather breeches and vest, his black hair pulled back into a short braid. Even at nearly forty harvests, Beltrann's chest and arms were larger and more heavily muscled than Nick's.

"Where's your master?" Nick asked Zen, more to bait him than to discern Jarret's whereabouts. Though Zen was Jarret's apprentice, he'd always rankled at the suggestion that he had a master.

Zen fumed and said nothing.

Nick chuckled. "Seriously, is he here? He might be able to help us make sense of these notes."

Beltrann went into the kitchen as Nick laid out the charred pages of the journal on the sitting-room table. The big man returned with two cups of steaming broth, some cheese, and bread. "I'm afraid Master Grannock is away on business." To Zen, he said, "You were out past your curfew. You shirked your studies."

Zen's expression soured. "Nick lost his home last night."

"And my mother."

"Aeron bless you," Beltrann said. "I'm sorry."

"Thank you." Nick related what had happened the previous evening in as much detail as his heart could stand.

When he finished, Beltrann said, "All this for a journal? What could be in it that someone would want so badly?"

Nick gestured to the remnants, each of which contained only bits and pieces of text, fragments of sentences beneath a title. He picked up one of the scraps and read it aloud.

> Portal of the Damned
> Devils Cauldron located somewhere...
> ...only revealed...
> ...noon on the equinox at...
> ...The Guardian of the...
> ...Great Sand near...
> ...Abyss before...

Finally, he said, "It doesn't make any sense."

"Look at this." Zen selected a scrap titled, "The Guardian."

The Guardian
Bronze statue with a cylindrical...
...land of the nomads among...
...dwarven forger named...
...two fingers tall at...

There were other pages too. Demonbane. The Shield of Faith. Medallions of Vexetan. The Codex of Mortaan. Mist Isles. Blessing of Alamain. "What makes this stuff so important that someone would kill to get it?" Nick asked.

Zen picked up several of the pages in turn. "These list a lot of powerful artifacts. No matter who's looking for them, any one of these relics would make it worth their search."

"Perhaps. But what if they aren't searching for artifacts? My grandfather wasn't. He sought understanding. Maybe these people are also trying to stop the Prophecy."

"Or make it come to pass," Beltrann said.

Nick dragged over a cushioned wooden chair and lowered his aching body into it. The scrapes and bruises from his fight with Jade's thugs had begun to make themselves felt once more. "Maybe they want to know what the Prophecy really says—which version is correct?"

"What?" Zen asked sarcastically. "You mean the one documented by reputable scholars or the tall tales told in taprooms? Which do you think is true?"

"I don't know. My grandfather used to tell us about the Prophecy when we were kids. At the time, the dark ending frightened us, so he told us there were other, happier versions foreseen by other prophets."

"Reputable prophets?" Zen asked.

"I assume so." Nick frowned. "No Prophecy scholar was more thorough than my grandfather. But we don't have enough of his notes to know what his conclusions were."

Zen returned the piece he'd been looking at. "He was trying to stop it?"

"That's my understanding. And maybe he found a way to do it. If he did, that would make this journal valuable enough to kill for." Nick sat back with a frustrated sigh. "I don't even know what the Prophecy actually says. I remember parts of the story, but Grandpa never told us all the details."

"If you want to find out," Beltrann said, "we can visit the Order of the Sage."

"Where's that?" Zen asked.

"In a monastery tucked into the hills on the far side of Traveler's Roost." He turned to Nick. "They have an extensive library. We might be able to piece together some of your missing information or learn the truth of the Prophecy. And you'll be safe there if someone comes looking for the journal again."

"How do you know about it?" Zen asked after a moment's silence.

"I was raised there. It's where I learned to read and write."

Gradually, a spark of hope began to form in Nick's soul. This one practical step might, in time, put some reason behind all this madness. "Can you take us?"

CHAPTER 3

Zen knew three things for sure about the men who'd attacked Nick: two of them were still out there, someone or something was working with them, and they had not yet found what they were looking for. Therefore, Nick was still in danger.

And, though Zen had learned much from Jarret, he didn't yet have the stamina to sustain a weaving throughout a prolonged battle. He was going to need help.

When Nick left to run errands in town the next day and Beltrann was busy in the kitchen, Zen paid a visit to Jarret's private study. The off-limits room was locked, of course, so Zen stood by the door and opened his consciousness to the weave.

Threads of magic appeared faintly in the ether around him. He reached out, as much with his will as with his hands, and began to weave a continuum of ice that conformed to the inside of the lock until he could actually turn the ice key he'd constructed. When the lock clicked, he pushed the door open and slipped through, releasing the ice back into the weave.

The study was dark, but Zen left the shutters closed, fearing a breeze might stir the items spread across Jarret's huge pine desk. Instead, he lit a lamp and began to scan through the organized piles of clutter.

Most of the stuff was mundane: notes regarding specific commissions, books of accounts, and the like. Shelves contained a variety of powders and other substances with which Zen was unfamiliar. A few minutes into his search, however, a wand of polished birch caught his eye. Though Jarret had never let him use such crutch devices during his lessons with the weave, Zen understood their operation—and their value. He slipped the wand into his robes.

He also scooped up a handful of scrolls, rolled parchment upon which Jarret had written incantations that could produce a variety of manifestations from the weave. What effects these particular scrolls would conjure, Zen couldn't determine without breaking the seals and examining them, but the fact that Jarret had sealed them told him the inscriptions were complete. For now, that was all Zen needed to know. He pocketed them as well.

Nick used the last of his coin to purchase a secondhand suit of armor—not pretty or even particularly well cared for, but serviceable. Then he said good-bye to his father and stopped by the jailhouse to confirm that the prisoners from the previous day remained in custody. He inquired about Sledge and his friend, who apparently hadn't been seen since the attack.

By the time he returned to Jarret's, Beltrann had packed a week's worth of food, which consisted of two loaves of bread and some dried fruits and meats from the remnants of the winter stores. Zen had gathered his own travel gear, including his flint, steel, and a complete set of tin cooking utensils.

The three set out early the next morning, leaving the house in the care of Melda, Jarret's housekeeper and cook. Beltrann was armed with a five-foot walking stick carved from compressed oak and Nick with his great sword.

The sun shone through the clouds most of the day and a cool wind kept the air fresh. They might have been out for a picnic, as pleasant as the weather was. Nevertheless, they avoided the road as much as possible, just in case Jade's men decided to make another try for the journal.

All the while, Nick couldn't shake the sense that he ought to be staying home to help his father rebuild the house. But Pa had several friends who could help with that. None of them, however, could make this trip for Nick. He had to do this himself. Until he understood why his mother had died, he would never find peace.

That evening, he began to collect wood for a fire while Beltrann unpacked the food. Zen settled himself into a corner of the camp and slipped into a trance-like state. His hands made gestures before eyes that held a blank stare.

"Now he decides to practice," Beltrann said.

Nick set down a load of kindling. "Practice what? His magic?" He began to clear a space for the fire.

"He calls it, 'tapping the weave.' I call it an excuse to get out of his share of the chores. When he's done, he'll be too tired to take a watch."

"Tired from that?"

"The weave does take something out of a mage. I don't understand it myself, but I've seen it in our master. And I respect Jarret enough to know that much of it is real."

Though Nick had seen Zen work enchantments, he'd never before seen this kind of sustained concentration from him. "Then we'll let him practice and we'll let him rest. Everyone needs a craft and I'll not fault Zen for his. The fact is, he saved my life with it the other day." He struck flint to steel and ignited a blanket of dry pine needles. "Besides, the work's half done anyway."

That night, they heard animals foraging in the woods around them. It had been a long winter, and the wildlife ventured near the camp on more than one occasion.

By the second night, they remained in the hills, but began to see plains to the west. Beltrann announced that they'd reach Traveler's Roost the following day.

Thrice, the troubling roar of a large predator reached them, distant but moving closer as the hour wore on. By dusk, Nick became convinced a large mountain cat had picked up their scent. And, as he was clearing space for the night's fire, a rustling of some nearby brush brought him up short.

He drew his sword and all three men stood ready.

Moments later, an unnatural silence descended upon the camp like a wet blanket, thick and suffocating. The trio searched the bushes and rocks for signs of danger. Then, just as Nick spotted it, a lion sprang for Beltrann with a sweep of its giant claws. The big man lunged to the side, smacking the paw away with his staff.

His heart racing, Nick darted in. He slashed the cat across the shoulder and side, cutting muscle to the bone. It roared and spun on him. A swipe of its claws grated across Nick's breastplate and sent him sprawling.

Beltrann whipped his staff over his head and slammed it down with a solid smack against the lion's hindquarters. The beast roared once more and fled. The whole event had taken no more than a few seconds.

"She won't make it far," Beltrann said.

"Too bad." Nick regained his feet, wiped his sword clean, and sheathed it. "We can't very well blame her for seeking food."

Zen stepped up beside him. "Just as long as we're not on the menu."

"Nice of you to join us," Beltrann said sarcastically.

Zen glared. "I was preparing the weave."

"Sometimes there's no time for weaving." With that, Beltrann returned to the provisions.

Nick patted his friend's shoulder in reassurance as he walked past on his return to the unfinished fire.

"He'll see," Zen promised. "Someday."

Whisper, a mere construct of air, insubstantial as the wind yet as physical as the ground beneath it, stalked the outskirts of Cedar Falls. Watching. Waiting. When the sun finally dipped over the horizon and the village settled down for the night, Whisper drifted through the quiet town. Anyone chancing to look out their windows into the narrow dirt streets could have seen nothing but the darkness.

When the construct reached the jailhouse, it peered through the small window. A single watchman sat inside, so Whisper collected itself, compressed its form tightly, hurtled forward, and blasted open the door.

The guard leapt to his feet, sword drawn and stance ready. "Who's there?" For a minute or more, he stared straight through the construct, seeing nothing.

Whisper moved slowly, careful not to disturb the lightweight articles on the desk and the dirt others had tracked onto the floor. By the time the guard closed the door, Whisper was already inside. The watchman gave one long nervous look out the window and turned back to his desk.

As he did, Whisper swept into him with a gust of wind so hard it hit the watchman with a solid impact. He staggered on his feet, his eyes flitting from one shadow to the next in a vain effort to locate his attacker.

Whisper hit him again. This time, the guard struck the floor and his sword flew from his hand. Slowly, he rolled over and began to struggle to his feet. When Whisper slammed him a third time, the watchman crumpled with a groan and lay still.

A hand formed of air, compressed by the weave and Whisper's will, lifted the keys and tossed them into Jade's cell, where she snatched them up. Her stay had apparently had its benefits. From the looks of her, the watch captain had provided his prisoners with a healer.

"It's about time." Jade released herself and her companion, then gathered the watchman's weapons and coin. Minutes later, Whisper and the fugitives vanished into the night.

Vinsous Drakemoor, clothed entirely in black, crouched among the manicured hedges at the edge of the Trondor palace grounds and studied the movements of the guards on the castle wall, deep shadows silhouetted against the darkening sky. An ebony mask concealed Drakemoor's fair skin from his dark bangs to the bridge of his nose and extended down the left side of his face, covering the cheek and jaw. He'd darkened his other cheek and the rest of his chin with soot.

Everything was ready. Tonight he would fulfill his latest contract.

He crept along the hedgerow, a mere shadow in the darkness, until he reached the base of the battlement. There he paused as footsteps on the stone above him passed by and faded away. Drakemoor slowly counted to thirty—exactly half the span of time between sentries—before tossing one end of his rope over the parapet. The grappling hook clinked and then scraped softly as Drakemoor took up the slack. Finally, the hook bit into the stone and he began to climb, a simple task for a man with the athletic build of a gypsy acrobat.

With the walkway at the top clear for maybe another fifteen seconds, Drakemoor hopped over the rampart and gathered the rope into his bag, just as the sound of boots drew near.

Drakemoor padded into the shadow of the watchtower, melted into the darkness, and waited. When the guard appeared, Drakemoor grabbed him across the nose and mouth, yanked his head back, and thrust a dagger through the soft tissue beneath the chin, through the roof of the mouth, and into the man's brain. In the same motion, he hefted the body over the parapet and into the bushes below. The motion took less than a second and left not a single drop of blood on the stone to alert the next man who passed.

Drakemoor stowed his knife and drew his sword, which emitted a palpable wave of silence that engulfed the air around him. The night, already still, became noiseless as death as he strode into the tower and began to snake his way through the royal palace.

Three guards intercepted him on the stair, apparently headed for the battlement. They rounded a corner and stopped in surprise. The lead sentry died before he could recover, his heart skewered on the tip of Drakemoor's blade. The others drew their swords and tried to shout an alarm, yet their mouths uttered only silence.

Pressing his advantage, Drakemoor rushed them. The defenders met him side-by-side and forced him to give ground. Blades clashed again and again, but the enchantment of Drakemoor's sword swallowed all sound so that none emerged to wake the keep.

Drakemoor drew blood first. The man he'd wounded dropped back, blood flowing freely from a gash in his sword arm, and turned to fetch reinforcements. Drakemoor shifted his sword to his left hand and drew his dagger. Before the fleeing guard took three steps, he tumbled to the stone with a blade in his back.

Alone, the remaining sentry was no match for the most notorious assassin in all the Civilized Lands. He stumbled down the stairs, offering a fighting retreat, while Drakemoor pounded away at his weakening defenses. As they passed the dead guard's body, Drakemoor bent to retrieve his dagger without missing a single thrust or parry.

And though the guard proved better than Drakemoor had expected, even better than most, he slowed as he took several nicks from Drakemoor's blade. Eventually the fight moved from the stairwell into the corridors near the royal residence. Ever patient, Drakemoor waited for the man to tire. Finally, the guard's sword dropped a little too low and it was over.

Drakemoor sheathed Silent Death, restoring the normal night sounds to the palace, and slunk down a corridor lit by widely spaced lamps mounted in decorative iron sconces along the wall. Two of every three lamps had been extinguished for the night, however, providing large stretches of shadow. At one point, a pair of servant girls passed him, unaware, in the gloom.

Finally, moments after picking the lock to the king's bedchamber, Drakemoor heard a distant scream. Apparently one of the servants had discovered the sentry's body. Unconcerned, Drakemoor studied his mark, now resting in final peace, and then opened the door and slipped down the hall to finish his grisly work.

CHAPTER 4

When Jade returned to camp, she reported directly to Alton, the leader of the expedition, an elf who'd exiled himself from Lorentil because he couldn't conform to elven ideals. There was more to his story, of course, but in their line of work, everyone had secrets better left unspoken.

Alton rose when Jade and her cohort strode into the firelight. Like everyone else in the Black Hand, he sported a studded leather glove on his right fist. "Jade, I'm pleased to find you well." His height, average for the males of his race, left him no taller than Jade's five-and-a-half feet. Ginger-colored hair hung down to the middle of his back. Most people mistook him for a human female until they saw the pointed tips of his ears.

Several bandits gathered around them, including Sledge and one other man who'd participated in the botched attack.

"Where's Cortell?" Alton asked.

Jade shrugged. "Dead." She turned toward the bundled supplies she'd left in camp while she was gone.

Alton grabbed her arm before she could walk away. "It seems you underestimated Mr. Mirrin."

"Not him. It was his mage friend I misjudged. I won't make that mistake again." She yanked her arm from his grasp and began to relate her version of the events. While they talked, Jade stripped out of her townsfolk costume to don more appropriate wilderness gear. She received several hoots and whistles from the men around her until Alton ordered silence. Jade ignored them all as she pulled on her leather trousers, heavy blouse, and riding boots. Her gear was as she had left it and her horse appeared to have been well tended in her absence. "The boy didn't know anything about the book. Did Whisper find it at the house?"

"No. So he torched the place, just in case it was hidden there. Unfortunately, a portion of it survived. It's now in Nick's possession."

"And you said *I* underestimated him."

"Whisper's tracked them out of town," Alton continued. "They're on the road toward Traveler's Roost. Which is convenient, actually."

Jade frowned. "Why is that convenient?"

"As best as we can tell, Sevendeath is also holed up there."

"Oh! That is convenient."

"I've sent some of the others to fetch him if they can. Or at least pick up his trail."

Jade studied him for a moment. "Alton, maybe we should forget about the journal. We came here specifically for Sevendeath, and splitting our forces is hampering both efforts."

"I understand, but the price Whisper has offered is too great to pass up. Besides, I believe we can do both."

She selected a spot near the fire and spread her traveling cloak on the ground as a bed for the night. "Just so long as we don't lose Sevendeath's trail again."

"We won't. That's part of my deal with Whisper. If we lose the trail while we're on this errand for him, he'll locate it for us again. He's done so once already, has he not?"

"True enough. When do we ride?"

"At first light."

"We have a couple hours of daylight," Nick said to Beltrann as they entered the town of Traveler's Roost, no more than a collection of buildings that had sprouted like weeds around a lodge the town's founder had built more than a century before. Most of the structures were dilapidated now, some abandoned altogether. "Shall we press on?"

"Either way, we should reach the Order of the Sage by tomorrow night."

"I could go for a hot meal and a comfortable bed," Zen said. Fortunately, the inn itself, The Roost, was among the few businesses that still seemed to be thriving.

Nick had seen no sign of pursuit since they'd left Jarret's place. "All right, then." He walked past a group of horses tethered at the roadside and hopped up the steps to the inn.

Inside, a quartet of ruffians were crowding the front desk. The best-dressed among them leaned over the counter. A heavy miner's pick, too shiny to have ever been used for its intended purpose, hung from his belt. His fat hand gripped a fistful of the innkeeper's blowsy shirt. "He goes by the name Sevendeath."

The woman and two men with him glanced toward the door. All four sported studded leather gloves, a symbol that seemed familiar from somewhere other than the ox of a man at the Cedar Falls market, though Nick couldn't remember from where.

"You sure he hasn't come in here?" the ruffian leader said.

Nick stopped at the door and gave the four a respectful berth. They weren't asking about him or the journal. They were after something else entirely. Better to keep quiet and see how things developed than to retreat suddenly and raise suspicions.

"Never heard of him," the innkeeper replied. "But I don't ask the names of my guests."

"Well then, you won't mind if we go up and look for him." The ruffian motioned his fellows toward the stairs.

"I most certainly would. You wouldn't want me to let anyone into your rooms. I extend the same courtesy to all my guests."

"Stop us if you can, then. We're not leaving until we know." With that, all four climbed the stairs to the second story.

Once they were gone, Nick approached the counter. "Trouble?"

The innkeeper grunted. "Probably, but it's my trouble, not yours. What can I do for you?"

Nick fished a silver coin from a meager purse at his waist and set it onto the counter. "One room. And whatever you've got to eat that's hot."

"You can take the room at the top of the stairs and down the end of the hall. If I were you, I'd wait until that bunch leaves, though. In the meantime, we're serving stew." He thrust his chin toward a tap-room off to Nick's left.

Above them, the ruffians started banging around like a stableful of agitated mules. A loud pounding, followed by the crack of splitting wood, came down the stairwell. The innkeeper winced and shook his head.

Trying to ignore the commotion, Nick chose a table and sat down. Beltrann hesitated, though, looking at the staircase to the upper floor.

"One thing my uncle taught me," Nick said. "Don't get involved in affairs that aren't your own."

"Lucky for you I didn't follow that advice." Beltrann leaned his staff against the end of the table and sat down next to Zen. "You two would still be wondering what to do with the shreds of that journal."

"Those guys," Nick said, "and the man they're looking for, are not our concern."

So he continued to think until the ruffians returned to the common room and marched up to Nick's table. The leader puffed out his chest toward Zen and spoke belligerently. "We're looking for an elf. Tall for his kind. Shaved, except for a black ponytail that reaches halfway down his back. Has a scar from his left eyebrow to his right cheekbone." His finger traced a line across his own face to illustrate. "Seen him?"

Behind the man stood the large woman Nick had seen on the way in. The animal hides she wore suggested she was an immigrant from the tribes of Cormont. Her stance was the most hostile of the bunch, though she had no weapons Nick could see other than her steel-studded leather glove and a sling tied to her belt.

"No," Nick said before Zen could reply.

"Which way did you come in from?"

"We came by the road, from the northeast." Beltrann pointed.

The leader glared at each of them for a moment, his expression seeming to call them all liars. "You see him, you let us know."

"Where will you be?" Beltrann asked reasonably.

"Here."

"Oh—" Zen stood.

Nick groaned inwardly at his friend's sarcastic tone.

"—so if we see him, you'll still be standing right *there*?" Zen pointed to the exact spot upon which the man stood.

"Mind your tongue, child." The leader placed his fingertips on Zen's chest and shoved him backward into his chair.

"Zen..." Nick said. Unnecessary violence could only bring trouble.

"What do you want him for?" Beltrann's tone remained calm, as though he was trying to smooth over Zen's insolence, but now he'd ventured into territory that was none of their business.

The leader considered his reply. "Let's just say we owe him vengeance."

"Why?" Zen asked. "Did he steal your woman?"

The leader's pick was in his hand in an instant.

"Take it outside!" the innkeeper yelled.

Zen scrambled from his chair as the pick smashed it to splinters. Another ruffian, wearing a well-used suit of black leather armor adorned with steel studs that matched the ones on his glove, drew his sword and circled behind Beltrann and Zen.

Beltrann lunged for his staff, but before he'd fully left his seat, the woman intercepted him. Her steel-studded fist smashed his cheek with an audible crunch. Beltrann stumbled backward and fell headlong over his chair. He lay dazed and writhing on the floor with blood streaming from a gash in his face.

Nick drew his sword as the fourth ruffian charged, leading the way with an arcing sweep of his blade. He deflected the cut. Forced into a defensive posture, Nick gave ground as the ruffian came on.

Zen had no time to grab his own staff as he sprang to his feet. He retreated to the taproom wall to avoid the broad sweeps from the leader's pick. From somewhere within the folds of his cloak, he produced a slender, polished wand, maybe half a yard long. Pointing it at the leader, he spoke a single word that sounded vaguely elfish. The hairs rose on Nick's arms as a sudden blue flash lit the room. A spark sizzled from the wand's end with a muffled pop and streaked toward the ruffian leader, who sprang away. The spark hissed across the taproom and scorched the clay plaster that coated the far wall.

The hide-clad woman was reaching to finish Beltrann when a fleet figure in black traveling clothes and with a long ponytail flying from the back of his otherwise-bald head sprang down the stairs. He rammed his blade through the back of one of the ruffian swordsmen, the man in the studded armor, pouring his blood onto the taproom floor.

"Sevendeath!" The hide-clad woman hefted a table that separated her from her prey and tossed it aside. A jab from her steel-studded fist fell short.

Sevendeath danced away, laughing. The woman howled in rage and pursued.

During the commotion, Zen's eyes lost focus and he began gesturing in the air. When the leader saw this, he launched a heavy downward stroke with his pick, forcing Zen to stumble around a table in a vain attempt to buy himself the seconds he needed to finish his weaving.

The leader split the table and brushed the pieces aside. As he came at Zen, the mage released two shards of ice. They sank into the man's chest and he staggered away.

Nick shoved his own sword through his enemy's defenses—and his gut. The man dropped his blade, lurched backwards with his hands across his exposed bowels, and crumpled to the floor. The reek of blood and spilled feces filled the room.

Beltrann wallowed among the feet of the combatants. He tried several times to recover his balance before he was finally able to stand. By then, he'd crawled halfway across the taproom and stumbled the rest of the way to the innkeeper's counter.

Sevendeath's sword slammed the woman's chest, but a steel breastplate beneath her hides absorbed the blow. Her next punch caused him to stagger back, but when Nick closed on her, she turned and fled.

He and Sevendeath pursued her to the top of the stairs, where she turned left, and left again, into a guest room with a splintered door. Without slowing, the woman wrapped her arms around her head and barreled through the window. Shattered glass rained down onto the packed-earth roadway below.

She landed on her feet just as her leader charged out the front door of the inn. The two gathered the horses from the hitching rail and galloped northward out of town.

When Nick returned to the common room with Sevendeath a few minutes later, Beltrann was leaning on the innkeeper's counter, imploring the man to help him. One of his eyes was swollen shut, his cheek split and bleeding.

"We can't stay here," Sevendeath said. "There are more of those guys about. A lot more."

"Who are they?" Nick demanded.

Sevendeath walked past the disemboweled warrior to the man he himself had wounded, found him alive, and sliced his throat. "Bandits. Call themselves the Black Hand."

Of course. Nick had run into them once or twice with his uncle. That's where he'd seen the studded gloves before. "I've never heard of them operating outside Palidor."

"Normally they don't, yet they chased me out of the kingdom a few weeks ago. I thought I'd lost them in Dreadwood Swamp, but somehow they picked up my trail again." Sevendeath pulled the glove off each of the bodies. "You'd think killing a few bandits would just increase the share for the rest of them." He held out the glove from Nick's kill for him to take.

Nick refused the trophy with a gesture. "How many have you killed?"

From a belt beneath his tunic, Sevendeath pulled a chain that held at least twenty black, studded gloves, each identical to the one he'd just collected. "They'll be back in force."

As they talked, Nick helped Beltrann into a seat. The big man dabbed blood from his face with a towel the innkeeper had provided. "You all right?"

"I will be. Give me a minute."

"Just rest," Nick told him, then turned to Zen. "Stay with him. I'll be back." He retrieved the sword, shield, and coin pouch from the bandit he'd disemboweled. If these men really were outlaws, the purse was fair bounty. Nevertheless, he gave most of the coin to the innkeeper to cover damages and then rushed to the provisioner's shack across the street.

"We're leaving," Sevendeath called after him.

Nick ignored the stranger. His friends wouldn't go anywhere without him. And if Sevendeath left on his own before Nick got back, so much the better. The last thing they needed was another reason for the Black Hand to pursue them.

He dumped the bandit's weapons onto the provisioner's counter. "How much for these?"

The merchant raised one eyebrow. "Are they yours to sell?"

Did it matter? "Of course they're mine."

"All right." He paused. "Two gold coins."

Nick scoffed. "They're worth ten times that."

"Not to me. Not right now."

Goblin crap. He hated bartering when he was in a hurry. He held out his hand and motioned haste with his fingers until the man dropped the coins into it, and then he hurried out the door.

"Ready?" Sevendeath said as soon as Nick returned.

"I thought you were leaving."

"I'm responsible for getting you into that scuffle—"

"No. I believe Zen did that all by himself." Beltrann leaned heavily on Zen's shoulder, holding his bleeding face with one of his own hands.

Zen elbowed the big man and he groaned.

"The least I can do is escort you to this monastery," Sevendeath said.

Nick scowled at Zen. "You told him where we're going?"

"He may be useful."

"We don't need an escort," Beltrann assured him, though his eyes seemed to have trouble focusing.

Sevendeath huffed. "Decide. Those bandits won't be gone long."

To Nick, the choice seemed clear. He'd seen Sevendeath fight. The group was stronger with him than without him. "Zen's right. We accept your help." Furthermore, if they split, and the bandits had to choose between a personal grudge and the journal, they'd likely come after the journal. The Prophecy was too important for him to believe otherwise.

"All right, then. Let's go." Sevendeath led the companions to the south, away from the direction the fleeing bandits had taken. Once they left sight of the buildings, he turned west into a broad valley that separated the monastery from Traveler's Roost. Scrub grasses covered a landscape dotted with dry-climate brush. "You guys go on ahead. I'll cover our trail and catch up."

Beltrann continued to struggle from the blow he'd taken and he relied on the others to carry his supplies. Eventually, as the sun began to descend toward a solitary peak that loomed in the distance, he began to walk on his own.

That evening, they came to a bridge that crossed a river at the mountain's base. On the far side, a trail led up a rocky, forested slope—the strenuous climb to the monastery.

Sevendeath came to a halt just before the bridge. "We'll cross in the morning."

"Let's cross now," Nick said, thinking to put the natural barrier between them and any Black Hand bandits who might be pursuing.

Beltrann shook his head carefully. "I'm spent. We can't navigate the trail in the dark anyway."

Without waiting for consensus, Sevendeath climbed a steep gully that led thirty feet up a slope to their right, and returned a few minutes later. "There's a small plateau just up there. It's shielded by a screen of brush and should give us a clear view of the valley when the sun comes up."

"All right." Nick slipped his arm around Beltrann and helped him make the climb. Once the big man was settled, Nick rounded on Zen. "You're taking his watch tonight, since you started the fight."

Zen gave him a sour look, but nodded.

When the camp was set, Nick joined the stranger, who sat on the edge of the bluff with his feet dangling over the side, watching for signs of pursuit. Nick could contain his curiosity no longer. "Your name is Sevendeath?"

The stranger shook his head. "That's just what the Black Hand call me. The first time I attacked them, I raided a sleeping camp and killed seven of them in a single night."

"You murdered men in their sleep."

He shrugged. "Why not? Everything's legal in the fight against evil."

Nick thought about that and, for the time being, chose not to dispute it. "What's your name then?"

"Rancid."

"Rancid?" Nick chuckled. "How'd you get a name like that?" After a moment, he swallowed his mirth. "I'm sorry. I meant no offense."

The waxing moon highlighted the scar on Rancid's face, giving his features a grotesque cast. "It's a long story," he said finally.

"We've got all night."

"It's not a story you'd care to hear." With that, Rancid pushed himself to his feet and stalked into the darkness.

CHAPTER 5

T he next morning, as Zen and Beltrann packed up their meager supplies, Nick peered with Rancid through the wall of shrubs at their back-trail. He thought he'd seen a cloud of dust on the horizon, but facing the sunrise, he couldn't say for sure... until a row of riders appeared at the top of a ridge. Nick could discern little about their weapons and gear, but they traveled light, not laden with goods as merchants would be. Then sunlight glinted from the right hand of the foremost rider.

"Baron's blood," Rancid spat.

Nick spun toward his friends. "We've got company. Black Hand. Nine of them."

"Should we hide or run?" Beltrann asked. His face was more swollen and purple than it had been the night before, but the fog in his eyes had cleared. He seemed more alert and energetic.

Rancid swept up his pack and settled it onto his shoulders. "If they found our trail off the main road, they'll find our trail up to this camp-site."

Nick scanned the cliffs nearby. The way they'd come up was the only way down. "If we stay here, we'll be trapped."

Rancid stood poised, ready to descend the steep ravine to the bridge below. "Then we make a run for this monastery of yours."

"It's a good six-hour climb to the Order," Beltrann said. "But the trail is hazardous enough that horses will give them little advantage."

Nick gave Beltrann's wounds a critical look.

"My head still hurts, but it no longer feels like there's an ax embedded in it."

"We'll have to move quickly." This was Nick's errand. These people were his responsibility. "Can you make it?"

"I must."

"All right then." Nick gathered his own pack and handed Beltrann's to Zen. Then he and Rancid helped the big man down the slope. Just as they reached the bottom, the bandits topped another rise, not half a mile behind. A cheer filled the air and the riders spurred their mounts into a full gallop. Nick led them over the bridge and into the rugged hills beyond. Within moments, the horses were out of sight once more.

The companions ran along the rough trail, scrambling over boulders and fallen trees, through deep furrows cut by the early spring runoff. For an hour or more, they fled the constant sound of hoof beats behind them, which at times came so close Nick could make out the curses of the pursuers as they urged their horses to greater speed despite the hazards.

Rancid smiled grimly when they heard the loud rustle of something heavy tumbling through the brush, accompanied by the scream of a rider.

Eventually, Beltrann's breathing turned ragged and he began to slow. By the time the riders came into view again, they'd closed half the distance.

Rancid rounded a bend and gestured to a deep cut in a near-vertical face on one side of the trail. "Quickly."

Before Nick could object on Beltrann's behalf, the big man stepped into the cut and began to climb. Rancid urged him on. The scuffling of Beltrann's boots against the stone knocked loose a steady rain of rocks and pebbles onto the others as they followed him up.

Rancid was still on the trail when they heard the bandits approaching from just around the last bend. He leapt into a patch of bracken on the far side. Beltrann and Zen had reached the top, but Nick was exposed and would certainly be seen if the riders glanced behind them as they passed. He held his breath and said a silent prayer to Aeron as the riders thundered by, the noise of hoofs and gear burying any sounds from Nick and the others. Moments later, the Black Hand rode out of sight.

As soon as the bandits were gone, Rancid scrambled up the cleft. He led the party along the shelf for a short distance until it broadened onto a steep but climbable hill, and from there, up into a thicket of ash trees.

Thirty minutes later, they heard the riders return.

"It's okay," Rancid said without slowing. "Even if they figure out where we left the trail, they won't leave their horses behind to follow. They'll go on to the monastery." He paused. "The problem is, they'll beat us there."

"I know a way," Beltrann assured them. "We can circle around and come at the monastery from above. That way, if the Black Hand set an ambush on the trail, we'll bypass it."

Agreed, the companions spent the day working their way up the broken mountain terrain, climbing higher and farther from the path with frequent stops as Beltrann became fatigued by the combination of his wounds and the exertion.

At dusk, they emerged from a pine grove and stood, looking down upon the monastery. A wall constructed of clay and wild grasses, kneaded together and baked into bricks, stood twelve feet high and wide enough to permit a watchman to walk them. Several buildings of similar construction hunched within the perimeter, many of which shared a wall with the exterior battlement.

Save for the sounds of night foragers, the clearing around the monastery remained quiet. The Black Hand were nowhere in sight.

"I don't like it," Nick said. The clearing was broad enough that the bandits, if they were hidden beyond the trees, could catch them on horseback before they gained entry to the compound. "They had to know we were coming here." Several monks walked on the walls. Maybe they would intervene if the bandits attacked. "Will they let us in after dark?"

"Probably not," Beltrann said.

"Then we'd better go now."

Rancid produced a rope from his backpack and they each descended the short cliff. Halfway across the clearing, a shout rose from somewhere down the trail, followed by a rustling of gear and the sound of hooves. One by one, the Black Hand riders emerged from the trailhead and spurred their horses to a gallop.

"Bloody baron," Rancid muttered, redoubling his speed.

Nick and Zen helped Beltrann, who seemed to have tapped some new well of strength and picked up his pace.

As the riders closed, a door parted the monastery's side wall and an elderly man wearing a plain brown robe and leather sandals beckoned them to enter. He shut the door behind them, giving only a glance at the Black Hand riders.

"This way." The old monk ushered them into a small room that contained several straw mattresses. "Rest here. Do not worry about the men outside. If they wish to enter the compound, they may make their request in the morning. I have locked the gate for the night." He tucked each of his hands inside the opposite sleeve of his robe and bowed. "I am brother Yucca. I will bring food and a healer. Tomorrow we will discuss that which brings you to our humble sanctuary."

Minutes later he returned with another monk, who applied a warm herbal poultice to Beltrann's bruised and lacerated face. Yucca set out a nutty sweet cake, the bread dense and filling, and a tea that soon put them all to sleep.

Nick woke the next morning when a rather unusual-looking acolyte pulled aside the animal-hide door covering and entered their room with a breakfast of fruit, freshly baked bread, and milk. The hairless olive-skinned girl, who appeared to be in her mid-teens, had a triangular face with high, angled cheekbones, a jutting chin, and flattened nose. She looked at him through pink eyes, narrow and slanted. Her disfigured hands and bare feet had but three clawed digits each, like the talons of some bizarre raptor.

She set the tray on a table, bowed respectfully, and left.

"Goblin's blood," Rancid said as soon as she was gone. He spat it like a curse.

Nick had seen many goblin slaves during his trips through Palidor. He'd even seen a few of their half-breed offspring. Though Rancid's may have been an accurate guess of the girl's parentage, she didn't look like any goblin-kin Nick had ever seen.

"What was that thing?" Rancid asked.

"Be nice." Nick walked over to inspect the food.

"She's a monk of the order," Beltrann replied. "That makes her a friend. And one to be trusted."

"I don't trust anybody." Rancid approached the food warily and sniffed at the pitcher. "Goat's milk." He poured some into a small clay cup, which he handed to Nick.

Nick glanced once at Beltrann, then downed the liquid. It was fresh and cold. "Can't argue with the quality."

Rancid grunted. "Unless it's drugged like last night's tea."

"It wasn't drugged." Yucca brushed the hide from the doorway and came inside. "We brewed it with chamomile and hops. I told you when

I served it that it would help you sleep."

"We thank you for your hospitality." Nick selected a cloth napkin from the food tray, piled it high with fruit and bread, and then returned to his cot. He sat cross-legged with his breakfast in his lap and sampled a grape. "The food is excellent."

"You are too kind." Yucca bowed. "We produce it all here at the Order. I am pleased that you like it."

"Elder," Beltrann began, his tone more respectful than any he'd used during the trip from Cedar Falls. "Let me introduce my friends." He indicated each in turn. "Nick Mirrin, Zenobrian Zersaash, and Rancid... Sevendeath?"

Rancid shrugged. "That's as good a name as any."

"I apologize for our unannounced arrival," Beltrann continued. "I hope we've caused no imposition to you. If we have—"

"Don't be foolish, brother."

"I wasn't sure you would remember me."

"Of course I remember. But even if I hadn't, all are welcome here. You know that."

Nick set his meal aside. "I'm afraid we must impose upon you for more than healing and hospitality."

"I expected as much. No matter where you're coming from or going to, our humble home is out of the way. Nobody comes here without a reason."

"We're looking for information," Nick told him, trying to make it sound important.

"What knowledge do you seek?"

Nick described the events of the past few days, his voice cracking more than once during the telling, and produced the remnants of his grandfather's journal for Yucca's inspection. "Beltrann said you have a library here, that you might be able to help us understand the value of these pages."

"We are sincerely saddened by your loss." The monk bowed. "Rest for today. There will be time tomorrow for that which you seek. And

I'm sure our scholars will enjoy the diversion."

Yucca turned to Beltrann. "You are looking better this morning. How do you feel?"

He touched his torn cheek gingerly. "I might bother you for a pain remedy later."

"Of course," Yucca replied. To the others, he said, "Would you like a tour of the compound?"

Rancid waved his arms at the walls of their cramped room. "Anything to get me out of this box."

"Rancid," Beltrann said.

The bandit hunter glared at him.

"Show some respect. These people have offered to help us."

Rancid snorted. "They've offered to help *you*. I have no interest in your scraps of paper, or the poem they refer to. I got you here. My business is done." He threw the curtain aside and stormed into the courtyard.

Nick folded the cloth and returned it to the tray. "Your offer is gracious. My mother was killed because of this journal." An ache formed at the back of his throat. "I need to know what she died for. And I'd like to get started right away."

After Nick's friends finished their breakfast, Jasmine, the deformed acolyte, returned and led them into the courtyard. Well-tended grounds surrounded a grassy field occupied by thirty or so monks engaged in exercises ranging from calisthenics to stretching, balance, meditation, and sparing. Chickens, pigs, goats, and rabbits ran free or stared out from hutches and pens. A fenced vegetable garden lined one wall. A well provided water for the community.

"An orchard extends down the hillside to the south," Jasmine explained. "We produce some of the finest fruits and vegetables in Meuribar."

"She's not boasting," Beltrann said. "She's simply stating fact."

"You mean, she's not *just* boasting," Rancid muttered.

If Jasmine heard him, she made no response.

Beltrann did reply. "She's informing. We are here to learn. Are we not?"

They passed a series of clay-walled workshops with heavy wooden doors. Those that stood open—those of the smith, carpenter, and leatherworker—weren't much larger than the room Nick and his friends had slept in the previous night. The smell of roasting meat wafted from the kitchens.

"All who live here," Jasmine continued, "are raised by the Order until they reach their twelfth harvest. In addition to academics, we're taught manners, respect, and morals—"

"Whose morals?" Rancid asked.

Jasmine paused briefly, but again continued without reply. "We're taught the value of hard work and a balance in all aspects of life."

"What happens at twelve harvests?" Nick asked.

"We are given a choice to leave or to become a monk and live by the creed." She recited her next words with an almost prayerful reverence. "Where there is inequality, seek balance. Where there is ignorance, seek knowledge. Where there is conflict, seek resolution.

"Those who stay to become monks," Jasmine continued, "are given the name of some flora and answer to no other for the duration of their training, and in many cases, for the rest of their lives."

"My path was a little different," Beltrann said. "I decided to stay, but not as a monk. I apprenticed in the forge and served as a smith for twelve harvests before I moved to Cedar Falls."

They came, at last, to the library. Beltrann turned the handle with a loud click and heaved open the door. "You'll forgive me if I don't join you. I have many old friends—family really—that I'd like to catch up with."

"Zen?" Nick motioned toward the library door.

Without a word, the mage stepped into the shadowy interior, a small room with perhaps a hundred well-preserved books. An impressive assortment indeed, Nick realized as he perused the shelves, probably one of the most extensive collections in the kingdom.

Finally, he noticed a shriveled old monk resting in the corner. Wisps of white hair hung from her pale, wrinkled scalp. She looked like nothing more than the dried husk of some woman who once was, until she shifted in her creaking chair.

"Welcome. I am Mum." Her voice rose with surprising strength. "You seek knowledge. Yes?"

"Where there is ignorance..." Nick said, remembering a portion of the creed he'd just heard."

"Bravo!" The old woman smiled, wide and toothless, and clapped her frail, spotted hands.

Jasmine introduced them. "They seek knowledge of the Prophecy."

"Be specific, dear."

"I'm sorry, elder." Jasmine bowed. "I mean the Last Prophecy of Mortaan."

"Well, that's a trick, isn't it." The chair, or maybe the old monk's joints, cracked as she climbed to her feet. She ran a bony finger down the spine of each book, squinting at the titles in the light of a dozen clean-burning lamps. While Mum was searching, Jasmine excused herself quietly.

"Ah, here it is," Mum said after a few moments. "The Codex."

"You have the Codex of Mortaan?" Zen exclaimed.

"Shhhhhh." Mum pressed a finger to her lips. Though they were the only ones in the room, it was, after all, a library.

"Unfortunately, it is only a copy," she said. "Not the original."

"Does it matter?" Nick asked.

"It matters a great deal, I'm afraid. You see, only the original, written by Mortaan's own hand, can be trusted to contain the text of the prophecies with integrity."

"May I see it?" Zen's voice held more than a hint of impatience.

"Certainly, young Zen." Mum laid the book carefully on a stone table in the center of the room and opened it. The script was written in the flowing hand of a scribe. She turned the pages until she came to the prophecy of interest, which resided in the middle of the book.

Nick frowned. "I thought this was the *last* prophecy of Mortaan."

"It is, and it is not. He wrote several predictions after he wrote this one, but this is the only one that has not yet come to pass. So, it is the last of his prophecies to be fulfilled."

Nick scanned the page. "But you're sure it will be?"

Mum remained silent for a time before answering. "Nick, if you ask that question of any scholar in the Civilized Lands, he must invariably answer, 'yes.' Mortaan's reliability as a prophet is faultless. All of his other predictions have come true. When the conditions are right, the time will come, and this prophecy will be fulfilled as well. Your grandfather, on the other hand, was not convinced."

Nick's head snapped up. "You knew my grandfather?"

"Oh, yes. He came here often. That is why I am so eager to work with you on this project. Perhaps I can lend insight into his work."

Nick's voice was barely a whisper. "I'd like that."

While they spoke, Zen examined the Prophecy. "How can you even read this?" He set the book down and pointed to the passage he'd been studying.

...the heroes of the land of will to bring the fight to The Master, but all will fear. And they will fail. falter before the Master, who cannot be harmed by any weapon. or another, forged of this world. The armies of darkness will. crumble, those of the civilized races, bringing forth the Age of Darkness from which there Will be no Enlightenment...

He looked up from the page. "It doesn't make any sense. The punctuation and capitalization are all messed up, leaving the sentences, and therefore the meaning, largely ambiguous."

"That is where I can help," Mum said. "I worked with Nick's grandfather while he struggled with these expressions. We pondered many interpretations, looking for hidden loopholes and alternative meanings." She placed her hand on a stack of pages, bound with a yellow ribbon inside a stiff leather cover. "These are my notes from those discussions."

She also provided Nick with a blank journal in which to record his own observations. This was the first time Nick had considered the Prophecy outside the context of a fairy tale about a distant future. He knew the common renditions that circulated in the ale houses, gossip circles, and fireside debates, but many of the details were new to him.

He spent most of the day just familiarizing himself with the text as it was actually written, with its garbled language and convoluted phrasing. "My grandfather doesn't mention the Prophecy itself in his journal, at least not in the scraps I have here."

"He believed the Prophecy would be fulfilled only if all its stated preconditions came to exist at the same time. He focused his efforts on those, not on the Prophecy itself, hoping to find a way to forestall each." Mum paged through her notes. "Ah, here they are: slave riots, a northern kingdom in civil war, demons emerging from the Devil's Cauldron, and a return of the dragons."

Nick transcribed the scraps of text from his grandfather's journal into his own and added notes. "The first condition is pretty common. Goblins are an unruly race. It seems like there's always some sort of slave disturbance somewhere. That's why my father never bought any. They're more trouble than they're worth."

"The events wouldn't be mentioned if they didn't stand out in the visions of the prophet," Mum said. "Your grandfather believed the riots would have to be widespread and violent to be taken as a portent."

Nick scratched the days of stubble that made his chin itch. "The only condition that reveals anything specific is the demons' rising from the Devil's Cauldron, a canyon somewhere in the Great Sand."

"There's also mention of a 'Guardian,' a statue of some sort, in the land of the 'nomads.'" Zen referenced the pages of a secondary text

Mum had pulled from the shelf. "This book says the Devil's Cauldron contains the ruins of an abandoned city. Maybe the nomads once lived there."

"I doubt it," Nick said. "That desert's a death trap. Nobody lives there. Nobody even goes through it if they have a choice. Yet that's where the demons are supposed to emerge." He paused. "There's a lot missing from the journal, but the text we have suggests this Portal of the Damned can only be located during an equinox."

"The spring equinox occurs in eight days," Mum pointed out.

"Yeah, but we don't know if it's the spring or fall equinox that's important," Nick said. "We've also lost any reference there might have been to a year."

"Maybe it doesn't matter." Zen stood and stretched his back. "Either way, I have no desire to go into the Great Sand. And, I'm not sure what we'd do if we found the Portal."

The discussion went on, and by late afternoon, Nick had learned several things he hadn't known before. Most notable was the fact that the medallions of Vexetan, referred to only cryptically in the journal, would be awarded to the Master's disciples. His "Chosen," as the Prophecy called them, would number twelve. And the medallions would allow the Master to guide them from afar.

Mum's notes said the word "guide" might suggest outright control, in this context. At a minimum, it implied some form of direct communication.

Zen took another turn at the Codex. "It says here that this man, the one touched by Vexetan, will become the 'Master of Air and Darkness.' Both 'Air' and 'Darkness' are capitalized. Any idea what that means? Is it a reference to apparition magic?"

"We concluded that an age of literal darkness will follow the Age of Prophecy, and that this 'Master' will rule it absolutely. The civilized races, if we're suffered to exist at all, will be subjugated by the goblinoids—goblins, orcs, trolls, and ogres—the races that Vexetan created long ago."

"The end of dwarves, elves, and humans," Nick muttered, struggling to get his mind around it all. "No wonder my grandfather was trying to stop it."

"And the Master of Air?" Zen pressed.

"The dragons will return." Mum shrugged. "If he controls them, his rule will include the skies."

"It could mean he'll have mastery of air itself, and perhaps of shadows too." A chill gripped the room as Zen passed one hand over the other, producing a small chunk of ice. "Mine is apparition magic. Every weaving I know how to do uses ice. Maybe this master's skill is similar, but with air rather than ice."

Nick remembered his father's words from just a few nights before. *The flames inside whipped around something fierce, like they was caught in a whirlwind or something.*

Mum stood, leaned over the closest oil lamp, and blew it out. Apparently she considered the day's work finished. "It could indeed, young Zen. It could indeed."

The following morning, Nick returned to the library with Zen and Beltrann. He began with a review of the remaining notes from his grandfather's journal, some no more than titles on scraps of parchment. They went through them, one by one, looking them up in every reference Mum could produce, until Jasmine came in sometime during the mid-afternoon.

She knelt in silence with one knee on the floor, her head bowed, and waited several minutes before Mum acknowledged her presence.

"What is it, child?"

"I apologize for the interruption, elder. Yucca has asked me to invite our guests to the wall. There is something that they, perhaps, will wish to see."

Nick and Zen glanced at one another, then looked at Mum.

"Of course, child. Thank you." Mum led the four of them into the courtyard and up the stone steps to the top of the east wall, where a dozen brothers and sisters of the Order stood, gazing outwards. Rancid paced in front of them all.

The nine riders of the Black Hand had gathered at the far edge of the clearing, Jade and Sledge among them, in addition to the hide-clad woman and the man who'd escaped with her from Traveler's Roost. Mounted side-by-side, they watched the monastery with unnatural interest.

"Look there." Yucca pointed.

Nick followed his gaze but saw nothing unusual.

"Do you see that pair of pine trees?" the monk asked. "Just to the left of the last rider?"

"Yes."

"Look just to this side of those trees. There is a distortion in the air."

"I see it," Zen said.

"I don't— Wait." Nick squinted at the spot. There was something there, nearly invisible. "It looks like heat rising from the road in mid-summer?"

"Yes," Yucca said. "But it's not. See the base of it? It stirs up dust as it moves."

"Like a little whirlwind," Nick said.

Zen quoted from the Prophecy. "The Master of Air and Darkness."

Nick whipped his head around to look at his friend. "You think that's an air apparition?" Fear sharpened the edge of his voice and his heart began to quicken.

"I'm sure of it."

Rancid stopped pacing. "How do you know?"

"I know what they can do." Zen pointed to the distortion. "Notice its size and shape, roughly that of a man. It's too constant to be a natural phenomenon."

"Could it be one of the twelve?" Nick asked. "Or am I just growing paranoid?"

CHAPTER 6

Balor Culhaven, Baron of Tawneydale, cousin to the late king of Trondor, rode into the capital five days after the assassination of King Ednar. He traveled with his personal guard, fifty strong, and approached with confidence. If the rumors were true, Ednar's sons had been murdered along with the king. Since Ednar had no brothers, Balor was next in line for succession.

Today he would submit his bid before the Ruling Council and, when the time came, they would affirm his ascension to the throne.

The heavy, iron-bound gates to the city of Trondor, capital of the kingdom of the same name, stood open. Recognizing his banner, the guards allowed him to pass without challenge.

As always, people crowded the narrow cobblestoned streets, going about their business amid the stone and clay architecture of the second largest city in the most populated human kingdom. Balor and his company thundered through the streets at a gallop, villagers scrambling to make room for his noble procession to pass.

Like the one at the city wall, the palace gate lay open. The guards stood aside to admit him into the courtyard as though they expected him, as well they should. But their worried glances as he walked his mare toward the palace entrance told Balor something was amiss. He handed the reins to a waiting groom, and his standard-bearer passed his flag to an honor guard. The banner, a silver unicorn against a blue background, would fly above the soaring marble and granite towers, alongside those of any other nobles in residence, for the duration of his stay.

A pair of the king's Home Guard stopped him outside the Ruling Council's meeting chamber. "Wait here, sir," the senior guard said. "I'll notify the council you've arrived."

Eagerness drove Balor toward the chamber doors, but he resisted it. Despite his need to learn the circumstances surrounding the death of his cousin's family, the formalities must be observed. So he stayed in the hall and tried to keep his feet still while he awaited permission to enter. Once he got it, it took an act of will to keep from crashing through the doors with a vehemence the council would have perceived as disrespectful.

Before him, a long, curved table spanned a third of the way around the circular room with seven council chairs arrayed behind it, such that each faced the precise center of the room. Six of the chairs were occupied.

Traditionally, these men advised the king, who retained sole decision-making authority. When the throne was vacant, as it was now, the council became the governing body. They ruled by majority vote until they could crown a new king.

Balor stopped short of the room's focal point, where all who addressed the council were required to stand.

Gremauld Santari, one of the council members, occupied the king's seat, the center seat of the seven. Gremauld's own chair stood vacant.

"What madness is this?" Balor demanded of the council as a whole.

"Silence!" bellowed Gremauld, who wore the gold crown and purple robes of the monarchy.

Thunder rolled through the room as the twenty guards surrounding the chamber each slammed the butt of his spear on the marble floor, punctuating the king's command.

"I have not granted permission to speak," Gremauld finished.

Although Balor didn't know how this man came to sit in the king's chair, the trappings of the throne were unmistakable. He stepped up to the red circle in the center of the floor, snapped his heels together, bowed toward Gremauld, and waited.

"We've been expecting you, Baron Culhaven," Gremauld said in a civil tone. "State your business for the council."

"I've come to confirm the news of King Ednar's death and that of his children, and if it is true, to present my bid for the throne."

Gremauld's features affected a sorrow that, from any other man, might have been genuine. "It's true. The king and his family were murdered five days ago. I am sorry for your loss."

"And what of the throne? My eyes tell me the council has already approved a bid."

"Your eyes do not deceive. I am king of Trondor."

"But—" Balor stammered. "The law forbids the council from approving any bid for forty days following the death of a king. All challengers must have time to submit their bids, which this body—" He indicated the council with open palms— "must authenticate before anyone, *anyone*, can succeed."

"Circumstances required that the succession take place immediately."

"What circumstances?"

"The assassin who murdered your kinsmen and mine has escaped into Faldor. To pursue him, we must send troops into that kingdom." Gremauld adopted a tone of exaggerated patience, as though offering an explanation was an act of supreme generosity. "The council can command troops only in the defense of Trondorian territory. Had we waited the usual forty days..."

"I see." A pause hung in the chamber as Balor assessed his options. Finally, he said, "Request permission to address the council, that they might advise the king in this matter." Custom allowed any significant issue to be presented to the entire council. Certainly, the succession to the throne was significant. Although no laws required this and Gremauld could refuse the request, Balor didn't think he would. Pride was considered to be a grievous fault in a ruler. No king who refused to hear from the council would garner respect from his subjects. Furthermore, tradition permitted the king to witness the arguments, but not to interrupt until the council had heard the subject's case and rendered its recommendations.

"Of course," Gremauld allowed cordially.

At present, the Ruling Council included Folton Culhaven, uncle to the late King Ednar; Pandalo Gundahar, the general of the Trondorian army; Nordock Marriten, the royal treasurer; and Rinten Garret and Keal Lansar, both personal friends of the former king. Gremauld, who had held the seat now empty, was husband to the late king's sister.

Balor addressed Folton directly, as he was the eldest member of the council. "Gremauld Santari has been approved as king?"

"He was crowned the day before yesterday."

"And what of the law? I am next in line for succession. You must have known I would submit a bid."

Folton nodded.

"It has been but five days since my cousin's death. I came as soon as the news arrived. My bid must be considered."

Nordock sat with his elbows on the table and his hands folded before him. "We do not have the authority to accept bids for the throne. It's no longer vacant."

"I submit that it is vacant." The statement came out more pleading than Balor had intended. He took a deep, settling breath before continuing. "Although Gremauld sits in the king's chair, his bid for succession could not have been *legally* accepted. For that, he must wait the required forty days. Therefore, the council retains authority, and Gremauld, as a member of the council, will cast but a single vote in the decision."

Nordock's eyes remained hard. Only his lips moved. "That law was suspended prior to the vote. The succession is legal, and therefore final."

"Gremauld has no legal claim to the throne. There's no precedent for an in-law to succeed."

"That is true," Folton replied. "The council will consider your petition and make a recommendation to the king. Even if that recommendation includes a reversal of the decision, it still must be approved by the king."

Balor stood, still and silent as a stone. Gremauld would never voluntarily relinquish the throne.

"I realize," Rinten said, "the proceedings that have taken place during the past few days are unusual. They are, however, legal. The offer on the table is the best the council can make at this time."

Stiffly, Balor bowed to Gremauld and requested leave so the council could deliberate.

"Of course, my cousin." The somber set of Gremauld's mouth failed to hide the grin of satisfaction in his eyes. "Stay this night and refresh yourself. You're welcome for as long as you like. And as you can see, there is an open seat on the council. I offer it to you. Will you consider it?"

Balor swallowed a throat-load of bile that rose within him and retired without a word.

Later that evening, Pandalo and Folton visited Balor's private chambers. These two, by their own account, had been overruled by the majority during Gremauld's ascension.

"The council is corrupt." Folton spat into the fire burning in the hearth along one wall of the sitting room. "Not at all like it was when I accepted my seat."

"What really happened?" Balor asked the old man.

"That's not entirely clear. Gremauld managed to secure three of the six council votes. He, of course, cast the fourth vote that brought his side the majority."

"And he accomplished all this with his claim about the escaped assassin?"

"I don't believe that argument alone won him the votes. It merely served as an excuse to make his proposal."

Pandalo stroked the bushy, peppered beard that, along with the matching mustache, conformed to the current style in Trondor. "Personally, I think he promised Nordock payment from the king's vault for his vote."

"What of Rinten and Keal?" Balor said. "They were two of Ednar's closest friends. Neither would have accepted a bribe."

"That's true. I've known them for a long time. Both are honorable men." Folton paused then, as if trying to decide how to make his next statement. "I don't know the truth of it, but it's been rumored that King Ednar voiced his wishes to Rinten and Keal. Some say that if none of his children could take the thrown, he preferred that it not go to you."

Balor's gut twisted. "Why in the name of all that's civilized would he do that?"

"It's not clear to me that he did," Pandalo said, "given Gremauld's reputation for treachery."

Folton cleared his throat nervously. He sat forward in his seat, but said nothing.

Balor sighed. "Come on. Out with it, old friend. If you have something to say, say it."

Folton stared into his wine for a long moment, and then nodded resolutely. He failed to look at Balor as he spoke. "You're ambitious. Maybe that made Ednar uncomfortable."

"Of course I'm ambitious," Balor spat back. "I'm a nobleman. We're all that way. Ambition is what drove us to become the ruling class. And it's not necessarily a bad trait. That same drive and determination that made us leaders also makes us effective *as* leaders. It's what we do with our power that matters." He paused. "I fear what Gremauld will do with his."

Folton nodded again, conceding the point, while Balor drained his wine. For the better part of an hour, the three discussed the possible plots of subterfuge that might have contributed to Gremauld's succession, but it was all speculation.

Finally, after a long span of silence, Balor asked Pandalo, "If I fight this, can I expect any support from the army?"

Pandalo picked up the bottle. He studied the remainder of the wine through the smoked glass for a few moments, and then split it among their goblets. "The soldiers are well aware of Gremauld's brutality, especially the incident in Dunshire eight harvests back."

Balor remembered it well. Gremauld had doubled the food tithe to further fill his own overflowing storehouses, then ordered the beheading of thirty-four farmers who had protested the increase. That example, as Gremauld had intended, brought the rest of the population in line. From then on, everybody paid whether he could afford it or not.

If that had been the end of it, it might have been forgotten. As a result of the heavy tax, however, a fifth of the rural population within Gremauld's territory had starved to death the following winter, while Gremauld refused to distribute any of his stores to aid them.

Even now, he justified that brutal decision by claiming that he'd simply culled the unproductive among the farmers. The fact that they might have fallen victim to poor soil, a bad run with the pests of that particular year, or a late frost—as opposed to their being incompetent growers—didn't seem to matter to Gremauld. The way he saw it, his township and the surrounding lands had been made stronger, and he would do it all over again, exactly the same way, if given the opportunity.

Balor had no intention of letting him cull the entire kingdom. He slammed his goblet onto the table, spilling a blood-red stain onto the rug beneath it. "The succession is illegal. The throne is mine. And I intend to take it back."

"I'm with you." Pandalo stood, clicked his heels as he came to attention, and bowed. "With as much of the army as I can sway."

Balor looked at Folton.

"I am too old," the man said. "But I will not stand in your way."

"Fair enough." Balor returned his attention to the general. "Gather what support you can and bring them to me at Twin Peaks."

While the company stood on the walls, pondering the intentions of the Black Hand and their unusual cohort, Rancid paced at the forefront of the crowd, where the riders could see him. He unhooked the chain of trophies from his belt and jingled the studded gloves of two dozen dead bandits before the watching enemy. When they didn't respond to the taunt, he strung his bow and launched several arrows, but the riders had moved beyond range.

"Why do you provoke them?" Jasmine asked.

Rancid turned. "What?"

"Where there is conflict, one should seek resolution." Her calm was maddening. "Those people out there do not seem hostile. Why do you provoke them so?"

"They're evil," he said as though that explained everything. When she didn't reply, he added, "They must be destroyed."

"Your hatred of them is evident. I think perhaps it gets in the way of your finding a rational response to their presence. In these situations—"

"Look!" Rancid brandished his string of gloves. "I know my enemy. My sword is my response." Spittle flew from his lips as he ranted. He made a sweeping gesture toward the courtyard. "Look at the might you have here. If you'd all charge out there with me, we could *destroy* them." He emphasized his words with a clenched fist. "But no. You sit here behind your walls, doing nothing."

"We do not know these people. Nor do we know you. They have done nothing to us."

Rancid wheeled on her.

"Perhaps they are legitimately pursuing a rabid murderer?" She eyed the chain of trophies. "We observe as is appropriate, so we may gain the knowledge necessary to determine the best course of action. We do not sit and do nothing."

Rancid muttered an oath and launched another arrow and harangue of taunts at the riders.

"You have too much passion. Emotion clouds your judgment."

Rancid pointedly ignored her.

"If you will excuse me," she said finally, "I have chores to attend to."

"What could you possibly have to do that is of any importance?"

"Your dishes." The girl spun and walked away.

The bandits remained outside the walls for the rest of the day. At nightfall, they dispersed from the clearing and began a round-the-clock vigil from several vantage points surrounding the cloister.

Nick returned to the library with Zen, Beltrann, a renewed sense of urgency, and a determination to take up his grandfather's work. If there was a way to forestall the Prophecy, he would find it. The survival of his race and that of the dwarves and elves depended upon it. And his grandfather's journal might have once contained the information he'd need to do it.

After a third day of study, however, they'd gleaned all they could from the monks. Nick had to learn more. He had to know the truth of the original Prophecy. And if the air apparition really was a Chosen, he had to wake the Civilized Lands to the events that might be coming.

Rancid spent his time pacing the battlements, harassing the Black

Hand, unable to leave the monastery while the bandits patrolled the perimeter.

That evening, they purchased from the monks the supplies they'd need for the next leg of their journey and declined supper in the modest dining hall. Instead, they sequestered themselves in a corner of the courtyard so they could discuss their options with some measure of privacy.

Brother Yucca brought them several apples from the orchard, a bowl of pan-fried turnip wedges, nearly too hot to touch, and a platter containing two pit-roasted hens—half a hen each. He laid the whole spread out on a large goat-wool blanket. It was a regular picnic, and it promised to be the most enjoyable meal any of them had had since this ordeal with the journal and the Black Hand had begun.

Jasmine exercised with her peers on the lawn, not more than thirty feet away. Her weapons were each a short, three-pronged affair. The center point extended maybe half a yard, while the other two, no more than six inches long, served the same purpose as the guard on a sword. But the *sais*, as she called them, had no sharpened edge—just a point at the end of each prong. They looked more like a roasting spit than like an actual weapon, but Jasmine appeared to know them well.

It seemed, too, that she could jump higher and spin faster than any of her peers, though that didn't keep a nearby elder from criticizing her on issues of form and technique.

"Nick," Zen began, "I mean no disrespect to your grandfather, but I think the events leading up to the Prophecy are too great for us to influence. If we want to do something, we should do something within our means."

Rancid produced his dagger—one of questionable cleanliness—and reached for the platter of fowl. Fortunately the meat fell from the bone at the slightest touch, making the dagger unnecessary. "Personally, I don't put much faith in this poem of yours, but if this Master is evil, we should kill him."

"We don't even know who he is," Beltrann countered.

"No," said Nick, "but my grandfather's journal gives us a unique set of knowledge."

"And—" Zen made a vague gesture toward the walls of the cloister— "if that construct out there is one of the Chosen, the Master considers something in it to be a threat. We need to figure out what that is."

"The Prophecy says no weapon forged of this world will harm him." Nick fished through the scraps until he found the page. "It mentions a sword named Demonbane. This sword's not of this world."

"Really?" Rancid's eyes got big. "Where's it from?"

"It was forged in the fires of the Abyss by an angel of Aeron."

Rancid rolled his eyes. "Oh, baron." He began to twirl his dagger in his fingers.

Nick continued. "It's hanging in the royal hall in Brinheim, waiting for the time of the demons' return, when it will be wielded by the queen's champion."

"Obviously, that's not us," Beltrann said.

"The Prophecy also said the heroes who bring the fight to the Master will fail," Zen added. "Regardless of any weapon."

"Maybe. But there's another version of the Prophecy, one in which the heroes defeat the Master and prevent the coming of darkness." Nick held up his hand to forestall Zen's objection. "Mum believes that rendition has been concocted solely to entertain peasants who are more interested in a happy ending than in an accurate account of Mortaan's prediction. Scholars of the text generally believe the darker version, but most scholars have studied only copies of the Codex. Maybe the few who tell of a positive ending have seen the original text."

"I believe there were prophets who foretold a happier ending," Beltrann said. "But none have Mortaan's reputation for accuracy."

Rancid continued to twirl his dagger, which wavered more than once.

Nick half expected it to fly off in some random direction. "That doesn't mean they're not right. Or that they don't agree with the

Prophecy in Mortaan's original codex."

Beltrann nodded. "Sounds to me like we need to find the original."

"There is a reference to it in my grandfather's journal, but he didn't say where to find it."

"Mortaan was an elf," Zen said after a moment. "Maybe the elves can help. We might even try to get an audience with Alamain."

Rancid's dagger became still for a moment, then started up again. "Who's that?"

"The High Priestess of Aeron. Head of the church and queen of the elves."

"Wait a minute." Nick shuffled through the parchment scraps again. "The journal mentions both her and Aeron."

"And the Mist Isles?" Zen continued.

Nick uncovered the page they had learned the least about: The Mist Isles, the legendary home of the fairies, who had left the Civilized Lands at the end of the Age of Magic, about the same time the demons disappeared. "Nobody's ever found them."

"No *human* has ever found them. What about the elves?"

Nick stared at the mage. The thought had never occurred to him. Suddenly, it seemed as though everything was pointing to Lorentil. The Master, if he existed, was a disciple of the god Vexetan. High Priestess Alamain was his greatest mortal enemy. "We're going to Lorentil," he said, "to find Alamain and elicit her aid."

Zen and Beltrann nodded their assent.

Nick collected his documents and put them away before finally attacking the food. "But first, we have to do something about the Black Hand and their construct."

Rancid slammed his dagger down, burying it hilt-deep in the mossy grass. "Now you're talking."

CHAPTER 7

ucca woke the companions well before dawn with Jasmine at his side. "It is time."

Nick sat up and rubbed the sleep from his eyes before rolling out of his cot.

"I have given much thought to the meaning of the past days' events," Yucca continued. "I do not know what they portend, but this sudden interest in your grandfather's journal tells me the Prophecy is somehow connected. And the appearance of the air apparition is cause for additional concern." He glanced at the others as they began to collect their packs and other belongings. "As far as we know, none of the Prophecy's preconditions actually exist today. Therefore, we must temper our actions with reason. Nevertheless, given the seriousness of the Prophecy, it is imperative that you pursue your quest with all available resources. As such, the Order has decided to send our copy of the Codex with you. You may need to refer to it."

Nick glanced at Zen, whose thin eyebrows were raised in surprise. "That's very generous. Thank you."

Yucca gestured to Jasmine, who stepped forward bearing a traveler's bundle. "Jasmine will accompany you to safeguard the book. She had planned to leave the Order during the coming season anyway, for reasons of her own, and her skills may be of some benefit to you." He turned to the young monk. "Aid them as you can. You may find some of what you're looking for along the way."

"Thank you, elder," she replied softly.

Rancid eyed Jasmine with suspicion.

"This way." Yucca led them through the cellars, beyond which a hidden tunnel with a dry, packed-earth floor extended into the mountain.

Without a word, Jasmine lit a torch and escorted the party inside. Rancid retreated to the rear of the party and slunk along at the edge of the light.

Nick walked alongside Jasmine. After a while, he asked, "I've never seen features like yours before. What is your race? I mean no offense," he added quickly. "I'm merely curious."

"I am not ashamed of my heritage. The truth is, I do not know where I come from. The monks found me on the doorstep of the monastery when I was an infant." She kept her eyes on the path ahead as she talked. "Nobody knows who my parents are, or were. A powerful mage who used to live in this region had a reputation for calling demons from the Abyss for his experiments. It was rumored he attempted to merge a demon with a human, but instead of achieving a single, combined entity, the result was a pair of hybrid twins. He disappeared around the time I was discovered. If I am one of the twins, I may have a sibling out there, somewhere."

"Is that what you're searching for? Why you planned to leave the Order?"

"That is part of it. I seek the truth about my past, who I really am. I may find a brother or sister in the process."

Zen stepped closer to the two. "It never occurred to me a mage could create a new life form."

"I consider myself human," Jasmine said, "despite my disfigurements. Any assumption to the contrary would be purely speculation."

They continued for a time. Finally, Zen asked, "How long do you think it'll be before the Black Hand realize we're gone?"

"They will know as soon as the sun rises."

Zen gave her a look of surprise. "That soon?"

"When Sevendeath does not appear upon the battlement to taunt them, they will know."

He nodded his agreement.

"But they will not find our trail easily." She paused. "This Rancid Sevendeath, he is an elf?"

"Elf-kin, I think," Nick said. "I can see some human in his features. But at times he behaves more like an animal. In battle, he seems to act purely on instinct."

"He has had a hard life, I believe," Jasmine said. "Harder, perhaps, than any of ours."

"Yeah, maybe." Zen's voice held no compassion.

They came to the end of the tunnel, which opened on the mountainside. Dawn was beginning to lighten the plains below. There was no path to give away the location of the opening, and it took the group most of the morning to descend the treacherous slope.

As soon as they reached the bottom, Nick led them northward across the plains. "Is this your first time beyond the monastery walls?" he asked Jasmine.

"I have been out many times for my lessons in healing herbs, but never farther from home than Traveler's Roost. I am hungry for knowledge of the lands." She looked at Nick with wide eyes. "Have you seen the other kingdoms?"

He nodded. "I've been to them all at one time or another, except for Cormont. My brother and I each traveled with our merchant uncle from our fourteenth harvest to our seventeenth—an apprenticeship of sorts in the economy of the Civilized Lands."

"You worked for him, then."

Nick gestured at the sword on his back. "As a member of the caravan guard."

"And your brother?"

"He chose to tend the horses. Eventually, he settled in Trondor and started a family there."

"Such noble work. You should both be very proud. I have yet to earn an honest living."

"Don't sell yourself short," Nick said. "I watched you at the monastery. You work harder than any of us."

The country stretched out before them, a rangeland of low, rolling hills carpeted in lush green grasses and dotted with orange sandstone bluffs, a beauty unique to northern Meuribar. Early spring wildflowers had begun to bloom on the southern slopes. In the distance, herds of antelope grazed with apparent disregard for likely predators.

At sundown, Nick thumped his heavy backpack onto the ground. Jasmine explored the campsite, examining the nearby vegetation. Beltrann began assembling a fire.

Rancid stormed up to him. "Are you crazy?" He kicked dirt onto the infant flames. "Put that out."

Beltrann stood, hands on his hips, and glowered at him. "We need it for cooking and it'll likely get cold tonight."

"You want the Black Hand to find us? They may be evil, but they're not stupid."

"We passed beneath a mountain. I think it's safe to assume we've lost them."

"Rancid's just being prudent," Nick said. "Dig a hole for the fire with a bank on the southern side and keep the flames small. Wait until full dark to light it, so the smoke won't give us away."

"I will prepare the meal." Jasmine held a handful of fresh greens, including rosemary, thyme, and several Nick didn't recognize. "If there are other chores to attend, I'll assist with those as well."

Dinner turned out to be the best Nick had ever eaten on the road. The blend of spices with which Jasmine seasoned the squash and smoked fowl tasted wonderful. Afterwards, he told her, "I think the rest of us can tend to the dishes. Do you mind taking a turn at watch?"

"I'll take a shift in the middle of the night," she said. "I'm not troubled by insomnia and, with my physique, broken sleep will affect me less than it would the rest of you."

"That's handy," Beltrann said. "I'll take the first shift so Rancid can come in and eat. Otherwise he'll keep us all awake with his constant pacing."

Nick wiped the cooking pan with a rag and packed it away. "That gives me the morning shift." To Jasmine, he said, "Wake me when the moon reaches its final quarter."

She nodded. "Of course. Now if you will excuse me, I need to re-center my focus from the distractions of the day." With that, she trundled off to a corner of the camp, settled herself with her legs crossed and arms folded before her, and slipped into a meditation that resembled a deep sleep.

Zen settled himself on the far side of the campfire. His arms gestured in the air, his lips moved soundlessly, and his eyes seemed to focus on nothing.

Nick handed Rancid a plate of food. "When you're done eating, it's your turn to do the dishes."

"What do you mean it's my turn? This is our first night. How can it be my turn already?"

"The rest of us have done our share of the chores. That makes it your turn."

Rancid grunted as he stared at the pile of utensils for a moment before gesturing at Zen. "Does he call that magic?"

"Actually," Nick said, "he calls it 'shaping the weave,' or some such thing."

"Weave? You mean like baskets?"

Zen stood and walked over to them. "Not exactly." He made a gesture in the air and a small, rough object that looked like a semi-transparent rock appeared in his hands.

"What's that?" Rancid asked.

Zen offered it to him, but Rancid yanked his hands away.

Nick took it. "It's ice. Right out of thin air."

"There's a pervasive energy about all that exists," Zen explained. "With proper training, a mage can learn to see it, like little threads tying everything together. We call it the weave. The threads can be untied and reconfigured to produce a variety of objects and energies. Some things, like that chunk of ice, are both object and energy."

Rancid took the ice then. He sniffed it, licked it tentatively, and threw it away. "So what? My father has a whole cellarful of the stuff, and he has no magic I ever heard of."

Zen gestured again and a cold fog descended over the fire. The temperature in the whole camp plummeted. Within seconds, the flames died and the coals went dark.

"Thanks," Nick said. "I was planning to use that to study Jasmine's copy of the Prophecy."

"Sorry. I guess you'll have to do it tomorrow." Zen unpacked his blankets as the night's ordinary warmth began to return. "I'm going to bed."

The camp remained quiet throughout the night and the five of them ate cold leftovers for breakfast.

By midday, they reached an eastern tributary of the River Grand, which marked the border of the kingdom of Faldor.

The river, deep and swift, was too dangerous to cross, so Nick led them upriver until they reached a narrow stretch that Jasmine claimed she could hurdle, a distance of at least twenty-five feet.

Rancid harrumphed. "Try it. I dare you."

Nodding, Jasmine set aside her bundle and performed a long series of simple stretches, which caused Rancid to throw up his arms and declare the whole charade a waste of time. The others, however, watched with anticipation as she paced out her runway on the southern side and inspected the far bank.

Finally, she grabbed one end of the party's rope and closed her eyes as if to focus all her faculties on this one effort. A moment later, she took a deep breath and launched into a graceful, loping stride toward the river. She sailed out over the water as if she was diving in, but ultimately cleared the far bank by a fair margin, landing with a smooth somersault and springing to her feet.

Nick shook his head. "Amazing."

Beltrann let out a low whistle.

Rancid grumbled something to himself, dropped his gear, and followed her at a full sprint. He cleared half the river—which was probably better than any of the rest of them could have done—and swam the rest of the way, spitting out water and curses all the while.

They secured both ends of the rope several feet above the water's surface, and each person pulled himself across with his gear. Jasmine brought her bundle across and then leapt the river two more times to retrieve the southern end of the rigging.

The next morning, the sky filled with clouds that spat at them throughout the day. The wind kicked up in the afternoon and by evening brought on a full-fledged thunderstorm. Rain blasted the party in stinging horizontal sheets. The few trees around were too sparse to provide cover and would probably attract lightning, so the party settled into a shallow depression that blocked some of the wind but soon began to fill with water.

Jasmine checked her gear to make sure her copy of the Codex was secure in its oiled leather wrappings.

Thunder and incessant rain made sleep impossible, and the collective mood began to sink into a pit as cold as the hollow they sheltered in. By the time the moon was full, Rancid gave up and stomped off in search of shelter. Visibility would have been no more than a few feet even in daylight. Nick didn't expect to see him again.

In the early hours before dawn, however, Rancid returned. "I found a better camp," he shouted over the howl and the constant splatter of rain.

"Shelter?" Nick yelled.

"At least from this baron-cursed wind."

Nick looked at his soaked charges, who hunched in a semicircle with their backs to the gale.

"Anything's got to be better than this," Beltrann shouted.

As one, they stood and plowed forward toward Rancid's already-retreating back.

Soon the sky began to lighten. Rancid brought them to a gully with a river running through it.

"You've got to be kidding me," Nick said.

Rancid studied the river as though trying to determine which way to go. Finally, he turned upstream and marched for a good quarter-mile without a word before coming to a recess in the near side of the bank. It was far enough off the main channel that a flash flood, in the very likely event that one should occur, wouldn't sweep into it with any force. The nook offered no overhead cover but would at least get them all out of the wind, which had grown so fierce they could barely stand against it. Without discussion, they all dropped in and waited for the storm to abate.

Vinsous Drakemoor, having done his part to put the Master's Chosen onto the Trondor throne, cantered into the city of Faldor on the night the storm moved in.

Suddenly, the medallion he wore grew warm against his chest. When he extricated it from beneath his soaked traveling cloak, it pulsated with a faint, rhythmic glow. Reluctantly yet irresistibly, he peered into its polished onyx center and saw there the face of the Master, who swept away Drakemoor's every conscious thought for the duration of the communication.

When the Master finished, Drakemoor tucked the medallion safely away and considered his new target.

Until that moment, he'd known nothing of Nicklan Mirrin, or of his grandfather's journal. But apparently Nick and his friends had escaped the Black Hand and it had taken Whisper too long to locate their trail. Nick now had a lead of several days and was headed in Drakemoor's direction, which was for the best. Whisper would probably lose the trail again in the storm.

Drakemoor turned his mare toward a barn that stood adjacent to an inn. He dismounted, shook the excess water from his cloak, and handed the reins to the waiting groom. If he'd been assigned Nick in the first place, he would have simply scaled the monastery wall and that would have been that.

The storm grew fiercer after the sun came up. Wind blew rain across the plains, over the heads of Nick and his huddled companions in gusts so strong no one dared to leave the ravine for fear of being swept away.

Predictably, the river rose in the main channel at an observable rate, and by midday began filling the alcove itself with water.

If sleep had been difficult during the night, it was impossible now. One by one, they all began to shiver in the cold mountain runoff, including Zen, who'd grown up in the frozen north. Finally, they had to submerge their gear and sit on top of it just to keep themselves out of the frigid pool.

By late afternoon, they sat in two feet of water. The wind had subsided and the torrent dwindled to a tolerable rain.

Once again, Rancid ventured forth to find a better shelter. This time, Nick went with him. The grass of the plains had soaked through and they walked in a veritable swamp, their feet sinking into the sodden ground.

Near day's end, the silhouette of a few scraggly trees rose against the deepening violet of dusk. Fortunately, the high ground beneath the copse, though wet, wasn't mushy like the surrounding plains, so Nick relocated the party there and they settled in for another night of discomfort.

He and Jasmine managed to secure a few hours of light, fitful slumber. For the others, misery overcame exhaustion and they suffered another sleepless night.

Finally, the sun rose to reveal a clear sky and the promise of a warm day. Though a persistent urgency nagged at Nick, they all needed to unpack their gear for a time and let it dry. Most of their rations were soaked and permeated with sand from the river. The Codex, wrapped as it was, had survived.

Nick and the others napped in shifts throughout most of the day, trying to catch up on lost sleep. Everyone but Jasmine complained of raw throats and headaches.

At one point, they all sat around a sputtering fire, which had taken Rancid two and a half hours to start and no small effort to keep burning. Jasmine steeped a medicinal tea over the tiny flames.

Huddled there, Nick wiped the back of his hand across his running nose and then on his damp trousers. "Why are you staying with us?" he asked Rancid. "You have no obligation and you don't believe in the Prophecy."

Rancid hesitated, his eyes bloodshot and watery.

"We don't need protecting," Zen said. "If the Black Hand track us this far, we can handle ourselves."

"*He* can't." Beltrann held his hands so close to the fire, it was a wonder they didn't burn.

Rancid spun on him. "Who?"

"You. That's what this is really about, isn't it? If the bandits come, you'll need our protection. Not the other way around."

"Yeah," Rancid said, a little too quickly. "That's it." He hung his head for a moment, his ponytail obscuring his scarred face, then looked up at Nick. "Can I stay with you until you reach Lorentil?"

Zen's eyes narrowed. "What are you playing at?"

"You know what the Black Hand can do." Rancid spoke directly to Nick, as if the others didn't matter. "They destroyed your home—"

"And killed my mother."

"Yes." Rancid seemed almost excited now. "That's what I mean. What do you think they'd do to me if they caught me?"

Nick looked around. Even a day after the storm had let up, everything was still soaked. "I don't think they'll be able to track us after a downpour like that."

Rancid didn't answer. He just stared at Nick's face and waited for his reply.

"What about you guys?" Nick said. "What do you think?"

Jasmine pulled the pot from the fire and sampled a spoonful of her tea. "We can always use the extra sword, albeit a rash one."

Rancid scowled but said nothing.

Finally, Nick shrugged. "Suit yourself."

When Nick woke the next morning, he sat up and tried to speak, but the words came out as a hoarse croak. The blinding sunlight stung his eyes and he grabbed his throbbing head between his sweating hands.

Beside him, Zen shook Beltrann to life with similar results.

Jasmine gave them each a cup of tea she'd brewed from the herbs in her medicine bag. "How are you feeling?"

Nick groaned. "Like I've been trampled by an ox."

"None of you is feeling well." She dipped out two more cups of tea and gave one to Zen, whose eyes appeared swollen. He repeatedly pulled a handkerchief from somewhere in his robes to dab at his raw nose.

Rancid coughed a long series of throaty hacks and finally spat a wad of mucus into the fire. He sniffed the cup Jasmine handed him, described it as a "foul-smelling concoction brewed by the kin of a demon," and refused to drink.

"It will make you feel better," Jasmine assured him.

"I feel fine." He held the cup at arm's length, as if he could actually smell the tea through his stuffed nose even from that distance. Nick hadn't been able to smell his at all.

"You do not look fine, sir."

Nick climbed painfully to his feet. "Just drink it."

Rancid gave him a long, cold stare, downed the tea in a single gulp that must have burned his mouth and throat, and then tossed the metal cup onto the ground.

Jasmine picked it up without comment, then turned back to Nick. "You and Beltrann are sweating with fever. The willow bark and peppermint will help some, but it will take several days to exorcise the sickness completely."

"I've seen no sign of pursuit," Rancid said. "And the storm has wiped out our trail. Maybe we should stay here for a day or two and rest."

Wobbly on his feet, Nick was in no condition to disagree. He nodded and settled himself back down by the fire, where he sat throughout the day and accepted, without comment save for a brief word of thanks, every form of remedy Jasmine saw fit to administer.

Jasmine apparently enjoyed her role as caregiver. It seemed to give her a sense of purpose within the group, a means to contribute. "We have little food," she said, after inventorying their supplies in preparation for lunch.

Nick nodded but said nothing. By then, his eyes had stopped feeling bloated and his head throbbed less often.

"I will hunt," Jasmine continued. "I have never done it before. Perhaps I will be successful." She trotted off toward a nearby grove of aspen and pine with an enviable bounce in her step.

Thirty minutes later, Rancid sprinted by and threw a fistful of damp grass onto the fire, in an attempt to douse the flames. "Riders! Those larder-rot, Black Hand bastards have found us!" Then to Nick, more quietly, he said, "Where's that demon-kin monk of yours? We're going to need her."

CHAPTER 8

The floor of the Devil's Cauldron was shaded in these late morning hours, the sun inching its way down the western wall of the canyon toward the vestiges of some old civilization that once sat at its base. Ka-G'zzin, a demon of immense proportion by human standards yet considered small by some of his own kind, dragged a young girl behind him through mounds of collected sand.

His crablike form rose to fifteen feet as he skittered on his four hind appendages, moving between crumbled buildings and along the buried streets of some ancient city. How any humanoid race could have ever lived in the oppressive heat of the Great Sand was a mystery, but not one that warranted Ka-G'zzin's attention. Personally, he found the desert to be pleasantly cool compared to the stifling temperatures of the Abyss, the demonic prison in which his kind had been eternally bound, consuming their existence in the fruitless pursuit of escape.

Yet even the Abyss was preferable to this slavery that Ka-G'zzin endured at the behest of a human mage. His only comfort was that if he performed his duty well, the demons would return and he would, one way or the other, be released from service.

As the sun reached its zenith, brilliance swept the valley floor. The cliffs above obscured all but a ragged ribbon of light, which moved across the ruins. The sun shone from the eastern end of the chasm, until the contours of the canyon walls and overhanging cliff tops began to gradually obstruct the rays, breaking up the ribbon of light into pools of illumination that became smaller and fewer as the hour approached. On this day of the equinox, at noon—according to Addicus, the time specified in the ancient texts—the ribbon shrank to a single, irregular patch of sunlight on a nondescript spot in the amorphous sandscape of the valley.

There lay the Portal through which the Master would bring salvation to Ka-G'zzin's brethren. But finding the Portal and opening it were two very different tasks. Today's activities would merely tell Ka-G'zzin where he must dig when the time came. He left his sacrifice lying in the sand and circumscribed the sunlit patch with one of the blade-like claws in which his foremost limbs terminated. The moment passed and the pool of sunlight dispersed.

Ka-G'zzin looked with satisfaction upon the shape he'd drawn. The marking was temporary. It would be covered by sand blown into the canyon from the dunes above, or perhaps get swept away in the first breeze strong enough to touch the valley floor.

The virgin he'd brought with him had been weakened by the days of desert travel it had taken to reach this valley. For Ka-G'zzin's purpose today, anyone would have sufficed. She was not a sacrifice for any god, but a mere practicality. He'd selected her out of convenience: a target of opportunity, walking through the countryside of Brinheim exuding the sweet smell of a ripe female, as Ka-G'zzin passed on his way to the Devil's Cauldron.

Her condition guaranteed she would attempt no escape. She hadn't the strength remaining in her, so Ka-G'zzin left her where she lay and set about his work.

He paced out the distance from the Portal to seven locations along the canyon's sandstone walls and the nearest structures of the ruin. Each time he approached the girl, he sliced her flesh, collecting a few drops of her blood on the tip of his bladed claw. He scribed a bloody symbol that told him the distance and direction from the mark to the Portal, so that he might find the location again.

When he was finished, he dragged the girl, muttering incoherently in her delirium, to a stone pillar and fastened her there with a heavy chain.

"Don't leave me," she said weakly, past her parched lips and swollen tongue, as the demon skittered away. "Please."

Nick looked up from the campfire to see the line of riders on a rise to the south. All nine were there and he could pick out the two women, Jade and the hide-clad female from Traveler's Roost, among them. There was no doubt. The Black Hand had caught up.

He cursed himself then. Of course they'd caught up. He and his party had barely moved since the storm had started. All the bandits had to do was maintain their direction based on the last tracks they'd seen and eventually they'd pick up the trail again. And here Nick sat, naive and contented, enjoying a day in the sunshine as though he was on a spring camping excursion in the hills near home.

The fire smoked heavily now, heralding their location for miles, but it didn't matter. The Black Hand had already found them.

Three dozen hooves pounded the earth as the bandits charged. By this time, the companions' supplies were arrayed for ease of use, not packed for travel. There was nowhere to run in any case. Today, they had no choice but to fight for their lives.

Nick pushed himself to his feet and drew his sword. Jasmine hadn't returned, leaving only four of them to oppose the Black Hand, and their defense would be scattered. Zen stood at the fire with Nick, staff in hand. His eyes lost focus as he began to tap the weave. Rancid scrambled to the base of a leafless tree, some fifteen yards to Nick's left. Beltrann had been resting in the shade of a nearby aspen and now stood between the fire pit and the charging riders, at the forefront of the defense.

Several trees along the southern edge of the campsite slowed the Black Hand and channeled their advance into three lines of approach: one on Beltrann's left, one on his right, and a third at the east end of camp. The lead rider, an elf with ornate armor and a small shield, barreled in from there, straight toward Rancid, a long-handled sickle raised like a banner above him. Just short of Rancid's tree, he yanked his horse to a stop and slid smoothly from the saddle. He strode forward with deadly purpose.

Rancid skirted the tree trunk, trying to gain some semblance of protection against a weapon that had at least twice the reach of his own.

The hide-clad woman from Traveler's Roost launched a sling stone at Beltrann, forcing him to dodge to the side. She, Sledge, and an unfamiliar man with a spear galloped past the big man toward Nick.

Zen nodded with a sneer of grim confidence, his staff standing in the soft ground and his hands poised in the air.

The five remaining bandits had stopped short of the grove and dismounted to fight on foot. Two of those were at Rancid's end of the camp. Beltrann would have to hold off the other three until someone could come to his aid.

Nick couldn't see the air apparition. Nevertheless, he had to assume it was there somewhere, and that he, Nick, was its target.

The pain in his congested head faded to nothing more than an unpleasant pressure as his thoughts focused on his immediate enemies. He parried a thrust of the spear and ducked an arc of Sledge's hammer, which whooshed just over his head as the charging trio thundered past him and Zen. The sudden movement brought back a momentary pain in Nick's temples. Nevertheless, he whipped his blade across the unprotected side of the female, and she screamed in pain and rage.

All three bandits dismounted and left their horses, which were bred for speed and endurance rather than for combat, to fend for themselves beyond the boundary of the skirmish.

Nick turned to face them, trusting Beltrann to warn him if any of the other bandits made it past him to come at Nick's back. His breath came in painful heaves past his raw throat. His sword felt heavy in his hands.

A hawk made of ice flashed into being, right in midair. At a gesture from Zen, the bird swept down upon the spear-wielder, pecking and clawing his face, drawing the man's blood and attention. Two frozen shards sped past the hawk and embedded themselves in the man's chest, toppling him before he'd taken two steps from his horse.

Jasmine raced toward the camp. Nick had never seen anyone—short of a man mounted on a horse—move so swiftly. For a moment, he marveled at the bravery of this girl who had chosen death in battle over the safety of her concealment in the woods. As Nick watched, Jasmine was suddenly slammed sideways into the trunk of a tree, as though she'd been hit by an invisible runaway warhorse. She impacted with a sickening crunch and lay, unmoving, in the grass.

Nick could spare no more attention for her or the apparition that had hit her. The hide-clad woman, having tied a knot in her tunic to cinch it around the cut in her side, came at him with her steel-studded glove raised. She ducked Nick's sword and came up swinging. Her blow knocked the breath from his chest.

All at once, Nick's training from his years with his uncle's caravan kicked in. He became aware of everything. His pain and his peril; Sledge, behind the woman; the ice hawk. The violent stirring of the campfire and the sudden shower of coals that leapt into the air, kicked up by a solid wind.

Nick spun away from both the fire and the woman as the construct swept past, whipping at the fabric of his clothing. Hot embers and ash rained down on the spot where he'd been standing. For a moment, the construct's turbulent passage drove a wedge between Nick and the bandits. He thrust his sword at the thing, but his blade swept through without effect. From there, the flowing grasses at the construct's base allowed Nick to track its movements toward his backpack—toward the remnants of his grandfather's journal and the information the enemy had been so diligently pursuing.

Nick didn't have time to ponder the chilling implications of that development. The woman came at him again, this time with Sledge at her side.

CHAPTER 9

Once Jasmine went down, Beltrann divided his attention between her and the approaching bandits. If the apparition could take her out so quickly, it could do the same to any of them.

A few seconds later, however, Jasmine staggered to her feet. She rose gingerly, holding her side, and limped forward. For a moment, she closed her eyes in meditation and seemed to will the pain away. Then, as if that was all the care she needed, she sprinted to Rancid's aid, intercepting one of the bandits with a flying kick that smacked the base of his ear and dropped him like a sack.

Beltrann forced his attention back to the three bandits who had dismounted and now approached him. One wielded nothing more than a studded glove, but both of his friends advanced with swords.

Suddenly a pair of ice shards zipped past him into the nearest swordsman's chest, causing the man to stagger back.

In that instant, Beltrann attacked. When it came to combat, he was neither well-trained nor well-practiced, but he'd received some instruction during his childhood at the monastery. And years of swinging a smith's hammer had built up respectable strength in his arms. He gripped his staff with both hands and swung it like a whistleball club. The skull of the off-balance swordsman shattered under the force of the blow.

When Beltrann raised his staff again, the remaining swordsman hesitated, then detoured around the far side of a tree. The other bandit, looking at Nick, began a sequence of subtle gestures and muttered incantations.

Beltrann charged him, swinging his staff in almost awkward fury, forcing the man to dismiss his weaving unfinished. This, he'd learned from Zen, was not only disorienting, but fatiguing as well. The mage retreated as Beltrann pressed on, leaving the swordsman to hurry after. His staff connected once. Twice. Beltrann's third hit knocked the mage to the ground, unconscious or worse.

Instantly, Beltrann whipped his staff behind him, expecting the remaining Black Hand swordsman to be upon him, but he wasn't. The man lay, unmoving, at Jasmine's feet.

A female, the one Nick had pointed out from the monastery wall as Jade, charged Jasmine, her cutlass raised to cleave the monk's skull. Without turning, Jasmine struck out with her clawed foot. She grasped the woman's sword arm with her talon and pulled it to the side. In the same motion, she scooped up a branch the size of her thigh—a piece of debris left by the storm—and cracked Jade's skull with it. Thank Aeron, Beltrann thought, for friends like Jasmine, with courage and skill borne of the Order and a physique like no other.

The tattered journal of Nick's grandfather drifted into the air upon the wind of the apparition, and then vanished from sight as the entity swept away toward the south, leaving its Black Hand henchmen to fend for themselves.

"Abort!" yelled the leader of the bandit gang.

At that moment, Rancid stepped around the tree and drove his sword through the elf, who stood gaping. He fell to his knees as Rancid withdrew the blade and severed the elf's head.

That left only Sledge and the woman from Traveler's Roost. Hearing the call from their leader, both spun from their opponents. Sledge struck Zen with his hammer as he turned.

The bandits' horses, waiting nearby, received their riders expectantly.

When the woman slowed to mount, Nick slashed his great sword across her back and she tumbled from her steed.

Zen, though dazed by the hammer blow, drew the birch wand from within his robes. He pointed it at Sledge and slurred a command word. A blue spark hissed from its tip and slammed into the fleeing bandit. With a grunt, the brute doubled over in the saddle as his mount delivered him beyond a screen of trees. The remaining horses followed.

Nick whipped around to the south and scanned the landscape fruitlessly for the apparition. "I guess they finally got what they came for."

Zen put the wand away, pushed up the loose sleeve of his robe, and inspected his bruised shoulder. It'd be purple by nightfall, probably all the way to the elbow, but nothing seemed broken.

Rancid pulled the studded glove from the dead leader's hand and discovered a gold ring beneath it. Without ceremony, he slipped it onto his own finger.

Nick looked worried as he scanned the prairie to the south.

Beltrann stormed up to Zen. "Where did you get that?"

Zen continued probing his wound. "From a war hammer."

"Not that. The wand." His tone was threatening. "Where did you get it?"

"I borrowed it from Jarret." Zen tried to shrug, but when he did, pain shot down his arm and across his shoulder blades.

Beltrann planted his fists on his hips. He towered over Zen, taking full advantage of his imposing frame. "What else did you take?"

Sheepishly, Zen reached into his pack and produced a handful of rolled parchment.

"Give them to me." Beltrann held out his hand and made a beckoning motion with his fingers.

Zen handed him two of the three scrolls. "Better that I keep one. I may save your life with it someday."

Beltrann hesitated. "Fine."

"Good. Now you're an accomplice."

"We'd better go," Nick said, effectively heading off the coming argument.

Jasmine staggered up, holding her ribs, apparently on the verge of collapse. Willpower alone seemed to have carried her through the battle; to defeat three of the Black Hand, saving the lives of both Rancid and Beltrann—not to mention her own—in the process. But she'd reached her limit. She dropped to her knees, panting. That one hit from the apparition would have probably killed an ordinary human.

Rancid too returned to the ailing campfire. "Looks like our little flower here won't be able to travel for a while."

"The lesson of today is that we need to keep moving. That thing may come back." Nick touched Jasmine gently on the shoulder. "How are you doing?"

Steeling her resolve, Jasmine pushed herself to her feet. "I am well." She walked to her bundle, teeth grinding with the effort to conceal her pain. There she selected a leaf from the herbs in her medicine bag and chewed on it for a moment, sucking out and swallowing its juices. Her features relaxed almost instantly. Then she eased her bundle across her shoulder and looked pointedly at Rancid's minor cuts. "You think you can keep up?"

He smiled and shook his head incredulously. "If you have shoes, put them on. Your tracks are too easy to recognize." Without waiting for a reply, he strode out of camp toward the north.

They reached the River Grand, much broader and swifter than the small tributary they'd crossed a few days before, and followed it into a region of rocky landscape that provided visual cover from the surrounding plains. When Jasmine, Nick, and Beltrann began to falter from either injuries or illness, Nick called a halt for the evening.

Food was in short supply, so Beltrann whittled a branch into a workable fishing pole. He affixed a hook and line from the supplies they'd purchased at the monastery and set about catching dinner.

Relaxing on the riverbank, he inhaled deeply of the fresh highland air. He'd never been on such a grand adventure. Because he'd been sheltered in the monastery for the better part of his life, leaving it had been the most exciting and frightening thing he'd ever done. Oh, what an enterprise *that* had been, venturing past Traveler's Roost and into the mysterious and alluring valley beyond, a land he'd seen only from the ridge-top before.

Cedar Falls was the nearest town in that direction. So when the time came, that's where Beltrann went. There he learned the value of coin, for he'd left the monastery with very little, and when it ran out, he sought work. Unfortunately, the village already had its fill of smiths. Beltrann was forced to change professions. He became a manservant for Jarret Grannock, who proved to be one of the most lucrative employers in the area. There Beltrann had stayed.

So much for the grand adventure.

Now he couldn't help but enjoy the quest, even through the long days, the storm, and the battles. He was finally seeing the lands.

Sounds from some nearby animal burrows drew his thoughts back to the present. Perhaps Rancid would make himself useful and kill some small game to add to their stores. As it turned out, though, he just frustrated Beltrann's own efforts. He came and stood nearby, watching him fish, with a look of confusion on his face. Beltrann kept about his task and said nothing. As an hour passed, Rancid began shifting his weight from foot to foot, then pacing back and forth along the bank. Finally, unable to take it any longer, he blurted, "Why don't you just shoot them?"

"What?"

Rancid brandished his bow. "Just shoot them!"

Dumbfounded, Beltrann gestured toward the river. "Be my guest."

In a huff, Rancid strung his bow and launched four arrows into the water without effect, before giving up and stomping away. Nick joined Beltrann then, with a handmade fishing pole of his own. He fitted a hook to his line and sat down.

"Odd fellow," Beltrann said, after a time.

Nick looked up. "I think the only thing he's ever hunted is the Black Hand."

Over the course of the evening, the two men caught enough fish for dinner but none for the road the following day. Nevertheless, the food couldn't have been more welcome. It was the first fresh meat they'd had since they'd left the monastery. As Nick cooked, juices dripped into the fire, sizzling with a sound that made their stomachs growl.

Jasmine, however, didn't eat. Instead, she spent the evening in a state of deep, self-healing meditation from which the others feared to wake her.

For six days the companions followed the river northward before the prairie gave way to hills. The river turned east along the elven border and snaked its way down from an isolated, snow-covered peak.

Zen gazed across the river into Lorentil, where the grass was lush and green compared to the dirt and scrub on the Faldor side. Trees forested the elven land. It looked exotic, but it wasn't the beauty Zen coveted. It was the elven magic.

Still, his stomach soured at the thought of crossing into the land.

"You okay?" Nick asked.

Zen startled. "Yeah. Why?"

"You look... I don't know."

"It's nothing." He paused. "My father was an elf."

"I thought you didn't know your father."

"That's the point. He left before I was even born." Zen looked back at the expanse of land behind them, the human lands, which he'd traveled from Trondor to Palidor in search of any magic he could acquire. Yet he'd never ventured within the borders of his father's homeland. "I guess I never forgave him for that."

Zen shifted his pack on his shoulders. "That hardly matters now." He marched up to the river's edge. Purpose compelled him to set aside his stale animosity, or at least endure it. Lorentil was supposed to be richer in magic than anyplace else in the Civilized Lands. It was only a rumor, but one he'd heard from many sources and one that rang true.

Nearby, the river plunged seventy-five feet down a sheer cliff at the base of the peak. By this point, it had narrowed to a hundred feet across, still too wide to swim easily, but continuing upstream was no longer an option.

"Have you been to Lorentil before?" Zen asked finally. "The city, I mean."

"Sure." Nick cleared his throat of congestion left behind by the fever. "We went maybe a half-dozen times in the three years I rode with the caravan."

"Did you transport anything enchanted?"

"Sometimes. Mostly we hauled mundane wealth, which is actually more dangerous. That's what bandits look for—coin. Most of the enchanted stuff they're either afraid of or don't know how to use, or both."

Rancid joined them on the bank. "Not the Black Hand. They seek magic to use against their victims."

Zen and Nick glanced warily at one another but said nothing. With luck, they'd left that danger far behind. Another lay before them: the river, and the elves beyond.

Rancid gazed into the pool at the base of the waterfall, its bottom concealed in murk. "Looks like a great place for crocodiles."

"No," Nick said. "It's too cold for them here, but there're worse things than crocs."

Jasmine set her bundle down in the lush grass along the bank. "That can't be helped." Over the past week, her ribs seemed to have completely healed. She no longer showed any signs of discomfort, either from her wounds or from the colder air they'd encountered as they moved north. "We must cross." She selected a spot near where the river drained the pool, yet was wide enough that the current ran slow. "Here, I think."

Together, the party inventoried their rope and came up with two hundred feet, enough to span the pool if they could get one end to the other side.

"We can make a raft with some of this deadwood," Nick said, "to keep the packs dry and my armor afloat."

Beltrann gathered up a few of the branches lying near his feet. "I'll help with the raft, if someone else will swim the rope across."

They all stood in silence, alternately eying the river and each other. Gradually, every eye settled on Jasmine. She was the most athletic. Surely she could swim.

"Very well." She tied one end of the rope to a tree, took the other in the talon of her left hand, and dove into the pool. When she surfaced on the far side, she climbed out and secured the line.

Around the companions, the sounds of the forest were abundant, with birds chirping and lizards and other critters skittering through the underbrush. Suddenly, the loud hoot of some large and unnatural bird carried across the river.

Zen glanced nervously at Nick, who said nothing.

Jasmine, alone on the far side, turned and peered into the woods.

For several seconds, she stood motionless, watching. She moved away from the river, toward the denser copse beyond, and then walked parallel to its edge, stopping every now and again to observe some feature beyond Zen's view. Finally, she returned to the bank and descended into the pool.

By the time she rejoined her friends, the raft was ready. Nick tested its buoyancy with a dummy load of rocks before committing their supplies to it. Jasmine checked the oilcloth on the Codex and tied the wrapping snugly with a spare piece of twine. She looped an extra length of hemp over the guide rope she'd secured across the pool.

Meanwhile, Zen continued to scan the woods on the far bank, unable to pinpoint the source of his unease but poised to tap the weave nonetheless.

Finally ready, Nick waded in, secured the raft to a line around his waist, and pulled himself along the guide rope. The rope sagged nearly to the water's surface and the raft bobbed awkwardly behind him, but he crossed without incident. Jasmine followed to bring the raft back for a second load but stopped halfway out of the water on the far side, frozen in her tracks.

A pair of elven archers stood near the edge of the trees with arrows nocked in their bows. Their armor and gear displayed a mix of natural colors, making the elves difficult to spot, even in the open.

Zen could see no others, but that didn't comfort him in the least.

CHAPTER 10

Jasmine stood in the icy runoff of the snow-capped peak with no weapon, no supplies, and ten feet of water to wade between herself and the shore as a third elf emerged from the trees. He also carried a bow but had it slung across his back. A thin saber dangled loosely from his hand.

Nick, whose pack and supplies remained piled on the raft, had unfastened the bonds that secured the gear, but his sword wasn't handy enough to draw. He'd become a pincushion if he made the attempt.

"That thing with you?" the elf asked him, fluent in the human speech, pointing his saber at Jasmine.

The elves must have been watching for some time. Jasmine was obviously with him. Therefore, the question was a test of honesty. If Nick answered yes, the reaction of the elves was, at best, unpredictable. But if he said no, he'd likely die for the falsehood.

Nick hesitated.

Jasmine spread her clawed hands where the elves could see them and began wading toward shore. "I am no 'thing,' sir." The talons she presented belied her statement, but she continued in a pleasant tone. "I am a woman. And though we appear different, I am much like yourself." She stepped from the water, shivering with cold as a breeze swept her dripping body. The wet fabric of her thin robe clung to her skin.

The elven leader looked her over, expressing a rapid progression of curiosity, lewdness, amusement, and finally disgust. "I've never seen such a creature as yourself."

"I am human, though not fully. And I make no apologies for a heritage over which I had no control."

One of the elven archers tracked her every move with the point of his arrow as she approached to a comfortable distance for conversation. "I offer no hard feelings for your reaction, and desire only friendship with you and your people."

The elf turned to Nick with apparent disregard for Jasmine. "For what purpose do you enter Lorentil?"

"To visit the Temple of Alamain. We seek the aid of the High Priestess."

"In what matter?"

"Recent events have occurred that we believe are relevant to the Prophecy of Mortaan. Alamain may be able to help us understand these events, and the Prophecy. We seek her guidance."

"Can you be specific about these events?"

"We were attacked in my hometown by a group of bandits who call themselves the Black Hand."

The elf's eyes narrowed at the mention of the gang, but he didn't interrupt.

"You've heard of them," Nick said, with no question in his tone. He described everything from the pursuit from Cedar Falls to the assault that followed the thunderstorm.

The sentry's posture began to relax during Nick's recitation and two additional elven guards emerged from hiding.

"How many Black Hand?" the elf leader asked.

"Nine, but only one remains, and he was badly wounded when he fled. He, too, may have died."

"And the entity you spoke of?"

"It got what it came for. I don't think it'll come after us again."

Nevertheless, the border guard sent one of his men to spread news of the danger and gave permission for the rest of Nick's party to cross into their kingdom. He spoke at length with Rancid about his personal success against the bandits. Zen provided additional details regarding the apparition.

Nick showed the elves his own notes, which included his copy of the original scraps from his grandfather's journal, while Beltrann repacked their gear for travel.

On their second full day in the kingdom of Lorentil, Nick and his friends arrived at Gloriettin, an elven village surrounded by a low stone wall that looked like a battlement except that it stood only four feet high. A tall arch at the southern end framed a heavy wooden gate. Nick could have simply hopped the wall at any point, but suspecting some enchantment, he led them to the gateway, where a sentry directed them to the captain of the guard.

Inside the wall, the town couldn't have covered more than a square mile. The elven residents walked with a casual poise that suggested both confidence and humility.

A trio of dwarves lurched from the Siren's Lair, a seedy tavern hunched along the main drag. The three scanned the street, taking no apparent notice of Nick's party, then staggered away, still drinking from the stout flagons they carried.

"Odd, repulsive lot," Rancid said. "All squat and hairy."

Zen motioned to the Siren's Lair. "Whorehouse?"

"An expensive one." Nick angled toward the guard station farther down the street.

"I would have thought elves above that sort of thing," Beltrann said.

"You'd be surprised. They don't condone slavery, though. Not even of goblins, whom they dislike just as much as we do."

Jasmine received looks ranging from curiosity to fear, the former from elves, the latter from the occasional humans they passed. "Abomination," one man muttered.

Jasmine frowned, but she made no other response to the comment. Rather, her eyes moved from sight to sight, as though consuming every detail.

The captain, when they found him, sat astride a mare at the crossroads marking the center of town, accompanied by another man in similar dress. The captain surveyed Nick's ragged band, his eyes pausing on their filthy clothing, ill-maintained equipment, and half-empty packs. "Welcome," he said, with no hint of sincerity.

More than a little self-conscious, Nick explained their errand.

"Looking for a guide to the capital, are you? Fine. You'll find food and lodging at the Sweet Maple. The general store's across the street." He pointed.

The provisioner, just leaving his shop, settled a heavy wooden bar across the door and snapped a padlock into place. He wore a silk blouse and fine linen trousers. Apparently supplying foreigners in Gloriettin was a lucrative business. The sign on the door said the store would reopen at dawn.

Nick and the others proceeded to the Sweet Maple. Once there, they secured a pair of rooms, stashed their belongings, and settled into a taproom table. Early as it was, the place was crowded, smoke already thickening into an opaque haze across the high ceiling.

By the time they finished dinner, a young elf girl with sparkling auburn hair strode in, wearing form-fitting travel leathers, and marched up to Nick's table. "I'm Daranelle Lillipor. Hear you're looking for a guide." She spun a chair around from the next table, dropped her petite body into it, and swung her boots onto the table, nearly upsetting the drinks. "Call me Dara."

Zen shifted, sitting straighter in his seat.

The girl appeared to be about seventeen by human standards. As an elf, that would make her probably forty or fifty. "I can take you to the capital, but I charge ten coins for the service. In gold."

"We haven't got much," Nick said. "Does that include your food along the way?"

"I'll provide my own. You needn't worry about that." She flagged down the serving girl and bought a round for the table—cheap ale, but it was wet and welcome nonetheless.

"How long will it take to get there?" Zen asked.

"That depends. Are we riding or walking?"

Nick took a sip and set the drink aside. "Walking, I'm afraid."

"Unless you're supplying the horses," Zen added hopefully.

Dara flashed him a look that managed to say, "Not likely," and "I might surprise you," at the same time. She turned back to Nick. "Two weeks."

Zen leaned forward and whispered to her, "Is there anyone in town who might be interested in purchasing an enchanted scroll?"

Dara laughed out loud, a girlish sound full of fun and teasing. "Probably, but not if it's a secret. If you keep it in your robes, nobody'll know what you've got to offer. It's not like someone's going to steal the thing."

Zen sat back with a chuckle. "You're something else."

"I'll tell you what. I'll see what I can do. For a ten-percent commission." Then, to Nick, she said, "You need supplies, I gather?"

He nodded.

"Very well. We'll leave here at noon tomorrow." Dara downed her drink in a single pull and hopped to her feet. She patted Zen on the shoulder as she passed him on his way to the door.

Balor Culhaven sat astride his horse, overlooking Twin Peaks Pass. The Sharktooth Mountains stretched in a ragged, double row of snow-covered pinnacles to either side of him, separating a slice of eastern Trondor from the rest of the kingdom by a natural barrier that became intraversable during the winter months. The pass itself, which had opened just a few weeks before, would provide a defensible position from which he could mount the rebellion.

It had been several days since Balor had walked out of the capital, and he expected Pandalo Gundahar to arrive at any time with whatever support he could muster from the regular army. The general had worked his way to the top, starting as a foot soldier. As such, he'd earned the respect of the troops, but asking the king's commanders to join a revolution was unprecedented in the history of the kingdom. Then again, so was the succession of an in-law to the throne, especially one with Gremauld's reputation for brutality.

Dalen Frost, a man of thirty-five harvests, fifteen of which he'd spent as a scout in the Home Guard, loped up the hill on his grey gelding. He came alongside the Trondor heir. "Your vanguard forces approach." His breath was visible in the cold morning air. "Three thousand horse, my lord, with General Gundahar at their head, flying the Culhaven crest. They'll arrive by noon today, if they're not delayed."

Balor frowned, silent for a long moment. "I had hoped for greater numbers."

The general arrived shortly before noon with the mounted men, each of whom led at least one spare horse on a tether. He nodded to Dalen and turned to Balor.

"Well met, Pandalo," the heir said. "I trust you are well."

"Yes, my lord. And I you." He bowed to complete the formal greeting.

"Tell me you have good news."

"In truth, the news is not as good as I'd hoped, but it's better than I'd feared. Marktel refused his allegiance. I've swayed a third of the regular men, but we're dangerously short in cavalry."

"Is this all we're to have, then?" Balor gestured to the company forming up by ranks in the pass.

"No, my lord. We've nearly eight thousand. I left the rest as a rear guard for the foot soldiers, who couldn't keep pace. I wanted to bring the news ahead."

"That leaves Gremauld with twenty-two thousand mounted men. They'll overtake our soldiers."

"Not likely." Pandalo smiled mischievously. "We stole what horses we could and scattered the rest. It will have taken Gremauld at least a day to recover them and another half to prepare them for the journey. I also left three thousand horse and as many light infantry in the Black Forest where it reaches out to touch the road. They'll delay the pursuit long enough for the others to arrive."

Balor nodded, some semblance of hope returning. "Anything else?"

"Though we'll fight the war outnumbered two to one, I've swayed better than half the archers and crossbowmen. We'll be able to defend the pass, at least until Gremauld realizes what he's up against." The general paused. "I'm sure the king has issued a call for the militia by now."

"We're days ahead of him. I sent runners to call up the volunteers from Tawneydale and beyond. I believe most of the southern townships will support me."

"I trust you're correct." Pandalo bowed again. "If I may have your leave, I've preparations to make."

Zen walked beside Dara as the party left Gloriettin and penetrated deeper into the elven wilderness. A strange haze began to fill the sky, diffusing the sunlight.

Rancid frowned upward at the bizarre phenomenon. "It's unnatural."

"It's part of the enchantment of Lorentil," Dara explained. "It imparts a subtle confusion upon all but elves who enter our lands. If you're welcome, the elves will guide you. If not..." She shrugged.

"That's all well and good for you," Rancid said. "But how do we know you're even leading us north?"

"You don't. In fact, I'm not. The capital lies both north and west from here." Dara winked at Zen. "I will take you north, if you wish it."

"It's all right, Rancid," Nick said. "The elves may harbor a want for coin, but they treat their friends fairly."

What Rancid muttered next was unintelligible. After that, he remained strangely quiet for the rest of the day. That night, however, he returned to his familiar routine of patrolling the camp while Nick studied the Codex, Jasmine meditated, and Beltrann cooked.

Zen moved off to one side with Dara and entertained her with various manifestations from the weave. She giggled like a girl of eight harvests when he altered his face with thick white eyebrows, a long, villainous mustache, or a beard fit for a dwarf—each made entirely of snow, but willowy and flowing in the manner of real hair.

"Isn't that cold?" she said, touching it.

Zen shrugged. "I grew up in northern Trondor. I'm used to it."

When the party began to settle down after dinner, Dara said, "We'll need two people up at a time throughout the night. There're beasts in these woods that can take out a lone sentry at a single stroke if we let them."

The following day, Zen asked her many questions about the elves and their ways, touching on the subject of magic only subtly.

He was still by her side two days later, when they reached Morrinia. "I haven't seen a single road or trail since we entered Lorentil," he said.

"That's another part of our defensive policy. We do everything we can to promote an environment that's easy to get lost in."

By the looks of it, they'd succeeded. The land was covered with a uniform blanket of wild grass and clover, generally flat, and dotted with enough trees to prevent a view of the horizon in any direction. Dense groves and large, loose forests appeared at every turn. The sun, shrouded by the persistent haze, had become useless for navigation.

"With towns as close together as these, there must be a lot of traffic between them. How do you prevent trails from forming?"

"Most visitors travel with an elven guide, though our laws don't require it, and each of us takes a slightly different route every time. Druids will quicken regrowth to conceal any trail that does begin to show."

They passed the gate into Morrinia, which was protected by a four-foot-high battlement similar to the one around Gloriettin. The villages were sisters—twins even—spawned of the same design. The provisioner's store sat in the same position as the one in the border town. Only the name on the sign convinced Zen that Dara hadn't led them in a wide circle back to the same place.

"We'll spend the night here," she said. "I may have a buyer for your scroll."

"Hush." Zen glanced back at the others. "I don't want an argument with Beltrann. He would rather I keep it."

She gave Zen a sly look and leaned close. "You are determined to sell?"

He bit his lip and looked at his feet. The enchantment Jarret had stored within the written words might come in handy someday, but Zen's purse was empty. "I must."

"Then check in and come to my room in an hour."

He did, and the two set out into town. The prospective buyer turned out to be an elf who lived in a cottage separated from the main street by a quarter-mile of residential dwellings. He may have been a practitioner of the weave or merely a dealer of enchanted wares. His shop was a ten-foot-square room attached to his house.

When Zen gave him the parchment, the elf unrolled it and inspected the text carefully, probably verifying the language and syntax. He examined the scroll's edges and the condition of the parchment. Zen smiled. The more carefully the elf studied the document, the more he was likely to offer. Jarret Grannock produced no cheap wares.

"Thirty gold coins."

Zen choked on the price. He'd apprenticed long enough to know the scroll's value, a full five times the offer. He pounded his chest with his fist to clear inhaled saliva from his throat.

"If you prefer," the elf said, "you may take a trade from my stock. I'll offer any scroll from this shelf, or two from there." He gestured to the referenced items.

Zen peeled back the title row of a few of the rolls and returned them to the shelf. He'd value them at less than the coin, but he was caught between a hydra and its hellhound. The shop was well stocked. The elf didn't need Jarret's scroll, or even want it—judging by his demeanor—unless his profit would be enormous.

Finally, Zen accepted the gold, paid Dara's fee, and returned to the inn, wondering if Morrinia really was on the way to Lorentil or whether she'd sidetracked them all for the sake of the commission. Not that it mattered. He'd asked for a buyer and she'd found one.

Zen didn't see her again until the following morning, when she knocked on his door at dawn. The party purchased a cold breakfast of cream and sweet cakes, and departed within the hour.

That noon, they entered a glen and discovered a man straddling a log, chewing on a loaf of hard bread and a handful of dried apples. An overstuffed backpack sat on the ground beside him.

"That's odd." Dara scanned the nearby trees. "Wait here." She approached the traveler as though she hadn't a care in the world.

Zen could hear none of the conversation from his distance, so he watched the two carefully. Dara motioned to the woods with a sweep of her hand and pointed back toward Morrinia.

The man, dark-haired and clean-shaven, dressed in a maroon overcoat and gray trousers, spoke at length. He gestured sparingly as he talked, exhibiting a peculiar economy of motion. Dara listened patiently before making her reply.

Finally, both turned toward Zen and the companions. The man stood, stuffed his leftover apples into his cloak pocket, and hefted the backpack onto his shoulders.

"This is Vinra," Dara said when she returned.

The man came to a stop behind her.

"Says he's a priest of Robala. He was traveling to Lorentil when he lost his way." She winked at Zen. "He'll be joining us if no one has any objections."

The man waited. An elongated bundle protruded from the top of his pack at his left shoulder, wrapped in a thick blanket and secured with twine. A sword and brace of daggers hung on his belt. One had an opal inlaid in the handle. The man had wealth, apparently.

When nobody dissented, Dara extended her hand, into which Vinra deposited a gold coin.

Beltrann shook Vinra's hand. "Robala must be a minor deity. I've never heard of him."

"Her," Jasmine said. "Patron saint of the wayfarer."

"She's more than a saint," Vinra insisted.

Nick stepped up. "She's no Aeron."

"Perhaps not," Vinra said, apparently without affront. "But she takes care of her own."

"What sends you to Lorentil?" Zen asked, hoping the question sounded casual, indifferent.

"I'm to deliver a sacred artifact to the temple and perform a 'Quelling of the Beasts' ceremony."

Zen's gaze went again to the bundle. It was too short to be a staff. A scepter, maybe. Enchanted? Probably. Divine? Perhaps. Ah, but could Zen acquire it? That was a question for another time. He shoved it into the same corner of his mind that remembered the ring Rancid had taken from the Black Hand leader in Faldor. One never knew what the future might bring.

CHAPTER 11

"Assassinated?" Zen exclaimed, when Vinra told him of King Ednar's death. He still considered Trondor home, and Ednar was the only king he'd ever known.

Dara nodded. "I heard that too. It supposedly sparked a revolution, brothers of the old king, I think. Some dispute over an illegal succession."

Nick moved up to join them. "A civil war? Is that what you're saying?"

"Didn't you know?" Mock astonishment lit Dara's face. "Wars are *never* civil."

Nick shot her a sharp glance.

"In a northern kingdom," Zen added, remembering the preconditions of the Prophecy.

Dara looked from one to the other, as though she realized she was missing some significance in the exchange. "It's fairly common. A king dies. Suddenly everybody sees it as their big chance. Rationality flies up the chimney. Swords clash."

Her own blade rang as she pulled it from its sheath. She might have been drawing it to emphasize her point, until a dark form passed over them, half hidden in the mist.

Seconds later, a huge horse flew into sight above them. No, not a horse. A beast. A hybrid. Part horse, part raptor. Wicked talons terminated its feathered forelegs. It had the head of a huge bird of prey. Only the hindquarters looked like those of a horse.

The creature dove at Beltrann, digging one set of claws into the man's shoulder. Beltrann spun and the second talon missed its mark. Nevertheless, the thing lifted him into the air. Fortunately, he was too heavy for the beast to carry with one claw, so it dropped him to the ground, leaving long rents in his shirt and skin. He tumbled once and lay still.

His heart racing, Zen drew Jarret's wand from within his robe and waited for the creature's next pass. Suddenly Dara shoved him to the ground, knocking the wand from his grasp as a second creature dove at him from behind. It plucked up Dara in his stead.

In response, she plunged her sword into the thing's belly. Her blade sparkled with energy. Tendrils of lightning hissed up its length, charging the air with a power that made the hair on Zen's arms stand up. Crackling waves of energy struck the beast, exploded within it, and sent it plummeting to the ground.

Splattered with blood, Dara dropped from its dead claws and rolled to her feet, ready for the next strike. The smell of charred flesh and fur soured the air.

For the moment, Jarret's wand lay forgotten at Zen's feet. His eyes were riveted on Dara and her sword. He'd never seen such power displayed in a weapon before. Sure, he'd seen weavings produce lightning, but to imbue an object with that kind of enchantment required more skill than any mage he'd ever known. And to find it in the hands of a young elf girl... What was the power of his paltry wand compared to—

to this?

A cry shattered his thoughts. A third creature had swept in behind Nick and nearly caught him off-guard. It soared up and passed beyond the screen of trees.

In the quiet moment that followed, Zen retrieved the wand and searched the small patch of sky. The trees were too close and the creatures too fast. "Are they gone?"

Vinra rushed to Beltrann, who was struggling to stand. Rancid took cover under a nearby maple. Nick, Jasmine, and Dara stepped to the center of the clearing and stood with their backs together.

A second later, the hunters returned. An arrow from Rancid's bow shot harmlessly past one of the beasts.

"They're agile in flight," Dara said. "But once they commit to a dive, they become vulnerable."

As if on cue, two of the beasts plunged at the exposed trio, who darted separately to one side or the other and lashed out. Jasmine spun, her taloned foot balled into a kind of fist, and cracked the ribs of one beast with an audible snap. Nick sliced a deep gash in the side of the other. As one, the raptors rose and vanished beyond the trees in search of easier prey.

After a period of silence, Beltrann came to his feet and walked gingerly to the others. His shirt hung in tatters. The wounds beneath looked as though they'd been weeks in the healing, rather than minutes.

"How?" Nick asked.

Beltrann gestured toward Vinra. "An elixir of some kind."

"Enchanted?" Zen wondered aloud.

"I'm a priest. It's my business to heal." Vinra glanced toward the sky. "Looks like the Quelling is overdue."

Rancid marched up, his bow still strung. "Come on. Those things are wounded. If we're quick, we can catch them."

Dara stopped him with a hand on his arm. "Leave them."

Rancid opened his mouth to retort, but Dara's fierce look gave him pause. "They'll attack some other innocents," he said finally, without his usual conviction.

Dara wiped the charred blood from her sword and sheathed it. "Perhaps."

"I don't understand," Nick said. "As a guide, aren't you supposed to protect the visitors in your lands?"

She placed a palm on Nick's chest—a gentle, almost affectionate gesture—and flashed him a broad smile. The skin on Zen's face flushed with warmth and an unexpected pique rose within him.

"Only the welcome visitors." She dropped her hand and turned back to Rancid. "The predators, too, are part of our defensive policy. We encourage them to thrive, and kill them only when necessary." She fixed her gaze pointedly on Vinra. "That's why you should never travel Lorentil without a guide. And a properly armed one, at that." She patted the pommel of her sword.

"In truth," she continued, "we were lucky. They usually wait until full dark, when we'd have been less prepared and unable to see them coming. But it's been a long winter, and food is scarce."

While she was speaking, Rancid unstrung his bow and strapped it once again to his backpack. "You mind if I harvest some feathers for fletching?"

"Not at all. Perhaps your arrows will fly straighter." Her easy smile dissolved any sting the words might have carried. "Take some meat too. Hippogriff breast is some of the tastiest you'll ever eat."

As they proceeded north, the air grew only marginally cooler and the patchwork forest didn't seem to change at all. After five days of monotonous trekking, the companions finally broke free of the trees into a broad opening dotted with smaller shrubs and bushes. For Zen, the sight couldn't have been more welcome. They'd wandered in the woods for so long, he'd begun to feel they really were walking in circles.

At Dara's suggestion, they constructed a bonfire in the middle of the clearing before beginning their almost ritualistic nightly routine, during which Vinra now excused himself to commune with Robala at every sunset. Ultimately, Zen and Beltrann settled in for the first watch. Two hours later, the moon began its nightly cycle.

Beltrann added wood to the fire, expanding the globe of illumination. In the freshened blaze, a pair of eyes glowed from within a shadow that moved with patient determination and absolute silence. As soon as Zen saw it, it rose and bounded forward. In the light, the animal resolved into a tiger that stood as tall as a man while all four of its paws were planted firmly on the ground.

Zen could have yelled out, but he was already chanting, fingers working the weave with the swiftness of one facing death. He spun tendrils of magic faster than he ever had before, shaping them into a fistful of razor-edged shards. They collected in his palm, one after another. Two. Three. Four. He'd never produced so many at once, but desperation drove him on. When he felt himself weakening and the tendrils of power beginning to slip through his fingers, he propelled the missiles into the charging cat.

The shards tore strips of skin from the tiger's face. It roared in agony, loud enough to wake everyone in the camp—and probably anyone else within ten miles. But the cat didn't stop. It lashed out with a paw the size of Zen's chest. Claws ripped into him like daggers and threw him to the ground.

The others sprang to their feet. Nick and Dara snatched their swords, and along with Jasmine, surrounded the cat.

It lashed out wildly. Its stinging claws raked into Nick and Dara. Jaws closed around Jasmine. Her bones crunched. She went limp and the tiger tossed her away like a discarded rag.

Zen fought the pain in his chest and tried to scramble clear of the destruction.

Battered and bleeding, Dara turned her blade upon the beast.

Lightning lit the length of the sword as it bit into the animal's side, and blue, glowing tendrils engulfed the cat's body.

With a deafening roar, the tiger whipped around to destroy the source of its pain.

Nick rushed in from the opposite side and drove his blade into the tiger's flank. Its hind leg collapsed beneath it.

It spun on him, bearing teeth the size of Nick's hand.

Then complete darkness engulfed everything. The effect seemed to have emanated from an object in Vinra's hand, a mere glint in the firelight before the black consumed it.

Zen got to his hands and knees, and crawled. His chest burned. It felt as though it had been shredded, as though his muscles hung in tattered ribbons that dragged along the ground as he moved. Logic told him that this wasn't so, but the darkness seemed to intensify the pain.

Rancid let out a roar of challenge from somewhere across the campsite. A noble effort, perhaps, to draw the tiger from the fallen.

Finally, Zen came into the muted moonlight. A globe of darkness had swallowed the fire, making it impossible to distinguish anything but the deepest of shadows. The battle had grown eerily silent.

Suddenly, the tiger sprang from the blackness and landed with a soft thud on the grass nearby. A low rumble rose from its throat as it looked down upon Zen like a barn cat contemplating a broken mouse that lay between its paws.

Again Nick charged, his great sword sweeping in an arc over his head. The cat backed away warily. Finally it turned and fled, limping into the night.

A quiver shook Nick's voice. "Where's Jasmine?"

CHAPTER 12

ick rushed to Jasmine as the light of the fire blazed once
again in the ravaged campsite. Her ribs had collapsed and
giant punctures dotted her chest. She was breathing, but in
shallow, ragged breaths that flecked her lips with her brown blood.
When Vinra knelt next to Nick, Jasmine's wild eyes darted fearfully
from one to the other, as though she recognized nothing.

She sucked at the drops of elixir that Vinra dribbled onto her lips,
growing stronger and beginning to sip on her own as her efforts
brought her closer to the bottom of the vial. Her breathing gradually
slowed and became less labored. Yet the wicked holes in her chest continued to bleed.

Finally, she closed her eyes and seemed to slip into a deep, deep
sleep. If not for the faint rise and fall of her chest, Nick might have
thought she had died. Instead, he recognized it as the same healing
meditation she'd used in the days following the Black Hand attack.

This time, though, he feared it wouldn't be enough.

With one of their two healers trying desperately to save the life of the other, Beltrann dressed Zen's wounds and those of the others as best he could until Vinra had finished wrapping Jasmine's torso with bandages from his pack. Then the priest stripped away the shreds of Zen's tattered cloak and cleaned and rewrapped the mage's wounds.

All in all, the tiger had done less damage than Nick had feared. The blind fury it had shown following Zen's ice attack was apparently just that—blind. Most of the scratches from the cat's six-inch claws were shallow and glancing. The cat had sought purchase in any meat it could as each victim was thrown beyond reach by the impact of its massive paws.

Even Zen, who'd taken the brunt of the initial attack, had escaped serious injury. None of his wounds were any deeper than his ribs. Vinra assured him that, despite the pain, he would heal quickly.

Meanwhile, Rancid and Dara constructed a litter to carry Jasmine.

"Is it safe?" Nick asked Vinra. "Can we move her?"

"We must. She needs more help than I can give her here. She needs a healer with access to Aeron's blessing."

"Your god not powerful enough?" Rancid asked.

"I haven't a high enough standing in my church for her to grant me the healing this woman needs. Yet we're unlikely to find a higher priest of Robala in Lorentil. Aeron is the god of the elves. We're in his land. Find one of his high priests and Jasmine may yet survive."

He took her by the shoulders and motioned Nick to grab her feet. "Move her carefully. She's still broken inside. If she was human, she'd be dead already."

Dara nodded, uncharacteristically quiet. "It's not far. We should reach the capital city this morning."

When they arrived in the city of Lorentil, the first thing Zen noticed was the noise. Wagons rattled by, wheels creaking and the mules' hooves clop-clopping on the wide cobblestone avenues. Musicians and charlatans of magic performed on every corner, and the bustle of the population—nearly all elves, this deep into their kingdom—contributed to the urban cacophony. The clamber was no greater than in other large cities, yet it was in sharp contrast to the peace of the elven wilderness.

"We need gold," Rancid told Dara as they entered the city. "We have no coin for food, lodging, or a healer. Where can I sell my hippogriff feathers?"

"Try the provisioner or armorer." She pointed out the general store as they passed. "The rest of you, take Jasmine to the Berryseed Boardinghouse. I'll bring a healer there." To Nick, she said, "The healer's fee will come out of my own."

At that point, the party split. Dara sprinted down the broad avenue. Nick and Beltrann carried Jasmine to the boardinghouse. And Rancid went into the provisioner's shop with the others, where his feathers fetched a modest sum. Zen replaced his shredded cloak, then left Vinra to find Robala's temple on his own. Zen had a more important errand to run.

The weave seemed alive everywhere in this city. He could sense it in the air, as both a physical and spectral presence that hooked him and reeled him in. He would come into power here. He could feel it.

Of course, that was just his hopeful imagination talking. To all outward appearances, these people were as ordinary as Zen himself. Some knew bits of the art. A few, perhaps, wielded true power, but Zen had no way to distinguish among them. The latter wouldn't likely associate with him in any case.

Zen was drawn out of his thoughts by the uneasy feeling that someone was watching him. He scanned the boardwalks in the dusky glow of the sun, which had already dropped below the tree line. People wandered by, heedless of his presence. Then he spotted her, an elven woman with the look of an angel, leaning against a storefront with one foot on the boardwalk and the other leg bent so the sole of her boot rested on the wall behind her. She had long wheat-colored hair and eyes the same frosty blue as Zen's own. Hers exhibited the almond shape typical of her race.

The woman stared at him, though not in a menacing way or even in a manner that suggested appraisal or curiosity. Her gaze was casual, perhaps inadvertent. Yet she was watching him. Her eyes moved with him, while her thoughts seemed elsewhere.

Then her gaze came into focus on his and she smiled ruefully, as though she hadn't meant to stare. Still, she didn't look away. When Zen stopped, his eyes locking onto hers, the elf's posture straightened and her expression turned to one of frank interest.

She stepped off the boardwalk and crossed the road to him. "Hello, stranger." She nestled his arm in her hands and sidled up in a much-too-familiar fashion. "I don't believe I've seen you before." Her head just reached Zen's shoulder as she looked up at him, her porcelain features marred only by a slight overbite. The imperfection, barely noticeable, somehow made her even more alluring. "You're not in a hurry, are you?"

Zen stared, openmouthed and speechless. Such a beautiful elven woman could have any man she chose. And she chose, apparently, to offer herself for coin. The realization stole much of her charm as Zen considered the things she must have done, and who she'd done them for.

All the while, his body responded physically to her warmth and intent.

"There must be something I can do for you."

"Yes," Zen heard himself say.

Her face lit up and she squealed with delight.

"I'm looking for magic." Zen's mind sorted through the possibilities. He had little coin to pay for her favors—and he wasn't interested in any case, despite what his body was telling him—but she must know people.

The woman drew her head back and examined his face carefully, her brow knitted.

Zen pressed his advantage while she was still off balance. "I have information that could be of value to someone in a position of influence."

She studied his expression. Her clothes were of obvious quality—a fine linen blouse, snug around the waist and loose in the chest, and pants of some tight-fitting, supple leather—both clean and in good repair.

"You have contacts, I'll wager. And from the looks of you, you could attract all sorts of men. I'll give you the information. In exchange, I want to know how I might acquire magic—artifacts, equipment, or knowledge, it doesn't matter—for a price I can afford."

"Let's go somewhere." The elf gave him a smile as she stepped away. The wicked gleam in her eye aroused fantasies Zen couldn't afford.

She led him to a large building that sprawled in the upscale end of town, beneath a sign that pictured a mug, a bed, and a roasted turkey leg. He must tread carefully. Maybe she was interested in his proposal. Maybe she thought he would trade his information for sex.

Then again, she might just walk him into a den of high-class cutthroats and thieves.

CHAPTER 13

R ancid spent the evening and most of the night plotting ways to convince Nick and his friends into coming to Palidor. With their help, Rancid could wipe the Black Hand out of the kingdom for good.

Nick had a score to settle with the bandits. If Rancid could get him to abandon this quest against a fairytale spawned in some long-lost age, Rancid could probably cajole him into joining his own crusade against the Black Hand. He could promise Zen magic from the bandits' treasure stores. Vinra might do it to make Palidor safer for travelers. The others, however, could prove more troublesome.

He was still pondering the problem the next morning when he, Nick, and Zen left for the temple of High Priestess Alamain. Rancid bothered to go with them only so he could find a way to discredit the Prophecy. Dara and Beltrann chose to stay with Jasmine, while Vinra went instead to the temple of Robala to perform his precious Quelling ceremony.

When they arrived, a priest admitted them into the temple, listened as Nick recited his story, and reviewed the notes in Nick's journal. He promised to request an audience for them at his earliest opportunity and asked them to return the following day for Alamain's reply.

When they got back to the Berryseed Boardinghouse, the three checked in on a sleeping Jasmine, then went down to the common room for lunch. The noon hour had brought in quite a crowd, and the whole place buzzed with talk of the Prophecy.

Ignoring the chatter, Zen went straight to the bar. He asked the elf behind it for directions to Glimmernook, the mages' college, and then excused himself.

Rancid, glad to have an opportunity to speak with Nick alone, led him to a corner booth and sat down. "Let me see that journal."

Nick unpacked the book and slid it across the table.

It was the first time Rancid had really seen it, other than from a distance as Nick had studied it every evening by firelight. Unsure where to start, he opened it to the page titled "Demonbane." The text included the transcribed entry from Nick's grandfather's burnt journal and several supplementary notes Nick had made at the Order of the Sage. "We should get this sword. It says here—"

A young serving boy approached the table.

"Lunch," Nick said, without asking what the kitchen was serving. "For both of us."

The boy nodded and hurried away.

As soon as he was gone, Rancid continued. "This sword was made to fight this battle. It's in Brinheim." Near Palidor. "What in the baron's name are we doing all the way up here in elf country?" Oh, what Rancid might do to the Black Hand if he got hold of this sword.

"It's not that simple—"

"Fighting evil doesn't have to be complicated. You take up a sword, find the evil, and kill it."

Nearby patrons began casting glances their way.

Rancid lowered his voice another notch. "If it's a special evil, you find a special sword." He motioned to the journal to complete his point.

Nick was silent for a time before responding. "Zen thinks Alamain can help us. And I tend to agree."

"I don't—"

An elf strode up to the table.

"Busy place," Nick observed.

The elf wore a green traveling cloak, still showing dirt from the trail, and carried a sword at his hip. Rancid had noticed him shortly after they'd come in, sitting at a table across the bar with a backpack at his feet and a longbow leaned against the wall. A guide, probably looking for work.

"Good afternoon." The stranger introduced himself. "You two appear to be a couple of hardened fellows."

"We like to think so," Rancid said.

"Well then, I've got some news that might interest you."

"How much is it going to cost?" Nick asked wryly. Nothing came free in Lorentil.

The elf smiled. "On the house. It seems there's been a run on mercenaries in Palidor. They're paying top dollar for anyone with a sword who knows how to use it."

"Why's that?" Rancid said. "Are the Black Hand getting out of control again?"

"It's never been a very safe place to travel," Nick added.

"No," the elf replied. "I understand the bandits have been unusually quiet."

Nick raised an eyebrow at Rancid. "Sounds like you made a dent."

"That or they're on their way here." The Black Hand had been known to cross into Lorentil on raids to grab elven females.

The elf looked back and forth between them with a perplexed expression. "I just came from Palidor, we didn't see any sign of them on the way in. As far as I know, they haven't crossed the border in years."

"Then why the sudden need for mercenaries?" Nick asked.

"Plantation owners are hiring. It seems the slaves are getting harder and harder to control." The elf stepped aside to let the serving boy distribute lunch, a slab of gamy red meat and a heap of stewed greens. "The thing is," the elf continued, "lately the slaves have been armed."

"Armed?" Nick's eyes shot wide-open. He glanced at Rancid, as though to confirm that he'd heard correctly. "Slaves?"

The elf nodded. "Nobody knows where they're getting the weapons. But they're *goblin* swords, if the rumors can be trusted— nothing made anywhere in the Civilized Lands."

Nick shook his head. "Doesn't make sense. Goblin imports are illegal, except for the slaves themselves."

The elf raised a placating hand. "I'm just repeating what I've heard. Anyway, if you want to check it out and need a guide to get you there, I'm staying here at the Berryseed." With that, he turned and left.

Nick remained silent for several minutes, then said, "That's two."

"Two what?"

"Conditions of the Prophecy."

Rancid shrugged. Two conditions didn't make a prophecy. Besides, he had the sword to think about.

Zen arrived at the appointed house twenty-four hours after he had met the elven tramp. "Irlyren sent me," he told the elf who answered the door, as he'd been instructed to say. His heart sounded like a heavy drum in his chest. If Nick and the others ever found out what he was doing... Well, they wouldn't understand.

But in Zen's own mind, his purpose was clear. Nick had been quite carefree with his journal, first at the border crossing, and then again at Alamain's temple, and the information in it had begun to circulate.

Besides, the enemy already had the journal. So now, the more people who knew what was in it—such that others might move to stop the Prophecy as well—the better. Zen had merely found a way to profit from the information's distribution. And, if things went well, that profit would come in the form of enchantments Zen could use to fight the Prophecy's fulfillment.

The doorman led him down a long hall in the private residence of some well-to-do Lorentil citizen. Zen didn't make the assumption that his customer was the owner of the house, though he very well might be. If he was, he must be as naive as Zen himself.

The doorman led him into a study. Behind the desk sat an elf, somewhat aged by elven norms but not yet old. He wore plain clothes, though not as rich as Zen thought the owner of the house might wear. When he looked up, he did so with a serious expression devoid of any identifiable emotion. Nothing about his attire or demeanor suggested that he was a mage, as Zen had hoped his buyer would be.

"Take a seat," the elf said after the doorman departed.

Zen moved toward one of two plush leather chairs that sat opposite the desk, and then stopped. "I'd rather stand." His voice shook slightly.

"Fine." The elf's expression didn't change. He just stared at Zen with the face of a bluffcard player. "What do you have to tell me?"

Zen scanned the dark corners of the room for hidden occupants, something he should have done when he entered. Fortunately they were alone. "I have information regarding the Prophecy of Mortaan."

"The girl told me that much."

"I believe it's coming true even as we speak."

The elf nodded but remained silent. Word might have already traveled this far since they'd shared it with the elves at the border crossing.

"We haven't discussed payment," Zen said finally.

"I have no way to gauge the value of the information until I've heard it." The elf seemed almost bored. "So I'll offer you this. You tell me what you have to say. I'll ask questions. You'll answer them or not, I don't care. Once I've heard everything, I'll pay you whatever the information is worth to me."

"What's to keep you from hearing the information and declaring it's worth nothing?"

"That is a dilemma, and I reserve the right to do so. For all I know, your information is worth exactly that."

The elf had penned him in already. He didn't seem to care if Zen walked away without saying another word, which wouldn't benefit Zen in the least. He'd have to trust the elf and see what happened. After all, his "product" cost him nothing to give. Finally, he said, "I'll give you some of the information and you can pay me what you think that piece is worth. If I think we're headed in the right direction, I'll say more, which you'll pay me for."

The elf shook his head. "I'm willing to do that if you like, but the magic I brought is of no small value and cannot be given piecemeal. I would be forced to pay you in coin, which would not ultimately buy the enchantments I might offer." He paused. "You didn't come here for coin."

No, he hadn't. So Zen agreed to the terms.

He didn't ask if the elf was familiar with the Prophecy. The elf wouldn't have come if he wasn't. He began by detailing the current events. The elf had surely heard about the Trondorian war, so Zen focused on those events that were specific to Nick and the journal. He told of the air apparition and its relevance to the Master of Air and Darkness, and watched the elf's face for signs of interest.

The stranger kept his emotions hidden.

Zen elaborated on the nature of the entity and explained that most apparitions were mere constructs, capable only of following simple commands or performing menial tasks. "This one's different, however. It's sentient. It makes its own decisions. Behaves independently. This suggests great power in the one who created it. That someone appeared to be among the Black Hand. The Master of the Prophecy might even be the leader of the bandit gang."

"How did you come to be involved in these events?" the elf asked.

"I'm working with some friends to prevent the Prophecy from coming to pass." He paused. "I'm hoping to attain magical power along the way."

"What if those are conflicting goals? Wait." The elf raised one hand and turned his head away. "Never mind. That's none of my business."

"If I have to choose between gaining power and stopping the Prophecy, which would I choose? Is that what you were going to ask?"

The elf nodded.

"Power." The word came out with ease and conviction, without hesitation or doubt. "Provided that the extent and nature of the power is sufficient to protect me from the effects of the Prophecy's fulfillment."

"What brings you to Lorentil?"

"The stolen journal makes a reference to Alamain's blessing, but the journal was damaged. The rest of the entry is missing, so we don't know what purpose the blessing is supposed to serve. It also mentioned a couple of relics related to Aeron. We're hoping the High Priestess will give us guidance." Nick had already given this information to a variety of others, so Zen gave it now without guilt or concern.

"What else did this journal say?"

Zen hedged a little here. "The Master's agent has taken the journal from us, so I'm working from memory." Indeed he was, but only because he hadn't brought any notes with him. He deliberately failed to mention that Nick had copied the text into his own journal and that he'd added notes since. That was information the enemy didn't have.

"It mentioned a number of items." Zen listed those that came to mind, including Demonbane and the Shield of Faith. He'd already alluded to those, so he couldn't omit them now. He also listed the Portal of the Damned—though not what he knew of its location—and the related Guardian. The Prophecy contained references to the medallions of Vexetan. They wouldn't be news to the elf, so Zen mentioned them. In the end, he included everything he could remember.

"What do you know about these items?"

"As I said, the journal was damaged. We had only vague references to work with. That's why we seek Alamain's help. We're supposed to see her before we leave the city. Perhaps tomorrow. I'll come back and tell you anything we learn." He paused for emphasis. "If I feel that today's compensation warrants an additional meeting."

"I see," the elf said. "Before we discuss that, is there anything else?"

Zen thought for a moment, then shook his head. "I think that's everything."

The elf nodded to himself, and then he reached under the desk and produced a leather sack. He carefully arranged the contents on the desk between them: several bottles, presumably of some enchanted elixir, each marked in the language of the elves; a few sheaves of parchment—scrolls—and an enchanted wand. The elf named the effects of the wand and elixirs and the titles of each of the scrolls. "You may choose two of these items to take with you. Come back after your talk with the High Priestess and I may offer more."

The offer was greater than Zen had expected or even hoped for. He selected the wand and a scroll, and agreed to the later meeting.

After Zen left, Gwyndarren, the elf, considered what he'd learned. The young mage had claimed, through Irlyren, that he had knowledge of the Prophecy that no one else had. Though that seemed highly unlikely, Gwyndarren had agreed to the meeting. One never knew what one might hear. He'd even brought a few of his enchanted belongings so he could play the game if it proved worth playing.

In the end, Gwyndarren *had* learned something of value—specifically the list of relics, which was the sort of information Gwyndarren had thought he was looking for. He'd heard of a few of them before. They were intimately associated with the Prophecy, and the Prophecy was well known. But Gwyndarren had only known *of* them, not *about* them, so he cataloged each bit of knowledge in the proper place in his mind. Yet that information was, in large measure, valueless. All of those things were mentioned in the stolen journal, which meant the Master of the Prophecy—the person most likely to pay top coin for the information—already had it.

Yet there was something else Zen had given Gwyndarren, something the mage had said without realizing its importance. Zen had told him he'd work for the Master's side, perhaps as an informant in the midst of the Master's enemies, for a sufficient price. Zen hadn't put it in those terms, of course, but he'd said it nonetheless. Thus, Gwyndarren had given Zen much in the bargain.

The problem was how to find the buyer. The only one who would care enough to pay, and the only one who could pay enough to make it worth Gwyndarren's while, was the Master himself. For Gwyndarren's price would be as high as Zen's—sufficient power to protect himself from the Prophecy's fulfillment.

Nobody even knew who the Master was. He was probably hidden by Vexetan himself, and therefore impossible for a mortal to find... if he existed at all... if Zen and his companions were right about the Prophecy's coming.

Still, somebody was after the journal for a reason, somebody with enough power to call and control a sentient apparition. That was the person Gwyndarren must find. That was someone who did exist. And Zen had told him where to look.

Among the Black Hand.

CHAPTER 14

"Here they come."

Balor turned from his maps and strode calmly to the blind he'd erected to conceal his command post from the approach to the pass. A cloud of dust rose from the plain below. "Are the troops ready?" he asked Dalen.

"More than ready. Pandalo's got them stoked. They're eager to fight."

"Not too eager, I hope. Timing will be critical."

The lead riders of Balor's rear guard galloped into sight, pushing their mounts for every ounce of speed, mere minutes ahead of the vast enemy cavalry. Fortunately, Pandalo had left enough horses behind for even the foot soldiers to make a mounted escape from the Black Forest.

Thunder rolled up the hillside as the pounding hooves of six thousand horses thundered into the canyon. Enemy riders poured into view behind them. "My god," Balor breathed. At twenty-two thousand, Gremauld's mounted troops alone numerically matched Balor's entire army. "How long have they been at that pace?"

"Hours. They're all but killing their horses," Dalen said. His hawk, Harriet, clung to his padded wrist with the message case still attached to her leg. Communications would be key if Balor wanted to ultimately win the revolution. The hawk had already proved her value in that capacity, as had Dalen.

While they watched, Gremauld's horsemen flooded the valley.

Balor's own riders had just passed the marker. He nodded to the captain of his personal guard, who, in turn, gestured to the herald beside him. The man raised a pole bearing Balor's banner and placed it in a slot prepared for the purpose.

Balor's men had commandeered every cask of oil from the township of Twin Peaks and emptied them across a wide stretch of the pass. At Balor's signal, several hundred flaming arrows arced through the air. In seconds, the valley below was ablaze. The fire forced most of Gremauld's troops to stop. But the lead horses, perhaps three thousand of them, got through.

Too late, Balor thought. He'd stationed Pandalo and twenty-five hundred foot soldiers beyond the blaze in case of that very event, but they wouldn't be enough to defeat the mounted troops who'd escaped the snare. Pandalo was already in trouble, but Balor could do nothing about it at that moment.

The remainder of the enemy horsemen piled up at the approach to the flaming barrier. Many plunged into the conflagration and burned. Frightened horses threw men to the ground, to be trampled in a sea of hooves. Confusion reigned as the horses behind plowed into the gathering mass of equine bodies. Gremauld's leader must have called a retreat, but nobody could hear over the braying of the animals, the roar of the flames, and the screams of the dying.

Then the slaughter began.

The signalman sounded the horn, which carried across the valley to the far hillside. In an instant, eight thousand arrows filled the sky, launched from hidden positions along both sides of the pass. They rained death upon the pretender's army. By the time the horsemen knew they'd been fired upon, thousands lay dead. Many others who'd lost their horses from beneath them scrambled to regain their feet before being trampled.

Seconds later, Balor's archers unleashed another volley, followed by a steady cloud of the missiles.

At close range, crossbowmen with stout bolts crouched at the base of each hill and tried to pick off Gremauld's knights, whose heavy armor couldn't be penetrated by lightweight arrows.

Those men in the rear of Gremauld's army pulled their mounts to a stop before becoming mired in the confusion and turned to flee the way they had come. As they did, Balor's own mounted men slammed into them from behind. The fighting there was fierce, the outcome uncertain. Balor's troops were fresh, his horses rested, while Gremauld's were near the limit of their endurance. But as the enemy juggernaut labored into motion, away from the flames, their sheer numbers began to overwhelm the rebels.

"Sound the retreat," Balor ordered.

The herald raised the horn and blew the command.

His cavalry wheeled on its heels and galloped from the canyon, the fresh horses easily outdistancing the spent mounts of the enemy. But the flow of Gremauld's men was now toward the west—the direction of safety.

Some of the enemy, who'd either dismounted voluntarily or lost their horses, swarmed up the hill to ferret out the wielders of the deadly crossbows. They, in turn, scrambled farther up the slope or took up swords to oppose their foes, who were great in numbers, cornered, and whipped into a desperate fury.

Balor had played his hand. From here on out, the advantage would go to Gremauld.

The day after his meeting with the mysterious elf, Zen took his new-found enchantments to Glimmernook, where he had another appointment to keep. He'd paid a brief visit there the day before and convinced a professor named Krielund that there was something special about Zen's magic—something worth studying.

"Let's start with the calling you demonstrated yesterday," the old mage said.

Zen and Krielund had performed identical callings, using identical gestures and incantations, but much of an enchantment depended upon the mage's intuitive perception of the weave. Where Krielund had produced a real, living badger from his calling, Zen had produced a badger constructed entirely of ice, not living precisely, yet alive in every sense that mattered. It snarled at Krielund's badger, who growled back, each animal connected to its mage by an invisible thread of the weave.

Zen agreed to repeat the calling.

"Before you do, I'd like you to put on a teaching ring." Krielund handed Zen one of a pair of golden circlets. "I'll wear the other. They'll allow us to read each other's foremost thoughts and see the weave constructed by the other. I'll be able to observe your enchantment."

"All right." Zen took the ring without hesitation. Krielund had promised to compensate him for his efforts, and he might learn something along the way that could help him understand and increase his own power. He slipped the ring onto his finger.

"Now close your eyes and focus on my thoughts."

When he did, a window opened into the professor's mind. Zen didn't share the elf's thoughts, exactly, but he could hear them, or at least some of them, separate and distinct from his own.

"Good." Krielund spoke gently, purposefully. "Now open your eyes and begin. Recite the incantation one phrase at a time and form the weave slowly. I want to see the shape and aspect of it. Don't proceed to the next phrase of the incantation until I give you leave to do so. If you have difficulty holding the pattern together, I'll help you."

Zen opened himself to the presence of the weave. This had been the most difficult part of the enchantment to learn, so many years before, because he hadn't had any formal training in how to do it. He'd talked to the mages who'd traveled through the mountains near his home, on their way to or from the arctic town of Icecap. The mountain pass, always covered in a thick blanket of snow, was almost impossible to traverse without someone who knew the trails. Zen, having grown up there, served this purpose. After the first couple of years, word spread and anyone seeking passage from the south stopped at his home, hired him as a guide, and made arrangements for him to meet them on the north end of the pass for the return trip.

He always asked if the traveler, or anyone in the group, had use of the magical arts. If so, he requested that the mage teach him along the way, rather than paying in coin. Most of his clients agreed, eager to hang on to their gold.

Afterwards, Zen worked to make sense of what he'd learned and to fit it into the things he thought he already knew. For years, he remained unable to tap the weave by himself, but he learned a little more, day by day, and he never gave up.

The first time he successfully tapped the weave, he was sitting on a snow-covered hillside overlooking the frozen sea. He'd been trying all day to "open himself to the magic," as his mentors had called it. Finally, he began to feel the flow of the weave around him—just a faint touch of its presence, but it was there. He reached out to it, without really knowing what it was, and grasped an object from the ether.

There in his hand lay a glistening piece of ice. The element was all around him, and he could have simply chipped some from the ocean below. But the ice in Zen's hand was special. Zen had created it from nothing—called it from the weave. He'd exhausted himself with the effort, yet he felt triumphant.

The following day, he repeated the feat, remembering how he'd attuned himself to everything around him. He focused on the weave and formed a frozen cube in less than half the time it had taken him the day before. But again he was spent. The magic seemed to drain something from him, a life force he didn't know existed, let alone understood.

Still he kept at it, and each day it came to him more quickly and easily than it had the day before. He formed simple shapes, then more complex forms, but always, his medium was ice. He didn't know enough to create from anything else. He tried occasionally but became frustrated. So at the end of the day, he returned to the one thing at which he knew he could succeed. The experience became addictive.

The following spring, a client taught Zen the calling he and Krielund now used. It was supposed to bring any one of a variety of animals from its nearby home. Zen had had only a few days to work with the mage, and he couldn't seem to establish the necessary connection to the animal. He could see it there, a ghostly shadow through a gilded screen of energy, but he could never quite bring the animal to him.

This weaving, too, he practiced over the winter, when the air had become too cold and the snow too deep to traverse the pass. Finally, he called a creature he'd connected with. Instead of arriving in its true body, however, it was formed of ice, as Zen's original successes had been. Zen was not disappointed by this. The shape he'd called was animated, and Zen was jubilant.

Over time, he built these little snippets of training into what he now understood of the use of the weave.

In the elven college, Zen shaped the weave and began to search through it for a badger from the nearby wilderness. While he searched, he listened to Krielund's thoughts as the professor examined his work.

Zen's use of the weave was sloppy, Krielund observed. The tendrils looped out in large hoops away from the focal point. They came back, passed through the focus, and shot out in some other direction. It wasn't the tight weave the professor always demanded of his own students, but he didn't scold Zen for the fact. Somewhere in this pattern lay the secret behind Zen's peculiarity. And today, Zen was not the pupil. Krielund was here to learn from him.

"Hold the pattern there," Krielund said.

Zen felt a stiffening of the braids as Krielund used his own magic to shore up the threads, to help Zen hold them in place while Krielund studied them. The pattern contained several dead threads, as Krielund called them, strands that escaped the central pattern and failed to loop back. Some of these simply ended in midair between the two men.

Curious, Krielund thought, *I didn't know they could do that.*

"Do what?"

"You see these here?" Krielund pointed to the truncated strands. "They seem to vanish into the ether. Pervasive magic is a whole, its weave continuous. Yet these strands come to an end, as though they're disconnected pieces."

Zen shrugged. He'd always had these dead threads in his pattern. Perhaps he'd tapped a form of magic with which Krielund was unfamiliar, some manifestation the professor didn't know existed.

"You may continue," Krielund said finally.

Zen did, still monitoring the professor's mind.

The power in the weave is strong, Krielund thought. *Perhaps that of a fifth-year pupil, but it's inefficient. With the proper instruction and a tighter pattern, this boy could perform a much more powerful calling.*

Eventually Zen found the animal he'd been searching for and reached out to it. The dead threads began to pulsate along with those that touched the animal. Within seconds, a badger formed of ice stood in the mage's study, sniffing the floor and looking very much agitated.

After the weaving, Zen released the animal. Krielund ordered an aid to fetch some hot blueberry wine for them to sip as they discussed what he'd seen and what it might imply about Zen's magic.

By the end of the day, they had only speculations, but they were based on experimentation and sound theory. Krielund had, at one point, followed the path of the dead threads and found that they didn't actually terminate but stretched into another dimension, into the material plane of water. Krielund theorized that they extended from there all the way into the pseudo-plane of ice, which would have been closer to their own world in the region of Icecap in the middle of winter. Zen had stumbled onto that connection first and had apparently used it exclusively to invoke the weave.

In the case of the animal calling, Zen borrowed the form and consciousness of the true animal but called material from the plane of ice to create the construct, rather than calling the live creature.

"I must admit," Krielund said after twelve hours of research, "you've given me much to consider. Constructs are a difficult trick to master all by themselves. But you've learned to combine them with traditional enchantments, to mold your own style of the art."

He collected Zen's teaching ring and returned it to the drawer with its mate. "Thank you for taking the time today to share it with me. It has opened a whole new direction for me in my research. If you're ever inclined to return to Glimmernook as a student, you'll be most welcome."

Zen didn't have the coin required for tuition or he would probably have abandoned Nick's quest and enrolled in Glimmernook that very day. As it was, he showed Krielund the wand and scroll he'd received from his elven contact the night before. "If I may," he asked, "I'd like to trade these to you, along with today's work, for something greater than you might have offered otherwise."

Krielund took the devices, scrutinized them, and nodded. "I have just the thing for you. It'll put you right in your element, you might say."

CHAPTER 15

Smoke filled the air from the still-smoldering valley as Balor listened to Pandalo's report. The general had done well that day on the eastern side of the flaming barrier. He'd intercepted the contingent of Balor's men who'd baited the trap, exhausted though they were, and turned them back to smash Gremauld's horsemen.

"In the end," Pandalo said, "we captured or killed every last rider who passed through the flames."

"The prisoners?"

"Disarmed. Sent under guard to the township of Twin Peaks. We can hold them there until the end of the conflict."

Just then, Harriet arrived with a dispatch from Dalen, who'd mounted up and followed the retreating army.

Balor untied the message from the hawk's leg and read it. "Seven thousand."

Pandalo nodded. "That matches our estimate."

"It says the retreating horses reached their limit just ten miles down the road. They'll probably continue west in the morning and try to meet up with the main body of Gremauld's army, which must be on its way by now."

"They're near enough. We can catch them by dawn."

"With some risk. This time our troops will be tired, and theirs rested. Still..." Battle frenzy would sustain Balor's troops through the fight, while Gremauld's men would be surprised and disoriented. "They've left us an opportunity we can't ignore. Prepare the men. Only two days' rations. We'll be back here, one way or the other, by tomorrow night."

He scribbled a note to Dalen and slipped it into the message case on Harriet's leg, so that by the time Balor arrived, Dalen would have all the intelligence necessary to plan the attack.

But when Balor got there, the enemy camp was deserted. "They knew we were coming."

"Maybe not." Pandalo's gaze scanned the smoldering remains of the previous night's cooking fires. "They may have recognized their vulnerability. If it were me, I too would have kept the men moving."

Balor grunted. If he pursued, he'd be making the same mistake Gremauld had made the previous day. "Come. We must return to the pass and prepare our defense. Dalen will keep us apprised of their movements."

During the three days that Nick and his friends waited for their audience with Alamain, Dara's healer, a priest from the high temple, visited Jasmine's room, where Nick spent most of his waking hours sitting beside her bed. Each time the healer came, Jasmine's condition improved. After the first day, she was able to stay awake most of the time. By the second, she began to sit up and talk. And when the time came, she insisted on attending the meeting with the High Priestess, so Nick helped her walk to the temple. Though she seemed tired and moved with care, she looked alert and smiled often.

Zen, for his part, sported a brand-new mage's staff with a rough-cut, translucent crystal that looked suspiciously like ice at its tip. He refused to say how he'd gotten it, only that he had traded for it at Glimmernook. Nick, knowing better than to get involved in business not his own, didn't press the point.

At the temple, the same priest who had received Nick on their previous visits led the party into a small foyer, beyond which lay the audience chamber. "We must observe silence for a few moments." He turned to Nick and the others and, grasping a rose-colored amulet in his hands, bowed his head and prayed. When he looked up again, he scanned his visitors with eyes that lacked focus, as though looking into their very souls.

When the priest came back to himself, he selected Nick, Jasmine, and Beltrann. "You three may see the High Priestess now."

"What about the rest of us?" Rancid demanded.

"Your hearts are not pure. You may not enter."

Nick frowned, but had no time to ponder the statement as the priest led the three of them directly into Alamain's holy presence.

Her chamber was small but ornate. Religious symbols—stylized stars and rays representing the light and purity of Aeron—decorated the walls, carved into the polished stone and inlaid with silver. A crystal chandelier that hung from the arched ceiling held some fifty burning candles made from the purest white wax Nick had ever seen. Silver candelabras framed a gilded throne, which sat on a white marble pedestal.

The priest ushered them to the center of the room. There, he announced Her Holiness, the High Priestess, and knelt before her. The companions mimicked his movements. After a full minute of supplication, they rose. "You have one hour," the priest told Nick. He closed the door silently behind him as he left.

Alamain herself appeared ancient, old even by elven standards—somewhere between five and seven hundred harvests, Nick guessed. Dressed in a pale pink robe, she rose from her seat, leaning on a polished silver staff with a star at its tip. As she walked up to Nick, her shimmering hair streamed nearly to the floor behind her. Wise, lavender eyes bored into his, as though she could read every truth, past and future, hidden there.

"Tell me your story, Nicklan Mirrin." Her quiet voice, hoarse with age, might have been a whetstone gliding across a silver blade.

She listened intently as he described his attack by Jade and the Black Hand at the Cedar Falls weekend market. He told of the burning of his home and the death of his mother, the chase to the monastery and what they knew of the mysterious entity that had pursued them all the way into Faldor. He included what they'd learned from the library at the Order or the Sage, the battle with the bandits, and the loss of the journal, leaving nothing out that had occurred before they reached the elven border.

"We haven't seen them since," he finished.

"And you believe this signifies the coming of the Prophecy." It wasn't a question.

Beltrann stepped forward. "There's more. The Prophecy foretells four conditions of its fulfillment. Two transpire as we speak."

"You are referring to the rebellion in Trondor." Again, it was a statement of fact.

"Yes, and we've heard reports from Palidor that goblin slaves have taken up arms against their owners—another of the preconditions."

Nick shot him a sharp glance for this overstatement. The elven guide had indicated only that some of the slaves had acquired goblin-made swords, not that the whole kingdom was in an uproar. "The remaining two conditions—the return of the demons and the dragons—we fear almost as much as the Prophecy itself."

"As well you should," Alamain said. "The times ahead will try us all, I'm afraid." Her eyes took on a sadness that nearly broke Nick's heart. She looked suddenly tired beyond exhaustion, old beyond even her years. Her gaze lost focus and she drifted into her own thoughts.

Nick waited a few moments for her to return. When she didn't, he was forced to interrupt her contemplation. They had only an hour, and his tale had already consumed half of that. "What does the church believe about the Prophecy?"

Alamain's eyes met his once more. "Because the Prophecy tells of the coming to power of Aeron's archenemy, Vexetan, the church has spent many resources over the centuries trying to understand it. Countless scholars have studied it for the whole of their substantial elven lives." She took a few steps away as she spoke. Nick strained his ears to hear the rest of her words. "Of course, no two scholars agree on how the text should be interpreted. So the church has developed a consensus understanding." She looked back at Nick. "Still an interpretation, mind you, of what the vision means."

"Do you think it'll come true?" he asked.

"Of course." She returned to stand before the trio. "Divination came to the races at the onset of the Age of Prophecy as a divine gift from the gods. They gave their vision to the seers as a warning of the events to come, not to prevent the future that was foretold, but to prepare for it."

Alamain became a teacher now, standing before her pupils, focused on her lecture. Her free hand waved in the air in emphasis of her points. "But the prophecies, especially those of Mortaan, are vague—obscure to the point of opacity. One must never know the whole of one's future, so the visions bestowed by the gods were left open to interpretation. Even Aeron himself doesn't know the whole fate of the Civilized Lands." She held up her hand to forestall any objections. "Oh, he can see much, and shows some of what is to come, but he has no sight into the schemes of Vexetan. And Aeron will not impart a vision until he knows how it will come to pass."

"But many of the prophecies are false," Beltrann said.

"I said the visions are true. I said nothing of the prophecies."

"But—" Nick began.

"The seer translates the vision into words, either spoken or script. Mortaan's gift was that he did so without assumptions or interpretation. All of the others, to varying degrees, chose to record their understanding of what the visions meant. Some were more accurate than others. Mortaan made no such translation. He recorded the visions as he saw them, in all their obscurity. Once a prophecy is fulfilled, the correct interpretation becomes clear, and the truth of the prediction can be seen."

Alamain looked at the faces of her pupils as though seeking some sign of confusion or understanding. She probably found both.

Finally, Nick voiced a question that had nagged him ever since Mum had described the coming Age of Darkness. "Do you believe the Prophecy is now coming to pass?"

"On that point, our scholars disagree. I do know that a High Priest of Vexetan has come to power and is moving against Aeron. I can feel his presence. This by itself doesn't portend the Prophecy. It's not the first time a disciple of the Dark One has moved against us, though this one has greater power than most."

"Do you know his name? Or where he is?"

She shook her head. "Vexetan has kept both hidden from us."

"The Prophecy calls him the Master of Air and Darkness," Beltrann said. "Does that mean anything to you?"

"The darkness, we believe, is a reference to the Age. He will become the Master of the Age of Darkness."

"And what about air?"

"On that also, the scholars disagree."

"Could it refer to the apparition we encountered?" Nick asked.

"Perhaps, but not likely. Apparition magic is pervasive in nature, not divine. It comes from the weave, not from the gods. It's outside the purview of the church, be it that of Aeron or Vexetan."

Nick took a deep breath. They were running out of time—not just for this meeting, but perhaps for the Civilized Lands as a whole. "Can you tell us anything about the sword Demonbane?" Nick asked.

"Ah, yes." Alamain thought for a moment. "Demonbane was forged in the Age of Magic as a weapon against the demons. After their imprisonment, the sword was left in the care of the kingdom of Brinheim."

"To be wielded by the queen's champion," Nick finished.

"Yes. In the event that the demons break free from their prison, Brinheim will be the first line of human defense."

"Does the queen currently have a champion?"

Alamain nodded. "There must always be a champion. If a need for the sword arises, it will do so suddenly. There will be no time to select a champion then."

"What about the Shield of Faith?" Nick asked, working quickly through his mental checklist.

"The Shield was made from the scales of a dragon and blessed by the High Priestess of the time. It rests now in our temple in Spitfire as a mere ornament."

"What was its original purpose?"

"To provide protection against the breath of a dragon."

"Will the church ever release it from the temple?"

She nodded. "If the dragons return and there is need."

Nick moved on, visualizing each scrap of his grandfather's journal. The key was there. It must be, or the enemy wouldn't have sought it. "What do you know about the Devil's Cauldron?"

Alamain didn't seem to mind the abrupt manner in which Nick conducted the interview. Perhaps she, too, felt the press of time. "The Devil's Cauldron is a pit in the middle of the Great Sand. The Portal of the Damned, the gateway to the Abyss, is hidden within it." She paused, as through deciding how much to say. "If the demons return, they'll do so through the Portal. It's the only gateway to their prison."

Jasmine had been so silent throughout the conversation, Nick had forgotten she was there. She spoke up now. "But demons have come into our world since their imprisonment."

"Yes. A calling can pull the body of a demon through the fabric of the world, and it may walk among us for a time. But it remains bound to its prison, and its body must ultimately return." She fixed Jasmine with a piercing gaze, as though her next words might hold some special significance for the monk. "Most of the mages who practice such magic eventually fall prey to the demons they seek to control."

Ignoring the apparent digression, Beltrann picked up the conversation where Nick had left off. "And the Guardian? Is it some statue that watches over the Portal?"

Alamain turned back, the moment between her and Jasmine lost. "The Guardian is a key that, if found, can be used to unlock the Portal."

"My grandfather thought it was in the land of the nomads," Nick said. "Do you know where that is? Somewhere in the Great Sand?"

"No. Nobody lives there anymore." Alamain's attention drifted from them and she paced the chamber thoughtfully. Finally, she looked up. "I would guess he was referring to Cormont." Then her tone changed. "Time is short, I'm afraid, and I have duties to which I must attend."

"What will the church do about the Priest of Vexetan?" Nick blurted before she could turn away.

"We will study and deliberate. Eventually, we will act." The sadness returned to her eyes. "But the church is an institution, and institutions are slow. When the decision comes, I fear, it will be too late."

"And what of us? What should we do?"

"As I see it, you have three choices. You may chose to prepare for the coming of the Prophecy. In that case, you must find the original text. Copies will lead you astray. At last report, the original Codex resided at the College of History in Eckland, Palidor."

Alamain continued. "Instead, you may choose to take the fight to the High Priest. But to do so, you must have a weapon that carries my blessing. Vexetan protects his servants. You'll not overcome his protections without it." She went silent after that. Again, she may have been deciding how much to reveal.

"And the third option," Nick prompted.

"You know," she said, as though expressing an aside, "the aspect of the Prophecy I dread most is the coming of the demons. The civilized races can no longer protect themselves from that kind of magic." She came back to the point. "You may try to prevent their release."

"And if it can't be done?" Nick asked.

"Then the Prophecy will no longer matter." She turned from them and walked to the back of the chamber, where a door opened at her approach. She stated this last remark with such finality that it left the companions speechless.

Jasmine was the first to recover. She turned to the door through which they'd entered. The others followed.

"Unless," Alamain said as Jasmine reached for the handle. As one, they all turned back to the High Priestess, who stood halfway through the doorway, which exposed a gilded hallway beyond. She didn't turn when she said, "Unless the fairies can be found and returned to oppose them."

"Is that possible?" Nick whispered, fearing to even ask the question. He couldn't afford false hope.

"Perhaps. There is one who may know how to find them. Return at midnight." Alamain stepped through the doorway and was gone.

CHAPTER 16

At lunch, later that day, Rancid sat with the others in the taproom at the Berryseed Boardinghouse.

"Searching for the fairy people is too much of a long shot," Nick was saying. "The way I see it, we need to focus on the Codex—go to Eckland and find out what the Prophecy really says."

"What?" Rancid choked on the morsel he had in his mouth. He'd expected a lot of things, but not the one thing he actually wanted.

All eyes turned to him.

Afraid his outburst might cause suspicion, Rancid decided to argue, at least momentarily, against his own desires. "Are you crazy? We can't go to Palidor." His mind raced through several excuses before finally settling on one. "The Black Hand are all over the place."

Nick set his mug down. "The elven guide said the bandits have been quiet."

Rancid fixed him with a cold stare. "And that doesn't scare the spit out of you?"

Nick shrugged but didn't answer.

Silence settled over the conversation as Rancid locked eyes with him. "They're planning something. I say we go for the sword." He stabbed another chunk of meat with his fork, shoved it into his mouth, and spoke around it. "Then we'll go to Eckland and get your poem."

Vinra was watching the exchange with frank curiosity and an amused smile.

"The sword won't help us," Nick said. "Only the queen's champion can wield it."

"The shield then," Rancid mumbled.

"The church won't give it up until the dragons return."

"So steal it."

Nick snorted. "We're not stealing anything. Besides, what are we supposed to do with a shield, beat the Master over the head with it?"

"We could go after the Guardian," Beltrann said. "Keep the Master from releasing the demons. That would buy us time."

The whole idea was absurd. They didn't even know what the thing looked like or where to find it. If it was in Cormont, it'd take months just to get there. Months during which the Black Hand could recruit new members. "The Master may already have it," Rancid said, finally.

Jasmine smiled at him from across the table, an eerie gesture in that lipless face. "You give up too easily."

"Yeah," Nick said. "Eckland is by far the easier objective and you say 'no' without even trying. What are you really afraid of? Not the bandits. You've killed so many they've had to scale back their operations."

Rancid washed another chunk of mutton down with a swallow of cheap, warm ale. "They're probably out looking for me."

"Why? Because you've killed so many of them?" Nick's food lay forgotten before him. "If you hurt them so badly, that's all the more reason for them to cut their losses. They ran you out of the kingdom. That should be enough."

"You've forgotten they're working for the Master," Rancid said quietly. "They'll come after us."

"The apparition wanted the journal. And it got it," Zen said. "It has no more interest in us."

Nick and his friends were trying to force Rancid into a corner. Slowly, deliberately, he backed into it. "We'll also have goblin raids to worry about."

"We can use that to our advantage," Vinra said.

Nick glanced his way. "You going with us?"

"If you don't mind. I have to complete a Quelling in Palidor as well. I can accompany you to Eckland and go on to the capital city from there."

Nick nodded. "We'll travel more safely with you than without."

"We can go in under the pretense of mercenaries looking or work," Vinra suggested.

Rancid shook his head, affecting a solemn manner. "We'll be recognized."

Fortunately, Nick wasn't fooled. "By whom?" When Rancid didn't answer, Nick raised his eyebrow. "Well?"

Rancid looked at each of them in turn. Then around the barroom, as if seeking help from elsewhere. He found none. Finally, he returned his gaze to Nick and dropped his defensive facade. "My father, the baron of Forlorn Keep."

"What has he to do with this?" Jasmine asked.

"I think he's a patron of the Black Hand."

Nick's eyebrows came together. "Wouldn't you know?"

Rancid shook his head and stared at the table. "He hated me. From the moment I was born, he kept me in the cellars under the kitchen with the garbage and made everybody call me 'Rancid.'" His voice remained low, nearly inaudible. "Until a year ago, I lived off the charity of the kitchen staff or discarded scraps from the baron's table." He glared at them, his hand gripping the handle of the dagger beneath the table, daring them to pity him.

"Where was your mother?" Zen asked.

"She was an elf slave."

"An *elf* slave?" Nick said. "I didn't know there were any elf slaves."

"There's not supposed to be. But my father has a weakness for the females. The Black Hand capture them on raids and bring them back. My father keeps them in the dungeons until he's through with them. Then he leaves them there to die. That's the kind of animal he is."

Nick spoke to him in a calm, reassuring tone. "We have to go into Palidor. You understand that, don't you? And you know the kingdom better than any of us do."

Rancid had to grit his teeth to keep from smiling. He'd take them to Palidor, all right. And he'd use them to rip the heart out of the Black Hand. "Okay. But we leave first thing in the morning, before I change my mind."

That evening, Zen met again with the mysterious elf who was willing to pay in enchantments for the knowledge Zen possessed. But Zen hesitated longer this time than he had before. The declaration the priest had made—that Zen's heart wasn't pure—had unsettled him. Zen had never thought of it in those terms. He had ambition, sure, but he'd never really done anything bad. Had he?

Perhaps the admonition was a warning that the strange elf was up to evil. *Does that matter?* Zen pushed the question aside. As long as he didn't give away any secrets, he had nothing to worry about.

Certainly he'd told the elf details about the enchanted artifacts and relics that surrounded the Prophecy, but he'd said nothing that Nick hadn't already told others. If this elf sought to learn those things, he'd learn them easily enough with or without Zen's help.

No, Zen could do no harm here. He was getting something for nothing.

He returned to the house in which he'd met the elf the first time, as he'd once again arranged through the lovely elven tramp, Irlyren.

The elf greeted him bluntly. "What do you have for me?"

Zen wondered again if the elf was up to evil. If he was, how would Zen know? Suddenly he wasn't sure he wanted to say anything. But he'd come here to do just that. He couldn't just walk away. Ultimately, the lure of the elf's magic, the items arranged on a table behind the desk, kept Zen in place. Yet what could he say that wouldn't betray his friends?

"Have you been able to use what I gave you last time?" Zen asked finally.

"A little," the elf admitted. "In fact, I'm hoping it will lead me to information that will help you in your quest."

"Really?" Zen's jaw slackened. "You want to help us?"

"Of course. I took what you said about the Black Hand to the guard house yesterday. Those bandits have been encroaching into the elven lands for years. The border guard is fed up. They want to take advantage of the damage you and your friends have done and the distraction you're providing."

Zen was dumbfounded. The elf was actually paying him for information that he was using to help them. It all sounded too good to be true. The priest's warning surfaced again. Maybe it wasn't a warning at all. Maybe it was an acknowledgment that Zen didn't know who he was trading with—a reflection of Zen's lack of moral certainty rather than a statement about his business partner. Suddenly that seemed likely.

"They need more specific information," the elf continued. "They need to know where they can find the Black Hand."

Zen wrestled his thoughts back to the conversation. Certainly telling the elves where to find the bandits could come to nothing but good. He told Gwyndarren everything Rancid had said about the location of the hideout, that the bandits operated in western Palidor and resided somewhere near Forlorn Valley. He mentioned that a baron, who presided over a keep of the same name, was probably pulling the strings or at least had a vested interest in the bandits, and might cause trouble. It wasn't much, but it was likely more than the border guard already knew.

"Excellent." The elf took a few notes to pass along. Then he returned to Zen's original question. "About the relics you mentioned last time, I'm researching them. If I discover anything useful, I'll pass it along."

"I'm afraid that won't be possible," Zen said. "We're leaving in the morning."

"I see. In that case, I'll need to know where you're going, so I can send word ahead if I learn anything."

The longer he spoke with the elf, the more easily Zen breathed. "We're going to Eckland, in Palidor. I don't know anything about it, or even where it is, exactly, but when we arrive, we'll probably stay at some mid-range inn."

The elf fished a roll of parchment from one of the desk's drawers and handed it to Zen. "Perhaps we can help each other."

Zen took the offering. "What is it?"

"It's a simple enchantment. If you learn anything that might be of use to me in researching the relics—or in anything else, for that matter—read the scroll out loud. Speak my name, Gwyndarren Lortannon, and then speak your message. I will hear it."

"How will you reply?"

"I won't. Not immediately. But I'll hear your words and act on them. If the need arises, I'll use similar means to contact you."

Zen nodded and tucked the sheaf into his robe. The two talked amiably for some time before Zen realized he'd told the elf everything Nick had related about their meeting with Alamain.

As requested, Jasmine returned to Alamain's chamber at midnight with Nick and Beltrann. Another elf was with the High Priestess, a small girl, an adolescent perhaps. She stood barely three feet tall, with long black hair—unusual for her race—and sharp, intensely elven features.

"May I present Aeriel," Alamain said.

When the girl came forward, she seemed neither timid nor subservient. She carried herself with an almost royal grace.

Alamain continued. "Aeriel is a direct descendent of the fairies."

"Aren't all elves?" Nick asked.

"That is a common misbelief, but no. As a race, elves have actually been around much longer—as long as dwarves and men. Fairies were created by Aeron during the Age of Magic to combat Vexetan's demons. Once the demons had been imprisoned, the fairies' purpose had been fulfilled. They fled the Civilized Lands, bringing the Age of Magic to a close."

Jasmine stepped forward respectfully and waited for Alamain to acknowledge her. "Nobody knows where they went? Did they leave our world entirely?"

"No. Not entirely. They went to the Mist Isles. A pair of islands north and east of the Civilized Lands. Their location is known, yet no one has ever found them."

"How can that be?" Nick asked.

"As their name suggests, a mist of the fairies' own making surrounds the islands. It's said that none but the fairies can sail through it without becoming hopelessly lost. No one has ever successfully done so."

"Then what hope do we have of finding them?"

"Aeriel may be able to help. She's been alive since before the current age began. She's half fairy."

Beltrann let out a long, low whistle.

"If it is Aeron's will," Alamain continued, "she will lead a ship through the mist."

"Then you can send a message to warn them of the demons' imminent return," Nick said. "That's great."

"The fairies have direct access to Aeron. They have no need for the elven church. Therefore, a message from me would be meaningless. They must hear your words from one who has witnessed the events you speak of. They will know your heart and understand its truths."

Apparently that was good enough for Nick. "I'll do it."

"No." Alamain placed a tender hand on his shoulder. "If the ship fails to find the islands, it may never return. And you, Nicklan Mirrin, have your own task before you."

"Will they accept me?" Jasmine asked.

Aeriel spoke for the first time, her voice as clear and sweet as if she was a single lily singing from within a field of wildflowers. "Your very blood will make them cry in outrage, despite the integrity of your heart."

For Jasmine, that confirmed what she had always feared. Her inhuman blood was, in fact, demon blood. She was the creation of some sadistic mage who liked to play with the denizens of the Abyss.

Meanwhile, all eyes had turned to Beltrann.

"That leaves me." He bowed first to Alamain, and then to Aeriel. "When do we leave?"

The fairy-kin motioned to the back door of the audience chamber, the door from which she and Alamain had entered. "A boat is already waiting to take us downriver to the coast."

CHAPTER 17

In a hurry to reach the rich market in Palidor before the goblin uprising subsided—before his dwarf-forged weapons would lose much of their value—Harimon Mirrin led his caravan into the deepening night, his long black hair whipping in the fresh breeze. The moon wouldn't turn full until after midnight, so Harimon's men had lit torches at the four corners of every wagon. Fortunately, South Bend wasn't far ahead.

His nose caught a hint of something on the wind. It was subtle and momentary, but it carried with it the stench of decay, death, and corrosion, a scent so foul even the memory of it nearly made him retch. Looking off in the direction from which the wind blew, he saw nothing and heard no sound.

"Trouble?" his guard captain asked.

Harimon hesitated, still peering into the darkness. "I don't know. I thought I smelled something."

"Campfire maybe?"

Harimon shook his head, trying to categorize the smell he'd experienced and the sensation that had accompanied it. The meat he'd had for supper turned foul in his stomach. "No, this was something different. Something... I don't know... putrid and gamy and—"

A scraping sound, stone on rock, reached him from somewhere off to their left. "You hear that?" Harimon asked.

Two other men joined them. The rest of the guards stood ready near the rear of the caravan. All nine of them—six guards, including their captain, two hired hands, and Harimon himself, shifted nervously. Only Harimon and his captain were mounted.

The sound came again. Not stone on rock, Harimon decided. Bone on rock. "Get them moving. I want to make Loran by the day after tomorrow."

Onward they clattered into the night, Harimon's battle ax now gripped in one of his strong hands.

A minute later, a dark shape took form on the road ahead, standing fifteen feet tall with crablike claws extended before it, spindly appendages armored in a glistening carapace.

As soon as it came within sight of the wagons, it rushed forward, moving with the speed and grace of a spider. Its eyes glowed a ghastly pink hew from sockets buried in its armored face. Spikes protruded along its spine.

A gout of fluid spewed from its mouth. The liquid, ignited by the torches, engulfed the lead wagon in an instant conflagration. A wall of heat washed over Harimon.

His guard captain spurred his horse forward, and two of his men charged on foot. Harimon would have turned the wagons around and fled from the monster, but the road here skirted the Great Divide—the massive, rugged mountain range that separated the Civilized Lands from the Wild Lands. The road was too narrow and the surrounding terrain an impassable tract of broken stone and exposed bedrock, so he charged with his men into the stench.

Fire from the burning wagon lit the scene with an eerie orange glow, giving the beast a hellish cast. This creature could have come only from the Abyss itself, though how the demon came to walk the Civilized Lands, Harimon could only guess.

The captain held his spear before him like a lance. Its tip struck the demon in the chest, but the beast didn't seem to notice. It plucked the man from his horse with four of its bladed pincers and ripped him asunder. Limbs flew in four directions, showering the horse, the demon, the road, and the two advancing footmen in a spray of gore. A glob landed on Harimon's cheek with a warm slap, slid down his face, and dropped onto his saddle.

The demon snatched the captain's horse from the road, tossed it casually into the air, and caught it in its mandibles. The mount squealed a strangled cry until its ribs collapsed. Then it fell silent.

Cautiously, the guards took another two steps forward. The demon dropped its meat and spewed a gout of saliva. One of the guards screamed. His armor smoked and began to dissolve. Within moments the man collapsed onto the ground, writhing, as demon spittle consumed his flesh.

Harimon didn't even consider trying to save his merchandise, though it had cost him all of last season's revenue just for a down payment. He'd find some other means to repay the dwarves the coin he still owed. At that moment, he cared only for his men. "Break away!" he called. "Leave the wagons! Flee!" He swung his ax at the monster, determined to hold it off while his men escaped, but they stood fast, refusing to leave without him. So he turned and galloped along the burning caravan, yelling for the others to follow.

He looked back to see if the demon was pursuing. It wasn't, but some invisible force struck the guard nearest him, threw the man from the ground and into the flames. This new creature sped past the wagon, whipping the fire into a frenzy. Running was no longer an option. The invisible newcomer was much too fast.

Harimon darted between the wagons to the opposite side of the road, leaving the unseen enemy behind, and continued down the line toward the back of the caravan. The lead team of mules broke free from the conflagration and ran headlong to their deaths at the claws of the demon. The second team, also near the flames, yanked and jerked until their efforts dragged their load off the road and into the adjacent crags, upsetting the wagon. Trapped in their harnesses, the mules went down as well. They lay struggling on the rocks, bleeding from the lacerations caused by their own panicked movements.

Mules all down the line tried to back up or bolt to the side, but harnessed as they were, they could gain neither freedom nor safety.

Harimon passed the last wagon and found his remaining guards lined up and launching arrows toward the stirring dust that marked the base of their invisible enemy. Several of the missiles seemed to hit the creature. They hovered in the air for a moment as though stuck fast into the thing, then went flying to one side or the other as the entity came on. The two grunt-workers Harimon had hired to assist with any menial tasks had disappeared somewhere in the commotion. They, at least, might survive.

The unseen force swept through the archers, slammed one of the men aside, and came straight for Harimon. The merchant raised his ax to face it, saving one hand to steady his horse. When the thing came close, Harimon swung at its insubstantial form, and the blade struck something—a subtle resistance. Still the thing didn't slow. It bowled Harimon's horse over, and he tumbled into the crags along the roadside.

The demon advanced, towering over the wagons, as Harimon struggled to regain his feet. When it reached the third wagon, the mules backpedaled their load, forcing the team behind to turn aside and flee. The rear wagon toppled. The third team lunged forward, pulling their wagon off the road. Their yoke broke loose and the mules struggled over the rocky ground toward safety.

Still the demon came.

The guards at the rear of the caravan stood together to face the invisible entity, swinging their swords toward any hint of stirring dust. The thing bobbed and swayed as though leery of the men, until it caught one with a glancing blow and knocked his sword free.

Leading with another gout of putrid spittle, the demon rushed into the fray. One guard fell, clawing at the dissolving skin of his face and neck until the corrosion laid his skull bare. The demon skewered the remaining guard, held him in the air on the end of a bladed claw, inspected him carefully, and then bit off his head.

Harimon charged. The bony plates of the demon's body were too tough to penetrate. But the joints between... there he might have more luck. His great ax came down with a crunch, slicing one huge pincher from the demon's massive leg. It wailed an inhuman cry and swept a bladed claw that caught Harimon in the chest and sent him flying—split from armpit to navel—into the crags.

As his life ran out of him, Harimon watched the invisible entity beat one of his downed men to a pulp against a fallen wagon. The demon had gone in search of the hirelings who'd fled.

Balor sighed, more relieved than annoyed, when Dalen's approach interrupted his inspection of the defenses. "What news?"

"Gremauld's army slept last night in Tawneydale," Dalen said. Smoke clouded the horizon from the direction of the city. "They've stripped it of food and supplies, and burned it to the ground."

Balor seethed. Pressure mounted in his chest and his temples throbbed. Tawneydale had been his home, the seat of his power. "Did the people get out?"

"Some of them. The men in the militia left to join those volunteers coming up from the south. As for their families, we warned them Gremauld was coming, but they couldn't have expected... that." He motioned to the smoke-choked sky to the west.

Balor's fists were clenched so hard his hands started to hurt. He flexed his fingers several times to work out the ache and began by stages to slow his breathing. "This is exactly why we can't let him keep the throne. Where is he now?"

"They left the city at dawn, headed this way."

That would put them at the pass in two days. "How many?"

"Forty thousand. Give or take."

The bottom dropped out of Balor's heart. His army hadn't been idle during the past week, but he couldn't imagine how it would hold out against a force twice its size. He continued walking the ridge, Dalen at his side.

"You there!" Balor hailed a corps commander. "Move your archers down." He indicated a strip of ground thirty yards below them on the hillside.

"But, sir, we've already dug our trenches here, and—"

"You see those trees?" Balor raged.

The commander looked, jaw hanging open as though he'd suddenly realized his insolence. "Of... of course, my lord."

"They'll obstruct the line of fire to your left."

"Gremauld will come from the right, my lord."

"They'll get past your position. You have to make that assumption."

"Then I'll have the trees cut down."

"No," Balor said. "They'll slow any advance up the hill." He scanned the surrounding terrain. "Besides, the line of retreat is better from down there. Move your line."

"Yes, my lord." The commander bowed and hurried away.

Dalen continued when he had the heir's attention once more. "The king has assembled ten thousand militia. They left the capital two days ago with a hundred veteran officers to lead them."

Balor blanched. According to the runner he'd received the previous evening, his own militia would number only three thousand—if they arrived at all. They had been forced to divert to Stunted Spruce Pass, a mere game trail passing through the southern quarter of the Sharktooth range, to prevent Gremauld's army from cutting them off at Tawneydale. From there, they planned to skirt the eastern foothills. The detour would take weeks.

Yet there was nothing he could do about that at the moment—nothing but make a few final adjustments to his defensive line before joining Pandalo in the command tent.

An overcast sky promised foul weather, the slate-gray of the clouds a perfect backdrop to match Rancid's mood as he contemplated a return to his homeland. If these obtuse, poem-chasing idiots wanted to go into Palidor, then he'd bloody well lead them there—right into Forlorn Valley, the heart of Black Hand territory. Let them use their swords for his purpose for a change.

He bent over Dara's map and pointed to a range of hills along the expansive border between Palidor and Lorentil. "This spot provides cover, in case the Black Hand are watching for us. If they're not..." He shrugged. "No harm done."

Dara nodded, tucked the map into her backpack, and led the party out of the city. As near as Rancid could tell, she never referred to the map again.

By midday, the clouds began dropping sprinkles and then torrents of rain.

It poured intermittently for several days, making travel uncomfortable but slowing them little. Vinra taught them the proper way to wrap and store their rations and important documents, in order to prevent losses like those they'd suffered during the tempest on their journey north.

On their third day, Rancid's paranoia, or some prescient sense within him—if such a thing existed—got the better of him. He began, at intervals, to lag behind the party and scout for signs of anyone who might be following.

He dropped back a good thirty minutes and waited. No one. Nevertheless, that strange sense continued to nag him, and he'd learned long ago to trust his instincts. So he continued to check their backtrail, dropping farther and farther behind each time, without any concern that he might lose his party. The wet, spongy ground readily accepted his friends' footprints and held them long enough for Rancid to track his way back.

On the afternoon of the fifth day, he discovered three shrouded figures on horseback trailing behind them. He could discern little of their identities. Each of the slight forms, hunched against the weather, wore a gray canvas cloak with a hood pulled low over his head. Elves. And with horses of obvious quality.

Most bothersome, however, was their lack of speed. Though mounted, the riders slogged ahead no faster than a man's walking pace, their heads bent before them as though to keep the rain from their faces... or to observe the soggy tracks of Rancid's personal army.

Once the riders had passed, Rancid circled widely around them and hurried to warn his friends.

"They might not be following," Dara said when Rancid caught up that evening. "They may simply be traveling in the same direction."

"All the same," Nick said. "I think we ought to change our course, just to be sure."

Dara thought for a moment, then nodded. "We'll post an extra sentry tonight. Tomorrow morning, we'll head straight east for a few miles before returning to our southeastern course. If we see them again..."

Satisfied, they all settled into their evening routine.

The following night, however, in the early hours of dusk, Dara spotted a small fire. "Quietly, now." She motioned them all forward. There, huddled over the sputtering flames, sat the same three elven riders.

"I told you," Rancid muttered.

Nick's finger shot to his lips.

Dara gave them both a glare. At her gesture, they backed off a few hundred yards. "You guys wait here."

"What are you going to do?" Zen whispered.

"Talk to them. Find out who they are and where they're going."

"I'll go with you," he said.

"If they're looking for *you*, they might not recognize *me*. Those robes, on the other hand—"

Zen straightened. "You can't go alone."

"Are you my big protector now?" Her words held no resentment or offense. Even Rancid had to admit the sincerity of her smile and the gratitude in her eyes.

"He's right," Nick said. "It's too dangerous."

"Well then." Dara took Zen's elbow gently in the crook of her arm. "Wish us luck."

Rancid waited for a few moments, and then followed.

Two of the riders turned from the fire and moved to intercept Zen and Dara. The third remained seated, cowl pulled over his head, poking at some small game he had roasting on the spit.

Rancid cursed the fact that the rain had stopped. Without it to help hide the sight and sounds of his movements, he didn't dare approach close enough to actually hear the conversation. And the meager gestures of both parties revealed nothing.

"Well?" he said when the two returned a few minutes later.

"They're just travelers," Dara declared, "going to Asnordyn, a small village on the border near Palidor. We'll pass through there ourselves."

"I'm not so sure," Zen said. "When we asked where they were going, the elf who claimed to be their guide hesitated before giving the name of the village, as though he'd momentarily forgotten it."

"Or was trying to come up with a plausible destination on the spot," Rancid said.

Zen nodded.

"They're lying." Rancid spat onto the ground. "They're following us. I knew it."

"That would be quite a trick," Dara said, "considering they've been in front of us for the past twenty-four hours."

"Maybe," Nick said. "We took a detour, and yet here they are. Doesn't that seem suspicious to you?"

Dara rubbed her forehead, thinking. "Perhaps. But they would've had to skirt east soon anyway to miss the small mountain range just south of here."

"How about their guide?" Zen asked. "Did you recognize him?"

"No."

"Should you have known him?" Nick asked.

"Not necessarily. Elven guides are a small community, but Lorentil's a big place. What's more, our suspicious friends are elves. They may not need a guide. Theirs may just be the one among them who's most familiar with the route." She paused. "No, it doesn't mean anything."

"You said we're going through Asnordyn?" Nick asked.

"I'd thought to stop there for supplies before leaving you at the border."

"In that case, let's detour far enough east that we shouldn't see them again. If we do, we'll know we're affecting their movements."

"That won't be necessary," Dara said. "They're mounted, so they'll make better time than we will. We can just wait here for a day and let them get ahead."

"I like that," Nick said. "The rain's let up. We can use the time to dry our gear, Rancid can hunt for some fresh meat, and Jasmine can pick us some greens." He gestured to each in turn. "If we run into the riders again, we'll know they waited for us."

After a little thought and a few words of discussion, they backed off about a mile and set up their own camp. As always, when in the elven wilderness, they posted double watches for the night.

The next morning, Rancid returned to the riders' camp and found it deserted. He watched it for a time, just to make sure the elves were really gone, before going in. When he did, he found what he should have expected—footprints from three elves and three horses. No supplies or implements had been left behind. So he returned to his own camp, no more comfortable or enlightened than he'd been when he left.

That day, the weather turned fair and held until they reached the village of Asnordyn on their nineteenth day out of Lorentil. They entered the town at midday, stopping just long enough to pick up a few supplies and whatever news they could gather. And to inquire about the riders.

Rancid went straight to the local stables. If the elves had passed through, the stablemaster would have noticed the quality of their horses.

"Sure," the stableman said. "They were here. Came in four days ago."

"When did they leave?"

"Well now. That's a difficult question. Perhaps I can recall something..." The elf scratched the side of his head in an exaggerated gesture of thought.

Rancid snorted. He didn't have much coin, nor did he have an inclination to haggle with the elf. "How much will it take to loosen your tongue?"

The elf nodded his satisfaction. "One gold coin to loosen my tongue."

Rancid dug into his purse and gave him the gold.

"And another to spur my memory."

"What? No way."

The elf slipped the coin into his pocket and shook his head. "My tongue is quite loose. You've gotten what you paid for. I simply can't remember when they left."

Rancid considered drawing his sword. Perhaps that would spur the elf's memory. If not, he could always take the loosened tongue in trade. He scanned the stable to make sure they were alone, and then thought better of it. He pulled out another coin and tossed it to the elf. "Now talk."

"What would you like to know?"

"Everything."

"That's an awfully broad request."

Rancid put his palm conspicuously on his sword's pommel. "When did they leave? You have nothing to gain by protecting them."

The elf stepped back with a nervous glance at the sword. "Certainly not. They left three days ago."

That was more like it. "Did you notice any markings of ownership on the horses?"

The stablemaster shook his head. "None other than their quality, which you've already mentioned."

"What about the elves themselves—were they wearing any insignia or tattoos?"

Still no.

"Maybe steel-studded gloves, like this." He displayed his chain of trophies.

The elf shook his head again, emphatically this time, eyes open wide. Maybe Rancid had struck a nerve.

"Do you know who they were?"

"I assure you I don't."

Rancid took a threatening step forward. "Did they mention the Prophecy of Mortaan?"

"Yes."

"What about it?"

"Th—they said they thought the Prophecy was coming. Th—that I should consider which side I would take in the upcoming war."

"What else?"

"About the Prophecy? Nothing." The elf's voice turned sarcastic. "They gave me the 'tip' in lieu of coin and laughed like they thought it was hilarious. I didn't take them seriously."

"What were they wearing when they came through?"

The elf looked confused. "Traveling clothes, like your own."

"No heavy, gray cloaks?"

"Not that I saw."

No matter. They'd have packed the cloaks away when the weather improved. Rancid relaxed his posture—the elf's tongue finally seemed to be appropriately loosened and his memory properly jogged. "Did they mention the Black Hand at all?"

After a moment's thought, the elf said, "Not that I heard."

Rancid didn't press the issue, though he remained skeptical of any seeming coincidence in the path the riders had taken. "Did they say anything about a group of travelers they met on their trip from Lorentil?"

"No. In fact, they didn't say they came from the capital. But they seemed concerned that someone would arrive before they left. I got the impression they were being pursued." He hesitated. "By you, I suspect."

Rancid left a few minutes later, trying to fit these riders into the story of his past so he might guess how they fit into his future.

CHAPTER 18

"That's absurd!" Pandalo exclaimed when Balor revealed his latest plan. "Military doctrine and countless historical events reveal the folly of splitting a force already outnumbered by the enemy."

"I see no alternative," Balor said. "Gremauld's army is too large for us to defeat, even from a defensive position. His militia, if allowed to arrive, will make him that much stronger. We cannot hold the pass."

"So you propose to defend it with half the men?"

"We hurt him badly on his first assault. He'll be wary. If we make a sufficient show of force, his own paranoia will buy us time."

"You're making an awfully big assumption, my lord."

Balor said nothing. Pandalo was right, and they both knew it.

"So we gain time," Pandalo said. "Then what?"

"We'll take our next opportunity, whatever that might be."

Dalen had been silent, listening, until now. "It can be done."

"I'm not questioning that—" Pandalo began.

"North Fork Pass is not far from here," the scout said. "I can get you through before Gremauld arrives. From there, it'll be up to you to intercept his volunteers."

"It's not the volunteers I'm worried about. Or their veteran leaders." Pandalo turned back to Balor. "I'm worried about this pass. You. And the men here." He took a deep breath and released it slowly. "If Gremauld discovers us, he'll come after half our army with all of his. Then he'll turn and finish off the other half."

Balor placed a hand on Pandalo's shoulder. "I understand your concern. But we won't win this war without taking chances. We have to bite at the pieces we can chew." He dropped his hand. "The decision's mine, and it's final. The very absurdity of the plan will prevent his suspecting our movements."

During those weeks in the elven woods, Nick could have almost forgotten about the Prophecy, except that every time his thoughts drifted toward home, he recalled the devastation he'd left behind there. Grief threatened to cripple him, but it was quickly replaced by a sense of urgency as sobering and real as his mother's death. If the Prophecy was coming, she was but the first innocent casualty.

Midmorning on the second day out of Asnordyn, Nick and the others finally reached the border of Palidor, where they paused to bid farewell to their elven guide. "I wish I could afford to give you something more," Nick said. "I can't overstate our thanks."

"That's quite all right," Dara said. "When I learned that the church was paying my fee, I doubled it." She jingled the heavy purse hanging from her belt. "They've compensated me well. You needn't worry."

Rancid overheard the comment. "Hey! *We* arranged for the church to pay."

"You did," she acknowledged.

"So if you ripped off the priests, we should get a cut."

Dara feigned shock and dismay. "That would be immoral."

Rancid opened his mouth to speak, but said nothing.

She continued, smiling now. "They agreed to pay my fee. Nothing more. If I give you a cut, then that part wouldn't go toward my fee. I'd have to return that amount to the priests."

Rancid found his tongue. "You overcharged the church. Where does that fit into your model of morality?"

She laughed and patted his shoulder. "Price is *always* negotiable. If the buyer can afford more, you charge more. That's simple economics."

Nick noted a gleam in Dara's eye as she turned away. The girl must have known the company was low on funds and she apparently enjoyed Rancid's distress. But she relinquished none of the coin. She was, after all, an elf.

Nick didn't fault her for her attitude. She'd come a long way with the group and was responsible for its survival against both the hippogriffs and the giant tiger. He and his friends would find the means to get by.

When they finally crossed the border, they did so in a region of hilly terrain that took the rest of the morning to navigate.

"The Black Hand will be watching for us," Rancid said when the hills began to taper off. "We have to assume that. We can't afford to underestimate them." His scan of the country ahead seemed more elaborate than necessary, as though much of it was merely for show. "Wait here. I'll scout the trail."

Jasmine offered to go with him, but Rancid shook his head. He put a finger to his lips and motioned for them all to get down. When he turned to leave, Jasmine grabbed his arm. He spun back, anger flashing in his eyes.

"You could be ambushed," she said in a whisper so low it was nearly lost in the gentle afternoon breeze. "You should not go alone."

Rancid yanked his arm from her grasp and stabbed a finger at the ground. "Stay here." Then he disappeared around a bend.

Jasmine turned to Nick. "I do not trust him."

"Nor do I, but he knows this area better than we do."

"That is exactly what worries me."

Rancid returned after the better part of an hour. "Just over the next ridge lies the main caravan route through Palidor, a favorite hunting ground of the Black Hand. For the moment, this side of the road appears to be safe."

They crept up to the thoroughfare and waited while Rancid repeated his performance on the far side, with the same result. From there they crossed into the hill country beyond.

Throughout the next day, they moved deeper into Palidor. That evening, Nick approached Rancid again. "Eckland is east of here. Why are you taking us south? The road would be faster."

"You're right." Rancid's reply was measured, his voice calm. "Our path lies to the southeast, but not so much east as you might guess. Remember, it took only twelve days to reach the city of Lorentil from the elven border, but twenty-one days to return. We've come a long way east already."

Nick listened patiently. Rancid was an odd character, but a capable scout.

Rancid continued. "That road carries every merchant convoy traveling from the capital city and port towns to the inland kingdoms of Brinheim, Meuribar, and Faldor. It's lucrative beyond compare for the Black Hand. And they'll always be found somewhere along it. I bring us south into the hills for the same reason we crossed the border in them. It's safer by far than any other option."

Nick had to admit that it made sense, and if he'd been making the decisions, he would have led the party into peril on that very road.

Before he could reply, Rancid addressed the company. "It'll take longer this way, perhaps several days longer. But we will get there." He waited for a gesture or word of acceptance from everyone before issuing a final note of caution. "I know the Black Hand. I know them perhaps better than anyone outside their brotherhood does. And I don't believe for a minute that we can avoid them altogether, no matter what path we choose. So keep low and stay alert."

With that, he led them away.

The demon Ka-G'zzin surveyed the highway between Glintbroc, the dwarven City of Gold, and Silversmith, a port town in the human kingdom of Meuribar. A constant flow of trade caravans snaked their way into and out of the pass. Whisper, the air apparition, hovered nearby, almost imperceptible even to Ka-G'zzin's demon senses. Somewhere in the tribal lands of Cormont, the Master had assured him, Ka-G'zzin and Whisper would find the key to the Portal of the Damned, but to get there they must pass through the dwarven kingdom of Gildstone. And the only way into Gildstone was through Glintbroc.

Unfortunately, this highway, perhaps the busiest stretch of road in all the Civilized Lands, provided the only approach.

Ships bypassed the dwarves all the time in their passage to Cormont, so the Master could have paid for passage with some unscrupulous captain, but he'd demanded that this mission be performed with the utmost secrecy. And with Ka-G'zzin's size and appearance, he had no way to arrange passage on a ship without attracting notice.

Therein lay the crux of Ka-G'zzin's problem. The road was packed with caravans—day and night—during the fair months. Lacking any other place to stop, the merchants set camp right on the road at nightfall. Ka-G'zzin and Whisper could force their way past the traders, but that would betray their presence. And by all reports, the walls of the dwarven city would be much more formidable than any trials they might meet on the road, including the battle he and Whisper had fought with the human merchant west of South Bend.

That had been an unfortunate incident. Oh, Ka-G'zzin gave no thought to the loss of life. What care did a demon have for the humans and their kin? Millions of the miserable things would die in the few months after the opening of the Portal, and Ka-G'zzin would savor every stroke he would deliver on behalf of his brethren.

No, he cared not for the merchants. He cared only that the incident had cost him one of his legs and had put the success of his mission—and therefore his own release from slavery—in jeopardy. Just to be sure that word didn't spread, Ka-G'zzin and Whisper had spent the following day tracking down and exterminating every creature who'd seen them, whether human or animal.

Ka-G'zzin hoped to avoid a replay of that incident on the Glintbroc road. Traffic was too dense. There would be too many witnesses.

Rather, he examined the land along the roadside. Passable, though it would get worse as they neared the dwarven border. He and Whisper could probably manage any terrain it proved necessary to cross, but it would cost them time. The demon's mandibles ground together in agitation. The traffic ahead made the delay unavoidable.

As the sun went down, the demon rose from his haunches and clambered over the rocks toward the cliffs of the Great Divide. He and Whisper had no difficulty of vision in the darkness and no need for sleep. They would travel as far as possible tonight, and if the road passed from sight by morning, they would continue through the day to recover some of the lost time.

One concern remained, however. Cormont was a large and sparsely populated kingdom. And according to the Master, the journal Whisper had stolen from Nicklan Mirrin merely suggested that the Guardian was there. To have any chance of finding it, they would have to at least have a starting point for the search.

He shook the thought loose. The Master had assured him that more information would be available by the time they arrived. And Ka-G'zzin had no cause to doubt.

orches and lanterns cast an orange glow over Halidreth's dimly lit cave. Rough-cut stone augmented the natural walls, giving the space a utility it had lacked before the Black Hand had moved in, and a variety of stolen furnishings provided a level of comfort that suited the tastes of the bandit gang.

Halidreth clenched his black-gloved fists when an orc entered the chamber escorted by two Black Hand sentries. He took a slow breath to subdue his mounting ire. Never did an orc bring good news.

"The orc demands to see the Chosen," one of the sentries announced.

Halidreth nodded at once. He led the men and their grotesque visitor, with its sickly green skin and lumpy features, through a short tunnel and into the chamber beyond. As they entered, the stench of the ogre, Groot, assaulted his nostrils.

The gargantuan goblinoid stood at the far end of the spacious cavern, flanked by three of his orc commanders. Orcs came and went regularly now, moving in the daylight under the cover of traveling cloaks, often accompanied by Halidreth's own Black Hand agents—much to their individual peril. In fact, the risk had become so great that Halidreth no longer allowed them to wear the symbol of their guild while in the company of the goblinoids.

"What you want?" Groot rumbled in a mockery of the language used by the civilized races. His deep voice grated like the thunder of a rockslide. Trickles of dust vibrated loose from the ceiling as he spoke.

"We get no swords," the visitor stammered. "They not come." His feet danced in place, betraying his agitation.

"AAAAAAGH!" Groot stomped across the room, his twelve-foot frame towering over the wretch. The cave shook with each footfall. He lifted the orc with one hand about the creature's chest and pressed him against the wall.

"Wait," the orc pleaded. "I give news. You kill me. But not before news."

Halidreth pursed his mouth and raised his eyebrows. He'd expected the creature to plead for its life, though it would have been a wasted effort. Groot's mind wasn't sophisticated enough to make the distinction between the messenger and the message. The plea the orc did make, however, gave an importance to his message that piqued even Halidreth's interest.

Groot relaxed his grip and waited. When the orc didn't continue, he said, "Speak."

The orc was panting now, short of breath, trying to regain some measure of composure. "Men take ships. Take swords. Kill orcs."

Groot gave a long rumble in his throat.

The orc continued. "Port closed. They stop all ships. Men go on board. Men search." He sucked in a rasping breath. "We get no more ships. No more swords. Not now."

Groot stared at the wretch, unmoving. Halidreth had known it would happen sooner or later. The goblin swords they'd put into the hands of slaves from one end of Palidor to the other could only have come from across the channel. The king didn't need to know how the swords were being distributed to stop their flow into the kingdom. It must have happened weeks before, if this orc had made its way here from the coast since then.

Groot dropped the orc and turned away, his green-tinged skin shining sickly in the torchlight. He paused for a moment, his head piercing the cloud of smoke suspended near the ceiling, then turned to Halidreth.

"Don't matter. We ready for next step."

Halidreth froze. Groot had never said anything about a next step.

"Goblins hide in safe place. Have many swords. Have ten tens of orcs. Now free rest of slaves."

Halidreth let out a breath he hadn't realized he'd been holding. This was, in fact, good news. Groot's orcs and goblins would have to conduct the raids. Any overt involvement by the Black Hand would lead the authorities here. And Groot wouldn't want that.

When the ogre had recruited the Black Hand to escort orcs across the kingdom by day and distribute swords into the fields of plantations at night, Halidreth had been forced to stop his band's normal operations. But Groot had offered the bandits more than twice the coin they could have expected to take—even in good times—and promised the service would be temporary. Perhaps now it was finally coming to an end.

As for the freeing of the slaves, Halidreth had no concern for that. The distraction would be beneficial. In fact, the king's patrols hadn't mounted an expedition into Forlorn Valley to search for the Black Hand since the slave riots had begun.

Groot turned to his orc commanders and gestured to the messenger. "Take him. Go."

Following the ogre's lead, Halidreth nodded to his own sentries. "Leave us."

As soon as the two leaders were alone and Halidreth had closed the door, Groot announced, "There is more news."

Halidreth waited.

"Meddlers come to Pal-dor." Groot still hadn't learned to pronounce the name of the kingdom properly. Two syllables seemed to be his limit in both vocabulary and pronunciation.

"Oh? How many are there?"

"Five now. One go back when get to Pal-dor."

"Do you know where they're going?"

"To Eck-land. They look for book."

Halidreth stroked his bald pate as his mind sifted through the possibilities. Eckland was a long way from Forlorn Valley, but he and his bandits knew the area well. It was rich territory, not far from the heart of the slave trade. "Is Sevendeath with them?"

Groot nodded.

A slow smile spread across Halidreth's face and the warmth of anticipation infused his body. "We'll have a little surprise waiting for him."

"No." The ogre strode across the chamber and settled into the stone chair the Black Hand had constructed for his use, along with all the oversized furnishings in the room. "They must get book. Then you kill them." Groot's huge, green hand clenched the odious medallion that hung delicately at his throat.

Halidreth didn't miss the implied meaning of the gesture. He had been threatened with the wrath of Vexetan's Anointed One several times since the ogre had come to him. Halidreth's power over the outlaw gang he'd founded so many years before had become as fine as desert sand. He couldn't seem to hold it any longer. Day by day, he felt it trickling through his fingers.

Like the grains in a handful of sifting sand, the numbers of his forces were also dwindling, a fact he attributed to Sevendeath. He would have his revenge, one way or another.

CHAPTER 19

The sun touched the western horizon just as Dalen emerged from the North Fork trail, with Pandalo Gundahar and half of Balor's rebels: an enormous human serpent that snaked its way, single-file, through the pass—ten thousand men strung out for miles. It would take Pandalo most of the night to bring them all in and form them up for the next day's march.

Supply wagons would never have made the passage. Instead, each man carried his own weapons and a share of the army's camping gear, cooking utensils, and repair implements. They led enough extra mounts for the army to subsist on horse meat in the days to come. There'd be no time to forage, hunt, or pillage for food.

After watching the army's slow progress for several minutes, Dalen drew his mount alongside the general's. "I must take my leave. I'm needed at Twin Peaks."

Pandalo frowned for a moment, deep in some inner thought, before responding. "Do what you must. May fortune speed your passage."

With a nod, Dalen kicked his mount into a run. He'd lose his light in less than an hour, but he meant to take advantage of every minute it offered. He had so little time.

Balor looked down upon Gremauld's army, which had settled itself at the mouth of the pass and for two full days just sat there.

His own forces—such as they were—had prepared as well as they could, but the constant vigilance and the awful specter of the vastly superior enemy began to take their toll on his men's nerves.

Why didn't they attack?

The north side of the pass, a steep slope composed of broken rock interspersed with towering cliffs and deep ravines, was ideal for concealing archers and presented Gremauld with an impassible barrier. The southern side, on the other hand, offered a gradual slope dotted with brush, trees, and outcrops of ragged stone. Defensible, to be sure, but not impassible. Gremauld had sufficient men at his disposal to rush the pass and still send a sizable force up the southern slope.

By contrast, Balor's forces had been reduced to a mere twelve thousand men, but more concerning was his lack of leadership. With Pandalo gone, and many of the commanders with him, Balor was left with only two captains and a handful of lieutenants to lead his troops.

Roltar, commander of the elite foot soldiers—thirteen hundred men trained for combat in any terrain—hustled up beside him. The man had led the Black Forrest ambush to a remarkable victory and was now responsible for defending Balor's vulnerable left flank.

In Dalen's absence, reconnaissance had also fallen to Roltar's men. "Still no sign of preparation, my lord."

"Perhaps he's decided a siege serves his purpose better than an assault. He has all of Trondor to supply his army." Balor had only the small slice east of the Sharktooth, and that had been barren since the first snow the previous fall.

Roltar bowed. "You would know better than I, my lord."

Balor studied the man for a long moment, evaluating. He was used to having Pandalo to confer with. Roltar, however, seemed more comfortable in the field. Tactics were his specialty, not strategy.

Balor returned his attention to the enemy. "More likely, he's letting anticipation erode our morale."

"If so, my lord, it's working. The men are restless. They're having difficulty sleeping. Quarrels among the troops are more frequent and violent than I've ever seen."

"They must be patient." Balor turned to the captain. "Keep them busy. Invent chores if you must."

Roltar bowed once more.

After the man left, Balor studied the army below. "What are you waiting for, cousin?"

A distant wail passed through the hills. Nick stopped short and his friends scanned the surrounding terrain. Rancid, however, pressed resolutely forward.

"What was that?" Nick asked him.

"The Black Hand." Rancid didn't look up as he answered. Instead, he turned down a gully into a dry wash.

"How close?"

"Who knows?" Rancid broke into a jog down the streambed. He had to yell over the rattling of gear. "They use those infernal horns. In these hills, there's no way to tell which direction they're coming from, or how far off they are. But we have to get out of sight. There could be a handful or a hoard of the bastards."

In his heavy armor, Nick struggled to keep up. The ground they covered was dotted with hoof prints, but Rancid was too far ahead for Nick to mention them, so he just tucked his head and pumped his arms and legs, using everything he had to keep pace.

Rancid finally brought them to a stop about a mile down the ravine, where a pair of oily, stagnant ponds and a few sickly trees blocked most of the wash. Here, the wall of the gully rose to twenty feet above the streambed in a nearly vertical rise on the eastern side. The western wall presented a higher, more gradual slope. Rancid turned, panting, and waited for everyone to settle in around him.

"It looks like the bandits use this wash as a thoroughfare." He pointed to the hoof prints. "But there's a choke point here, and cover on the slopes."

Nick surveyed the walls. A couple of cottonwood trees and some large clumps of barberry grew nearby. *An ambush?* He narrowed his eyes at Rancid and waited.

"I don't know what that horn meant," Rancid said. "I've heard them constantly during the past year and have never been able to de-cipher the coded calls. But I've no doubt it's the Black Hand." He looked from face to face, his breathing slowing now with the brief rest. "If they've spotted me, they'll pursue. If they do, they'll come down this wash. We can either waylay them or hide, depending on the size of the group."

"And if they're not following?" Jasmine asked.

He shrugged. "Then they won't come down the wash and we have nothing to worry about."

"What if it's not the Black Hand?" Nick began to catch his breath now as well.

"We let them go."

Nick inspected the site again. It was a good spot for an ambush. And Rancid was right. He might have been seen. Based on Rancid's history with the Black Hand, they would respond in force to his reap-pearance in Palidor.

Nick nodded. "Agreed."

The five of them took up positions on the margin of the ravine and waited, listening for additional horn calls. They heard none. After what seemed an age, a cloud of dust drifted over a nearby ridge, around which the streambed snaked through a valley. Whatever the source of the cloud, it was in the wash and headed their way.

Before long, the drumbeat of hooves began to shake the ground. Nick crouched at the base of the western slope, behind the stout trunk of a scrub oak, and waited.

Moments later, four riders appeared. One man rode out in front, then a pair, with another trailing. Their stride was an easy canter in the soft sand, their gazes directed forward rather than toward the ground as they would be if they were following tracks. But they were bandits, all right. A studded black glove adorned the right hand of each.

As the first rider neared the spit of sand between the pools, he must have seen something—a rustle of bushes perhaps, or a glimpse of one of Nick's companions. He slowed and glanced at the sides of the ravine, as if he was unwilling to pass through the narrow stretch. Finding a sheer face on his left, the man veered right, toward the more gradual slope, well beyond Nick's reach.

In another circumstance, Nick might have let him pass. His uncle had taught him to use his sword only if a fight became unavoidable. But this was different. The Black Hand had killed his mother.

He gripped his sword's hilt in both hands, ready to charge. Then Vinra began mumbling from somewhere behind him, praying to Robala, and a globe of suffocating blackness engulfed him.

The rider cursed. His horse stumbled as it reached the steep bank in the darkness. Nick crept toward the sound until he emerged from the globe. The blackness engulfing the western slope had discouraged the remaining bandits from choosing that route. The men—no, one man and two women, all hooded—had to run the gauntlet.

As the now-leading pair of Black Hand raced between the stagnant pools, Zen came to his feet atop the eastern cliff, brandishing his staff, and called an elven command.

A frigid wave of air swept from its crystal tip. Even from a distance,

Nick felt the bite of it, as if he'd fallen through the ice of a frozen pond. His exposed hands became so cold they could barely hold his sword. Both riders screamed. One passed the pools and spurred her horse southward. Frost clung to her cloak and the mane and tail of her mount. The second horse succumbed to the cold. It collapsed in a frozen heap, spilling its ice-covered rider to the ground.

The trailing bandit slowed her horse and looked frantically for an alternate path. Finding none, she risked Zen's wrath and charged between the pools, her horse leaping the dead animal. She made no effort to assist her downed companion, who was struggling to rise.

"There's no valor among thieves," Rancid cried as he darted into the fray.

Nick flexed his frostbitten hands and followed.

As the trailing bandit passed over her downed companion, Zen would have liked to have hit her with another icy blast from his staff, but it had its limitations, and he didn't dare tax them until he knew better what they were.

He turned, instead, toward the lead rider. The woman crouched low over the neck of her horse and urged it to reckless speed. Though she'd already fled beyond Zen's range, he couldn't let her get away. If she informed the Black Hand of Sevendeath's return, the bandits would descend upon Nick's little group in droves.

In desperation, he risked a new weaving, a variation of a calling he'd picked up during his day at Glimmernook. It was dangerous in the extreme to attempt an unpracticed weaving under the stress of battle, but this one wasn't exactly unpracticed. He'd studied the incantation and gestures on the way down from Lorentil—even performed the weave in earnest once or twice on quiet nights in the camp. This time, though, he must pull the weaving together from memory rather than from his notes.

Focusing his energies, he began to chant. The weave came to him instantly, and he sent it in search of an animal. Not just any animal, but a bird of prey—one he'd seen the day before, after passing into the hills. Within moments, the raptor entered his awareness. He grasped it with tendrils of the weave and copied its form.

Unlike a calling, this morph used his own body to manifest the animal's shape. His staff, pack, and other gear joined him in becoming that which he'd sought and captured. Slowly, his vision shifted from his own to that of the bird, a strange and disorienting sensation that passed as quickly as it had come.

Zen examined himself to make sure he was whole. His body, what he could see of it, was there—his, yet not his: no longer a body of flesh, but of frosty, snow-covered ice. Color notwithstanding, he looked like the real hawk.

With a screech, he launched himself into flight, where he gained a commanding view of the battlefield. Nick, Rancid, and Jasmine charged the fallen bandit, who still stumbled among the deadfall that littered the wash.

Rancid buried an arrow in the back of the trailing rider. The woman tumbled from her mount and lay still. Two riders down. Two escaping.

Zen banked toward the frontrunner, who was easily a half-mile down the wash, racing toward the south. He pumped his wings. In this form, flight felt natural. Yet he gained only slowly on the woman, with no idea how he'd stop her when he caught up.

Worse, the farther the chase pulled him from his friends, the riskier it became. Eventually, the woman turned in her saddle and scanned the landscape behind her. When she saw Zen, she studied him for a long time, then pulled her hood back and scanned the rest of the sky. Without slowing, she raised her crossbow and launched a bolt.

Zen veered upward. The missile slipped past, mere inches below his left wing.

As Nick approached the bandit they'd trapped between the stagnant pools, the man's movements became more and more desperate. Finally, he leapt into the western pool—the larger of the two—and disappeared, taking with him his halberd—a wicked-looking, long-handled ax.

Ripples disturbed the leaves, clumps of algae, and brackish film that covered the pool, concealing everything beneath its surface. Nick motioned to the others. Together, he, Rancid, Jasmine, and Vinra took up positions around the pool and waited for the bandit to resurface.

When he did, he heaved himself out of the filth, dripping and spitting, and rolled instantly to his feet. Within a few running strides, he slipped a piece of parchment from a water-tight document case hanging at his belt, spoke its enchantment, and leapt fifty feet to the top of the western embankment.

"Goblin's blood," Nick muttered beneath his breath.

Jasmine plucked a throwing star from a pouch at her waist and threw it. The small, barbed disk sailed into the trunk of a cottonwood with a soft thud as the man ducked behind it. From there, he darted away from the lip of the ravine and disappeared from sight.

Jasmine sprinted in pursuit. Nick trudged after, too heavily laden with his armor to keep up. If Jasmine caught the man, she'd need help against the halberd the slippery rogue had managed to retain throughout his flight.

Moments later, Nick gained the top of the rise, leg muscles burning, and glanced back at the others. Vinra had lost his footing on the slope and struggled to regain it. Rancid thrust his sword into the woman he'd felled from her saddle. Zen was nowhere in sight.

Nick pressed on. As he burst through the trees into the open, his hopes plummeted. The rider who'd topped the embankment at the beginning of the battle had turned back. He now charged Jasmine at a dead run, swinging a spiked, iron ball on the end of a heavy chain.

Nick's eyes grew and he redoubled his futile effort to make up the distance.

Jasmine, with a *sai* in one hand, closed on the runner before the horseman arrived.

Her quarry drew up short and spun on her, swinging his halberd.

She dug her clawed heels into the ground and came into the weapon's arc off-balance. Floundering, she raised her *sai* to block. The bandit's blade sent her small weapon flying into the brush. But it had deflected the blow.

After that, Jasmine seemed unable to breach the man's long defensive reach. She dodged and twisted around his strikes, waiting for an opportunity to grapple the weapon from his hands.

Nick gave them a wide berth as he passed and took up station in front of the charging horse. The bandit's lips twisted into a wicked sneer that revealed broken teeth. A gleam in his eye suggested overconfidence. Indeed, many men would have been an easy target for the rider and it had been three years since Nick's days as a guard for his uncle's caravan, but he'd fought mounted bandits many times before.

The thunder of hooves filled his ears. Vibrations from the ground reverberated up through his feet. He smelled the hot breath of the horse. Dust swirled around the shadow of the spiked ball plummeting toward his head.

Nick ducked, thrusting his blade into the air to intercept the chain of the morning star. The ball whooshed past so close he could smell the oiled links of the chain. He tightened his grip as hard as he could with both hands and prayed his blade would hold. Bolstering his strength by the force of will alone, he braced himself for the blow that would hit him next.

As the chain wrapped around Nick's sword, the horse's full momentum gathered him up and ripped him from his feet. Still, the sword flew from his hands, and he landed with a thump that blasted the air from his lungs.

For a moment, he wallowed in disorientation. Then the dust cleared and he looked up to see what he'd accomplished. His sword lay a short distance away. Next to it sprawled the bandit's morning star, a threat Jasmine would no longer have to face.

But the horseman was still mounted and armed. Just behind his saddle rode a quiver of javelins—as deadly a weapon as any in the hands of a mounted foe. The rider didn't reach for them, however. Using both hands, he pulled his mount to a halt beside his cohort and bent to heave the man onto the horse's back.

Just then, a white hawk swooped at the rider, its shape wavering unnaturally as it spread its wings to slow its descent. A shimmering blue-gray robe fluttered into being, enveloping the full weight of Zen's suddenly-human form as he appeared in the air above the bandit's head. When the rider reached down for his friend, though, Zen sailed over him and tumbled to the ground in a cursing heap of cloak and staff.

It was all Nick could do to keep from laughing, the mighty ice mage humbled by his own weaving, but his mirth lasted for only a moment, during which the second rider settled himself astride the horse.

With a yank of the reins and a spur of the heel, the bandits would be gone.

Regretting the need, Nick scooped up his sword and sank it to the bone in the horse's leg. It and the riders tumbled to the ground.

Rancid and Vinra arrived then, and the bandits never got up.

As soon as they were dead, Nick knelt by the horse, its eyes wide and chest heaving as it labored to stand on its nearly-severed leg. "I'm sorry." He thrust his sword into the dying animal's brain, putting a merciful end to its misery.

While Rancid collected his trophies, Nick helped Zen to his feet. "You all right?"

The mage nodded. "One got away."

"Then we'd better go. If she saw Rancid, she'll gather help and come after him. Our best chance is to keep moving."

"There's more. She was the woman from Cedar Falls. The one who approached you about the journal and later rode with the air apparition."

"Jade?"

Zen nodded.

"I thought she was dead."

"It was her. I'm sure."

CHAPTER 20

Gwyndarren entered the Black Hand hideout unarmed, on foot, and surrounded by bandit warriors. His two riding companions had been unwilling to venture into Palidor without knowing his purpose and destination. Reluctant to reveal either, he left them at the border and entered Black Hand territory alone.

Until then, the ride had been uneventful, marked only by an unexpected meeting with Zen and his companions in the elven woods. Not wanting Zen to recognize him, for fear the mage would guess his game, Gwyndarren kept his hood pulled over his features and tended the meal while his friends dealt with Zen.

After that, Gwyndarren had quickened has pace to avoid another chance meeting.

Now, as the guards led Gwyndarren into the chamber, the bandit leader—bald, muscled, and well-dressed in silks and fine linen—came to his feet. "What's this?"

One of Gwyndarren's captors stepped forward. "This elf has demanded to see the Master."

The leader stepped away from his throne, a stone seat padded with plush velvet cushions. The incongruous combination gave the throne an air of primacy and practicality that was reflected in the rest of the room's furnishings. Beneath the throne lay a semicircular platform with three steps ringing its perimeter.

"'Master' can mean many things." The bandit stepped to the edge of the dais and looked down upon Gwyndarren. "I assume it's not a reference to an owner of slaves, because my men are well paid."

This was the crucial moment. Gwyndarren had had no fear throughout his trek and no hesitation to engage those he sought. He'd rode confidently through the bandits' territory, carrying more coin than any man ought. When the outlaws discovered him, he tossed his purse onto the ground, spilling his gold before them.

Grinning and salivating, the men advanced with murder and robbery in their eyes.

"There's more where that came from," Gwyndarren shouted, making no move to defend himself. "But not on my person."

The bandits moved close enough to prevent his escape and paused to hear his next words.

Gwyndarren smiled. A gang with the reputation of the Black Hand would employ no amateurs. They wouldn't plunder for paltry sums if it would cost them the opportunity for greater riches. "I seek the Black Hand." From the gloves each man wore, he'd found them. "I have a business proposal. I offer information in hopes that an alliance might be forged between us. An alliance that will ultimately profit us all." He motioned to the discarded purse. "I make that payment, as a sign of my sincerity."

Several tense minutes followed, in which Gwyndarren feared little for his life. They wouldn't kill him before he'd made his offer, which he'd do only in the presence of the Master. Besides, as an accomplished swordsman, he had no reason to fear these four.

But now, in the throat of the bandit's lair, he hesitated. They'd brought him here without the benefit of a blindfold, so he'd learned the location of their hideout. That narrowed the possible outcomes. The bandit leader would believe Gwyndarren's offer was both genuine and valuable, or he'd kill him where he stood. Perhaps both.

A heavy, iron-banded door sealed this chamber from the deeper recesses of the complex. Behind Gwyndarren, several guards stood between him and the well-hidden mouth of the cave. And if the man standing over him was the mythical Master, his power was far greater than Gwyndarren's own. Fighting, if it became necessary, would not be an option.

Gwyndarren would live or die by the next words he spoke.

"Well?" The bandit leader's voice was low and menacing. "What sort of master do you seek?" The leader's mouth, framed by black hair in the shape of an arrowhead that pointed toward the ground, twisted into a sardonic grin. He looked like an ordinary man, not an immortal as Gwyndarren believed the Master of the Prophecy to be, but the leader's head was shaved, not naturally bald. He might have removed the lock of white hair by which the Prophecy said the Master could be identified.

Calmly, the Black Hand leader drew a dagger from his belt, descended the steps, and placed the blade against Gwyndarren's neck.

Gwyndarren's hands remained free and the guards made no move toward him. He could have stopped the knife if he chose, but it would have been a short-lived defense. Better to demonstrate trust and bravery.

"Speak or die." The man's breath, which warmed Gwyndarren's face, reeked of stale ale and bad cheese.

No, this was not the master he sought. He was master of the Black Hand, perhaps, but nothing more.

Gwyndarren phrased his proposal carefully. "You seek an elf-kin named Sevendeath." It wasn't a question. He knew from Zen that this was so. "I can help you."

"How?" The bandit pricked the skin at Gwyndarren's neck.

"There's a mage among Sevendeath's comrades whose loyalty is untrue. He seeks power. And he'll sell out his friends to get it." He locked eyes with the bandit leader. "I can contact him."

"A mole?" The bandit withdrew the dagger but kept it in his hand, ready to use, as he considered the possibilities. His next question should have been, "At what cost?" Instead, the leader asked, "What does that have to do with the Master?"

"*The* Master," the bandit had said, tipping his hand for Gwyndarren to see. This man knew the Master of whom Gwyndarren spoke. "I have a proposal for the Master as well. Though I don't know where to find him, my sources have led me here." He locked eyes with the bandit leader. "Help me contact him. I'll help you kill Sevendeath."

This was a dangerous game. Gwyndarren had only Zen's allegiance to barter with, and he was selling it three ways. First, as an offer to the bandit leader in exchange for assistance—and his life. Second, he'd offer it to the Master when he found him. Third, he counted on it for himself. And he didn't yet know if Zen's traitorous remarks were sincere.

"Sevendeath has left Palidor." The bandit leader mounted the steps to the platform. "I have no further interest in him."

A stab of fear pierced Gwyndarren's heart. There were two men in the room whom he couldn't see without turning, and the leader had just dismissed his proposition. Thus, a sword might already be plunging toward his back. "He's returned." The words rushed out, giving the statement an unwanted tone of desperation. "He travels to Eckland with his friends."

The leader stopped. He turned slowly to face Gwyndarren. "I know he rides to Eckland. I've arranged a surprise for him there. But your knowledge of that fact proves the truth of your claim." He nodded to a guard behind Gwyndarren.

Then everything went black.

Dalen Frost strode through the king's camp with confidence as he approached Gremauld's command tent, despite the wary looks of those acquaintances who knew he'd departed the capital with the rebels. Those looks were offset by the nods of acknowledgement he received from the few men who knew him well enough to trust him in spite of the apparent circumstances. Gremauld would be among the latter. For it was Gremauld who had sent him, at Dalen's own suggestion, to serve the heir and report back.

Wearing his uniform as a scout of the king's Home Guard, rumpled and misshapen from weeks of neglect at the bottom of his travel pack, Dalen paused at the entrance and allowed the sentry to announce his presence. Then he passed through the flap without challenge.

Inside, the king's commanders were attempting to plan their strategy with very little information. These men included Dornell Cratten, captain of the Home Guard; Slovcca Hammond, leader of what remained of the king's cavalry and knights; Gallamon Wyman, newly appointed general of the king's army, having replaced Pandalo Gundahar; and three captains of the footmen, who Dalen could identify only by the insignia of rank on the men's breasts.

Gremauld looked up as he entered. He spread his arms in greeting. "My friend, it's about time. I trust you're well."

"As well as can be expected, your majesty."

The commanders shuffled impatiently as Dalen and Gremauld began the necessary formalities. But this time, even the king carved right into the heart of the matter. "Where have you been? We've waited two days for your report."

"My apologies, your majesty. I was unavoidably detoured, but you'll be glad for the news I bring."

Slovcca paced back and forth throughout the exchange, face turning red and knuckles whitening. Finally, he could contain himself no longer. "Your news," he roared, "would have been more timely had it come before my horsemen arrived." The large man strode up to the scout, looking more than ready to put his white knuckles to use.

Harriet squawked and fled from Dalen's arm to the back of a nearby chair.

Twenty Home Guards, standing sentinel around the perimeter of the tent, stepped forward with swords drawn. Prone to escalation, violence was not permitted in the presence of the king.

Dalen looked back calmly, with a reply on his lips, but he held it for the proper time.

Slovcca returned to himself. He glanced once at the guards and stepped away from Dalen, head bowed. "Forgive me, your majesty."

Gremauld nodded to the guards and they returned to their posts, becoming silent sentinels once more—mere shadows at the edge of one's vision.

"Come." The king beckoned Dalen to a large table in the center of the tent. A canvas map of Trondor was spread upon it, held at the corners by daggers thrust through the canvas and into the wood. "You must be thirsty and we have much to discuss."

A servant brought a mug of warm ale for the scout and a goblet of port wine for the king.

"What can you tell me of the traitor and his army?"

"The news couldn't be better. Balor has split his forces. Half remain to guard the pass and occupy your attention. The remainder march west to destroy your militia."

Gremauld's commanders murmured their disbelief and satisfaction.

"Then we have him," General Wyman declared.

Slovcca stepped forward. "You were sent into Balor's camp to provide intelligence. Why did you not warn me of the ambush? I lost two-thirds of my men that day." His voice shook with suppressed fury.

Dalen faced him squarely. "First of all, I was not sent into Balor's camp. I volunteered. Second, I was unwilling to compromise my position of trust for the sake of a battle that wouldn't determine the war's outcome."

"Fifteen thousand men!" Slovcca roared. If he'd had less pride, he might have been in tears over the loss.

In truth, Dalen felt for the man, who was, in the end, responsible for the deaths. But his pity didn't extend far enough for him to withhold his next comment. "It was a massacre indeed, but one you could have avoided. Only a fool would run headlong into an unscouted chokepoint knowing an army the size of Balor's lay somewhere ahead."

Slovcca huffed and turned away.

"How are his forces deployed in the pass?" Wyman asked.

"I don't know. I went with those who plan to intercept the militia. Balor will have reassessed and redeployed his men after we left. Nevertheless, I can tell you what types of troops remain, and their numbers."

Wyman turned to the king. "I recommend we take the pass tomorrow, then turn back and catch the rest between us and the militia."

Dalen wheeled on him. "It may take days to overcome Balor's defenses, and Pandalo has a full day's head start. If you leave now, the militia will delay him long enough for you to catch up. Wait, and you'll arrive too late. The volunteers will be lost."

"Is Balor with them?" Wyman asked.

"He's here, in the pass."

Wyman turned again to the king. "We can't let him escape."

"There's more," Dalen continued. "Pandalo will continue west. He intends to take the capital."

Gremauld hesitated, then shook his head slowly. "Trondor is invincible."

"It's invincible," Dalen said, "because Pandalo made it so. Nobody knows more about the city, its defenses, and its vulnerabilities." He paused for emphasis. "And *he* believes he can take it."

"I'll send a runner to warn the militia," Slovcca offered. "They'll delay the rebels for a day or two, at least."

"Either way," Dalen said, "it'll take Pandalo time to crack the city's defenses. If you hurry, you can stop him. He's counting on secrecy, and on Balor to keep you occupied here for as long as possible."

"Excellent." To Slovcca, Gremauld said, "Send three of your fastest messengers to warn the militia. General, prepare the army. Tonight we move."

"With pleasure, your majesty." His excitement was palpable as he passed from the tent—palpable and infectious, for it seemed everybody there shared it. Including Dalen.

CҺAPCER 21

"There you are," Rancid said to himself when he came across tracks on the day after the ambush. He bent to examine the prints of several horses—eight, maybe. Yes, eight. He was sure. One might find a traveler or two in these hills, perhaps a party as large as four, but more than that in a single group had to be the bandits.

During the next few days, he found signs of Black Hand activity with increasing frequency. He followed them as closely as he could without alerting the others, scouting several hundred feet in front of the party to buy himself time to make the necessary inspections. Eventually, he began to see a pattern that suggested he was closing in on the Black Hand hideout.

The problem was, he should have seen more of the bandits by now. They ruled these hills. Infested them. His party should have had several clashes and killed dozens of the thieves by now. Yet the Black Hand remained strangely absent.

On the third day, Rancid found something he hadn't expected. Goblin tracks, a dozen or more. And humans as well—heavy ones—and a horse. The tracks led to the northeast. His father's keep lay in that direction and this fertile basin contained a multitude of plantations, all of which employed goblin slave labor. But if the tracks had been left by a slave caravan, they came from the wrong direction—from that of the Great Sand. Furthermore, every trader in Palidor knew better than to brave the Black Hand here, where the bandits were thickest. The whole thing didn't make sense.

He hurried back to the main party and found them huddled in a knot around Jasmine.

"I am telling you, I heard something," the monk said as Rancid arrived.

"Heard what?" he asked.

"Voices. A shout, back that way." She pointed. "It was faint, distant, but I definitely heard it."

"Not distant enough if it could be heard," Rancid said. "Wait here. I'll check it out."

"Hold on." Nick turned to Zen. "That hawk trick you did the other day was pretty slick. Can you do it again? Scout from the sky?"

Rancid frowned. He could retain control of the party's movements only through the filtering of information. "It's too dangerous. What if they decide you're lunch? Wait here." He moved off in the direction Jasmine had indicated.

Voices reached him as he approached the backside of a small rise a few minutes later, so he stepped carefully to avoid twigs, dry leaves, gravel, and other sources of unwanted noise. Goblins, the language told him, but not just goblins.

A deep guttural voice spoke in a tongue he'd never heard before yet somehow understood. "Keep up, Murkba, or we leave you here."

A horse appeared at the top of the ridge and Rancid ducked into a mound of boulders. From there he examined the rider. Not a man, but something else, olive-colored and slimy, with hooked teeth, sunken eyes, bushy brows, and an upturned nose. It looked like a goblin, with its greasy black hair, sickly pallor, and misshapen legs. But it was much too big to be a goblin—larger even than most men. It had a muscular build, wielded a wicked flail, carried a sizable shield, and wore chain armor. This was no slave.

After a two-minute survey of the countryside, the rider called to someone beyond the ridge. "Get the goblins moving. We're late." It spoke in that weird language, but again Rancid understood. The ring on his finger—the one he'd taken from the Black Hand elf the day the whirlwind stole Nick's journal—had grown warm.

Curious, Rancid removed the ring and the rider's words changed to something more like, "garble, garble, muck muck, something-or-other..." Pure unintelligible drivel. He put the ring back on with a fierce, almost savage elation. This was an information filter he could use. Just then, the rider pulled his horse around and descended from view.

Gradually, the hoof beats faded until the screech of a hawk drowned them out. A white bird circled the area once, then swooped to land nearby. Rancid rolled his eyes as Zen transformed beside him.

"What did you see?" Rancid asked grudgingly.

"Fourteen goblins and six..." Zen pursed his lips as he labored for the right word. "Six of something else—like goblins, but bigger—including one on a horse."

"I saw him. You'd better warn the others. I'll stay here and keep an eye on them."

Zen transformed again and flew away.

Unsatisfied with his vantage point, especially when he compared it to Zen's, Rancid eased himself to the top of the rise and into a bramble thicket to get a view of the other side.

Until that moment, he'd held out some hope that the rider and his kin were some form of goblinoid slavers, selling out their own inferior cousins for a quick turn of profit. But all fourteen goblins carried goblin-made swords. Many wore a shield or armor. These were *escaped* slaves, and the mutants were likely responsible for freeing them.

Rancid's first instinct was to fight. A small group of goblins and one of the big mutants loitered just below him. He might dispatch the mutant with a single, well-placed arrow. And the goblins, only recently freed and armed, were no warriors. Rancid could rush them, kill as many as possible, and then flee from the larger group, drawing them all to Nick and the others.

But there were too many. The odds weren't favorable enough. And Rancid hadn't survived to slay twenty-seven Black Hand thieves by acting foolish. He did check to see if any of the creatures wore gloves. Though he'd never known the bandits to consort with goblins or their kin in the past, he hadn't known them to consort with air apparitions either. These were strange times.

None of the wretched beasts wore the Black Hand symbol. But the mutants were clearly from the Goblin Isle. That made them evil—to be slain on sight by royal decree. And yet here they were, deep into the Civilized Lands, well armed, accompanied by runaway slaves in the hills of Forlorn Valley, traveling in the direction of the baron's keep.

Maybe the Black Hand weren't working with the mutants. Still, Rancid would've bet good coin that his father was responsible for it all.

The sounds of movement behind him announced the arrival of Nick and the others. What in the burning fires of the baron's kiln were they doing there? Zen was supposed to alert them, not bring them. A warning and a taunt of stupidity rose in him, but he could voice neither. His companions were too far away, and the goblins too close.

Quietly, he nocked an arrow and, drawing back his bowstring, took aim at the nearest mutant. He hadn't seen the rider since it had disappeared from sight several minutes before. If it flanked them, or worse, brought reinforcements... He never finished the thought. If that happened, Rancid would simply hide there in the brush. Why should he die because of someone else's stupidity?

He looked back at the others, who were searching the rocks and brush where Zen had left him. Eventually they moved around the side of the ridge and passed from sight. Then, as the small cluster of goblins below turned northward, toward the rest of the rabble, a loud crack sounded from the direction of Rancid's friends, the distinct sound of a branch snapping underfoot. *So much for stealth.*

The goblins and mutant stopped as one and turned toward the sound.

"What was that?" one goblin said.

Rancid swore silently to the nine hells about his bungling companions stomping through the hills like dwarven stonecutters.

"Go find out," the mutant ordered, and a pair of goblins started south to investigate.

Rancid's arm began to shake from holding his bowstring taut for so long, but he didn't dare relax the weapon now. Holding his breath, he fought to keep his aim steady and awaited the outcome of the goblin's search.

Suddenly a snowy white deer pranced into view, snapping twigs and churning up gravel as it went. The animal stopped at the top of the hill when it saw the approaching goblins.

Something wasn't right about the animal. It paused a moment too long, as though it wanted to be seen, turning to flee only after the goblins whooped and leapt after it. In that split second, Rancid recognized an unnatural intelligence in the deer's ice-blue eyes.

The mutant called the goblins back from their chase and Rancid's respect for Zen's magic reluctantly climbed a measure higher. With a sigh, he relaxed his bow and began to massage his exhausted arm.

Still, the mutant was cautious. He called to the larger crowd ahead and they hailed their mounted scout. To Rancid's dismay, the rider returned to its previous perch on the rise and scanned the landscape. Then it turned its steed and began a slow sweep of the ridge.

Rancid, tucked in the bramble at its very summit, crouched directly in the path of the rider. The mount snorted and jerked its head as it passed Rancid's hiding place, stopping there. Its breath huffed in Rancid's ears. He held his own, moving not a muscle for fear of discovery, as the horse turned and looked him in the eye.

The rider jerked the mount's head forward once more. He kicked it into motion and continued along the ridge, spending an eternity at the southern tip, searching for signs of danger. Rancid didn't breathe easily until the mutant turned north and rode away.

"There's nothing here," the rider said as it passed the others. "You waste time. We must go."

Rancid waited a full ten minutes after the goblins and their guardians departed before climbing out of the bramble. When he reached the southern tip of the ridge, his friends emerged from hiding as well.

"That was close." Nick brushed dust off his clothing as he climbed from a boulder patch.

By then, Zen had returned to his natural form. "What were those things?"

"Orcs, I'd guess," Nick said. "I recognize them from stories."

"Ever seen one?" Zen asked.

"Nobody has, except for the slavers who harvest goblins from their own continent." He cast a nervous glance toward the north. "I can only guess what they're doing here."

"We'd better keep moving. They might come back." Rancid resumed his southward trek. He didn't look back to see if the others followed. Better to be done with the bandits and move on as quickly as possible.

Jade strode into Halidreth's audience hall. "Sevendeath's on his way here."

Halidreth excused the orc captain with whom he'd been negotiating, obviously relieved to be rid of the brute. "By 'here,' you mean Palidor," he told Jade. "He's going to Eckland."

"No. I mean this hideout. He's within a day's ride."

Halidreth's brow creased. "You're mistaken. Groot assures me he's going to Eckland."

Jade placed her hands on her hips and glared at the leader. "Groot's a fool. I've been trailing Sevendeath for the past three days. He's tracking us. He's coming here."

"You saw him? You're sure?"

"Oh, yes. I saw him, and his demon-spawned consort too." Jade would never mistake either of them, not after they'd left her for dead, baking in the Faldor sun and being eaten alive by insects. She'd lain there for days with her skull pounding, drifting in and out of consciousness, before Drakemoor had shown up and nursed her back to health, resupplied her, and made her fit for travel before going his own way.

Before this was over, Jade would see both Sevendeath and the demon monk dead.

"Where is he now?"

"He wasn't five miles from here when I left them, but he doesn't know where we are. It may take him a couple of days to actually find the entrance."

Halidreth's brows shot up and the edges of his mouth curled as if he was grudgingly impressed. "He's getting bolder. He wouldn't have dared to challenge us on our own turf last winter."

"He brings powerful allies. And you've sent more men than we can spare to eastern Palidor to intercept him there. You underestimated him."

"Nonsense. Fetch the elf."

"Come." One of Halidreth's guards led Jade toward the heavy banded door to the catacombs beyond the audience chamber.

As she pulled it open, Halidreth added, "You'd better bring the Chosen as well."

The darkness was complete, save for the stinging blaze of torch-light each time an orc guard pulled the stone door aside and tossed Gwyndarren a skin of water, loaf of bread, or chunk of rotten meat. If they had delivered the meals at the usual times, Gwyndarren had been caged for nearly a week, but he couldn't tell for sure. The complete absence of sunlight had wreaked havoc on his body's natural clock.

In the meantime, he drank the water and ate the bread to keep himself alive. He tossed the meat, whose stench threatened to turn his stomach, into the corner with his bodily waste. The combined reek kept him in a constant state of nausea, and by the time the guards heaved him from the cell, his clothes hung loosely from his shoulders.

The pain in his skull had receded to a tolerable sting, and that only when he touched the wound. Blood still matted his hair. That which had dried on his clothes made them stiff and uncomfortable.

This time a woman accompanied the orcs, and she was beautiful. It wasn't her looks—either face or body—that made him think so, for he'd never been attracted to the rough features of humans. And the visage of this particular female was more severe than most. What drew Gwyndarren to her was the fact that she was there at all.

She was the first person from a civilized race he'd seen since Halidreth's guards had clubbed him. Her presence now spoke of his salvation. So he craved it.

"Halidreth wants to speak to you." Her voice was as harsh as her features, but her message made his soul sing.

When they entered the audience hall, Gwyndarren confronted the enormous bulk of an ogre—an ogre, in the Civilized Lands!—along with an astounding profusion of goblin kin. How had they gotten this far inland without being discovered? Surely if the king became aware of their presence, he'd mount an expedition to eradicate the scourge from his lands. Gwyndarren tucked that fact away, in case he found a use for it later.

The bandit leader, speaking from his throne on the dais, gestured to the ogre. "This is Groot. He's intrigued by your proposal."

As the ogre turned toward him, the glowing medallion against his throat seemed to suck in all the world, leaving nothing but its presence in Gwyndarren's mind. *A Chosen.* This was the one he must convince, the one with which he must bargain. At that moment, he completely discounted the bandit leader. He'd come one step closer to the Master. Halidreth no longer mattered.

"Intrigued?" Gwyndarren's mind was slow from lack of nourishment and from this sudden, favorable turn of fortune.

"Not in so many syllables," Halidreth was saying, "but Groot likes to explore his options."

Gwyndarren ignored him, preferring to deal directly with the person in control. Intermediaries always cost him something. And this one—he touched the sore spot on his skull—had already cost him plenty.

But again Halidreth did the talking. He told of Sevendeath's coming and of the elf-kin's formidable company. "Your ice mage is with them. Groot suggests we test him before we offer him to the Master." He paused. "You do intend to offer him to the Master, do you not?"

Gwyndarren winced. Was he that transparent? He nodded. Here and now at least, honesty would likely serve him best. He smiled for the first time since he'd arrived. "I know just how to do it. It'll serve your immediate need and it will test Zen's loyalty, as well as his guile and influence."

CHAPTER 22

Balor stood atop the rise as the enemy formed up for an attack in the shadowy illumination of dawn. This day was shaping up to be the trial of his life. Perhaps even the end of his life. Hope had failed him. Gremauld had separated his army into two forces the day before. One half, perhaps a little smaller than the other, headed west down the road toward the city of Trondor, toward Pandalo and the detached portion of Balor's army. The other half remained behind and busied themselves with preparations for an assault on the pass.

The fact that Gremauld had split his forces could mean only one thing. Balor had lost his gamble. And with it, the war.

Even so, his forces were as ready as they could possibly be. They'd dug a great trench—a dozen feet wide and ten feet deep—across the narrowest part of the pass, a mere third of a mile across. This they fortified with pointed wooden spikes. Behind that stood a breastwork of crisscrossed timbers, sharpened on the west-facing end to slow any mounted or foot assault that made it across the trench.

Half of Balor's men were lined up behind the barricade in anticipation of the onslaught. His best archers hid among the recesses on the hillside overlooking the battlefield, with orders to shoot any officers or mages they could identify. Roltar and his elite footmen waited in the forest on the southern slopes to repel any flanking attack. Finally, the remaining troops and the mounted men, Balor held in reserve to drive back the forces he knew would eventually break through the line.

It wasn't enough—not nearly enough—he realized, watching the enemy form up. There were thousands of them. Tens of thousands. And Balor's defenses already lay in ruins, remnants from Gremauld's first strike, which had come during the night.

Hundreds of horsemen had approached through the scorched valley. A sentry had spotted them a few hundred yards from the barricade and blew a warning. The alarm, though truncated by the sentry's death, roused the defenders.

Gremauld's horsemen lit their torches and raced forward. Hidden pit traps collapsed beneath several of the attackers and they disappeared from the line. The rest hurled their torches into the barricade, but the green wood didn't catch easily. Archers behind the line fired into the darkness, but the retreating horsemen had become mere shadows in the night.

Seconds later, another wave rushed the trench, this time a thousand, by Balor's estimate. They stopped short as the others had, and hurled flasks, jugs, and occasionally, small barrels of lamp oil across the void into the buttress. Flames roared into life and devoured the barricade. The defenders spent the night dousing the flames to save what they could of their fortification.

When morning came, Balor surveyed the damage. The charred and weakened breastwork lay broken and stark in the sunrise, completely consumed in places—compromised everywhere. Gremauld gave them no time to rebuild.

The agonized cries of men and horses rose from the open pits, a third of which had been sprung. Many would die in those that remained, but not enough to make a difference.

Balor had sent too many men with Pandalo in his run around Gremauld, but if Pandalo could destroy the militia and stay ahead of the enemy, perhaps there was still hope.

Having seen enough, Balor descended the slope and deployed most of his combat mages to the front line, which his commanders and mages both recognized for the desperate move it was. Because mages' weavings were small in scope and short in range, they were generally reserved for skirmishes involving small numbers of men. In a large conflict, like the one that would take place today, they must move to the front line to weave their enchantments, which would mark them as valuable targets.

They, and their contributions, would be short-lived.

Has it come to this already? each seemed to be thinking. He gave them no explanation. None was needed.

The morning hours put the sun behind Balor and into the eyes of the attackers. So Gremauld waited until it rose high into the sky before he launched his assault. Then a mighty cry sprang up from the army and seven thousand armored troops charged ahead, swords brandished in the air and shields raised against the rain of defending arrows. Every fifth man carried a ladder to aid in crossing the trench.

Two hundred yards behind, another seven thousand men rushed forward. Thousands of arrows arched over their heads and into the defensive line.

Dozens of Gremauld's first ranks fell to the concealed pits. Thousands more pressed on.

Balor had twenty-five hundred crossbows along the front, more than three for every two feet of the line. Half of them knelt in front, the rest stood behind. They fired in waves. A good many struck the defenders. The mass of oncoming bodies was impossible to miss and the light armor of the infantry was as nothing against the stout missiles. Many more bolts, however, stopped in the outstretched shields that protected the unconcerned attackers.

Swordsmen stood ready behind the crossbows. Behind them and on the hillsides, archers loosed arrows into the unprotected ranks of the second wave. Hundreds fell, dead or wounded, in the first seconds of the battle. The ditch filled, end to end, with clambering bodies, struggling against gravity and the defenders, to gain purchase on the east side. The impact of metal on metal rang through the valley and echoed from the rugged northern wall of the pass.

Flares of blinding light lit one sector, lightning flashed in another, as Balor's mages joined the fray.

Gremauld's second wave reached the trench and crowded the first, still stalled at the barrier.

Beyond them, the pretender's horsemen galloped forward, fifteen hundred strong. Balor frowned. Surely they didn't think to jump the trench, not with the barricade behind it. Damaged though it was, it would prevent any horse from clearing the combined obstacle.

"My lord." The commander of his reserve forces pointed to a portion of the line, where Gremauld's men began to pour through.

Balor ordered some of his reserves forward to fill the breach. Two more points weakened. He released his reserves a few hundred at a time, knowing that once he'd committed them all, the next breach would crumble his defense.

The charging horses reached the trench and galloped across as if the ditch was a mirage. That could mean only that a mage, one well concealed among the mass of enemy soldiers, had aided their passage.

The horses leapt the charred logs that remained in their way and smashed through the thin screen of defenders.

Balor spurred his own gelding into motion, followed by fifty of his personal guards and his remaining cavalry. By the time he arrived, thousands of enemy soldiers had flooded through.

He crashed into the fray, carving a path with his sword. The mass of men and horses slowed him enough for his own men to catch up and flow around him into the enemy. Swords, shields, axes, and armor rang against one another. Three of Balor's personal guards—three of his friends—died in his defense. Bellowing a roar of anguish, he pressed on.

Balor passed beyond the horses and drove into the enemy footmen. A dozen men rushed him. Then one of Balor's own, one of two mounted mages he'd held in reserve, appeared at his side, immersed in the weave. The faces of the rushing men went blank, as though in a deep trance. Their fellows overran them, trampling them in the confusion. Balor's knights swept the rest away.

Most of the men around Balor were his own now. Perhaps the breach was closing. But no, the barrier was still a long way ahead. The enemy had encroached farther into his ranks than he'd realized. Huffing from the exertion, he rallied his men around him and pressed forward once more.

His mage wove an enchantment on a knot of enemy knights. Suddenly panicked, the knights turned and fled back the way they'd come, shouting a message of failure and defeat. Gremauld's soldiers hesitated. Many turned and ran. Balor charged into the gap. His sudden gain of ground lent credence to the fleeing knights' cries.

Then it happened. From nowhere, an arrow buried itself in Balor's chest—a stray from the fighting or a lucky shot from an enemy archer, it didn't matter which. Breathing became suddenly, painfully impossible. His body weakened and he coughed a fit of blood into his hand— his sword hand—which was now empty. He must have dropped the weapon somewhere.

Grasping the arrow in his blood-slick grip, he yanked it free, further tearing the internal tissues. He could no longer breathe. Blood ran freely from his mouth and down his chin. His right hand and his chest both burned with a fiery pain. His vision narrowed, and he tumbled from his mount.

CHAPTER 23

A nudge awakened Zen. The night was overcast, the moon and stars obscured. He could just make out a person's silhouette against the coal-colored sky above him.

"Someone's coming." Vinra's whisper was barely a breath in his ear.

Zen rolled out of his bedding and groped for his staff as the priest moved off to wake the others.

Once he'd risen to a crouched posture, he didn't dare move. Their camp sat atop a steep hill jutting from the landscape amid several similar formations where the wind had eroded the soft earth, leaving the more durable rock behind. Nick had chosen the location because the bandits couldn't climb the cliff unless they were willing to leave their mounts below. As it was, a single misstep could send Zen tumbling down the fifty-foot drop to the valley floor. And if he stood, someone might spot his silhouette against the clouds. Many creatures could see better in the darkness than he, the goblinoid races among them.

A rattling of gear, the creak of leather straps, and the muted steps of booted feet rose from the valley beneath. Close. Too close. He squinted but could make out nothing in the darkness. Nobody but bandits would travel in the middle of the night or in total darkness.

Quietly, Zen spoke an incantation to tap the weave. To his sight, the night lightened. The whole of the valley, cast in pale grays, took on the hue of a moonlit, snow-covered landscape.

Yet his friends still groped in the darkness. Zen's vision alone could penetrate the night.

Nick stumbled up beside him on the unseen ground, sending a rattle of pebbles over the edge.

Zen caught his arm. He swore noiselessly as the sounds below settled quickly into silence. *That's it. They know we're here.*

He peered past the lip of the cliff. Below, nine goblin slaves, having escaped from their master, wielded crude swords. They hesitated for a moment, then bolted away. Zen watched until they were gone.

Two bands of runaway slaves within a span of twelve hours. And yesterday, a half dozen orcs as well. Apparently Rancid hadn't overestimated the dangers of Palidor. The sooner they got to Eckland, completed their business, and departed, the better.

A cry rose from the king's army as they launched the attack, but Roltar could see none of the valley from his position just south of the pass's entrance. Instead, he scanned the field below him. Within minutes, a contingent of Gremauld's forces advanced up the hill in a flanking maneuver.

The trees and terrain forced the approaching line to break up and ascend the hill piecemeal. Roltar's own men, scattered about the area in knots of four to a dozen men, hunkered in tactical positions, ready to engage the enemy. He would coordinate their movements as necessary with a prearranged system of whistles and bird calls, but his men needed no individual leadership. They were trained to fight independently.

Before long, several men approached through the trees. Roltar crouched within his camouflage and signaled to the other three men in his knot to prepare.

The advancing men stepped softly, as though they knew the enemy was near. One man placed his foot within arm's reach. Without standing, Roltar buried his dagger into the man's calf, all the way to the bone and a good way through. Every man in the victim's company spun toward his cry of alarm and pain.

At that moment, Roltar's men stepped from their concealment and loosed arrows into the startled group. Three crumpled to the ground.

His blood up now, every sense heightened with need, Roltar rose over his bent victim and severed the poor man's head.

Together, he and his men engaged the remaining seven opponents, sword on sword. Roltar, holding the high ground, chose an adversary and advanced with confidence. The enemy soldier stumbled, fell backward, and rolled out of the way of Roltar's descending sword.

But Roltar didn't press the advantage. He had more immediate concerns as another man charged him. Roltar danced around his opponent, from rock to log to rock again, forcing the man to divert attention to his own footing. Then Roltar had him.

He pulled his sword free and spun to face his first opponent, now back on his feet. But the man stumbled away with an arrow in his throat before Roltar could engage.

Roltar scanned the area for another opponent. All lay dead or dying. One of his own men limped on a bloodied leg, so Roltar signaled another to help the wounded man back to a safe location. His remaining man, a close friend named Hapgood, moved forward with him to locate additional prey.

Within minutes, the two came upon a group of at least eight advancing foes, who spotted them and charged. Roltar and Hapgood fled up the hill. Cheers rose from the king's men as they took up the chase, which wouldn't last long. All Roltar needed was an advantageous point from which to make a stand. Shortly, they came upon a rock face, some thirty feet across and twelve feet high. Without slowing, they sheathed their swords and bounded up the cliff. In a single fluid motion, they gained the summit and spun toward their enemy.

Ten roaring men charged into view. The defenders had their bows off their shoulders in one heartbeat. Arrows flew in the next. Two of the attackers dropped. The rest crouched warily and began to back off.

Roltar whistled. A knot of his own men arrived shortly and pushed the attackers back down the hill.

The sounds of fighting surrounded them now, near and far. He smiled at his friend. They were in their element, a replay of the Black Forest ambush. And like that previous skirmish, the enemy outnumbered them at least three to one.

Only this time, retreat would mean defeat for Balor. It would allow a flanking maneuver, which the heir was counting on Roltar and his men to prevent.

And this time there were no mages. Roltar had expected Gremauld to employ his weavers here, rather than in open combat along the valley floor. He didn't have time to consider the implications of their absence. And, frankly, he didn't much care.

He scurried up a pine to reconnoiter the landscape and the disposition of forces—both his own and Gremauld's—and spotted an enemy contingent advancing without challenge. He whistled to a knot of his own men farther up the slope. When one looked toward him, he signaled the number of advancing men and pointed in their direction. The soldier nodded and moved his team to engage.

As Roltar clambered down, he heard a signal for help from one of his own men. So he and Hapgood hurried out onto a rock outcropping where they could see in the direction of the call. Below, a group of Gremauld's men fought their way up the hill, led by a captain named Andlan, an old rival who had beat Roltar out of his last promotion.

Andlan had rallied at least thirty men to him and now pressed purposefully forward, engaging all who dared to enter his path. He faced defender after defender with his great ax and brushed them all aside. Andlan's own men died by the dozens, but those who followed were heartened by their leader's boldness and success. Scores flocked to his lead, faster than the accumulation of dead and wounded around him.

Roltar launched an arrow at the enemy captain, as did Hapgood. The distance was short and the shots clear, yet both arrows missed their mark. They fired again, and missed.

This time, Andlan ordered his own men to return fire.

The two defenders had time to take just one more shot. Roltar's arrow soared wide. Hapgood's shattered against Andlan's chest. Roltar knew then where the king's mages were: safe in the enemy camp, having spent their energies to protect the officers going into battle.

Dropping his bow, Roltar sprang from the outcropping to the battlefield below. He whistled an urgent plea for any man within earshot to converge. Then he drew his sword to engage.

Andlan marched forward, taking obvious pleasure in the challenge. His ax was a heavy weapon, slow compared to the lightning quickness of Roltar's saber, but his enchantments more than made up for the imbalance. One enchantment confused Roltar's perception as soon as he stepped into its field, distorting Andlan's apparent location until he became a shifting mélange of opponents, all moving in choreographed synchronicity.

Yet Roltar's fourth swing connected, cutting the man across the cheek. The blow hit hard and should have cleaved off the top half of Andlan's head. Instead, it left only a shallow cut across his face, revealing yet another of Andlan's magical protections.

The dance continued for several minutes. Defenders flowed in from all sides to oppose the growing threat. Finally, Andlan swung his ax in a sweeping overhand strike.

Roltar raised his sword to—

Balor woke to sunshine filtering through the fabric of his tent and a pain searing in his chest. He remembered pulling an arrow from his breast and striking the ground beside his horse. His mage had thrown up an energy barrier to shield him as his cavalry swept the enemy back toward the barricade, borne by the momentum Balor himself had made possible. There his memory ended.

Warmth pulsated from the ring on his right hand as its healing power worked to mend the remaining damage to his tissues. He gritted his teeth against the pain, rose from his cot, and padded gingerly through the flap of the tent. Winded from even that small effort, he leaned on a hitching rail for support. The sun, low in the eastern sky, told him he'd slept through at least one night.

Weak though he was from loss of blood, he could breathe. And he was fairly sure he could sit a horse. He could command.

He'd lost his gelding and sword somewhere in the fray, however, so he commandeered replacements for both, mounted up, and cantered to the front. His men had pushed Gremauld back to his own side of the pass, where he was preparing for another attack.

Strengthened more every minute by the power of his healing ring, Balor rode the length of the demolished barricade to let his troops know he'd survived and to hearten them for the coming assault. As he passed, he separated those he needed for the reserves from those he condemned to the front line.

When he reached the end, he received a report from an unfamiliar soldier, who introduced himself as Hapgood. He learned of Roltar's death and of the enchantments that had brought him down. The southern slope, Hapgood reported, could not be held for another day.

Before Balor had time to ponder that crisis, a cry rose from Gremauld's army, who charged the pass with a zeal that foretold their victory.

Balor raced to join his cavalry. By the time he reached them, they were already needed to repel a spearhead that had broken through the center of his line. Though his strength was fading, he led the charge.

Shortly after his cavalry slammed into the spearhead, an enemy soldier emerged from the throng and extended his hand as though commanding Balor to stop. A cobble materialized in the air before him, a single stone suspended by the weave. A second stone appeared, several feet down the line. Then a third. A forth. A dozen. A hundred. Thousands. Within a span of seconds, a stone wall twenty feet high and hundreds of feet long isolated Balor and his cavalry from the front—withholding his reinforcements from those who needed them. Sounds of the slaughter reached him from the other side.

But a contingent of enemy horsemen had been trapped on the eastern side of the construction, apparently not by accident. The lead rider broke away from the pack and spurred his horse through the screen of defenders toward Balor. He suffered numerous direct and forceful strikes from swords, axes, and arrows, but he ignored them all in his fixated charge toward the heir.

Balor recognized the enchantments woven around this rider as those that Hapgood had described—those that had devastated Roltar's men the previous day. This crazed rider was a suicide assassin, fortified to deliver a single, killing stroke to the challenger to the throne.

Balor watched in fascination as the man drew near. He struggled to raise his sword, but it had grown too heavy. Loss of blood and the exertions of the morning had left him depleted in ways he didn't care to acknowledge.

The attacker came at him with a grimace so foul and menacing he looked like death itself approaching.

Before he arrived, however, a mage behind Balor completed a weaving. His incantation ended in a single exclaimed word that swept past Balor like a physical presence. "Die!"

The assassin's face stretched into a silent scream as his flesh tightened and split, dried and flaked off in bursts of ghostly powder, revealing the muscle and bone beneath. Still the man came. Muscles in his arms shone through the disintegrating skin until they too began to erode.

Just as the last of the tissues disappeared from the rider's bones, his sword struck Balor's armor with no force left behind it. When the war horse collided into Balor's mount, the bones of the rider swept forward and lay scattered in the dust like so many vestiges of some long-forgotten battle.

When Balor turned to thank the mage for his life, the man slumped in his saddle, pulled his horse weakly around and urged it toward the rear, his magic spent.

A minute later, the enchanted stone wall fell, disappearing as quickly as it had formed. The mage who had erected it teetered on the sword of a defender who, seconds later, fell to the ground with a pair of arrows in his back.

Balor's presence at the front bolstered the resolve of the rebels. Together, they held the barricade for half the day before Gremauld's men broke through at multiple points and Balor had no reserves left to commit.

Ultimately, the pretender's army filled the pass with a flood of death.

CHAPTER 24

As the companions were setting up camp, a voice invaded Zen's mind, one he knew as Gwyndarren's. *A quarter mile west of your campsite is a hill with three walnut trees at its summit. Meet me there during your watch tonight. I have something for you.*

It seemed odd that Gwyndarren should be in Palidor and that the elf should know Zen's surroundings so intimately, but Zen shrugged it off. If Gwyndarren had that kind of power, so much the better. Especially if he offered Zen something he could use.

Vinra had gone off to commune with Robala, Jasmine was stretching before her nightly meditation, and Nick was bent over his own journal and Jasmine's copy of the Codex, studying.

Zen approached Nick. "I need some space tonight. I'm working on something big."

Nick looked up from the pair of texts in his lap. "Nothing loud, I hope."

"No."

"Stay in sight."

Zen didn't. He used his hawk form to locate Gwyndarren's hill before the light faded. Then, after a suitable interval, he returned to the camp and settled in to get some sleep before his watch.

In the early morning hours, while he and Nick were supposed to be warding their friends from opposite ends of their silent camp, Zen slipped away to make the rendezvous.

"I trust you're well?" the elf said.

Zen approached and the two clasped hands. "We must be brief." Even with his ghostly night sight, it had taken him much longer to arrive than he'd expected, and he still had to find his way back before sunrise. "I'll be missed if I'm gone long. You said you have something for me."

Gwyndarren chuckled. "Ever the opportunist. I like you, my friend." He pulled a silver vial with a cork stopper from a pouch at his waist.

Zen could discern none of its details in the darkness. "What is it?"

"Mist, collected from the isle of the fairies. Pull the stopper and it'll cloud the area with a veil so thick it'll bury the sun." He smiled as he passed the bottle to Zen. The faint gleam of the elf's teeth shone through the darkness. "Interested?"

"Yes," Zen said without hesitation. If the mist really did come from the fairies, this was a rare gift indeed.

"It's yours," Gwyndarren said, "for a small favor."

For such as this? Zen waited for the price, sure it would be more than he could afford.

The elf continued. "Your guide, Sevendeath, leads you and your friends against the Black Hand. Are you aware of this?"

"Of course. He leads us against them at every opportunity, and kills them without question or compassion. But that's no concern of mine—I have no love for the Black Hand—as long as he gets us to Eckland."

"That's my point. He's not taking you to Eckland. It lies north and east. Sevendeath leads you south. He's searching for the bandits' hideout. That's where he's taking you."

Zen considered the possibility. It had been weeks since they'd crossed into Palidor. Their path had been erratic since they'd come into the hills, but always generally southward. If they were in eastern Palidor, as Rancid claimed, they should be in much more populated territory. A simmering fury began to warm Zen against the night's chill, but he was angry with himself more than with Rancid. "That I didn't know."

"Consider it free information. But you must turn him aside. Return your party to a course for Eckland and forget the bandit lair. Do this, and you may keep the bottle. Fail, and you'll die with Sevendeath at the behest of the Black Hand. For they know you're coming and they're prepared."

But Zen's was a cautious greed. "What is your interest in the Black Hand?"

"None. I care nothing for the bandits. But for now, their purpose serves ours—yours and mine. And Sevendeath's vendetta against them is detrimental to your quest." Gwyndarren paused, as though he'd heard something in the darkness. "His hatred serves no one, least of all himself."

Zen nodded, recognizing the truth in the elf's words. As for the deal, he'd made up his mind as soon as he'd seen the vial, but the choice would've been simple even without the prize. Nick sought the Codex and the prevention of the Prophecy. And Zen supported that goal as long as it didn't interfere with his own quest for power. The Black Hand would only cost them time, and perhaps their lives. But he had one more question. "How did you find me?"

"I have means. Do you still have the parchment I gave you?"

"Of course."

"Good. Keep it safe. You'll need it later." He looked over Zen's shoulder. "The horizon grows lighter. You must return."

The next morning, as Rancid gathered his gear for the day's march, Zen grabbed him by the arm and nearly heaved him from his feet. "We need to talk." The tone in the mage's voice was as cold as his eyes.

Rancid scrambled to keep his feet as Zen pulled him to where the others had gathered. Confused expressions met them both as Zen deposited him amongst their party. "Let's talk about the course we've taken since we crossed the border."

"I told you before—"

"I know what you told us, but the farther south we go, the less I believe your lies."

"Hey." Rancid held up both hands in his own defense. "I've lied to no one."

"We're farther from the road than we need to be and more west than you would have us believe." Zen made the claim with the conviction of a man certain of his facts. This was no idle speculation.

Rancid's eyes narrowed.

Zen continued. "You forget that some of us are well-traveled. These hills and the frequent cloud cover do much to hide our true course, but I've seen it from the air. This is not the way to Eckland."

"But it is." Rancid put as much authority into his voice as he could muster. Only Nick had questioned their course since they'd crossed the border, and he too had a reason to hate the Black Hand. It was the others, Jasmine and Vinra, whom Rancid must sway to his side. And they seemed uncertain, awaiting the outcome. "Once we skirt these hills we'll turn east, straight toward Eckland. If the Black Hand think we're in Lorentil, they'll never suspect us here." That was certainly true. In fact, Rancid was counting on it. He could never prevail if the bandits knew he was coming.

The stalemate continued for several minutes before Nick finally intervened. "Excuse us for a minute." He took Rancid's arm, more gently than Zen had, and led him from the others.

Once again, Rancid welcomed the opportunity to speak with him alone. If he could gain Nick's trust, he might buy himself the day or two he needed to find the hideout. He was close. The signs told him that much. And he wanted it so badly he could taste blood in the air.

When they'd gone far enough, Nick sketched a rudimentary map of Palidor in the dirt with a stick, based on what he knew of the kingdom, presumably from the years he'd spent with his uncle. He faced Rancid with a neutral expression. "Where are we? I want to see how far from Eckland you've taken us."

Rancid hesitated.

"Zen is right about one thing," Nick continued. "This is taking longer than any of us expected. Our food is beginning to run low."

Rancid had concealed his plan by answering questions vaguely and refusing to justify his actions, but Zen's ability to scout beyond Rancid's horizon made him privy to too much.

After a pause of several heartbeats, Rancid stabbed a finger at the drawing, indicating a location near Forlorn Keep. "I chose the long route, away from the caravan road, to avoid the Black Hand as much as possible."

Nick stared at the map, chewing his lower lip.

Growing nervous with the silence, Rancid added, "Raiding caravans on the road is their way."

"Wouldn't this route have been safer?" Nick traced a path north of the one they'd taken. "A guide of your skill should be able to find a safe route that's... more direct."

Though Nick had made the statement tactfully, it stuck like a dagger in Rancid's pride. Every indignant retort that came to mind, however, would only make him sound desperate, so he said nothing.

Nick continued gently. "It hasn't made sense to me, with your hatred of the Black Hand, that you'd leave them alone. You may be leading us around their hunting grounds but I don't believe you're avoiding them." He paused.

Still, Rancid remained silent.

"The scouting party we ran into the other day was a long way from the road." Nick pointed to the map. "You knew we'd run into them here. You told us in Lorentil they make their home in this valley.

"Rancid." Nick waited for him to look up. "I may be quiet, but I'm not stupid. And I too have a score to settle with the Black Hand. Or have you forgotten that they killed my mother?" His voice was a harsh whisper, laden with grief. "What sword blade are you walking? I deserve an answer, if for no other reason than because I want them dead too."

Nick's eyes showed pain and smoldering rage, emotions Rancid recognized as his own familiar companions. But did that mean Rancid should trust him, just because he fought well and hated the Black Hand? What else was there besides fighting and hatred—ability and motivation? When it came down to it, nothing else mattered. Isn't that what drove him—drove him to hunt, drove him to kill, and drove him nearly mad? Maybe Nick would understand.

"You're right." The words rolled from Rancid's lips, tinged with guilt. "I've led you past their raiding area and deep into their homeland. If I'm right, we're within a day's ride of their main camp." He pleaded now, his plan exposed and his need desperate. "They're evil, Nick. We must wipe them from the land. I think the truth of their leadership and the power behind the slave revolts lie here, in this valley."

Nick at least seemed to be listening, so Rancid kept the words pouring. "Stopping the slave riots would put a wound in your Prophecy, maybe prevent it from coming to pass. And we're fighting evil. Running to Eckland to find a book is as meaningless as Jasmine's creeds. I thought taking the long route, killing a few Black Hand, and maybe throwing a rusty dagger into the Prophecy was a good plan."

Rancid deflated then, and because he respected Nick, he did something he'd never done before. He apologized. "I'm sorry. I should've told you. You hate them as much as I do. I'll plot a safe path out for you and the others and then I'll go hunt the bastards down and kill as many as I can." He looked away before Nick could see the emotions that haunted his soul.

Nick put a hand on Rancid's shoulder. "Let me talk to them. I, too, am convinced that the bandits are involved with the Prophecy. They wouldn't have come for my grandfather's journal if they weren't. But the Codex is important too. We must know the true Prophecy if we're to have any hope of stopping it." He glanced toward the others. "Since we're here, perhaps we can spare the time to find the hideout if it doesn't take long."

"No. You mustn't tell them. They'll refuse."

"I won't let you lead them like lambs to the slaughter. If we take on the bandits, we'll do it with everyone's consent, and with proper planning and preparation. Personally, I think we should locate the hideout, map its location, and report it to the authorities in Eckland. Let them do the dirty work so we can be on our way." With that, he marched back to the others.

Rancid hurried to follow.

Once there, Nick related the substantive portions of their conversation and asked for opinions.

Zen spoke first. "I thought there were a hundred or so Black Hand. We can't defeat them all."

Rancid's smug smile concealed the reservations he felt inside as he jingled his chain of trophies. "Much fewer now."

"Where are they?" Jasmine swept her arm across the landscape. "If we are so near, why do we not see them? Do they not have scouts? Or sentries? If they despise you as you say, why do they not come en masse against us?"

Good question, and one Rancid had pondered for many days. But he didn't have the answer, so he made one up. "They've been ravaged beyond my original estimate. Now they're vulnerable. We must take advantage of their weakened state."

"Maybe they've moved," Vinra suggested.

"We've come this far," Nick said. "I thought we'd give him one more day. If he finds the hideout, we can evaluate the risks. If they do have a tie into the Prophecy, and I believe they do, we need to find out what it is." He looked at the others.

"Fine," Jasmine said. "But if there are more than ten bandits, they are too many for us."

Rancid squared off with the monk, his voice raised. "We can take twenty. You've seen them fight. They're cowards."

Jasmine's tone remained unperturbed. "They retreat when they face a losing battle. We should do the same."

Rancid stiffened at the veiled slight to his judgment. His hand flexed several times, hovering near the pommel of his sword.

Zen stepped between them. "I have an idea." He pointed down the path they'd been traveling. "Does this trail lead toward the bandit camp?"

Rancid's eyes narrowed in suspicion. It was Zen's observations that had put him in this predicament. "I think the general direction is correct."

"Good. Take the others as far as you like down the trail. I'll search from the sky. We'll cover more ground that way. If we don't find the camp today, we go to Eckland. Agreed?"

The others' nods of assent told Rancid he'd lost his gambit. Though the Black Hand base was close, he wouldn't likely find it in a day. So be it. He'd fought the bandits by himself before. He could do it again.

Zen took to the skies in his hawk form, flying southeast along the trail, searching the ground for any sign of the Black Hand or their hideout. But he had no idea what he'd do if he found it. Would the camp be too large for his friends to attack? Would he find a small and unsuspecting camp? No, not unsuspecting, not if what Gwyndarren had said was true. That posed another question. Was it true? Had

Gwyndarren really spoken to the Black Hand as he'd implied?

None of the answers mattered, of course. Gwyndarren had paid him well for a task that served Zen's own purpose and that of his friends—except for Rancid. And Zen cared little for him. Rancid had never bought into their quest anyway. He'd ridiculed the Prophecy, squandered their time, and used them all for his own selfish ends. As before, Gwyndarren had given Zen something for nothing.

Once he'd flown beyond sight of the party, Zen turned eastward. Tomorrow, the whole group would come through this territory on their way to Eckland. So instead of wasting the day in search of a camp he had no interest in finding, Zen scanned the countryside for signs of danger. He noted any landmarks that he'd be able to see from the ground. They would tell him later if Rancid's course stayed true.

He returned to his friends eight hours later, his energies spent, and sadly reported that his search had come up empty. "All I saw were some tracks, old ones, in a dry wash, like the ones we found last week."

"What do you know of tracks?" Rancid said. "Show me where. I can follow them to the bandits' hideout."

Zen shook his head. "I searched the area for miles in every direction. There wasn't a soul to be seen. I think your bandits have left."

"That's it then," Vinra said. "We move on to Eckland."

"No." Rancid's fists balled on his hips. "You gave me a day to find them. It's only mid-afternoon, and a day is twenty-four hours long. Go out again tonight. If they keep a fire, it'll be obvious from the air."

It took unwavering concentration for Zen to maintain a weave as complex as a morph. "I'm spent." When he was still miles from camp, he'd feared he'd have to land and walk the rest of the way back. Ultimately he'd held on. Now he had nothing left. "I need rest."

He turned to Jasmine, who'd been the most adamant about returning to their original purpose. "Physically, I can travel, but I won't be able to tap the weave until I've rested."

"For how long?" she asked.

Zen's mind was fogged with the morning's exertions. "I don't know. Several hours, at least."

"Okay," Nick said. "We gave Rancid a day to find the camp. And although he's stretching our agreement, I'm inclined to honor it. We'll camp early tonight and wake you before dawn. You can try again then."

Grudgingly, Zen accepted the deal. Early morning was Zen's watch anyway. So Nick covered it alone while Zen went out again. But he saw only two fires within ten miles of their camp. Neither belonged to the Black Hand.

As soon as he'd reported, Jasmine shouldered her pack. "Then we go east."

They strode a hundred feet before Nick turned back to Rancid. He hadn't moved—hadn't even lifted his gear. He simply stood there, watching Nick and the others walk away.

Finally, Nick said, "You coming?"

CHAPTER 25

T hree days later, Nick gazed out upon a broad, fertile valley, decorated with a patchwork of plantations—the growers of Palidor, the population most impacted by the slave riots. Rancid had escorted the party through the hill country that surrounded Forlorn Valley, and past the baron's stronghold, on their way to Eckland at last.

The shining sun added to Nick's sense of freedom as they left the dangerous hills behind. Though the party's provisions had run low, water would be plentiful in the basin, and Rancid and Jasmine could hunt and forage for sufficient food to sustain them.

Rancid had agreed to come only because he believed the bandits had moved east. He would find them, Rancid had vowed, and one by one, he would eliminate them.

Nick's own hatred of the Black Hand was more subdued. He worried primarily about the fate of the Civilized Lands, and the bandits played only a secondary role in the Prophecy. They worked for the Master or for one of the Chosen, hence their interest in the journal, but they weren't the root of the evil.

For days, the companions' trek through the fertile basin proved pleasant and uneventful. At times, they were questioned by plantation guards. Each time, Nick explained that they were working for bounty, searching for Black Hand bandits and goblin runaways. The string of trophies weighing down Rancid's belt lent credence to this claim, and the guards allowed the party to proceed.

A week passed, as did the fertile lands, and the companions climbed into the high country of eastern Palidor, a landscape more suited to ranching and livestock than to growing and harvesting.

Because the use of slave labor was universal in the kingdom, the ranchers were not immune to the uprising. At one point, Nick and his party came across a burned-out ranch house, the embers still hot and smoldering.

Eight dead lay among the ruins, two goblins and a human family, including a small girl of four or five harvests, run through with a goblin sword.

Nick turned away from the grisly sight with bile in his throat and fist clenched at his side. More deaths of innocents. More houses reduced to ash. Based on the condition of the bodies and warmth of the ruins, it had all happened within the past forty-eight hours. His eyes found Jasmine's. "Search the grounds." The tool shed and feed barn, at least, remained intact. There were bound to be useful tools, food, coin, or other supplies about, and the dead would have no use for what little remained. "Take anything we may need. Vinra and I will bury the bodies."

Rancid was already scouting for tracks.

"I'll take a look from the air," Zen offered. "If there's danger nearby, I'll find it." When he returned, he reported a second casualty, another ranch, a few miles north.

It was dark by the time they'd buried the victims, having left the goblins to rot in the next day's sun. Nick slaughtered a lamb from the orphaned livestock to sustain them for as long as the meat kept. With a renewed sense of urgency, he allowed the group a mere four hours of rest and resumed their journey when the moon turned full.

As dawn brightened the sky, they came upon a third house, this one still standing. Ranch hands moved among the buildings, beginning their morning chores. Slaves went about their tasks with a manner of dour resignation, seeming to accept their destined life of servitude, perhaps oblivious to the unrest around them.

A boy, barely out of adolescence, dropped his dung-caked shovel and ran inside, raising his voice in alarm. Nick stopped the party then and waited for the men of the house to emerge.

Three stepped out onto the porch.

"Stay here," Nick told his company. "We don't want to frighten them."

"Bit early, ain't it?" said the foremost of the ranchers.

Nick closed half the distance to the men. "We bring warning."

"Is that right?" The speaker rested his hand on the pommel of a sword.

Though the rancher tried to keep the gesture casual, Nick perceived the nervousness in it. The other two men weren't armed, though two nearby slave wardens were. Nick pointed back the way he'd come. "We found two burned-out ranches within ten miles of here. Goblin attacks, it looks like. We thought you might like to know."

"Tell me about it," said an unkempt, surly man in the back of the trio. "One of them was mine." He spat onto the ground. "Now I got nothing."

"Mind if I ask what happened?" Nick ventured.

The man chewed his lip for several seconds before responding. "I went to the co-op for supplies with two of my men. When we got back, the house was gone and my family dead, murdered by goblin trash." He spat again, dark liquid through blackened teeth.

"I'm sorry. Some of the tracks lead this way. We thought we'd better warn you."

"Appreciate the gesture," said the man with the sword, "but everybody hereabouts knows of the riots. Getting to be too many to count now."

Rancid walked up behind Nick. "You know of the Black Hand?"

The rancher's eyes narrowed. "What of 'em?"

Rancid hefted his chain of trophies. "We're hunting bounty, runaway slaves and Black Hand bandits. Seen any in the area?"

The man gave him a measuring look, taking in the deep scar on his face, before settling on the numerous black gloves. "They pretty much leave us alone here. Not much wealth in a ranch, except for the livestock. They don't seem much interested in that."

Nick glanced at the horse barn behind the house, then took a step forward to regain the rancher's attention. "You wouldn't happen to have a few horses you can spare? We've only a few coins to pay, but it would greatly aid our efforts against the goblin rebels."

"They seem to be congregating in the east," Rancid lied. "We've been tracking them all the way from Forlorn Valley, but without mounts, we fall farther behind every day."

This time, the rancher took stock of the entire party. "I'll tell you what. I got a few draft mares. They ain't no use around the house, and it ain't wise to take the wagon out 'til all this blows over. You use 'em to hunt goblins, I'll give 'em to you." He paused. "You need food?"

Nick nodded.

"I got some jerky and dried apples. Sell 'em to you cheaper than you'll find in town, what with the food getting short and all."

The rancher's wife packed a sack of provisions and the boy bridled three horses.

"They'll live off the land if you let them," the rancher said. "Won't need to carry no feed that way."

Nick thanked the man and paid what he asked for the food, and the party headed out once more.

"**M**age done it," Groot told Halidreth the day after Sevendeath's company turned east. "They go Eck-Land."

It required significant effort for Gwyndarren to keep a smug grin from his face. He'd never had any doubt. The task was simple enough, and it hadn't forced Zen to betray his friends. As such, it was a poorer test of loyalty than Gwyndarren had advertised. Therefore, he'd need to test the mage in earnest before presenting him to the Master as an agent of evil. It'd be suicide to offer him up before Gwyndarren himself knew for sure where Zen's loyalties lay.

And though Zen had never voiced any hesitation during their deals, Gwyndarren's instincts told him to proceed by stages, upping the stakes and the level of betrayal—as well as the threat of repercussions for unwillingness or failure—with each successive test.

"What of Sevendeath?" asked Sorowyn, Halidreth's elven lieutenant. "Did he go with them?"

Groot nodded slowly, almost ponderously. "Him go too."

"Pity. Alone, he's less of a threat. And I want another crack at him."

"You'll have it," Halidreth told him. "But right now, we can't afford the distraction. Better that he goes with the others."

Gwyndarren did smile now. He doubted Nick and his party could have beaten the hoards of goblins and orcs that now infested the Black Hand warren, but he'd saved the bandits a great deal of inconvenience. In doing so, he'd proved his worth to Groot and taken one step up the ladder of power. If Gwyndarren played his Hand right, he and Zen could go far indeed.

Halidreth continued. "Sevendeath now walks into our teeth."

"Leave him 'lone," Groot said, "'til friends find book. Then kill him."

Halidreth shot the ogre an acid glare. "Fine. As soon as his friends recover the Codex, we'll run them down and kill them." He gestured to Groot. "You'll have your book, Sevendeath will trouble us no more, and we can return to the caravan road."

"You're assuming the Codex is in Eckland," Gwyndarren said.

Halidreth glanced at Groot before addressing the elf. "Alamain told Nick Mirrin that it is."

"You must not be sure, or you would've gone after it yourself."

"The authorities would never give us the Codex, and we're not inclined to break into the College of History archive to get it."

"Still, what if it's not there?" Gwyndarren snapped his fingers as though he'd just had a thought, and then proposed a plan he'd formulated carefully over the past several days. "Zen will know if they find the book. We need only arrange a signal. Let him tell the Black Hand when his friends are ripe for slaughter." Now *that* would be a test.

"No!" Groot bellowed, wresting control of the conversation. "Drake-moor be in Eck-Land. He find out. He tell Hand."

"Just so long as we know." Halidreth turned to Sorowyn. "Take some men and go to Eckland."

Sorowyn nodded. "I'm due there soon anyway."

"Make sure you arrive before Sevendeath. Rally the patrols. Groot will arrange for Drakemoor to meet with you. Have everyone ready in case they do find the Codex."

Sorowyn wheeled toward the door.

Then Halidreth added, "Spare the ice mage."

Nick and the others traveled northeast for most of the day. Riding ahead on one of the horses, Rancid scouted the easiest passage over the landscape. Nick and Zen shared a horse. Vinra rode the other. With her hybrid physique, Jasmine had no difficulty keeping pace on foot.

Late that afternoon, Rancid came to an abrupt stop at the top of a shallow rise. The long black ponytail flying from his otherwise-bald head made him easy to recognize.

A voice beyond him yelled, "Sevendeath!"

Rancid wheeled his mount around and pointed to his chain of Black Hand trophies. Without stopping his horse, he leapt to the ground and ducked behind a pinion tree. There, he drew his sword and waited for the bandits to charge over the rise in pursuit. Nick pulled his horse to a stop. He and Zen leapt off and scrambled for the sparse cover of a few scraggly sage while Vinra and Jasmine did the same.

A minute passed, then two. Nick looked at Zen, who shared his expression of bewilderment. The shout had come from nearby. The bandits should've engaged by now. After all, they'd seen only Rancid, who'd always worked alone in the past. Yet the bandits were cautious and, as the most-feared band of outlaws in all the Civilized Lands, they weren't stupid. Perhaps they recognized an ambush, albeit an impromptu one, when they saw it.

The hoof beats of several horses drummed from the other side of the rise. Nick tensed, tightening his grip on his great sword. But the sound receded, moving off to the north, retreating or, more likely, flanking.

Nick eased himself to the top of the rise with Zen by his side. Rancid crawled to join them. There, they watched ten horsemen on strong, fleet mounts cantering down the shoreline of the wide Omensong River. The bandits, identifiable by the studded gloves they wore, were indeed moving away, but they weren't running scared. "Why are they leaving?" he asked Rancid.

"Cowards." Rancid waved his sword for the others to come forward. "Let's go get them."

Nick shook his head. "We'll never catch them. Their horses are faster than ours."

Zen stood. "They're not beyond our reach yet." He planted the butt of his staff in the dirt and began to chant. The crystal atop it began to glow and pulsate. A storm cloud gathered above the riders, now a quarter mile away, and built to a thick gray mass.

"No!" Nick yelled.

In seconds, a hailstorm the likes of which Nick had never seen before erupted, catching three of the riders in a deluge so thick it obscured the victims from sight. Two of the three rode from the storm, cursing, their battered mounts bleeding. But Zen could sustain the weave only briefly. Several bandits gathered near the perimeter of the unnatural storm and waited for it to subside. When it did, the third bandit struggled to his feet beside his dead horse, accepted a hand up onto another bandit's mount, and they all galloped away.

"Why are they running?" Nick asked again.

Rancid didn't answer. He stared intently at the retreating band, eyes narrowed and nostrils flaring with each angry breath.

Nick tried again. "They couldn't have known we were with you, and yet they let you be. Why?"

Rancid threw up his hands. "How should I know? They chased me through Dreadwood Swamp and the length of three kingdoms. Yet when I come to them, they walk away as if they don't even know me." He kicked a rock and sent it skittering down the hill. "I don't get it."

Nick kept an eye on the bandits until they faded into the distance.

"They're between us and Eckland," Rancid said. "That poses some problems, but none I can't handle."

"Better keep an eye on them," Nick told Zen. "Make sure they don't double back."

Moments later, the mage took flight.

By then, Jasmine had joined them on the rise. "Well, Rancid, it seems they are not out for your blood after all."

He wheeled on her with his sword in his hand and his voice full of coiled tension, a snake ready to strike. "Don't bet on it. They'll be back."

Nick stepped between the two, hands spread to keep them separated. "We've already had this discussion."

Jasmine raised an eyebrow and spoke calmly to Rancid. "Well then. What do you propose we do now?"

"Wait."

"I'm through waiting for you." She turned and walked back to Vinra, who had already gathered the horses.

"We wait," Nick said, "until Zen returns to tell us where the bandits have gone. We don't want to walk into an ambush."

Jasmine wheeled on them, but said nothing.

Finally, Rancid pointed his sword toward the north. "Go then and die. That will serve your quest as well as the Codex will."

Jasmine looked then at Nick. "How long will Zen be?"

"Half-hour, maybe."

She spun without a word and walked away.

Nick broke the silence that followed. "What do you really think?"

Rancid snorted. "I think she's an idiot."

"I meant about the Black Hand."

Rancid stared north down the river for several heartbeats, then sheathed his sword. "Caution above all." He met Nick's gaze. "They're cunning, and those we met today aren't rookies. They'll have us dead before sundown if we're not careful."

About twenty minutes later, Zen came back. "The river turns east about four miles downstream, just before a line of hills that parallels the river."

"The Ogre's Belt," Nick said.

Zen nodded. "The bandits turned and continued up the river-bank—"

"Toward Eckland," Rancid finished.

"Maybe we can cross the Omensong," Zen suggested. "Cut the corner and avoid the bandits altogether."

"No," Nick said. The river was seventy-five-feet wide, swift, and too deep to see the bottom. The few trees provided by the landscape were too small to construct a sizable raft. As such, any attempt to cross would probably cost them at least a day and their horses, if not some of their lives. "We'll stay on this side."

"That's fine," Rancid said. "I'll scout ahead. I know their ways. If they set an ambush, I'll find it." With that, he began to walk away.

"On foot?" Nick asked. "Grab your horse and ride."

Rancid spun on him. "You question me at every turn. I'll take you to Eckland, and I'll get you there safely. But for the next four days we'll be caught between the Ogre's Belt and the Omensong, a narrow passage in which the bandits will be able to predict our path." The scar on his face grew red, accenting the anger in his eyes as he waved a hand at the terrain. "This isn't Forlorn Valley. It's flat for miles, broken by gullies and ridges ideal for an ambush. I can't approach them on horseback without being seen." He turned to Jasmine and his volume dropped to a deadly whisper spoken through clenched teeth. "We must do this my way."

Jasmine marched up to him. "How can we not question your actions? Or your intent?"

"She's right," Nick said. "You've given us cause."

Rancid faced him with sadness in his eyes. Without a word, he strode to his horse, mounted up and rode west—the way they'd come.

Nick watched him go with one eyebrow raised, unable to reconcile his feelings. Certainly they were close enough to find their way to Eckland alone, but there remained the Black Hand. He didn't for a moment believe the bandits would simply ride away.

CHAPTER 26

Sorowyn led his Black Hand downriver between the Omensong and the Ogre's Belt, the band of hills that separated the high desert from the lowlands. Their luck this day had been good, despite the loss of a horse. He'd intended to meet with the Black Hand already in Eckland and join the coordinated hunt for Sevendeath and his companions. He'd never imagined Sevendeath would save them all the trouble of the search.

While the Ogre's Belt was far from impassible, crossing it would add days to Sevendeath's journey, and it would put him onto the caravan road, where Black Hand patrols would likely spot him. Therefore, if Sevendeath was headed for Eckland, he'd most likely come through the Omensong valley.

Even so, Sorowyn had lost more than one friend to Sevendeath's unpredictability. Every mile he rode away took more willpower than the mile before. He longed to turn his Hand around and finish the task that he himself had nearly accomplished when he'd scarred Seven-death's face the previous fall.

Sevendeath had assembled a company of able warriors, but they were only five—if the reports were true—and Sorowyn had some of the best the Hand had to offer. Still, he had more to consider than the Black Hand's collective desire for revenge. There was the Chosen. And the Chosen wanted the Codex. *So be it.*

Sorowyn pulled his horse to a stop and gathered the Hand around him. He pointed the jagged blade of his sword at Jade. "This is where you get off."

Jade nodded. Without a word, she dismounted and unpacked a few necessities from her saddlebags before giving her mount to the men who'd been forced to share. Then she turned to Sorowyn for instructions.

"Sevendeath will come this way. I suspect he'll stalk us all the way into Eckland. If he does, our tracks will give him an incentive not to stray. But if he goes north through the Ogre's Belt, he'll do so here. Either way, we must determine his strength and track his movements."

The sparse vegetation would make cover difficult to come by for most people, but Jade wasn't most people. She nodded. "It's late. They'll camp soon. I'll backtrack in the night. If I'm lucky, I can snag Sevendeath's horse. That'll slow them down and speed my return."

"They owe us one anyway," said a surly orc-kin waiting nearby.

"Just be careful," Sorowyn said. "We need the information more than we need the horse."

Jade gave him a long look of exaggerated patience.

Because anything else he had to say might also come across as condescending, he turned his horse and led the rest of the Hand away. When he looked back ten seconds later, Jade had already vanished into the scenery.

Just before dark, the ice mage hit them again. A storm cloud appeared from nowhere, gathered above them, and dropped hail the size of a mace's head. Sorowyn's own mage, Minshara, collapsed in the deluge, along with two of the mounts. Another horse and two Black Hand scrambled to safety after the hail began.

"Fan out!" Sorowyn bellowed, knowing the effort was futile. "Find him." He wheeled his horse around, searching the growing shadows for a human form. The only substantial cover lay on the far side of the Omensong, but there was no movement there save the flight of a startled white hawk, spooked by the roar of the tempest.

Within seconds, Sorowyn's company swept through the surrounding scrub, flushing out any form of life from every hiding place. They found no one. Meanwhile, a Black Hand priest of Vexetan, the only healer among them, raced to tend the wounded.

By the time his men gathered around once more, both Minshara and the other victim were back on their feet.

"I couldn't help the horses." The novice priest gestured to the two slain animals. "I'm sorry."

"It can't be helped." To the Hand, Sorowyn said, "Double up. Let's ride." He wheeled his mount north to put some distance between his band and the far side of the river. The ice mage wouldn't catch him twice if he could help it. "And spread out."

"You!" He pointed his weapon at one of three rookies in his group. "Make best speed to Eckland. Report our position, and that of Sevendeath, to the Hand there. You know where to find them?"

The young elf nodded curtly.

"Tell them to gather the scouts throughout the city. They must be ready when Sevendeath and his friends find the Codex."

Jade moved north, away from the path the Hand had taken, slunk into a ravine, and waited until dark. When night came, she backtracked, taking her time and keeping to the shadows as the moon became full.

At last she saw him, a ghostly figure moving across the darkened landscape. Sevendeath patrolled a crescent-shaped path across her own, but he seemed unwell—his path meandering, his steps unsure, as if he was drunk, delirious, or exhausted.

Tempted as she was to draw her crossbow and take him down, her orders overruled such an action. Instead, she bided her time. When Sevendeath reached the extreme of his patrol pattern, she slipped past to locate the enemy camp.

When she found it, she eased silently closer until she could make out the figures of two sentries in the darkness—the priest and the monk. Reaching out to the clump of sagebrush beside her, she gripped a branch and gave it a deliberate shake, then crouched—stock-still— to await the response.

Within seconds, the camp came alive with activity. The sentries roused Nick Mirrin and the ice mage, who quickly gathered their weapons and joined their friends, peering into the gloom. Jade stayed just long enough to ensure that everyone was roused. She counted them as they climbed from their sleeping bundles, and then slipped away, using the noise from the camp's stirrings to cover her retreat.

Carefully, she circled around Sevendeath once again, unable to keep from smiling. Nick and his friends would lose hours of sleep now, remaining awake, probably until dawn, to make sure Sorowyn wasn't planning some sort of attack.

She found where Sevendeath had tethered his horse—a shoddy beast without a scrap of gear, save a bridle that the elf-kin hadn't bothered to remove for the night. She walked the animal a safe distance into the night, then mounted up and rode south, away from Sorowyn and the Black Hand. By morning she was well behind Sevendeath's party, where they wouldn't think to look for her.

The next night, she could catch up to Sevendeath and confirm he'd kept to his course along the river before reporting back to Sorowyn.

Nick let his companions linger until noon to recover from their broken sleep of that night and the brief rest they'd had the night before.

As the others broke camp, Jasmine went in search of edible and medicinal plants, and returned a few minutes later with a pouch full of fresh pinion nuts. "I saw Rancid about a quarter mile downriver. He said he drove off a bandit that scouted our camp last night, but lost his horse in the process. He advises us to move cautiously."

Nick grunted. "Where is he now?"

"Scouting ahead."

"I figured he hadn't really left us, especially when last night's disturbance wasn't followed by an all-out Black Hand assault." The timing would have been perfect for a raid, with half the camp sleeping, Nick out of his armor, Zen spent from his attacks on the bandits the previous day, and Rancid gone.

"You think he just ditched the horse so he could track on foot?" Vinra asked. "Or do you think that really was a bandit we heard last night?"

"Who knows?" Though Rancid's behavior often defied Nick's form of reason, it was comforting to know he was still with them. "Everybody ready?"

"I'll check the area." Zen morphed into his hawk form, a transformation he couldn't have done just two months before but that now seemed as commonplace as Nick's donning his own armor. With a screech, he took to the sky.

By mid-afternoon, they rounded the bend in the river and turned east. They saw nothing more of Rancid or the Black Hand until late that evening, when they came across a meadow covered in dense grass and dotted by an occasional cottonwood. A tributary ran south from the Ogre's Belt into the Omensong, preventing an unseen approach by any bandits ahead of them. "We'll camp here," Nick announced. The others immediately broke into their nightly routines.

"Pssssst," Jasmine hissed a few minutes later, while foraging for herbs.

"What?" Nick whispered.

As he moved up beside her, she pointed into a thicket of thorn-berry. Curled up inside his blanket next to his stacked gear lay Rancid, issuing the slow, rhythmic breathing of one in deep slumber.

"Leave him," Nick said. "Tonight, we'll watch his back."

Sometime during Zen's watch the next morning, Rancid slipped away. He returned shortly after noon. "Goblins ahead. Just over the next rise. Two dozen of them, refreshing their water supply at the river."

"Orcs?" Nick asked.

"Just goblins."

"With goblin-made swords?"

Rancid nodded. "They've posted sentries, but we can slip past them."

He began to lead the others in a circuitous path around the rabble, but as soon as they got close, Zen strode to the top of a rise and showed himself. What did he have to fear from runaway slaves?

The alarm rose among the goblins and, emboldened by their recent victory over their masters, they charged the lone elf-kin on the hill.

Zen grinned in fierce satisfaction as he thrust the butt of his staff into the earth and called forth his wrath. The chill pulsed through him in harmony with the thrumming of the staff's crowning crystal. He gathered the weave and added a measure of his own life force. Within moments, a cloud formed and darkened over the creatures.

Heedless, the goblins rushed forward.

A euphoria of power swept through Zen as the cloud released its hail, pounding upon the skulls of the slaves, its sound deafening. When the storm subsided, nine of the miserable things lay dead in its wake. But Zen wasn't through. A fire burned within him. This was the meaning of power. The power to kill. The power to spare. The power to feel and say and do anything—to *be* anything. That kind of power wasn't his yet, of course. This was the mere tip of what he could become. And yet, the staff gave him a taste of it.

At the edges of his consciousness, his friends signaled for him to stop, but he paid them no heed. Six goblins perished in a second storm. The survivors scattered and fled.

Burning through his reserves, Zen called upon his staff and the weave once more. When the third storm subsided, he leaned forward and let the staff take his weight.

Nick and Vinra circled around from behind, taking the horses to flank the fleeing slaves. Rancid too was there, beside Zen on the hill, launching arrows at those he could see. When the dust settled, at least twenty of the creatures had been slaughtered. The remnants would threaten no one now.

Jasmine helped Zen to a rock that was large enough for him to sit on, near the river's edge.

When Nick returned, he thrust a live goblin toward the group assembled around Zen.

Rancid darted forward with fire in his eyes and a dirk in his hand while the wretch struggled to his knees. "Where are the Black Hand?"

The goblin's eyes widened. He fought against Nick's grip. "Not know Black Hand."

Rancid's eyes narrowed and he twirled the blade slowly before the goblin's face. "Don't lie to me. I'll stick this through your left eye."

The goblin moved a hand to cover his face, then hesitated. His hand wavered as though he wasn't sure which eye to protect. Finally, he plopped the hand over his right eye and pleaded, "Not lie. Not know."

Nick spun the creature to face him. "Where did you come from?"

"That way." The captive poked a stubby finger toward the north.

"From a ranch?" Nick asked.

The goblin shook his head emphatically.

"A plantation?"

The creature stared, brow scrunched in thought.

"A farm?" Nick tried.

A nod.

"North of the Ogre's Belt," Nick told the others. Then he turned his attention back to the prisoner. "You came across the hills? How long ago?"

Rancid whipped the slave around before he could answer. "There were many men on horseback. Did you see them?"

"Saw. We run away."

"When?"

"One day go."

Rancid gave Nick a puzzled look.

"Yesterday?" Nick guessed.

The prisoner nodded again.

"How did you escape your masters?" Rancid asked.

"We kill them."

"How?"

"With sword."

"Where did you get the swords?"

"We find them."

"Where?"

"In field."

"Somebody must be leaving them," Nick said. "Importing the swords and distributing them for slaves to find."

Rancid stared at the prisoner as though considering what more to ask. The goblin trembled.

"On a plantation," Nick said into the silence, "slaves outnumber their wardens ten to one. With the goblins suddenly armed, the wardens wouldn't stand a chance."

Zen's strength began to return. "Not without a mage."

When Nick glanced at him, pain and hatred shown in his eyes. "Where would they find a mage? How would they afford one?"

Nick collected a goblin sword from the ground and pointed the tip of it to the north. "Go."

"You stop to pick up a sword—" Zen thrust the crystal tip of his staff at the goblin's face— "you'll not take another step."

Its eyes wide, the goblin fled into the hills.

When he was gone, Nick inspected the weapon, a gnarled blade with a greenish-gray cast. "Definitely not from the Civilized Lands. I'd thought maybe the swords were fakes. But these are genuine goblin make. They came from across the channel."

"Not an easy thing to import," Vinra said. Goblin goods had never been legal anywhere in the Civilized Lands.

"No," Nick said. "I wouldn't think so."

CHAPTER 27

Fearing an ambush outside Eckland, Rancid led the party into the Ogre's Belt. From atop the central ridge, the thin ribbon of the caravan road was visible on one side and the glittering Omensong on the other. Because the thoroughfare was no safer than the riverbank, Rancid kept to the hills for two days until they dipped into the pass that cradled Eckland Road.

Within minutes of stepping onto the hard-packed roadway, a thundering of hooves and the creek of wagon wheels descended upon them from behind. Rancid spun around, sword drawn.

Nick stood in the road, his arms spread wide before a pair of runaway drafts hauling a cart, spilling potatoes at every bump.

"Whoooooooa!" Nick hollered at the galloping pair.

The horses reared, trying to avoid this man who stood rock-steady in their path, but the weight of the wagon forced the beasts onward. At the last instant, Nick darted left and the horses veered right, clambering past on the rocky shoulder, missing him by mere inches in their headlong rush. By then, they'd slowed considerably. Jasmine leapt forward and wrestled them under control.

As the horses settled, a wiry old man loped up and leaned forward with his hands on his knees, sucking in deep gasps. When he could finally speak, he did so between heaves of his chest, "Thank you... good sirs... Don't know... what... spooked 'em."

It took several minutes for the old farmer's breathing to settle. When it did, he eyed his horses in annoyance, then looked back at the merchandise scattered on the ground for more than a mile behind. He shook his head. "That's the better part of a week's harvest. Don't know what I would've done if not for you folks."

Nick put a reassuring hand on the old man's shoulder. "Happens to the best of us. No harm done. We'll walk you into town. There're bandits about."

"So I heard." He scanned the road, scratching his balding scalp. "Truth is, they're more interested in coin than potatoes. It's on the way back I'll be in danger."

"Nevertheless." Rancid joined the two. "We'll make sure you arrive safely." It wouldn't hurt to be in a merchant's company when they reached the city gates. In times like these, there were bound to be questions.

The old man's face darkened then, as he caught sight of Jasmine's features. Her pointed chin, bony jaw, and unnaturally high and long cheekbones gave her away as something inhuman. But, what she was, the man seemed unable to discern. He looked suddenly as though he'd rather have lost his horses than be seen with her, especially with rampant rumors of goblinoid races on the mainland. Reluctantly, he nodded.

Rancid took care to conceal his bald pate beneath the hood of his cloak and to bury his chain of trophies within its folds before approaching the gate. He couldn't be sure what the Black Hand might have offered for news of his arrival.

When the guard asked the merchant about his companions, the old man eyed Nick, caution sparring with gratitude in his expression. He may have been a simple potato farmer, but he'd been down the road a time or two, and he understood the consequences of vouching for strangers who later caused trouble. Finally, he shook his head. "I met them on the road an hour ago. They've been kind to me, but I don't know them."

The guard waved the old man through, then turned to Rancid, who was nearest to the gate. "State your business."

Checking to see that his gauntlets remained hidden, he answered the guard with conviction. "We seek passage to Gabby Creek."

The guard eyed Rancid's scar with some suspicion, then glanced at each of the others. Jasmine had turned her head away as she conversed quietly with Nick, her hands concealed within the robes of her Order. Shoes covered her taloned feet. Zen hid his features behind a snow-white beard, giving him the appearance of some other mage entirely.

"On what business?" the guard asked.

Beyond the gate, Rancid saw that nearly everyone on the streets was armed, so the party's weapons shouldn't cause the guard undue alarm. "We're from Forlorn Keep. My father, the baron, has opened a new brewery. I'm to negotiate a business contract with the merchants downriver." He waved a hand toward his companions. "The Black Hand are thick in the Valley. Thus we're forced to travel in numbers, as I'm sure you understand."

The guard held Rancid's gaze in silence for several heartbeats, a trick used to unsettle liars. But Rancid met his stare with steady confidence, never uncomfortable with a lie told for his cause. *All is legal in the fight against evil.*

"I recommend the Whiskey Trader," the guard said finally. "It's a tolerable lodge just off the marina. They give an honest merchant a fair shake."

With a nod, Rancid led his procession through.

Two blocks into town, Zen stopped outside a clothier's shop. "I need to change. If there're Black Hand in town, they might recognize my robes."

Nick followed him in, returning with directions to the Palidor College of History. "Zen'll meet up with us later."

"So will I." Vinra squinted at the horizon. "It's almost sunset. I must pay my respects at the temple."

Several blocks later, Rancid recognized six bandits from the banks of the Omensong. They had removed the studded gloves of their brotherhood, and with that simple action, had melded seamlessly into the populace.

He nodded to Nick. "There."

"I see them."

"And you do nothing?"

Nick waved his hands at the passers-by. "What do you propose we do out here, among so many?"

"Kill them. They're sure to have their studded gloves on them somewhere. That will justify their deaths to the authorities well enough."

"And if they don't?"

Rancid hesitated.

"We should at least determine their purpose," Jasmine said.

The bandits turned a corner and vanished from sight.

"Quickly," Rancid said.

Nick huffed. "Very well. You two follow them, but keep your distance. I'll find boarding for the horses and locate the College of History." To Jasmine, he said, "Keep him out of trouble."

Rancid didn't wait for her reply. He was already running, but Jasmine caught up well before he rounded the corner.

From there, the bandits strolled down the boardwalk as if they hadn't a care. They collected their horses from a nearby stable and rode toward the north gate. Rancid thought to follow and make trouble for them with the guards, but once the bandits were mounted, keeping pace would have made the two conspicuous. Instead, he and Jasmine paid a visit to the stables.

When they entered the barn, the owner took in Jasmine's features by the smoky light of a lantern suspended from the ceiling with a length of hemp. He gave a grunt and planted his pitchfork into the wooden plank at his feet. "We're closed."

Jasmine stopped immediately. When Rancid took two more steps, the stablemaster raised the pitchfork at him. "I said, 'we're closed.'"

Rancid halted then, but not from fear of the man, who meant nothing to him except as a source of information. "Why do you do business with Black Hand bandits?"

The stablemaster glared at Jasmine. "I know trouble when I see it. You've no horses. You're not here as customers."

"We're here to collect our mounts," Rancid replied.

"You've none in my care. I'd remember either one of you. Now take your cross-bred slave and get off my property."

Rancid raised an eyebrow and glanced back at Jasmine, then looked past the man into the stalls beyond. He could see only two of the horses in residence. Neither was the draft the bandits had stolen from him.

"May we see your horses?" Jasmine asked calmly.

"No. You have no business here and I'll not discuss that of my clients. You'd want the same consideration, I'll wager."

"We would like to buy a horse," she said.

"They're not for sale."

Rancid leapt forward. He grasped the tines of the pitchfork and wrenched it from the stableman's hand, causing him to flee the barn yelling, "Guards! Guards! Guards!"

He shook his head, tossed the fork to the ground, and then walked the length of the barn, searching for any horse he recognized. Finding none, he returned to the monk. "Let's go."

Che companions decided not to stay at the recommended Whiskey Trader tavern because Rancid feared the Black Hand might get word of their presence from one of the guards. Instead, they opted for the only inn they could afford, the Copper Kettle, a cockroach- and flea-infested dive in the worst part of the wharf district.

Wanting no part in the planned academic activities, Rancid departed the inn before dawn and slunk along the harbor, which was active even then. Fishermen and merchants loaded cargo or supplies for the day's toil. Dock workers and even the harbormaster's watchmen were on duty. But one boat, a river barge named the *Craven Gull*, seemed to have just arrived. It was the only boat on the pier whose crew was unloading, rather than loading, cargo. The harbormaster's men hauled the merchandise off to one side for inspection—opening, emptying, and repacking every crate, apparently taking the search for goblin contraband very seriously.

Then a slight figure, cloaked in black, emerged from the *Craven Gull's* hold and crossed the gangplank to where the merchant huddled with the watchman in quiet conversation. Rancid approached them, walking by with his cowl gathered around him as if to ward off the morning's chill. As he passed, the cloaked man slipped a small leather sack to the merchant and the faint jingle of coins carried to Rancid's ears in the predawn stillness.

It was a rare merchant who conducted honest business in the darkest part of the night.

Stepping onto the boardwalk along the storefronts, Rancid ducked into a shadowed doorway from which he could observe the men unseen. Though the merchant might have simply been delayed during his journey and only now arrived, it wouldn't hurt to find out for sure.

A few minutes later, the cloaked figure shook the merchant's hand and nodded to the harbormen. Then he scanned the length of the street before boarding the barge again and disappearing into the hold.

He returned to the deck, trailed by four massive figures, each with his cowl pulled so low that it completely concealed his countenance.

Even at a distance, though, Rancid could discern stout musculature, height greater than that of the average man, and arms a little too long for a human. Together, the four departed the barge and followed the cloaked figure up the road and out of sight.

Creeping behind the gang, maintaining at least a two-block distance, Rancid followed until they entered a darkened alleyway that reeked of urine and rotting fish, where the Black Hand elf, Sorowyn, waited with half a dozen saddled horses. All six mounted and rode back the way they'd come.

Rancid glanced frantically around him. Finding no place to duck out of sight, he forced himself into a casual stride as the riders passed, not daring to draw attention to his presence. He bowed his head to hide his features from the all-too-familiar bandit, but not before catching sight of the face of one of his charges—the face of an orc.

After breakfast, Zen went with Nick and Jasmine to the College of History. The gray, stone-block building stood stark and oppressive among the smaller clay-roofed structures nearby. Bronze letters set into the wall above the arched entryway identified the place. And the iron-bound oak door revealed the seriousness with which Palidor took the protection of its records.

Nick crossed the grounds of the courtyard and tugged on the handle. Despite its obvious weight, the door moved silently and opened to a lamp-lit foyer beyond. Stepping into the gloom, they approached a rotund clerk seated behind a large cherry-wood desk.

"How may I assist you this morning?" he asked.

"We're looking for a book," Nick began.

The scholar smiled proudly. "No library in the Civilized Lands has a greater collection."

"We seek the Prophecies of Mortaan," Nick said. "The original text."

"I—" The scholar stopped short when he caught sight of Jasmine's inhuman features. Wrenching his eyes back to meet Nick's. "I... um... I expect Master Windel will be in sometime this morning." He glanced at Jasmine again. "He... uh... should be able to assist you in your research."

"Actually, we're not here for research," Zen said.

"Then I suspect you've come to the wrong place."

"We're just looking for the one book."

The clerk waved his hand. "Yes, yes. As I said, Master Windel should be able to assist you. He usually arrives sometime mid-morning. Until then, you're free to make use of our collection."

After thanking the man, the three passed an ornate archway into a grand hall containing two rows of long tables and a wide gallery between them. The curved ceiling, supported by carved granite pillars, displayed an elaborate collage of historic or fictional scenes. A huge rug muted their footsteps on the stone floor. Individual study rooms occupied the perimeter of the gallery, the simplicity of their doorways incongruous beside the ornate openings to each library wing.

Zen eyed the collection of books with more than a tingling of power lust. "I can tell you which books are enchanted."

Nick looked around dubiously and leaned close. "Weaving might not be permitted in here." He nodded toward an observing acolyte.

The boy, perhaps eleven or twelve harvests, was probably too young to know much about the weave. So Zen turned back to Nick with the corners of his mouth curled up in a sly sneer. He began chanting before his friend could protest.

This time, when he tapped the weave, he didn't draw it to himself or try to manipulate it. He simply opened himself to it and gazed at the emanations of the books around him. Every book, without exception, shone with a faint pervasive glow. Zen stood amidst a library tenfold vaster than the one at Glimmernook. And every book enchanted. He swooned with the magnitude of the possibilities. But no, it was impossible. He couldn't afford to let his greed blind him to the truth.

There must be another answer.

This was a historical archive. Some of the books were nearly two thousand years old, yet all remained in remarkably good condition. Their aspect must have been that of a preservation enchantment.

Zen didn't let his disappointment distract him from his task, however. He focused instead on the nature of the enchantments and limited his scrutiny to the top shelf—the oldest of the texts. There, some of the tomes radiated more brightly than the others, and with a different aspect—that of the divine, the magic of the gods, entirely separate from the weave. These were the truly enchanted texts. Climbing a rolling ladder he found nearby, Zen pulled them out and placed them on the table. The Codex of Mortaan wasn't among them.

Nick slumped into his seat. "It's not here."

"If you had the original text, would you keep it on the shelf?" Jasmine asked.

"No," Nick said after a moment's thought. "I guess not."

The companions thumbed through the available books, more to pass the time than to obtain any specific information, until Master Windel arrived. By then Vinra had finished his morning prayers and had joined them as well.

"I understand you gentlemen need assistance," Windel said. "I'm delighted. It'll be a welcome diversion from the daily tedium of my studies. Nevertheless, my work is important and any time away will delay it, so I must charge you for my services. For a single gold coin, I'll assist you in any way I can for the duration of the day."

"Actually," Zen said, "our needs are simple. We seek the original Codex of Mortaan, but it's not on the shelf. Do you know if you have it?"

The scholar glanced at the mage before turning to Nick. "Do we have a deal?"

Nick dug into his pouch for one of his last remaining bits of gold and handed it to Windel.

"Very good," the scholar said. "Wait here."

Windel returned with an elder whom he introduced as the archive superintendent.

"Why do you seek the Codex?" the old man asked.

Nick told him, "High Priestess Alamain advised us to seek the original. She believed it to be here."

The man was silent for a time, so Jasmine unwrapped her own tome and laid it carefully on the table. "We have a copy. We wish only to make a comparison."

The superintendent nodded slowly. "I believe you, but I'm afraid we no longer have the book you seek."

"But you had it?" Nick's face brightened despite the seemingly bad news.

The superintendent's eyes became distant, unfocused. "For two generations, it was on loan to this library, but... oh, it must have been ten years ago now, the owner requested its return." His gaze settled on Nick. "Naturally, we complied."

"Who owns it?" Zen was almost afraid to ask.

"King Ednar." The old man's eyes turned sad. "The late King Ednar of Trondor, and a very close friend."

"Do you think it's among his estate?" Nick asked. "Or would he have lent it to another?"

The superintendent blinked away the moisture in his eyes. "I would guess it's in his personal library. But if the rumors are true, the throne is in contention. The new king may not yet know what he possesses."

"Trondor's a long way from here," Nick said, turning to his friends, defeat evident in his voice.

"Isn't this the only first-hand account you've had of the Codex?" Vinra asked. "It's but a journey away, and every step will bring you closer."

Nick wheeled on him. "It's too far—"

"Shhhhh." Windel glanced at the library's patrons around them.

Nick's voice dropped to a harsh whisper. "We're running out of time, and everything we need is scattered to the far corners of the Lands." He sat down, resting his forehead in his palm.

Jasmine secured the bindings on her tome and slipped it back into her pack. "While we're here, there are many things we might learn. And we've already paid for the good scholar's time."

"Speaking of time," Zen said to Vinra. "Don't you have to be in the capital for some sort of ceremony?"

The priest shook his head. "I just came from the temple. Your zealous friend's detour into Forlorn Valley cost me that honor. When I failed to arrive on time, the church sent another priest."

"I'm sorry," Nick said.

"Don't be. At this point, Robala is much more concerned about the Prophecy. Between the civil war in Trondor and the slave riots here, two of the prerequisites have already been met. According to the church elders, worse is coming. They've asked me to aid you in any way I can." He turned to Nick. "If you'll have me."

"We welcome the help."

Jasmine added, "Your healing gifts surpass my own. We will need that skill in the future, I fear."

"Not to mention a reliable guide," Zen said.

By the time Vinra excused himself for his evening prayers, the four had gone through their list of relics and learned something of each. The histories of Demonbane and the Shield of Faith were consistent with the information Alamain had given them in Lorentil.

The Guardian of the Abyss, the key to the Portal of the Damned, had been given centuries before into the care of the wandering tribes of Cormont, as safe a place as any, or so the rulers of the time believed. Presumably it remained there, too far away for Nick and the others to pursue. Zen was glad for that. The accounts he'd seen painted the tribes as primitive savages. He couldn't imagine much personal gain from a journey to such a backward and unsophisticated place. At least it would make the statue difficult for their enemies to find. Of the Guardian itself, they found little record, only a picture that depicted a bronze statue of an elven warrior holding an intricately decorated shield before him.

Jasmine borrowed a fine quill and purchased a single page of sturdy parchment. On it, she sketched an impressive likeness of the emblem etched on the Guardian's shield. On the back of the page, she drew a map of the Civilized Lands from an atlas available in the archive.

Of the Codex of Mortaan, they learned nothing more that day.

Vinsous Drakemoor crouched in the deepening shadows outside the College of History. A slow smile spread across his face as the last of the visitors departed and a fat clerk bolted the door for the night.

The assassin melted into the shadows and slunk to the entryway, where his black mask and outfit would allow him to vanish in the gloom. He slipped his slender hand into the lining of his cloak and fished out his picks. Working by feel alone in the dark, it took but a moment for him to defeat the lock. His first instinct was to open the door a crack and peer inside, but light pouring from within would betray him to anyone who might observe from the street.

Instead, he drew his sword to cloak himself in silence, swung the door wide, and walked casually through. The foyer was deserted, except for the portly man behind the desk, who shot to his feet, his eyes wide and staring at Drakemoor's mask and drawn sword. He opened his mouth to scream, but no sound emerged. His chair flipped over backwards and rebounded from the cut-stone floor. It too was silent. Then, in a display of immense strength or desperation, the fat man flung the huge desk forward, books and all, and fled toward the gallery.

Moments later, all became still once more and Drakemoor sheathed his sword. He padded across to the clerk's body, pulled the knife from the back of the man's neck, wiped the blade on his milky robes, and moved to the gallery door. The college was still and quiet. Confident that his entrance had alerted no one, he dragged the clerk by the feet back behind his displaced desk. Then, having determined from outside that this was the only exit from the archive, he waited.

An hour passed before voices approached—two of them, both male, one elderly. Moments later, the men rounded the corner from the gallery. The elder paused just inside the door. "That's strange. Where's—" The cold steel of Drakemoor's dagger against his throat froze the old man's words.

The younger scholar turned. He stood, mouth agape and eyes fixed on the blade that threatened his superior.

"Now," Drakemoor said conversationally, "let's find Mortaan's Codex."

CHAPTER 28

The next morning, rumors spread quickly of murder at the College of History. Nick and the others, including Rancid, who had returned sometime during the night, rushed to the library and found it closed.

"What's happened?" Nick asked the guardsman posted at the entrance.

"Three men were killed here last night."

"Might I ask who?" Jasmine said.

"The superintendent, one of the scholars, and a reception clerk. You'll have to come back tomorrow. I'm sorry."

Concerned, Nick thanked the sentry and drew his friends away from the doorway.

"It was the Black Hand. I know it," Rancid said, his tone a little too emphatic, a little too desperate, for Nick to believe he was at all certain.

"Whether it was or not," Nick said, "we have to assume the enemy knows where to find the Codex."

"Well then," Vinra said, "we have two options. We buy horses—fast horses—and race overland to Trondor, or we secure passage aboard an ocean vessel traveling north around the continent."

"But—" Rancid began.

Nick raised his hand to head off another tirade about the evil of the Black Hand. "Either option will require coin we don't have." Still, they had to reach the Codex before the enemy did. That book would be a more valuable source of information for either side than his grandfather's journal ever was. "We need to find out as much as we can about travel times and costs."

"I have a few contacts in town," Zen said. "I'll see what I can do about the coin problem."

Zen sifted through his backpack and extracted the roll of parchment Gwyndarren had given him. Maybe the elf could provide some form of magical transportation to Trondor. A translocation perhaps, a gateway between two places. That would come in handy. In fact, Zen decided, he should begin working on just such a weaving. But Gwyndarren had told him to use the parchment only when Zen had information the elf might find interesting enough to buy. What would he do if Zen used it merely to ask for help?

He shrugged his concern away. It was time to find out if this was a two-way partnership.

"Gwyndarren Lortannon," he intoned after reading the incantation aloud in the old elven tongue. "I must speak with you. Come to the Copper Kettle tavern in Eckland, room six." He pondered what to say next, wanting to bait the hook without making false promises. Finally, he said, "You may be interested in what I have to say." Then before releasing the weave, he added, "Come immediately, if you're able. I'll be waiting." If he was lucky, the elf would be in town already. If not, Gwyndarren might have a way to arrive presently. After their strange meeting in Forlorn Valley, nothing seemed beyond Gwyndarren's resources.

As he rerolled the parchment, the text on the top third of it faded into invisibility. He tucked it, with its two remaining identical inscriptions, into the bottom of his backpack and went downstairs to watch for the elf's arrival.

Less than half an hour later, Gwyndarren strode through the doorway, wearing a fine silken blouse and black trousers of a durable fabric, looking very much out of place in the dive. He scanned the tables as though seeking signs of trouble before entering. Zen rose, crossed to the stairs, and climbed them to room six. The elf entered a dozen paces behind him.

"Well met, my friend." Gwyndarren extended a hand in warm fellowship.

Any concern Zen might have held for calling him melted away in that moment.

"I can't say I approve of the accommodations." The elf frowned at the mud-stained floors and infested bed linens. He picked up a pillow by its corner with the tips of his thumb and forefinger and held it up for inspection. When he dropped it back to the bed, it released a cloud of fine dust and a sizable cockroach. "Not the sort of place you said you'd be."

"Rancid picked it. Purely on the basis of cost, I think. But it does lend credence to the name he uses."

"Indeed it does, my friend. Indeed it does." Gwyndarren glanced at the sheets once more before turning to Zen. "Forgive my manners, but I think I'll stand while we conduct our business."

Zen sat in a rickety chair in one corner of the room, symbolically reversing the positions the two had held during their meetings in Lorentil. "You asked me to contact you if I learned anything," Zen began. "We have a new lead on the Codex."

"Then it's not here, as you expected?"

"No. It's in Trondor. And we believe others seek it." As soon as the words escaped his mouth, he realized he should have negotiated a price for the information. Yet he couldn't berate himself too badly for the slip, for it was driven by his need. "I'm hoping you can provide an enchanted means of travel. It'd shave weeks off our journey."

Gwyndarren was already shaking his head. "I have resources—enchanted objects, information, connections, and even coin—but I'm not made of magic. And what you ask is great magic indeed. Greater even than your enemies possess, I suspect."

Zen's shoulders slumped. "I just thought maybe—"

"That is the kind of power you seek to have, is it not?"

Zen nodded, silent.

"I'd be disappointed if you aspired to something so easily attained that I might already have it. In fact, our partnership would be profitless for us both if you did. Nevertheless, I can help you."

Zen's eyes brightened.

Gwyndarren glanced around the room once more. "What you need is coin. You'll never outpace your enemies on foot, especially to such a distant place as Trondor. Particularly if you continue to follow that misguided friend of yours. He has cost you much time already."

"I wouldn't call Rancid a friend."

"Nor I. But he may yet be useful."

Zen ignored the statement and brought the conversation back to his immediate need. "You said you had coin?"

"Yes, but not for free." He faced Zen squarely, adopting a businesslike tone. "You have several items of considerable value, but due to their enchantments, Eckland has no market for them. I'll offer you a fair price for any you wish to sell, even those I gave you at no cost."

Zen frowned at the prospect of selling magic he'd worked hard for months to attain. Power was worth more than any amount of coin, but Gwyndarren was right. They couldn't expect to beat the Chosen to the Codex on foot. And he was right about something else too. Since they had arrived, Zen had seen no sorcerers or vendors of enchanted wares anywhere in town. There wasn't even an alchemist worthy of the name—only the Herb Garden, with its healing roots and exotic teas. When it came to magic, Eckland was a burned-out city in a burned-out kingdom.

Ultimately, Zen parted with the wand he'd stolen from Jarret. He could admit to himself that it had in fact been theft, even if he hadn't been able to admit it to Beltrann. But it was justified by their need, which plagued them still. Besides, Jarret would benefit from the forestalling of the Prophecy as well as anyone would. What was a minor wand against the weight of the Prophecy?

When Gwyndarren left him, Zen lay on the bed with a bag of gold settled on his chest, the weight of the coins matching the heaviness of his heart. He played this dangerous game for one thing: magical power. Now he'd sold some of what he'd acquired, and when they arrived in Trondor, the coin would be gone. He must find a way to make this game profitable if he wanted to continue to play.

Then again, the wand he'd sold was only his by deceit and the coin he'd gained would allow him and his friends to compete with their enemy. It was an investment in the success of both of his quests—for he would gain nothing if the Chosen beat them to the Codex. Furthermore, the coin he'd acquired gave him something Nick and the others needed and could now get only from Zen. Was that not, in itself, a kind of power?

Jade gasped and leapt for her sword when the figure appeared noiselessly beside her. "For the sake of the Master, don't do that again! How did you get in here?"

Drakemoor said nothing. He just smirked beneath the three-quarter mask that covered most of his face and, if the rumors were true, some grotesque deformity.

"What of the book?" she asked finally.

"It's not here. If it were, the superintendent would have told me. He believes it to be in Trondor, in the disputed royal library."

"We'll have to follow Sevendeath and his party there." Jade's fist clenched around the hilt of her sword. "That scoundrel borrows more time at every turn."

Drakemoor shook his head. "I just came from the wharf. They've booked passage on the *River Troll* to Gabby Creek. From there, they hope to reach Trondor by sea."

Jade's eyes widened. "Then we have to kill Sevendeath now, before he escapes us again."

Drakemoor's eyes turned cold. "I'm more concerned about the Codex. As you should be."

Jade growled low in her throat, the sound audible only to herself. "Have you informed the ogre?"

"I was waiting until we were together. He may have instructions for you." Drakemoor pulled the medallion from beneath his cloak. Holding it in his hands, he focused his gaze and called Groot by name. A soft glow began to emanate from the ornate gold frame and a mist clouded its onyx center. "I have news."

Jade couldn't hear the ogre's reply.

"The Codex is in Trondor," Drakemoor continued. "In the king's library. If I'd known, I'd have picked it up on my way out of the palace."

There was a brief pause.

"No. The war occupies the Chosen there and he's a long way from the capital. But I'll send warning."

Another pause.

"I also have news of the Guardian... The scholars told me all they'd learned for the enemy... Yes. Much more, though it took the scholars most of the night to find it." He pulled his dagger from its scabbard and twirled it absently about his fingertips. "It's amazing what one can accomplish when given the proper incentive."

A longer pause followed. The ogre had more for the Black Hand to do. Jade could feel it. Though she had a mind to refuse, she knew she wouldn't dare. So she stood quietly, arms crossed over her chest, and chewed on her lips.

"Of course I did," Drakemoor continued, speaking to the medallion. "Once they'd discovered the whereabouts of the Guardian, it wouldn't do for them to go blurting it to the others. Now would it?"

Just then a soft knock sounded from the door. "Come in, Gwyndarren." Drakemoor tucked the medallion away and turned to Jade. "I've asked the elf to join us. We may need help from the ice mage."

CHAPTER 29

"It's a fool's errand," Rancid insisted for the third time, glaring at the others in their dingy room at the Copper Kettle. "The book is here. In Eckland, somewhere."

"Why do you believe so?" Jasmine asked in a tone of calm reason.

Rancid threw his hands up and strode to the door. Then he wheeled on them once more. "Are you all idiots? They killed the scholars for a reason."

Vinra lay on the bed with his hands tucked behind his head. "Obviously."

Rancid met his gaze. "To keep the true location of the book secret. That's why."

"Very likely," Jasmine said. "But I subscribe to a different interpretation. I believe it means our enemies are mere hours behind us in their search for it. And they killed the scholars once they'd learned the Codex was in Trondor, hoping we had not already made the same discovery." She paused. "That means they are now a day ahead, assuming they left immediately after learning of the book's whereabouts."

Rancid huffed. "What better place to send us on a fairy chase than clear across the continent to a kingdom mired in war? By the time you return, the Prophecy will be fulfilled."

Nick sat forward in the rickety chair. "It's not that far by sea. And the enemy must first locate the Guardian before he can bring the Prophecy to fruition. From what we know, it's as distant as the Codex, and better hidden. Besides, without the *original* Codex, the Master may be working toward the wrong Prophecy, and we may be chasing legends."

"And what of the Black Hand? They're a part of this poem of yours. I know it. We should stay here and challenge them. That, at least, is a solid objective."

The room settled into silence.

"He's got a point," Nick conceded. "I too am convinced the bandits have a hand in this."

"I agree," Zen said. "But I think they've already played it, having imported weapons, supplied the slaves, and incited the riots—"

"But they're not done." Rancid waved his arms. Could the others not see? "They've been smuggling orcs, and who knows what else. They're assembling an army."

"I think that's a stretch," Vinra replied.

"We must not ignore the importance of knowing the true Prophecy," Jasmine said. "If there is a way to avert it, it will be found in the original Codex. Without that, we're ignorant."

"The Prophecy says there will be twelve Chosen. Suppose Sorowyn is one of them? If we kill him and take the medallion, that'll avert fulfillment."

"It says the Master will give twelve medallions away," Nick countered. "It doesn't say all of the Chosen will live to see fulfillment."

"There is value in disrupting Black Hand operations here," Jasmine said finally. "But we must pursue the Codex. If no other course of action is revealed, we can return to fight the Master's bandits."

Rancid folded his arms across his chest and planted his butt firmly on the edge of the bed. "I'm staying. I'll do what I can against the Black Hand. At a minimum, they must have a safe house here in Eckland. Maybe I can shut it down."

"It's settled then." Nick stood. "We must hurry. The rest of us have a boat to catch."

The group spent most of the next day riding a barge down the Omensong to the coast. Late that evening, Zen trolled the streets of Gabby Creek in a disguise he'd constructed from the weave and a borrowed set of Vinra's traveling clothes. During that foray, he identified only one provisioner with any kind of enchanted wares. Unfortunately, their cost was too high for him to afford and the enchantments too minor to risk stealing.

So when he received a message from Gwyndarren, it lightened his mood. *Meet me at the Smuggler's Cove at midnight, on the corner of Harbor and Sea Hag. Second floor. Room D.*

Now that was an offer Zen couldn't refuse. Perhaps he'd recover some of his losses from Eckland.

Later, in Gwyndarren's room, he inspected the delicately strung chain of white-gold beads and pale blue gemstones. "What is it?"

"It's a headband," the elf said. "The sigil will help you control the weave."

"I don't need help—"

"It will preserve your strength and improve your stamina—just a little at first, but increasing as you practice."

Zen stared at it, speechless. Jarret could never have imbued an object with such an enchantment.

"You said you wanted power." Gwyndarren gestured at the headband. "This is no mere trinket that will eventually be consumed by its own magic. This will augment that which lies within you." He waited for Zen to look at him. "This is power. Direct, raw power."

Zen's hands went cold. "At what price?" He could barely make his mouth form the words.

The elf smiled—a wry, almost-sincere gesture. "Very little for such a wonder as this, for it was difficult in the extreme to acquire."

Zen waited for the ax to fall.

The elf became suddenly serious. "Soon, you will meet one of the Chosen. When you do, you'll take no action against him."

Zen tried to keep the panic from his face. "You will arrange this meeting?"

"I apologize. I misspoke. You'll not meet this Chosen so much as you'll cross paths with him. I don't know when or where it will happen. I certainly can't foresee the circumstances of the encounter, but with the course you and your friends are taking, a confrontation seems inevitable."

For the first time, Gwyndarren's price wasn't free. This would require Zen to betray his friends' trust in favor of his own pursuit of power. Not that that bothered him much, as long as he didn't have to look Nick in the eye afterwards. As far as Zen was concerned, this was a quest for power. It didn't matter which side he ended up on.

Besides, if Zen was lucky, he wouldn't actually have to pay the price. As soon as he took the headband, he would board a ship for the opposite end of the Civilized Lands, leaving Gwyndarren far behind. "Okay—"

The elf stopped him with an upraised hand. "Before you speak further, let me be clear. I do not ask that you aid the Chosen in any way. In fact, it's better if you don't. I ask only that you, yourself, do not take action against him."

"And if he attacks me? Then may I act?"

"Of course. I wouldn't leave you defenseless. If you stay your staff, however, he should have no reason to harm you." He gave Zen a stern look. "But take warning. If you fail in your promise, you'll die with those whom you choose to defend."

Zen glanced at the elf's neck, checking for a chain or necklace of any kind. "Are... are you one of the Chosen?"

Gwyndarren laughed. "No. Nor do I work for them. Or the Master. I'm merely trying to save your life. You can't imagine the strength of the forces that oppose you. If you stand against them at that moment—even with the headband—you won't have the means to prevail."

The magnitude of Gwyndarren's prediction began to sink in. Was the elf guessing? Or bluffing? Certainly Gwyndarren knew more than he was letting on. Zen's heart became a rock in his stomach. The Chosen had set a trap for them. Gwyndarren was either trying to save him from it, or drop him into it.

"Who *do* you work for?" he said finally.

"I work for myself and no other."

"You give me an object of inestimable value, and all you ask in return is that I save my own life? What's in it for you?"

"It's an investment, for we both seek the same thing." He crouched before Zen's chair to bring his head level with that of the seated mage. "Neither of us will achieve it alone, so we must work together. I have contacts within the circles that seek to fulfill the Prophecy. You have contacts with those who seek to prevent it." Gwyndarren's eyes brightened with anticipation, as would a child's imagining his first tap of the weave. "Together we can accomplish amazing things. Just look at the headband. I had no such fortunes before we began. I give it to you now as a means to accomplish your own ends. By this, I hope to ride the hem of your robes to the acquisition of true power." His eyes lost their luster. "But that cannot happen if you challenge the Chosen before you're ready."

He patted Zen's knee as he stood. "Think on it, my friend. What say you?"

Zen nodded, more sure this time. "I'll do it."

"Excellent." Gwyndarren strode across the room and opened the door. "When the time comes, don't forget my warning."

As soon as the mage left, Gwyndarren collapsed onto the bed and massaged his forehead. Would Zen do it? His hesitation had been obvious enough, but it had become necessary to up the ante. At this point in the game, he'd convinced the Black Hand, even to the point of giving him the headband. Now he must convince the Chosen, both Groot and Drakemoor. For that, the test required a true betrayal of trust, or else it would be no test at all.

CHAPTER 30

Three days after his friends departed, Rancid crouched in the shadows of his alley and watched the *Craven Gull*. The crew had loaded its cargo the evening before, which told Rancid that his long surveillance was coming to an end. He wasn't disappointed.

Just before the sun broke over the horizon, Sorowyn emerged from a side street and strode down the pier toward the barge.

Rancid rushed from the darkness and threw back his cowl. "Sorowyn!"

The elf turned.

"You're up to your usual foul pollution, I see," Rancid yelled. "Too bad you won't be there when the king's army seizes everyone and everything at your Black Hand hideout in Forlorn Valley."

To the captain, he shouted, "I've informed the authorities here and in Gabby Creek that you've been licking the bandits' feet. At least you'll have the choice of being neutered here or downriver."

Apparently unimpressed by Rancid's bravado, Sorowyn simply mounted the barge's deck. The captain glanced nervously at the elf while his crew loosed the moorings and poled the *Gull* from the dock.

Rancid whipped a prepared arrow from his quiver and ignited the tip with his flint. He aimed at Sorowyn's heart and let the flaming missile fly.

The elf sidestepped and the arrow sank into one of several cargo crates stacked on the deck. The merchant and two of his crew raced to extinguish the flame. And as the boat eased into the current, Sorowyn's mouth spread into a broad smile.

With a curse, Rancid turned back to the alley to find his way blocked by two Black Hand bandits, brazenly displaying the studded gloves of their order. Quickly he took the measure of each. A lithe elven female stood in front, brandishing a sword. Her stance and the way she gripped the hilt betrayed her inexperience. Her companion, an orc-kin mage, was another story. Though there was nothing about his garb or equipment that set him apart as a mage, he made no move toward the club strapped to his belt, and he'd taken refuge behind the novice elf. Was this all the Black Hand had left to send against him? So be it. He would cut down the girl before the mage could so much as tap the weave.

As Rancid's sword cleared its sheath, a crossbow bolt whizzed past his head from a rooftop to his right. A black-haired woman began loading another bolt. Jade!

That bastard of a Black Hand cur, Sorowyn, had set him up.

Crouching, Rancid maneuvered the amateur girl into a position between himself and Jade, but with her size, she provided little cover. The girl parried Rancid's first jab and struck out—a standard maneuver, easily countered. Behind her, the mage began to chant in a dark, guttural tongue. Rancid sidestepped, feigned, and struck. The girl collapsed, sucking desperately to draw a breath into her punctured lung.

Shouts rose from down the street—several distinct voices hollering garbled curses intermixed with Rancid's name—but with two immediate adversaries, he didn't dare look.

He thrust his blade into the mage in mid-weave. When the orc-kin fell, the shouts suddenly died. Suspicious to a fault, Rancid peered down the street.

Nothing. No one. A mere illusion of sound.

Yet the distraction had done its job. A crossbow bolt ripped through Rancid's shoulder and knocked him to the ground. His sword flew from his hand and clattered onto the cobblestone roadway. Pain seared through him. Without daring to rise, or even to lift his head, he scrambled to the base of the building, out of Jade's line of fire. From there, he fled down the alley.

Jade's footfalls pounded on the wooden rooftops in pursuit.

At the far end, the passage opened into a broad roadway. *Baron's blood!* He scanned the street for options. Then, gritting his teeth against the pain, he raced across the opening. Just before he reached the far side, a second bolt shattered his arm and left the limb dangling.

As the awakening community began to populate the streets, Rancid gathered up the material of his cloak, wrapped it around his wound, and dashed into an abandoned warehouse he'd scouted several nights earlier while searching for signs of a Black Hand smuggling cache. Jade would undoubtedly report the deaths of two innocent citizens in the harbor district and would supply Rancid's description to the guardsmen as that of their murderer.

As Whisper swept along the cliffs of the dwarven range toward the flatlands in the heart of Gildstone, the Master contacted him through the medallion. "Every fall, the tribes of Cormont come together in a month-long celebration during which they trade news and goods. But that is not the main reason they gather. They compete to determine the tribe most worthy to steward the Guardian of the Abyss. Learn which tribe won the challenge this year and you'll find the Guardian."

Drakemoor had apparently learned much in Eckland. With a renewed sense of purpose, Whisper doubled his speed, racing toward Cormont to do the Master's bidding. Ka-G'zzin skittered along at his side.

Balor's army survived the defense of Twin Peaks Pass only because he'd positioned his troops as much to facilitate retreat as to defend the pass. Immediately, he began fighting a delaying action south through the foothills along the eastern face of the Sharktooth range.

By the end of the second day, smoke from the town of Twin Peaks poured, thick and black, into the clouded sky. Gremauld would spare nothing in the town, despite the vehement protests Pandalo had endured from the residents when he commandeered the goods Balor had needed for his failed defense of the pass. Gremauld would care only that Balor's supplies had come from there.

Fortunately, no other townships lay between Balor and his destination for Gremauld to plunder.

Now, after a month of retreat, the pretender nipping his heels the whole way, Balor led his haggard army into Stunted Spruce Pass, where three thousand militia joined him.

With the choke point of the pass folding in around him, his men would gain a well-earned respite from the daily rigors of pursuit.

Dalen Frost was there as well.

"Well met," Balor said. "What news?"

"Only the best, my lord. Pandalo and his detachment have arrived at the west end of the pass. The pretender's militia have been disbursed, given leave to return to their homes and families on their parole to refrain from combat until the issue of kingship has been decided."

"Very good. What of Gremauld's troops?"

"When they arrived too late to save the militia, they feared we'd gone on to take the palace." Dalen chuckled. "They returned to the capital while we came south to keep our appointment here with you."

After a pause, Dalen said, "And you?"

"We suffered heavy losses in the pass." Balor breathed a sigh and shook his head. "You disappointed me. You were supposed to turn *all* of Gremauld's troops back toward the capital."

"Gremauld is no fool. He recognized the opportunity we left him when we split our forces." Dalen spread his hands in a gesture of helplessness. "If I'd been more adamant during the king's council, I'd have overstepped my role as informant and Gremauld might have suspected. The best I could do was intercept the runners he sent to warn his militia."

Dalen knelt before his lord and bowed his head. "For this failure, I'll resign my post, if you ask it."

Balor grasped Dalen's shoulders and pulled him to his feet. "Don't be foolish. You know I can't do that. If not for you, we'd all have died at Twin Peaks. How long before the western half of Gremauld's forces arrive to box us in?"

"Weeks, I'd guess. And he'll likely leave a large contingent behind to garrison the palace."

Balor turned his face toward the late afternoon sky. "Come. We must get everyone into the pass by nightfall."

Nick stumbled off the ship in North Reach after seventeen days at sea, anxious for a hot meal and bath. In that order. He led his companions past two inns on the waterfront before stepping into a more respectable-looking place near the center of town.

"Grab a table," the bartender growled. The place was already beginning to fill with the evening's allotment of rabble. "Reeta," the man hollered into the kitchen. "Table."

A moment later, a young serving girl, probably the bartender's daughter, came to take their order.

"Whatever you have that's hot," Nick told her.

"And fresh," Zen added.

"I'm fresh," said someone from behind Nick as the serving girl walked away.

He turned toward the feminine voice, expecting to find a local whore looking to pick up tricks. "Dara! What are you doing here?"

Beltrann stood at her shoulder.

"Well, there's no accounting for haste." The lithe elven guide spun a chair around from an adjacent table. "Didn't I leave you guys in Palidor?" She plopped down and settled her boots—still dusty from the road—onto the table in front of Zen. "What are we drinking?"

"Oh, I'm sorry." Zen sat up hastily and waved down the serving girl. "Let me buy you a drink."

Dara laughed. The sound carried in the crowded taproom, causing several heads to turn their way. "Yes. Why don't you?" When the waitress arrived, she ordered a twisted licorice, spending the last two silver coins in Zen's purse. Then, tossing Zen a brazen wink, she proceeded to buy a round for the rest of the table. "What'd you do, ditch Rancid?"

Zen nodded.

Beltrann dragged up a chair and sat down. Somehow the big man's presence in North Reach didn't seem to bode well.

"Were you successful?" Nick asked. "Did you find the Isles?"

He grunted. "For all the good it'll do."

Zen wrenched his attention from Dara's exquisite face. "You talked to the fairies?"

"Sort of. I talked to Aeriel. She talked to them."

"They're not going to help us." Nick made it a statement, rather than a question.

"No. They've either forsaken or forgotten their duty to protect the civilized races from the ravages of Vexetan."

Vinra leaned forward. "Even against the demons? Didn't Aeron create them specifically to fight the demons?"

"We do not fight the demons. At the moment, there seems no battle to fight at all. Just this looming fear of the Prophecy."

Nick sat back to make room for Reeta to serve heaping plates of meat, mashed turnips, and gravy, steaming with an aroma the likes of which he hadn't smelled since he'd left home. "But they're coming. Did you tell them the demons are coming?"

"I told them everything we believe about the Prophecy. They didn't want to hear it, let alone listen."

"That's it then," Vinra said. "We must pray the Master never finds the Guardian."

The conversation went silent for a time as everyone began to eat.

"How did you find us?" Zen asked between mouthfuls.

"Alamain said you were aboard the *Gale's Darling*, on your way here." Dara shrugged. "I guess there's not much you don't know when you can talk to a god. Beltrann and I have been here for several days, waiting for the ship's arrival."

"And for a commission before you head back into Lorentil," Nick guessed. "Why make the return trip for free?"

"Actually, the church has paid me to accompany you, but Alamain didn't say where you were headed."

Vinra gave Nick a look. After what Rancid had done in Forlorn Valley, maybe they'd be better off without a guide.

"Into Trondor," Zen blurted before Nick could stop him. "The original Codex wasn't in Eckland. We think it's in late King Ednar's personal library."

Dara cocked an eyebrow at Nick. "Word on the street is, the war has moved south, just a day or two from the border. You're not likely to get past it if you're bound for the capital."

"I don't think we need an escort," Nick said. "I know my way around Trondor well enough. And so does Zen."

"I've already accepted the coin," she said. "It would be bad business for me to default on my contract."

"What's the harm?" Zen took Dara's hand. "We can always use a good sword."

"She was commissioned by Alamain herself," Beltrann added. "I'll vouch for that. And she did well for us in Lorentil."

"Then it seems settled," Vinra agreed.

"All right." Nick finished the mead Dara had bought him and thunked the tankard onto the table with a note of finality. "Welcome back. Both of you. We'll leave tomorrow morning. Without the fairies' help, a proper understanding of the true Prophecy has become more important than ever."

CHAPTER 31

Rancid emerged from the warehouse in Eckland two weeks after his run-in with Jade. His wounded arm had begun to heal, but the limb remained useless, bound to his chest as much to keep it out of his way as to immobilize it for healing. With luck, it might one day regain both movement and strength, but for now...

The night was dark. Oil lamps burned at sparse intervals along Cooper Street. A wooden sign nailed to the nearest lamppost proclaimed Rancid to be the murderer of two Eckland citizens. There was no sketch, but the written description was sufficient to condemn him, should he be spotted by an alert citizen. He had to get out of town, but the gates would be too closely watched.

He stuffed his chain of Black Hand trophies into his backpack, pulled his cowl over his face, and walked the length of Harbor Street downstream until the east gate came into view. Then he ducked between the stacks of crated supplies, worked his way in hiding to a shadowed pier, and pilfered an empty cargo pallet.

With this as a makeshift raft, and the moon not yet full, he kicked as far out into the Omensong as his legs would take him before he drifted past the walls into the Palidor wilderness.

The next day, he slept in a shallow gully under a blanket of uprooted sage. It was like old times—Rancid Sevendeath, alone, on the warpath against the mighty Black Hand. But he was through preying on the weak, injured, or careless among them. This time he would take the battle to where they lived.

He circled the city and found a perch that allowed him to view the western gate from a safe distance. Sorowyn had used this gate at least twice in the past month. He would use it again.

The six companions, Dara among them, left North Reach the day after the *Gale's Darling* arrived. On the way out of town, Nick stopped a small party of refugees, a family of four with two overburdened mules. He gave them some water, a silver coin, and a recommendation for the inn where he and his friends had stayed. "What news from Trondor?"

"It's bad," the oldest man among them said. "You don't want to go that way." The stubble on his face was about a week old, and they all smelled like they hadn't bathed in at least that long.

A woman beside him nodded.

"I'm afraid we must," Nick replied. "We have business in the Trondor capital."

The man shook his head. "Whether you plan to go by way of Twin Peaks or Tawneydale, you can't get through on the road. The pretender king has burned both cities to the ground."

"Tawneydale's been destroyed?" Nick's gut twisted, as it had when he'd first seen smoke rising over his house. "My brother and his family live there."

The old man nodded. "Some people may have gotten out."

"Which way did you come down?" Zen asked.

"We're from Twin Peaks. After hearing that Gremauld razed Tawneydale—"

"And let his soldiers rape the women and girls—" the woman added.

"—We had no mind to take chances. When Gremauld overran the heir at Twin Peaks Pass, we fled the city. By nightfall, thick black smoke smothered the air over the town."

"We tried to get through the mountains to Brenden Falls," the woman said, "but all the passes are blocked. If you want to reach the capital, you'll have to travel far to the west."

The man reached out to give Nick back his silver. "We packed little, but we do have coin."

Nick held his hand up to refuse. "You keep it. You've been generous in your speech."

"Where you're going, you'll need it more than we will." He inclined his chin toward North Reach. "Our journey's almost over. Yours has but begun."

"Would that were true." Nick took the coin and returned it to his purse. "Thank you again."

The next day Nick and his company crossed the border into war-torn Trondor. After having heard tale upon tale of Gremauld's atrocities, Nick chose caution over haste. He stayed to the west of the Sharktooth range and kept to the wilderness, planning to skirt the armies and circle wide into Tawneydale. Then he could find out what had happened to his brother before moving on to the capital.

Before long, a cold rain began to fall. The wind drove the mist into them like grains in a sandstorm. It wasn't the deluge they'd endured on the banks of the River Grande, but it slowed their passage for two days, until the clouds lifted enough for them to see the mountains once more. Vinra closed his eyes and let the sunrise bathe his face. "Feels good, doesn't it?"

"It'll be hot by mid-afternoon," Zen added as he joined them. "I prefer the cold. It feels more like home."

After breakfast, they gathered the gear, doused the fire, and moved out over the plain, hoping to reach Tawneydale by week's end. Based on everything they'd heard, they should have good roads from there to the capital. An hour and a half later, though, the bellow of a field horn sounded and several riders topped a ridge to their right. With but a moment's delay, eighteen horsemen charged onto the plain.

"Recognize the banner?" Nick asked.

Vinra nodded. "Baron of Tawneydale."

"Balor Culhaven," Zen added. "The rebel."

Keeping one eye on the riders, Nick continued walking. They had no business with the rebel army. The riders seemed to think otherwise, however. The leader and the standard bearer came to a stop twenty paces in front of Nick. Sixteen others formed a semicircle behind the first two. Their horses seemed fresh.

"Well met, travelers. What's your business in Trondor?" The leader's intelligent eyes surveyed the group with military efficiency. A sand-colored hawk landed on his leather-padded forearm.

"Our business is in the capital," Nick said warily.

"Then it's business of mine. Anyone who seeks the capital in these times, seeks the home of the enemy."

"We're not going to the palace," Vinra said. "We seek the Temple of Robala."

The man grunted. "Be that as it may, I have orders to bring you before the heir."

"Us? Specifically?" Zen asked.

Nick placed a restraining hand on his shoulder.

"Any trespassers of consequence," the rider said. "You're not refugees. You march toward war, rather than away from it. And you're well armed. Come with us."

Nick looked at his companions. Vinra shrugged. The rest stood mute.

"Very well," Nick said finally. They didn't seem to have much of a choice in the matter. "You have spare horses?"

"You'll ride with my men." He waved his hand and six of the riders came forward. Within minutes they were all mounted and galloping toward the Sharktooth range.

As they approached, the plain yielded to hills and the hills to mountains, becoming at times a narrow trail among forested bluffs. By late afternoon, Nick began to see rebel sentries among the steadily roughening terrain. At nightfall, the camp emerged. A plateau dropped away before them and a thousand cooking fires appeared as though they were stars in the sky. The lead rider brought his horse around a boulder patch and began a steep descent down a dozen switchbacks to the valley floor. In the throng of soldiers at the bottom, some of the men wore Balor's insignia. Most had no uniform at all. Many looked up, but none challenged their passage.

"Nicklan Mirrin."

The riders stopped and Nick spun toward the voice. "Marik!" He leapt off the horse and wrapped his brother in a huge embrace. "Blessed Aeron. How are you?"

"Well, for the time being."

"Thank the gods. When I heard what Gremauld did to Tawney-dale..."

Marik spat. "That son of a rabid cur. You don't know the half of it."

Around his brother, Nick saw very few civilians, and no children. "Your family?"

Marik's eyes hardened and he spat again. "Dead."

Nick stepped back and studied his brother's face. "Oh, Marik—"

"All of them. Dead. Gremauld's men killed everybody. Burned everything. They raped the women, the children." He fell to his knees, sobbing. "Ronna."

"They raped Ronna? At only eight harvests?" Nick clenched his fists. It was all he could do to suppress a wail of rage. "That bastard."

Marik sobbed into his hands. "I wasn't there to stop them. I couldn't even kill her to spare her the suffering."

"Where were you?" Nick asked. If Marik had been there, he would have died to defend his family.

"Balor's militia needed hostlers, so I volunteered and came south. Nobody imagined Gremauld would do something like that. I only heard..." He couldn't finish the sentence.

Nick scanned the army around them. So many men there. So many families torn apart. So many homes destroyed and lives lost because of this war. And this was just the prelude.

"I'm sorry for your loss." The lead rider prompted the column into motion. "But we must go. We've delayed too long already."

"I'm sorry." Nick climbed back onto the horse. "We'll talk later."

They threaded their way through Balor's army, which, though quiescent, seemed charged with anticipation, and came to a halt beside a large blue tent with silver trim. "Wait here," the lead rider said. He dismounted and strode inside.

When he returned a few minutes later, he told Nick, "You have leave to enter. As for the rest of you, come with me." He waited for Nick to dismount, then led Zen and the rest of his friends into the darkness.

Nick glanced at the tent guards, suddenly aware of his solitude among an army of strangers. As one, they pulled the tent flaps aside to reveal a richly carpeted interior. Warmth that Nick could feel even from a dozen feet away wafted from the opening. He swallowed once, gathered his courage, and stepped inside.

The smell of incense filled the air. A small fire burned in a pit to his left, the smoke drawn out a vent in the ceiling. A man whom Nick took to be Balor Culhaven sat in a plain, hard-backed chair behind a simple map table with two other men. Around the perimeter stood a half-dozen guards.

"I'm told you travel to the capital," Balor said.

"We seek the temple of Robala."

"You're a shabby liar. Not even Dalen believed that tale."

Nick stared at the heir.

"Sit. Be honest." Balor motioned to a nearby seat. "There's no reason to travel through embattled Trondor for a temple of any divine spirit. You could have gone to any of the Civilized Lands. Why not go to Faldor, or Lorentil?"

Nick held his breath. An attempt to deceive the king, or in this case the rightful heir to the throne, could be cast as treason and cost him his life. Balor, through patience or compassion, had decided to stay the executioner's sword for at least long enough to hear the truth.

What Nick said next would cost him his life or his quest if Balor was not the man Nick assumed him to be. "We're looking for a book rumored to be in the royal library."

"And for this you cross a battlefield? How am I to distinguish one lie from another? For all I know, you are spies for Gremauld."

"The original Prophecies of Mortaan are worth the risk."

"Are they? Your tongue will—"

"Do you know the Last Prophecy of Mortaan?"

Balor gave him a hard look. "I've heard the popular renditions." Though Balor spoke calmly, his eyes hardened around the edges.

"It's coming. And soon."

Balor said nothing.

"This very war is one of the preconditions, along with the current slave riots in Palidor, from whence we've just come. This thing is about to explode and take all the civilized races with it." Nick forced himself to sit. The fatigue of the day's ride, the exhilaration of speaking to the royal heir, the possibility of his own execution—just a gesture away, should Balor wish it—and his certainty of the truth of his statements filled him with a restlessness he could barely contain.

Balor must have heard it in his voice, or maybe he felt it in the air between them. "What would you do if you found this book?"

"Look for a way to stop the Prophecy."

Again, Balor didn't speak.

"For that we need to know the truth of it. It can't be copied accurately. No other book will do."

Balor watched him closely, seeming to study his features, but Nick suspected his thoughts were elsewhere.

"Will you help us?" Nick said finally.

"Perhaps we can help each other."

CHAPTER 32

"Demon!"

Chell looked up from her baby sister, who was playing on the banks of the Gorgon packing cakes of mud and grass, copying the work of the fathers on the guild house.

"Demon!" The call was clear this time.

Chell's brother Tolar, with two harvests beyond her own, leapt to his feet and sprinted up the hill toward the village, eyes wide with fear.

Chell laughed. What a tadpole. Nobody believed in demons. The elders had just made them up in the scattered years to frighten their children into obedience.

Little Leardra's face screwed into a mask of distress. "Ech! Ech!" She stretched her hand toward the fleeing teen.

"It's all right, dear heart. He'll be back. He's just going to check on Daddy."

The baby tried to stand but yet lacked the strength in her legs.

"Ech! Ech!" She crawled a few feet up the hill.

"Demon!" Booms of the tocsin drums echoed from the valley wall, punctuating the warrior's call. Others shouted now. Chell's mother called her name.

When Chell scooped little Leardra into her arms, the baby bawled and kicked her feet, still trying to get to Tolar. She slapped mud from her hands into Chell's face.

What nonsense. Nobody believed in demons... did they?

Her mother cried, "Chell! Come quickly!"

Boomboomboom, boomboomboom. The drums grew louder. More insistent. Others, farther away, joined the chorus.

"Chell!" Her mother ran down the hill. "Lana, Taro, all of you, go to your homes. Quickly."

The children splashed from the water and scattered. Chell climbed to her feet. "What is it?"

"Come." Her mother took the baby, grabbed Chell by the wrist, and dragged her up the hill.

The drums grew deafening. "Is it really a demon, Mama?"

"I don't know. Hurry."

When they topped the rise, the plateau looked like an ants' nest that someone had kicked, people scrambling everywhere. The footfalls of a hundred moccasins joined the drums as every warrior heeded their call.

Boomboomboom, boomboomboom.

Her father ran up. "Get them out of here. Where's Tolar?"

Her mother shook her head and looked beyond him into the turmoil of the village.

"Never mind. I'll find him. Just go." He disappeared into the chaos.

Just then a wave of liquid washed over the nearest tent—Chell's, and that of her family. The fabric began to dissolve. The center pole shattered and a sudden wind whipped the canvas into flight. Shards of clay pottery and stones from the fire pit lay scattered on the ground. Leardra screamed a piercing cry that left Chell's ears ringing.

Towering over Chell, not fifty strides away, stood the... the... what was it? All big and scaly. Shiny black pincers snapped beneath bulbous insect eyes that seemed to see everything at once and yet focused solely on her.

The monster swept a handful of warriors aside with its massive claws. Then it skittered sideways, stepping like a crab yet swift as a spider. It batted away swords and axes that came at it like reeds of thatch at an unfinished roof. Chell's mind reeled in horror, willing her to scream, but her body didn't respond.

Her mother grabbed her arm again and ran.

Still Chell couldn't tear her attention from the monster. Acid burst from its mouth and struck a warrior—she couldn't see who, his back was turned—and the man fell, writhing, to the ground.

Eight warriors thundered into the fray on horseback, Tolar, her brother, among them. They hurled spears into the monster's bony armor. Most glanced harmlessly aside, but Tolar's found a soft spot between the armored plates and sunk deep. The monster reared on its four hind legs and wailed an inhuman cry that froze Chell's heart.

She stumbled as her mother dragged her over a fallen tree. Beyond lay a steep climb up a short hill to where the families were gathering. Chell hurried to the top, then turned again to the battle below.

The riders charged while the warriors mustered at the monster's feet. Chell, too far away to make out faces, recognized her father by his bright red tunic. He was their chieftain. He would make it go away.

Acid struck another rider. His scream of agony carried all the way to the waiting hill and he fell to the ground. Blood stained his dissolving tunic as he struggled to stand.

The demon's eyes swept the battlefield for another target.

Those eyes... A chill crawled up Chell's spine. Could no one escape those demon eyes?

The monster snatched another rider from his horse with its pincerlike jaws and danced away, snapping its claws at the warriors on foot. Her father swung his mighty ax at the armored beast. It staggered. A cheer rose from the throats of the warriors. They rushed forward and, for a moment, it seemed they must defeat it, until it leapt above the crowd, skittered a hundred or more strides to the north, then turned to face the men once more.

"The Idol!" shouted one of the elders, the medicine man.

Half the warriors stopped in mid-stride and turned toward the sacred tent.

The idol?

The tent lay on the ground, smashed as her own tent had been, its contents scattered. An object floated into the air. Chell couldn't see what it was from this distance, but it looked small—no bigger than her own forearm. It rose higher, swept northward on an unseen wind, and vanished.

The demon, nearly forgotten now, worked its way toward the mountain ridge from which it had apparently come. Its eyes shifted wildly as if it sensed a rage building within the stunned warriors but couldn't locate its source. Chell had seen the rage before. And she sensed it too, an almost palpable determination that characterized the men of her tribe and that had made them the champions at the autumn challenge the last three years in a row. If she was the demon, she'd run too—eyes or no eyes.

The rage broke past the throats of the warriors and their collective scream shook the pebbles at Chell's feet. A hundred moccasins and two dozen hooves pounded the ground in pursuit.

The monster reached the base of the cliff and clawed its way up. It was fast—the cliff face no obstacle. At the top, it turned and fixed its eyes on the lead warrior—her father—who'd outpaced even the horses.

Oh no! The eyes.

Her father slowed. His skin became pale and his movements stiff. The warriors swept past him to the base of the mountain and began to climb.

The monster fled.

When Chell looked back at her father, he stood motionless. All of him—his body, his clothes, and even his great ax—had turned gray as stone. He'd become a statue, immortalized in mid-stride. She couldn't get her mind around it. She simply stared at the monument. Her father. The greatest of her people.

Slowly, he toppled forward, rocked gently, and came to rest.

Tolar dropped to his knees beside his father's petrified body, spread his arms to the heavens, and wailed.

Her mother gasped. She too fell to her knees, hugged Leardra tight, and wept.

Within minutes Tolar rallied the warriors and pursued the demon. But it was too fast in the rocky terrain. Even Chell could tell they'd never catch it.

"Mama," she said, "what's an idol?"

ChAPTER 33

ick pulled back the flap and confronted the expectant faces of his friends in the smoky light of the visitors' tent, unable to believe what he'd just agreed to do. He hadn't spoken for the rest of them, of course—they would have to decide for themselves—but Nick had made his commitment, even though it was suicide.

The others seemed to sense his foreboding, or perhaps they read it plainly on his face. None said a word as he passed through the flap and crossed to an empty cot, ignoring a table laden with fresh, roasted fowl and cheap wine.

Dalen, the rider who'd escorted them through camp, followed him in. Nick had thought about talking to his friends alone before asking Balor's scout to join them, but Dalen was part of the bargain and he had information Nick would need to convince the others to go along.

Nick lowered himself to the cot and sat in silence, staring at his feet, while contemplating his next words. Finally, he raked his hands through his hair and looked up at Zen, the one person besides Dalen who might actually agree to this absurdity. "Balor will help us, but he doesn't have access to the royal library. Only Gremauld can grant that privilege."

"Then we'll ask Gremauld," Beltrann said.

Nick didn't even look at him. "Gremauld sits on the throne of Trondor, but according to the rumors, and to Balor himself, Gremauld's kingship is invalid. He achieved it through bribery and deception."

"That's true," Dalen said. "He's not even in the legal line of succession."

"What does the legality of his succession have to do with the Codex?" Jasmine asked.

Nick faced her squarely. "Gremauld stands between us and the library."

"So we ask his leave to use it," Beltrann repeated.

"Balor has offered us an opportunity to help him supplant Gremauld and return the throne to its rightful lineage. By doing so, we'll gain his favor and give him the authority to grant us access to the Codex."

Dara balked. "You want to help him win the war? This war's of no concern to us, and we know nothing of rightful succession."

"Besides," Jasmine said, "if we mire ourselves in the conflict, it will only delay our trip to the capital."

Nick wheeled on her. "This is the quickest route to the Codex. It won't do us any good to reach the capital if we can't get into the library."

Zen set aside the bone of a quail he'd been gnawing on and wiped his hands with a moistened towel. "What does Balor want us to do? He has his own mages. With thousands of men on both sides, what difference can we possibly make?"

"We're strangers here. Gremauld's men wouldn't recognize us, or our association with Balor."

Jasmine raised a hairless eyebrow. "We're to become spies?"

"Not spies, exactly," Nick said.

"Then what?" Anticipation shone in Zen's eyes.

"He wants us to kill Gremauld."

"The king?" Beltrann blurted, half choked by a laugh of incredulity.

Jasmine shook her head. "It can't be done."

"I'm all for adventure," Dara said. "But this is crazy."

Zen was silent, his gaze unfocused, his thoughts turned inward.

"How do we get to him?" Vinra asked.

"I can get you in to see him," Dalen said.

All heads turned toward him.

Balor's scout settled himself on the floor among Nick's companions. "Gremauld believes I'm loyal to him. With a sufficient pretence, I can get you an audience."

"And what then?" Beltrann said. "We walk in and kill him, just like that, and then walk away?"

"Obviously we need to work out some of the details," Nick admitted.

"What does Robala have to say about all this?" Jasmine asked Vinra.

He shrugged. "The church has bade me to join your quest. I believe Nick's right about this being our quickest option. If we refuse, Balor can hold us here indefinitely. Furthermore, ending the war would once again open the passes to travel, for quest and commerce alike."

"Balor must have people more qualified for this sort of task," Jasmine said. "We are not soldiers."

"Balor has many capable warriors," Dalen said. "But they're all known by someone from the other side and may be recognized as rebels. If they're recognized while in my company, then I too will be compromised." He leaned forward and addressed Jasmine with the congeniality of a long-time companion. "You underestimate your abilities. You carry yourself with enviable grace and balance. Though I'm among the elite of the king's Home Guard, I would not wish to face you unarmed." He gestured to Nick and Beltrann. "You've two strong warriors among you. And even I have heard of the ice mage."

Nick glanced at Zen. His friend had grown up in Trondor, but to be known by an officer of the Home Guard...

"With a proper plan," Dalen finished, "you'll have the deed done before Gremauld's men can respond."

Dara held Zen's arm. She looked into his eyes and seemed more awed than frightened by what she saw there. "You plan to do this, don't you?"

"Trondor's my home. If I can help right the throne..."

"Can you supply us with the uniforms of Gremauld's army?" Vinra asked Dalen.

"If we need them, I can slay enough of Gremauld's sentries to provide what we need. But to do so would induce unnecessary risk. If you're recognized as strangers, and the monk certainly will be, the uniforms will only raise suspicions. You gained access to Balor's tent as outsiders. You can do the same with Gremauld's."

"Why don't we just ask Gremauld for access to his library?" Beltrann said again. "He can give us permission where Balor cannot."

Nick unhitched his sword and laid it on the cot beside him. "Balor invited us to do exactly that. He suggested we go to Gremauld with the truth of our quest. And that if he grants permission, we should accept it. Otherwise, Balor's offer stands. If we kill the pretender and give him the authority, he'll grant access."

"Gremauld will say no." Dalen sounded sure. "He has more to worry about than your petty quest, and he won't trust your motives. Furthermore, if he's working for the Master of the Prophecy, he'll have you executed for trying to stop it. If not, he'll at least detain you until the end of the war so your access to his archives can be properly supervised."

"How well do you know Gremauld?" Zen asked.

"Well enough to know his only concerns are self-serving."

"Could you teach me to mimic his gestures and the way he walks?"

Dalen's eyes narrowed and he gave the mage a long, measuring look. "Enough to fool the masses, though probably not his friends."

Nick suppressed a smile. He could always count on Zen, if not the others. "I'm more concerned with the layout of Gremauld's tent—numbers of guards, where they'll be posted—"

"I'll fetch some parchment." Dalen slipped through the opening and disappeared into the darkness beyond.

"We are discussing this as if it has already been decided," Jasmine said. "We have it on the word of one man that Balor is the rightful king. Is that sufficient reason to murder? Even if he is the rightful king, does that make him the one we should support?"

"Did you suggest the assassination?" Beltrann asked. "To avenge your brother's family?"

Nick shook his head. "Balor did. As I understand it, he's held this pass for some weeks. Half of Gremauld's army is trapped on the eastern side. The other half marches down from Trondor. Within the next few days, they'll have Balor penned in and Balor will lose the war."

"That explains his desperation," Beltrann said.

"Let me finish. If Balor took his men through the pass, he could defeat the eastern half of Gremauld's army. Then he could turn and squash the approaching men. That would win the war, but it would kill thousands of his own men and tens of thousands of Gremauld's, all of whom are his countrymen." Nick stood, unable to contain his passion, for it was indeed a great thing Balor was trying to do. "He sits here, day after day, risking defeat, to save the lives of the men fighting against him."

"If we kill this man," Jasmine replied, "even if he is evil, then we take that evil into ourselves. Is the Codex worth betraying our own morals?"

Nick found himself swayed by Rancid's refrain. *All is legal in the fight against evil.* Was it true? He didn't know, but that didn't lessen his conviction now.

"Gremauld is evil," he said. "But even if he wasn't, the war itself is tragic and should be stopped if at all possible. Families, children, will starve or freeze to death because the fields aren't being plowed or harvested, because their burnt homes aren't being rebuilt. Because all the able men in the kingdom are mired here. If killing one man will prevent further battles and thus save thousands of lives, it'll be worth it. I'd sully my soul to see the smile on a child's face when his father comes home safe and sound.

"Doesn't your own creed say, 'Where there is conflict, seek resolution?' This would resolve an enormous conflict." He turned to the others. "Day after day, these people kill their neighbors. Are they evil? Gremauld and Balor may be more evil or selfish than the common soldier, but according to everyone we've talked to, from North Reach to here, Gremauld had the Ruling Council vote on the kingship before Balor—the legal heir—had even heard of King Ednar's death." His voice cracked as he tried to hold back the flood of emotions that filled him. "My god, can't you see why Balor came to the capital with an army behind him? The question of who assassinated Ednar must have been high in his mind, especially after seeing the rapid rise of Gremauld. I don't think Balor expected this to degenerate into a full-on civil war. And now he's trying to stop it with a minimum loss of life. He could surrender, but what would happen to the people who've supported him?

"In war," Nick continued, "you either choose a side or stay out of it all together. The Codex is in the capital with three separate armies between us and it. We can't stay out of it. Besides, to go after the book and ignore all of this is just wrong." He drew a line in the dirt floor with the tip of his sword. "I've chosen my side." His voice rose to an impassioned crescendo. "Because it's the right thing to do."

Without hesitation, Zen stepped across the line to join him.

Vinra stood and strode up beside them. "I too believe Balor is the rightful heir. Whichever path puts him on the throne with the least amount of bloodshed is the right one. And as dangerous as it is, this *is* the quickest path to the Codex."

Jasmine crossed the line as well. "We need no reminder beyond the deaths of the librarians that time pursues us."

Dara drew her sword. Tendrils of lightning licked the blade. "What is life, if not an adventure? I'm in." She stepped over the line.

Only Beltrann remained.

"Doubts?" Nick asked him.

"Many." He rose to stand with Nick. "But we began this together."

"Whether or not Balor is the rightful king," Nick said, "or whether he'll be a good king, only history will remember. Yet with this single act, we give Trondor a fighting chance for a future."

Dalen stepped in through the flap and spread a large sheet of parchment on the table. He drew an octagon in its center with a sharpened piece of charcoal. "This is Gremauld's tent. It's located in the center of his camp, in the hilly region just beyond the mountains." He sketched the geography of the region. "We'll be safe in the pass. Balor retains a garrison at the far end. Beyond that, we'll rely on my reputation to reach the tent and gain entry.

"Once inside, you'll find Gremauld, likely one or more advisors, and his honor guard of twenty swordsmen."

"How good are they?" Dara asked.

"Most have more glitter than grit, but you'll be wise not to underestimate them." He drew the furnishings and began to mark the locations of the soldiers.

"How much is passage back to Eckland?" Jasmine asked as she watched the forces grow.

Dara glanced at Nick. "Twenty men are too many."

"We're only going there to kill one," Zen reminded her.

Nick's eyes never left the map. "And we shall kill only one."

"If you're successful," Dalen continued, "you'll be fugitives until Balor can assume the throne and pardon you. You can avoid this by leaving no survivors or credible witnesses, but the mage is right. You must kill Gremauld and flee as quickly as possible. I'll create a diversion, if I can, to cover your escape."

Nick's forehead creased. "You won't be with us?"

"I'll enter the tent briefly when we arrive, but I'll not go in with you. If I did, I'd have to fight against you or reveal my true allegiance. I'm not willing to do either."

Nick swallowed hard and glanced at his friends, fearful that they'd change their minds.

"Remember," Dalen said. "Once Gremauld is gone, you'll make your request to the Ruling Council, some of whom are among Gremauld's advisors. If any are in the tent at the time, you must kill them as well or they'll identify you later."

"How will we know?" Zen asked.

"I'll tell you just before you go inside." He spread his arms. "That's the best I can do. If there are no council members who can dispute me, I'll vouch for your innocence, should the need arise."

Dara spoke tentatively into the silence that followed. "If we kill your king, won't the second-in-command take his place?"

"Perhaps, but he'll lose the support of the army. A few men among his advisors are fiercely loyal to Gremauld. But the soldiers who fight for him are loyal only to the throne. Most despise the man, especially after what he did to Tawneydale and Twin Peaks. They'll not give their allegiance to a man who's not their king. Within a few days, the soldiers will head back toward the capital."

Nick stared at the map. "We'll need supplies."

"And coin," Dara said.

"And magic," Zen added.

"Balor has authorized anything you need." Dalen gestured to Zen. "We're gathering our battle mages. They'll have tonight to create any enchanted scrolls you may require. But we leave at first light. Nightfall is the best time to act and it'll take the day to traverse the pass."

"Remember," Nick said as Dalen reached the doorway, "non-lethal enchantments against everyone but Gremauld."

"I'm late for my prayers," Vinra said as he followed Dalen out.

The tent descended into silence. Only then did Nick acknowledge the food on the table, amid the leavings of the others, who'd quenched their hunger during his meeting with Balor. Still, he couldn't bring himself to eat.

CHAPTER 34

T he plan was sound, Zen told himself over and over as the party snaked its way through the narrow passage of the Stunted Spruce. Zen would present Balor's battle plans. Then they'd immobilize Gremauld, stupefy the guards in clumps—if Nick and his friends could stay out of the way of the weave—and Zen would do what had to be done.

Yes, the plan was sound. Except for one thing.

"If Dalen is working for Gremauld, he'll betray us before we ever get inside," Jasmine had said.

True, but Zen wasn't worried about that. Not that Dalen wouldn't do it. He might. But at that moment, an entirely different problem consumed Zen's thoughts.

Twenty guards. With Gremauld and his staff, Nick and his friends would be outnumbered nearly four to one. And the fools insisted on using non-lethal tactics.

Together, they carried more enchanted scrolls than they could use: hypnosis, morph, and of course, the moonglyph. If they couldn't do the job and escape within about a minute, they'd all die no matter what means they used. And the placement of everyone within the tent would be as critical as the timing. But they had it all worked out. The plan was sound.

Unless Gremauld was one of the Chosen.

Gwyndarren's warning echoed across the thousand miles from Palidor. *You can't imagine the strength of the forces that oppose you.* Zen had thought he'd understood. The Master and twelve powerful minions of darkness arrayed against the pitiful strength of Nick's company. The prospect was daunting. But Zen grew stronger every day, and soon he might be strong enough.

But an army? Did the Master command an army already? Gremauld's army? Gwyndarren was right. The enemy forces were overwhelming. They might be able to kill the king, but they couldn't fight the entire army.

Therefore, Nick's plan counted on surprise. If Gremauld found out they were coming—and he might know already—it'd all be over before it began.

Where would that leave Zen? On one side or the other, of course. But which one? If Gremauld was a Chosen, Zen had promised not to take action against him. His friends would stand alone against twenty enemy warriors. Zen would betray Nick, his best friend. Or he'd betray Gwyndarren, his steadiest source of power. There was no telling what recourses the mysterious elf might bring to bear if Zen broke Gwyndarren's trust. And Zen wasn't ready to find out.

On the other hand, to betray Nick would be to murder him. The plan would crumble, and Nick would die.

There must be a way out—something that would save him, his friends, and the Chosen—if only Zen was clever enough to find it.

Nick and his friends waited while Dalen conversed quietly with General Pandalo Gundahar, the man in charge of the rebel garrison defending the eastern entry to Stunted Spruce Pass.

When the scout returned, he spoke a few instructions to his hawk, released her into the air, and then turned to Nick. "Not a word until we reach the tent."

They dismounted and walked their horses for several miles as Dalen led them into the rocky woods that hemmed the pass. Dense conifers hid their movements, Nick hoped, from Gremauld's patrols. It was dusk by the time they skirted the sentries on the northern side of the king's army, where Dalen stopped to don his Home Guard uniform. That done, he put one finger briefly to his lips and led them in.

Within minutes, a sentry challenged them. But the guard backed down when he saw who approached. "I'm sorry, sir. It's just—"

"Say nothing more," Dalen replied. "I'd have taken your head if you hadn't challenged. Stay alert, the rebels are close."

"Yes, sir." The sentry faded back into the shadows.

The party threaded its way, single-file, through the waiting army as it went about its evening chores. Cooking fires blanketed the valley, one every fifty feet as far as Nick could see. Zen had changed his features. Nick would have gladly done the same. The shadow of Jasmine's cowl concealed her face. Her horse's reins disappeared into one of the voluminous sleeves that hid her clawed hands.

Then a staunch man with a week's beard and well-used plate armor stopped the procession. "Any word of the others?" he asked Dalen.

Another man nearby looked up from his chores and met Nick's gaze. His eyes ran the length of Nick's body, then narrowed. He looked once at Dalen, then peered at each of Nick's companions.

"They're but four days out," Dalen told the armored stranger in a reassuring tone. "It won't be long now."

The other man, the one by the cooking fire, adjusted his grip on his utility knife and lit a torch in the fire. "You!" He waved the brand at Jasmine and strode purposefully forward.

Nick searched his mind for options. He could stop the man, if he must, but not without causing a scene at least as damaging as the one he would prevent.

"Come," Dalen hollered back. "The king awaits." He spurred his horse into a canter. Nick and the others hurried to keep up, leaving the suspicious cook to draw his own conclusions.

A few minutes later, they reached a clearing. Gremauld's octagonal tent, thirty feet on a side, sat in the middle of the untenanted void. Only two guards now separated them from their mark. Two guards, and whoever was stationed inside. Dalen slowed to a walk and led them halfway across the gap before bringing the whole procession to a halt. "Wait here." He dismounted, and with a nod to the guards, vanished inside.

The scout would tell Gremauld one of two things. He'd say Nick and his friends were mercenaries who'd waylaid one of Balor's messengers and stolen the rebels' battle plans, which they'd now offer to the king in exchange for his favor. Or he'd tell Gremauld of the assassination plot.

If he did the latter, Nick and his friends were finished. Dalen would return to Balor and claim that they'd failed, and Balor would be none the wiser.

Nick glanced at the guards, then back the way they'd come. They'd penetrated at least a mile inside Gremauld's camp, with many hundreds of loyal soldiers to pass before reaching any semblance of safety. And the enemy was thickest at the mouth of the pass, near their designated rendezvous point.

The hair on the back of Nick's neck stood on end. What was keeping Dalen?

Finally, the scout emerged. There was no shout of alarm or rushing of the guards. Yet Dalen approached with a look of concern. "Only one of you may enter. I'm sorry."

One of us? Dalen might as well have given up the plot. One couldn't possibly succeed.

"I'll go." Zen climbed down from his horse.

It made sense: if any of them could do it alone, it was Zen. And he had the document. But Nick wouldn't let his friend make the sacrifice. He dismounted, along with the others. It had been his decision to do this. None of his friends had wanted to come. He'd talked them into it. If Nick went in alone, maybe he could get one well-placed sword-stroke before he died. And if Zen remained here, the others might escape. "Give me the orders. I'll go."

"It's better if I do it." Zen gave him a meaningful look.

"On my open grave, you will," Vinra said. "You'll not get the king's favor alone. *I'll* take it in."

Nick caught on to his ploy. *Brilliant.* "Why? So you can take it for yourself? I'm the one who killed the messenger. I'm entitled—"

"Come now, you'll all get your share of the credit." Zen took two strides toward the tent.

Then Beltrann stepped into his way. "We go in together, or not at all. No other way is fair to the rest of us."

"What does it matter? We'll share any reward. It makes no difference who hands him the document." Zen began to walk around him.

Suddenly, Beltrann's fist slammed Zen's face and decked the mage. He winked at Nick. "I've always wanted to do that."

Nick shot the big man a disgusted look and knelt beside his friend, who rolled over and climbed to his knees, blood streaming from his nose.

"I'll kill him." Zen reached for his staff and the parchment.

"Hold!" King Gremauld stood in the opening of the tent. "What is this?"

"It seems they can't agree on who will present the orders," Dalen said. "They feel it's not fair to the others if one gains your favor alone."

Zen climbed to his feet.

"Fine." Gremauld turned to one of his guards. "Kill them and bring the parchment to me."

Zen stepped forward, holding the document. "With a single word, this will go up in a handful of smoke and ashes."

Gremauld stared at him for several seconds. "Very well. But my favor will be less than it might have been otherwise." He turned to Dalen. "They may enter."

Dalen bowed low and returned to the party.

"You must keep your weapons sheathed. If you reach for them or make any sudden movements, the guards have orders to kill." Dalen fixed his eyes on Zen. "Any hand gestures that are interpreted as weaving will induce the same result."

He gave them each a hard stare, then turned to Jasmine. "Out of respect for the king, you must all lower your hoods. Walk to the center of the tent, before the table. Drop to one knee and bow your heads. Remain there until the guards permit you to rise. Do not approach the king, advisors, or guards."

His voice dropped to a whisper. "Two of the Ruling Council are present. You'll recognize them by the embroidered emblem on each of their shoulders. Good luck."

Without waiting for a reply, Dalen led the horses away into the darkening camp.

Zen wiped his sleeve across his face and it came away dark with blood. For just a moment, he thought he'd found a way out. Whether Gremauld was a Chosen or not, Zen could pass off the orders, claim it was too risky to attempt the assassination, and the whole lot of them could be on their way. With Gremauld's favor, they could pass freely through his army. Zen might even be able to gain permission to use the library, especially if Gwyndarren's connections with the Master made Zen known to the king. But only if he entered alone.

He gave Beltrann a sour look and wiped his nose again. Now he was right back where he'd started. And his nose was probably broken.

Slowly, Zen made his way to the tent, his mind working once again to devise a solution. Betray his friends? Betray Gwyndarren? Not if he could help it.

He passed the threshold and surveyed the guards inside, one every twelve feet along the perimeter. They stood at attention, armed in ornate chainmail and jeweled swords. Blessed Aeron, there wasn't a chance. Gwyndarren was right. They were too many.

A heavy map table, easily fifteen feet long and six feet wide, dominated the back half of the tent, just beyond the clear area designated for visitors. Behind it stood Gremauld and his advisors.

Zen scanned them for any sign that one was a Chosen. It didn't have to be Gremauld. If Zen was lucky, it would be one of the advisors. He'd made no promise not to attack a friend of the Chosen—only the Chosen himself. But none of the men wore a medallion or sinew headband that he could see. They didn't make any kind of signal or gesture that might give them away as a Chosen. Their exposed hands and faces showed no incriminating tattoo, though Zen didn't know what such a mark might look like. He even checked for a streak of white hair among the men.

He walked forward until he reached the table's edge, pushing the boundary of where Dalen had instructed them to stand. For the sake of the plan, they'd need as much space around them as possible. Then he knelt and waited.

Gwyndarren had said Zen would know the Chosen when he faced him. Though it was early, he'd seen no signs. The document in his hand provided some minor comfort. He'd be asked to stand before presenting it to Gremauld. Then he could take one last look before making his decision.

Focused wholly on this dilemma, Zen missed the king's word to stand. Rather, he came to his feet when his friends rose around him. Maybe this wasn't the meeting Gwyndarren had alluded to. Seeing no enlightening signs or signals, Zen took a deep breath and presented the parchment to the king.

Gremauld examined the document carefully before opening it. Though the seal had been broken, Gremauld would recognize it as Balor's. And the orders inside had been written in the heir's own hand, just in case Gremauld could recognize the script. In all respects but two, the document was authentic.

Zen scrutinized Gremauld with the same attention the king gave the document. Then he saw it. Around the pretender's neck, a small bit of chain hung down inside the king's chest plate. But Zen couldn't actually see the medallion. He had no proof.

Gremauld opened the parchment and began to read. The battle plans were, of course, fake, but there was something else too. There was the moonglyph.

Zen adjusted his grip on his staff. To the Abyss with Gwyndarren. Without proof, Zen could always claim he hadn't known.

Nick entered Gremauld's tent just to Zen's left. He located their prey—the pretender king and his council flunkies—and noted the positions of the guards. The weight of his sword pulled at his belt. If all went well, he'd never have to use it. But if he must, he'd use only the flat of the blade. He'd kill no one today but those he must in order to stop the war. True to Dalen's word, everything stood exactly where it should be, right down to the furniture. Everything that is, except for Beltrann.

Balor's mages had been very specific in their instructions for activating the scrolls. And the hypnotic effects were such that they must all stand in the exact center of the tent in order to avoid falling prey to their own enchantments. Beltrann had moved too far to the right.

Worse, his and Dara's hands were empty. They were supposed to have enchanted scrolls in their hands, disguised as additional rebel documents. Once the moonglyph was activated, they'd have but a fraction of a second to immobilize the guards. Beltrann had to disable those on the right and Dara the ones on the left. With both unprepared and Beltrann out of position, the guards would escape long enough to join the fray. Then it'd be too late.

As Gremauld opened the parchment Nick wanted to scream at Beltrann and Dara, but even a whisper at this point would give them away. He could do nothing now, except what they'd come here to do.

When Gremauld's eyes swept over the moonglyph that Balor's mages had enchanted the document with, his body shuddered almost imperceptibly, his eyes froze, and his skin turned the milky color of moonlight. His body went as still as the moon in the night sky.

In that instant, Zen spoke a low murmur and his staff erupted in a blast of cold air that slammed into the king, his advisors, and the guards behind them. All but Gremauld staggered. A frozen mist coated their hair and beards. One advisor went down.

The temperature in the tent plummeted. Nick's knuckles ached with cold as he whipped his sword from its sheath.

As he'd feared, Dara and Beltrann reacted too slowly. By the time they pulled the scrolls from wherever they'd hidden them and began their clumsy incantations, the guards were already in motion.

Vinra, too, had apparently seen the blunder. He spun to face the soldiers behind them, sword in hand. When he launched himself at them, Nick winced again. The priest had agreed to stay out of the fighting, to remain in the protected center and pray to his god for deliverance and for the healing of those in need. Now he too had encroached upon the designated enchantment zone.

Shouts erupted from somewhere outside, but distant, somewhere to the west—Dalen's diversion.

Orc's blood. The plan was in shambles. The guards to the right drew their swords and rushed at Dara and Beltrann. Those behind engaged Vinra. One of the men by the door slipped outside with an alarm on his lips. The men behind Gremauld had been caught in the throes of Zen's staff. But those on the left, three of them, closed unchallenged. Nick broke and ran, bull-rushing the guards all the way back to the tent wall. Suddenly, he couldn't remember why he'd agreed to do this.

CHAPTER 35

With the space Gremauld had cleared around his command tent, the nearest of the regular soldiers had been camped at least a hundred yards distant, and they might already be moving away toward Dalen's diversion. Still, Jasmine and the rest of the party had maybe thirty seconds to get this done and get out.

She spun in tandem with Vinra to hold off the guards behind them—six men—too many to delay for long, yet perhaps the two of them could give Zen that thirty seconds.

The guards charged. Vinra parried once, and then a glancing blow soaked his sleeve with his own blood. He locked swords with his assailant, grabbed the man's wrist, twisted him off balance, and threw him into the swing of another's sword.

A globe of red light filled the space in front of Jasmine. Dots of light sparkled within it like embers popping in a cooking fire, getting brighter, and soon becoming a brilliant, blinding white. Inside it, four guards gazed in wonder at the spectacle, their swords forgotten in their fascination of the weave.

Jasmine wrenched her gaze away from the mesmerizing display before it reached its full intensity. With that quarter covered, she sought another target. A badger of ice rushed at a guard in a corner near Beltrann, who tossed his spent hypnosis scroll aside. Another blast of cold swept Gremauld, who remained paralyzed by the moonglyph. Thick layers of ice coated his hair and clothing. A guard and the two councilmen crumpled in the blast, their dead eyes staring from frozen faces.

Dara gave up on her scroll. She had no safe place to invoke its enchantment in the mayhem. Guards pressed her and Vinra, but Nick looked desperate, off balance and bleeding from at least two wounds.

Jasmine whipped a throwing star from her belt and hurled it at one of Nick's opponents. It bounced harmlessly off the guard's mail, but it distracted him long enough for Nick to fall back a step and regain his footing.

One guard lay dead at Vinra's feet. The priest cried out as a sword struck him across his side. He staggered backward and fell to his knees. Jasmine lunged in front of him to prevent the guard from following through with the kill, though she probably should have let him. From the looks of his wound, the job was already done. It would only take longer for Vinra to die this way.

Lightning shot down Dara's blade and ripped through one of the guards. Three down.

Jasmine ducked an incoming sword stroke and kicked her own opponent in the gut. He doubled over, but she had no time to finish him. There were too many.

What was keeping Zen?

She glanced over her shoulder in time to see two of the guards pull Gremauld to relative safety beneath the map table. A third leapt onto the top of it to challenge Zen. For a moment, it looked as though they'd saved the pretender, but Zen inverted his staff and spoke the incantation again. A wave of frost washed over Gremauld at point-blank range, but the move left Zen defenseless. The guard on the table ran him through with a sword.

A painful gash tore across Jasmine side as she rushed to engage Zen's killer.

Vinra struggled toward the table as well. With his wound half-healed and an empty elixir bottle at his feet, he scrambled to save Zen as though he'd suddenly remembered his role in the original plan.

Dara, her sword whipping and flashing, fell back before the press of guards.

As soon as Jasmine and Dara moved away, Beltrann swept his globe of sparkling lights across the back of the tent to the other side, catching several more guards in its enchantment. Those the globe had left behind began to recover, but only slowly, staggering into motion, their eyes blinking. The men looked around uncertainly, as though trying to remember where they were.

Shouts reached Jasmine from outside, close now. Angry. And the clamor of armor and weapons. She leapt onto the table and grappled with the soldier there. He proved strong and ready. Immediately, he pulled her off balance, then struck her skull with the pommel of his sword. Jasmine reeled, the ice badger shattered, Nick cried in agony, and the remainder of Gremauld's guard rushed forward.

A sword ripped through Nick's side. He'd long since given up on the flat of his blade, but that didn't matter. Three skilled soldiers were too many. And more were on the way. Shouts from outside told him Gremauld's army would soon flood the tent. Even if he never made it out, at least he could finish what he came here to do.

The cold from Zen's staff may have already killed Gremauld, but Nick had to be sure. Turning his back on the soldiers, he dove for the table and the phony king beneath it. The enemy blade struck again. It came down on his back and ripped through his armor, slicing muscle, bone, and lung. When it hit Nick's breastplate, it forced him to the ground ten feet short of his target. Breathing became impossible. He spat a spray of blood and in that instant, he knew the blow had killed him. He felt it in his very soul.

But he felt something else too—a strange sensation of beastly rage and survival instinct. A warmth spread from his shoulder as a wave of magic pulsed through him. Feathers and fur, hooves and talons, became his as the weave remade his tissues—rent or whole—into something else, something inhuman. In that instant he was transformed.

He became a hippogriff.

As the sensation passed, his consciousness remained. His body ached where the sword had ripped through it, but the damage had partially healed in his remaking.

Dara pulled her hand from his shoulder and dropped a scroll to the ground, its morphing magic spent. "Let's get out of here."

Nick glanced about for his sword. It was gone, reformed with his body, clothing, and supplies. Guards from the tent perimeter rushed the floundering would-be assassins. Footsteps pounded the ground outside.

Zen stared at him, at first uncomprehending, and then the mage's eyes began to focus. He lay in a pool of his own blood, his enchanted disguise gone. But Vinra knelt over him with the satisfied look of a boy who has bested his older brother at the flip-chip table.

From somewhere in his robes, Zen produced a small silver bottle. He pulled the stopper and a fine gray vapor spewed forth. In seconds, Nick could see nothing beyond arm's length.

He crawled under the table, grabbed Gremauld with his mighty beak, and stood, throwing the table aside as he did. A guard cried out in surprise and came down with a thud somewhere in the mist. Jasmine landed lightly beside Nick.

She and Dara leapt onto his back. Pain from the reminder of his wounds stabbed through his entire body. With a muffled squawk past Gremauld's paralyzed form, Nick turned to flee.

He stopped. The fog was too dense, his bearings confused.

Which way was out? Shouts of anger and oaths of bewilderment sounded from everywhere around him. The tent wall couldn't be more than ten yards away in any direction. Still, he was lost. He groped his way forward for an eternity and stumbled, at last, into the wall.

The canvas ripped before him, sliced by a blade from above, and Nick forced his way through. Scores of soldiers rushed the tent, the first wave entering even now. He glanced back at his two riders, then launched himself into the air on his powerful new wings.

He climbed as quickly as he could. Arrows whizzed by him in his first few seconds of flight, then died away as he lost himself in the pitch of the night.

When he reached a safe altitude, he turned back to look for the others, Zen, Vinra, and Beltrann. They should have been right behind him. He circled for a minute more. Warriors came out of the tent now. The drama inside had apparently played itself out. Still, his friends were nowhere.

He moved the pretender from his beak to his talons, circled once, and released a piercing cry into the night.

"**M**ake way, make way!" Dalen shouted as he pressed through the milling soldiers. "Out of my way!"

He reached the mouth of the tent and pushed the guards aside. The smoke vent in the ceiling had been opened and the fog had cleared. Four guards lay slain, and three of Gremauld's advisors. He checked the bodies again. Nick Mirrin and his friends were not among them.

"Where's the king?" he asked one of the guards, who sat on a barrel just outside the opening with his head in his hands.

The man didn't meet his eyes. He merely shook his head and put it back into his hands.

Dalen gazed into the tent and scratched his head. Where was the proof? Balor would require proof.

As if in answer, a heavy weight fell from the sky. The tent collapsed with the impact, snapping several support timbers with a mighty crack and throwing up a rush of air and a cloud of dust. When Dalen looked again, the shattered body of Gremauld lay broken and twisted before him, his frozen gaze staring from the ruins of the collapsed tent, as if to accuse him of murder.

CHAPTER 36

Τhe innkeeper in North Reach pocketed the coin Gwyndarren
had given him. "Yeah, she was here. An odd looking one,
that. What is she? Goblin-kin?"

"Demon-kin."

The innkeeper recoiled. "Yeesh. I don't even want to know who'd
mate with one of those. Anyway, she's not here. The whole lot of them
went into Trondor, I think."

"I already know that much." Gwyndarren grumbled, his attitude
tweaked by the chafing of his backside. He'd hardly been out of the
saddle for a month and he still hadn't caught up to Zen and his friends.
"Did that disfigured monk have a mage with her, an elf-kin in shimmering gray robes?"

"Yeah. Him and some others."

"How long ago did they leave?"

"Let's see now..." The old man scratched his head for an interminable period.

Come on, come on. I haven't got all day. It was all Gwyndarren could do to keep from grabbing the man and shaking the information out of him.

"A couple of weeks, I'd say."

Gwyndarren ran out of the tavern, climbed onto his horse and eased his worn thighs into the seat. Two weeks! By the Master's grace, Zen might have found the book already. And if the mage left Trondor before Gwyndarren caught up, he might never see him again.

On the other hand, Trondor was a big place. Maybe Zen hadn't met the Chosen yet. Maybe it wasn't too late after all.

A s Nick approached the mouth of the Stunted Spruce, the sounds of battle drifted up from below. Pandalo had pressed a spearhead attack into the unprepared Trondorian camp—Dalen's diversion. The bulk of Gremauld's troops scrambled to respond, shoring up the front with hasty formations of unarmored troops, wielding whatever instrument of death they could reach.

Pandalo fought at the forefront of the battle, his sword flaming like a signal fire. But he had only a few hundred men, and Gremauld's defenses stiffened quickly.

Nick passed over him and let out an ear-splitting screech. The job was done. Pandalo could pull his troops back.

Nick turned, swept over the hills, and sought a campfire deep in the woods, where it could be spotted only from the air. There! The rendezvous. And not a moment too soon. The enchantment's weakening, the ache of Nick's body, and the turmoil in his soul sapped what little strength he had left.

He landed heavily beside the soldier who waited near the fire. The spare horses whinnied and pulled nervously at their tethers as Nick shook off his riders. His legs collapsed and he sprawled on his side. Quick breaths stirred the dirt beneath his nostrils and one talon clawed weakly at the ground. Nick clung to his animal form, unsure whether he could survive the reverse transformation without the aid of their healer. Maybe Vinra would arrive in time.

Then, with a clop of hooves and a screech of pride, another hippogriff alighted nearby.

"How about that?" Zen climbed from the back of the beast with Beltrann at his side. "Six for six. I wouldn't have thought it possible."

Nick's animal form slipped away. His head felt light, and the taste of dirt filled his mouth. He spat twice, pushed himself to a seated position, and inspected his beaten body. Vinra crawled up beside him and helped to remove his mangled armor. Nick's clothes were soaked with the blood of several wounds that still seeped. Each breath produced a piercing pain like a dagger in his lung. An invisible hand seemed to twist the blade whenever he inhaled. Yet he was alive.

Vinra handed him a vial of clear syrup. "Drink up. It's my last one. After what we've done, I'll pray for many months before I regain Robala's favor and the gift to make more."

Nick drank and the pain in his chest eased to a hot, searing agony. He stood, testing his legs and balance, then nodded. The others looked about as well off as he. Zen's robes were torn from shoulder to midchest and soiled with a deep red stain. Vinra also bore the mark of his brush with death. Jasmine and the others looked weary and blooded, but grateful to have survived.

"It is done?" asked Balor's soldier.

Nick nodded.

"Then we must ride to clear the mountains by morning. General Gundahar will hold the pass if the enemy attacks tonight."

The following night, Dalen arrived in Balor's camp with confirmation of Gremauld's death. He handed Nick a purse full of coin for the bribes and supplies they'd need in order to reach the capital city through territory occupied by Gremauld's army.

Nick, his mane of blond hair now shaved to the bare scalp in an attempt to hide his identity, gave most of the coin to Zen in repayment of their passage to North Reach. The rest he distributed among the group. Dalen also supplied them with enough field rations for their journey and Nick with a replacement suit of plate armor.

"It'll be best if you make your request of the council before news of Gremauld's death reaches them," Dalen said. "We'll leave in the morning."

In the morning? None of them was in any condition to travel. "Can the council grant us access to the library?" Nick asked.

"No. They have the authority of governance in the king's absence, but the library is private. It belongs to the king, not to the people."

"Then why—"

"News of Gremauld's death will travel swiftly. If you come under suspicion, then your arrival before the news will weigh heavily in your favor. Do you have any further business here?"

Nick nodded solemnly. "I've not had time to inform my brother of our mother's death."

"Do it tonight, and without a word about yesterday. We ride at dawn."

The next day, Dalen donned his Home Guard trappings and escorted Nick's party through the contingent of the king's royal army that was bound for the Stunted Spruce from the capital. To them he said nothing of Gremauld's death. Once past, he switched uniforms again before riding into Tawneydale, where the surviving villagers held no love for the pretend king.

When they arrived, Nick couldn't believe his eyes. The whole town was gone, or nearly so. Anything that would burn had been reduced to a pile of ash. The few residents who'd refused to flee to Faldor watched the companions ride by with expressions that ranged from resignation to despair.

Nick took the time to find his brother's house and livery. Both had been reduced to their foundation stones. If the bodies of his relatives had been there, someone had removed them.

Speech felt awkward in the somber silence and Nick said nothing until they were on their way out of town. There, a girl of maybe thirteen harvests stood by the road with two small children in hand.

Nick stopped beside her. "Where're your parents?"

The girl glanced about until she spotted Balor's crest on Dalen's uniform. She returned her gaze to her feet. "Our father fights with Balor."

"And your mother?"

The girl looked up. A fierce defiance flared in her eyes. "She tried to stop those murderous bastards from burning our house."

"I'm sorry." It was all Nick could say. He looked back at the ash-covered village. "My brother lived here with his family." He sat in silence for maybe a minute, lost in his own thoughts—seeing the ruins of his own farmhouse and the charred corpse of his mother as though they lay before him.

Without a word, he emptied a few coins from his purse into her hand, then spurred his horse into motion.

"Why would Gremauld do this?" he asked Dalen after they left the girl.

"Tawneydale was the seat of Balor's power."

"And Twin Peaks?"

Dalen shrugged. "That's who he is... was."

Nick shook his head solemnly. The needs of these people were beyond any of them to heal. Nevertheless, they helped where they could, and by the time they left the township behind, little coin remained among them. Except for maybe Zen, who might once again be called upon to provide for the party.

They traveled north until they were just beyond sight from the capital city's walls. There, Dalen brought them to a stop, wearing again the uniform of the Home Guard. "I recommend the Hostler House. I'll give you two days to meet with the council before I bring the news."

With that, Nick and his friends rode at last into the capital city of Trondor, a city of high battlements and stone buildings. A city built for war, dominated by the enormous palace of the late King Gremauld.

Jasmine remained at the inn to hide her features from those who might later recognize her description. Nick and the others proceeded to the palace.

"You must wait for the king's return," said the head councilman, a bookish-looking man with a glass monocle. Only two other council seats were occupied.

"When might that be?" Nick asked.

"When the war is over, I'd imagine. Next."

And that was the sum of his first audience with the Ruling Council.

Their wait wasn't long, however, and when rumors of Gremauld's death began to circulate, Nick returned to repeat his request.

Day after day, Rancid watched, subsisting on rations and supplies he'd accumulated during his night forays into the streets of Eckland, taking anything his need justified.

Eight days into his vigil, Sorowyn appeared. As he had last time, the bandit escorted a company of orc warriors, who rode up river in the dark of the early morning, hooves pounding the trail as if to separate themselves from the township as quickly as possible.

The outlaws thundered past Rancid's concealment, a location he'd chosen for its proximity to the trail and a mud flat through which the horses shoes would leave distinct and detailed prints. At first light, he inspected the tracks of his quarry. At least three of the seven horses carried the same stamp of craftsmanship on their shoes, the stamp of a smith in Forlorn Valley—an uncommon stamp this far east. One of the prints revealed a bent nail in the horse's shoe, hammered flat by the smith who'd installed it or by the miles of road the horse had traveled since. Another had a chipped hoof, long since healed. Rancid smiled. With so much to go on, the tracks wouldn't be hard to follow.

Over the next several days, he trailed the bandits on a stolen horse to a rendezvous that the riders had made near the bend in the Omensong, at which point Sorowyn, the lightest of the original seven, had circled back toward Eckland. The orcs continued west with a new contingent of riders.

Intent on the bandits' lair, Rancid followed the orcs. Day by day, he drew closer to his father's valley, but the tracking had slowed him down. By the time he passed the township of Noble, he'd fallen at least two days behind.

His wounded arm, though still useless and strapped to his chest with a sling, had ceased to cause him pain.

The tracks skirted the southern tip of Forlorn Valley and snaked their way into a forest-choked hill country, where trees pushed their way up through a gravel-strewn landscape that made tracking difficult. Rancid dismounted and walked before his gelding, carefully picking out the occasional impressions from the bandits' mounts. It took two days to cover as many miles. Then the trail opened into a basin that held a dry pond bed, where a dozen clear prints had been pressed into the damp earth, some with the same smith's stamp he'd seen outside Eckland and one that contained an impression of the familiar bent nail.

Ultimately, the trail disappeared into a rocky, vine-covered hillside, a mere two hours' ride from where Zen and Jasmine had forced Rancid to give up his previous search for the Black Hand hideout.

Rancid observed the area from mid-afternoon until well past dark. If there had been bandit sentries about, he'd have spotted them. Nevertheless, he waited until the moon was nearly full to approach. He moved through the trees until nothing stood between him and the vine-covered opening but a short stretch of narrow, rocky trail.

As he crept along the path, a dozen feet from the cave mouth, his foot slipped on the loose shale and a rain of pebbles clattered down the slope.

Rancid froze, his eyes locked on the vines before him.

A moment passed, and then the branches moved. *Baron's blood.* Rancid tossed a rock over the opening, into the bushes on the far side.

The vines shifted again.

Rancid slipped his dagger from its sheath and plunged through the barrier. His shoulder plowed into the chest of a man. He whipped his knife toward the sentry's throat, but the man twisted and Rancid's own momentum carried him past the bandit to land in a heap on the cave floor.

Like a cat, Rancid rolled to his feet and faced his enemy. Having lost his dagger somewhere in the darkness, he drew his sword.

The sentry did the same, the soft ring of the blade against its sheath unmistakable in the darkness. As he advanced, the bandit produced an object from his belt—a horn, by the shape of its silhouette against the screen of vine-filtered moonlight.

Rancid swatted it away before it reached the bandit's mouth. The man's sword came up in defense, but Rancid captured the blade in a circular motion that locked their pommels. Shoulder first, he slammed the man into the wall.

The scant illumination in the cave's entrance lit only the side of the bandit's face. His fetid breath blew warm against Rancid's scarred cheek. The tunnel beyond remained quiet and still. Slowly Rancid began to smile. In that moment, the sentry swept Rancid's feet from beneath him and sprinted down the tunnel.

Rancid caught a glint of moonlight off his lost dagger as he clambered to his feet. He swept up the knife and rushed to follow.

A torch flickered in an alcove just around the first bend. Rancid sprinted past, relieved to find the niche vacant. As he rounded a second bend, his quarry came back into sight. The bandit had paused at the end of the tunnel to pull open a massive, iron-bound door.

Rancid launched the dagger, which sank into the sentry's back with a sick thump. No sound escaped the man's throat as he dropped to the floor.

Lamplight and voices filtered though the slim opening from the chamber beyond. As Rancid crept forward, a deep, guttural voice rumbled from somewhere inside. "...Chosen of Trondor."

Tempted now beyond prudence, Rancid eased the door open a few more inches and peered through the crack between the hinges. An orc and two Black Hand bandits came into view.

"All the way up in Trondor? What do you expect me to do?" The bald man Rancid had come to believe was the Black Hand leader spoke with deference to an ogre. How the bandits had smuggled such a beast into Palidor, Rancid couldn't imagine. Yet here it was, easily twelve feet tall, with an actual medallion of Vexetan, exactly as Nick's notes had described it, hanging on a chain around its thick neck.

By the blood of the baron. The Prophecy was true.

CHAPTER 37

"Request denied," said the bookish man, the chair of what was left of the Ruling Council. "We told you that the other day."

"No," Nick said. "You told us we had to wait until the king returns. I came back because I've heard rumors that Gremauld is no longer the king."

"He's not. Request denied. Next."

The guards stepped forward to escort Nick from the council chamber.

"On what grounds do you deny my request?"

"We need no grounds. Guards."

Two men grabbed Nick's arms and pulled him toward the door.

"You didn't even vote," Nick yelled back. Then to the others, "What purpose do the rest of you serve here?"

"Wait," said an old man to Nick's left. "He's right, Nordock. We should vote."

The guards stopped.

"Then we need to hear him," said another man, resigned. "We cannot vote in good faith until we know his purpose."

Nordock huffed. "Very well."

Nick straightened his tunic and returned to the center of the chamber, where a small circle on the floor marked the proper place from which to address the council. There, he delivered his rehearsed lines. "I myself am merely a sword, hired by the monastic Order of the Sage. My charge is a scholar and monk of that order. She is studying the economic and trade history of the two most lucrative kingdoms in the Civilized Lands: Palidor and Trondor. The resulting thesis on the strengths and weaknesses of the two contrasting economies will benefit all the civilized kingdoms. Including Trondor."

"We're to believe this?" Nordock asked his colleagues.

"We have come from Palidor just two weeks ago on the *Gale's Darling* into North Reach." No merchant would sail into Trondor, for fear of having both their ship and cargo confiscated by one side of the conflict or the other.

"Then you have documents to support your research," the old man stated, rather than asked.

"We do, sir, but the notes are not mine. I do not have them with me."

"Very convenient," Nordock said.

"I need only return to the Hostler House and fetch them from the monk. I'll bring them before you tomorrow."

Nick and Jasmine spent that night fabricating an economic journal in Jasmine's own hand. Nick dictated the content from what he'd learned from his uncle Harimon and his own experiences within the slave-driven, bandit-infested economy of Palidor. By morning, they had filled a journal with notes that the council barely glanced at before granting access to the library.

"On one condition," the old man said. "Before you leave the capital, you will allow our scholars to transcribe your notes, and have the monk sign a writ to contribute a copy of her final thesis to the library."

Nick bowed. "The Order of the Sage is grateful for your generosity and hospitality." He wasted no time before gathering his companions, just in case Nordock suddenly changed his mind.

When they entered the royal library, twin hearths blazing by the door infused them all with warmth. Rows of shelves, eight on either side of the room, consumed half of the ground floor. Between them stood two rows of tables. A man of maybe twenty harvests studied under the light of a hundred oil lamps burning in a dozen chandeliers above. A plush gold and red rug muffled their footsteps. The second floor, open in the middle where the chandeliers hung, held a matching set of bookshelves.

They had no librarian to help them this time, so Nick shrugged at his friends, selected a shelf, and began reading titles. The others fanned out to cover the rest of the room. Vinra and Dara went upstairs. No one spoke. None needed to. They all knew what they were after.

At first Nick tried to discern a pattern among the collection, some hint as to how the books were arranged—by title, subject, author, age—but there seemed to be no organization at all. Zen searched the sister shelves across the room. The mage's mouth moved and his hands traced intricate patterns in the air. Of course. The Codex would be enchanted. No need for Zen to read the titles. But he couldn't search the entire library that way. So Nick turned back to his own shelf and began scanning the spines for really, really old books.

As he worked his way from shelf to shelf, Nick realized that there were quite a number of people there. He counted a dozen, besides himself and his friends, hidden away at tables tucked into the corners of the library. Three men sat together near a stack of backpacks and supplies, including weapons. Nick craned his neck to see what the men were reading, just on the off chance... But he backed away when one of them noticed his scrutiny.

He moved then to the next shelf and started the search anew. By mid-morning, he began to fear the book might not be there. What then? What if the Chosen had beaten them to it after all? Just as doubt began to supplant hope, Dara charged, with a rumbling of footsteps, down the staircase from the balcony, her face flushed with excitement and a sizable leather tome clutched in her hands. "Guys! Guys!" she whispered harshly.

"Shhhhhh," hissed a nearby scholar.

Because the secluded corners of the library were all occupied, Nick motioned her to a table in the center of the room, as far from watchful eyes and vigilant ears as he could find, and all his friends gathered around him. Dara set the tome down and backed two steps away, as though she feared its opening.

Nick stared for long seconds at the book's worn, hide-bound cover, adorned with dark steel edging at its corners and down the length of its binding. There was no title on the outside—no writing at all, in fact. Chills ran up Nick's spine and set the hairs of his arms on end. The atmosphere crackled with anticipation.

Unable to quiet his heart, Nick reached for the book.

"Wait." Zen began a chant that only added to the charge Nick already sensed in the room around them.

"What makes you think this is it?" Vinra asked Dara.

"I don't know. It just feels—" Her whole body twitched as though shaking off the creepies.

The scholar who had been studying at one of the nearby tables glared at them for a long moment, then gathered his materials and moved elsewhere.

"We should keep our voices down," Jasmine said.

"And set up a perimeter." Vinra motioned for Beltrann and Dara to move a couple of tables down in either direction.

"Well?" Nick said when Zen's focus returned from the weave.

"It's enchanted with some divine magic. It doesn't appear to have any protection born of the weave." His face scrunched into a frown. "Though I sense an aspect of deception."

"To keep it from being copied," Nick guessed.

"Maybe." Zen looked doubtful.

"Is it safe to open?" Vinra asked.

"Be my guest."

Zen hadn't exactly answered Vinra's question, but Nick reached for the book anyway. He hadn't come all this way for nothing and Zen would stop him if he thought there was any danger. Still, his hands froze inches from the book, his fingers trembling. He had to take a deep breath and muster his courage even to touch it. If this was the original Codex of Mortaan, and if it said there was no hope, did he really want to know?

"Go on," Zen whispered.

Nick touched the cover and his sweat moistened the aged leather. The binding creaked in protest as he pulled it open to reveal the first page. "From my mind's eye..." it said. Scrawled nearly illegibly across the bottom were the words, "Ageus Mortaan." Nick turned past the introduction to the first prophecy. The handwriting matched the signature on the previous page.

Jasmine set her copy of the Codex onto the table and opened it to the same page.

The spacing between the words—very erratic in the original, with many of the lines incompletely filled and broad gaps between others—contrasted with the text in Jasmine's copy and told Nick the original was indeed authentic. But what about the content? Nick began to compare.

After half a page, it became clear that the content was the same in both books, yet different. That is to say, the subject matter was similar enough to convince Nick that they foretold the same Prophecy, but in the copied translation, the scribe had embellished the text to such an extent that several wholly-new interpretations might be adopted. Was that the nature of the enchantment—that it caused the scribe to ramble onto the page in the midst of the translation? A sudden, new hope filled him. What inaccurate interpretation might have been derived from the ramblings added to Mortaan's last prophecy?

The ancient pages crackled as he fanned through them to the section of interest. Halfway there, the crackling stopped. A sudden and complete silence flooded the library. Nick glanced at Zen, assuming his friend was playing with the weave. But the ice mage just stared, his eyes wide and horror-struck, across the room.

Nick followed his gaze to see Vinra carefully place a black mask over three-quarters of his deceitful face. The shroud of the ceremonial sword the priest had carried throughout their journey lay in a discarded heap on the floor. Before him, Beltrann stared sightlessly at the chandelier, his arms and jaw slack.

Vinra gripped the sword in one hand, slid it smoothly from Beltrann's back, and let the big man topple, lifeless, onto the table.

CHAPTER 38

Vinra's face disappeared behind the smooth black mask, the hallmark of notorious assassin Vinsous Drakemoor. But for Zen, the shock of Beltrann's murder paled beside that caused by the medallion hanging around Vinra's neck. Here was the Chosen of whom Gwyndarren had spoken, the man Zen had vowed not to oppose.

Vinra, the priest of the wayfarer who'd become somehow lost in the elven wilderness, the friend who'd traveled with the party since Lorentil and had spent the last five months studying the strengths and weaknesses of his adversaries, the assassin who'd severed Zen's verbal connection to the weave with the simple act of drawing his sword...

Zen stopped his mind's accounting of Vinra's betrayals. This treachery ran deeper than any of those. Much deeper. Vinra had not only neutralized Zen's magic, he'd neutralized Zen himself. Gwyndarren had assured Drakemoor that Zen wouldn't interfere. Why else would Vinra display the medallion so brazenly after concealing it for so long?

And the silence of the sword's enchantment—for Zen recognized its source as soon as Drakemoor had drawn the weapon—guaranteed that no one beyond the library would hear the battle and come to their aid.

The weight of the crystal headband felt suddenly heavy on Zen's forehead. The decision he had feared was at last upon him. Who now to betray? Yet he could do nothing, one way or the other, in this damned silence. He began to back away. The enchantment must be limited to the region around the sword. If he could escape its influence, he could...

Do what? Gwyndarren was obviously a man of resources, not a man to take lightly. And he had his uses. Zen and his friends would never have escaped Gremauld's tent without the fairy mist Gwyndarren had given him. But if Gwyndarren's warning proved true—that the enemy was too great—to betray Nick would be to let him die at the hands of Drakemoor.

Zen rapped the end of his staff on the hardwood floor as he moved. When the sound of its knock reached his ears, he'd be free to make his choice.

Time froze as Drakemoor met Zen's gaze with a slight, knowing smile on his face. Then, in a black flash of motion, Drakemoor lunged at Nick.

The sound of the staff—a sudden thunder—brought Zen back to the moment. His hand ached, he'd been gripping the staff so tightly. With the utterance of a single word, he could bring its frigid power to bear on Drakemoor. But in the chaos, he'd also engulf his friends in its deadly power.

Though Zen was no connoisseur of sword play, he'd never seen a blade as swift as Drakemoor's. But Nick was good, too. And Dara. And Jasmine. Could the assassin beat them all? If not, and if Zen chose to stay out of the fight, how would he explain his quiescence?

Then he remembered the moonglyph and the spent scroll he'd used to contact Gwyndarren in Palidor. Before he even realized it, he'd made his decision.

Nick barely had time to draw his sword. The sheer weight of the weapon pulled at the tissues of the weeks-old wound in his chest. Still, his blade deflected the strike.

Vinra parried once and swung again, with much greater swiftness and skill than he'd ever let on and a hand quicker than Nick's heavy sword could hope to match. His blade came at Nick's chest, an assault of raw strength with a complete lack of finesse. The sheer brutality of it caught Nick off guard. He couldn't block in time. The blade struck his breastplate and the force of the blow knocked him back.

The utter silence gave the bout an unreal quality as disorienting as Vinra's betrayal itself. Nick collapsed against a bookshelf, sword dangling from his hand, and scrambled away. By then, Vinra had moved on.

Jasmine ran for her backpack and stuffed the Codex and its copy inside, for Vinra must be after the original.

Zen stood on the periphery of the library's main floor with a scroll in his hand, but something didn't seem right with the mage. Zen wasn't moving, and his skin showed the same pale coloring as Gremauld's had when the late king was under the enchantment of the moonglyph.

Vinra engaged Dara in a silent dance of swordsmanship, lightning sparking in jagged tendrils up the length of Dara's blade. For a moment, she seemed to hold her ground, and then Vinra began to tax her defenses.

Nick struggled past the pain. As he climbed to his feet, an odd weight pulled at him. His breastplate dangled awkwardly from a single unbroken clasp, hampering his movements.

With one glance at the combatants, Nick dropped his sword and began to work the final buckle free.

Dara's flickering sword darted past Vinra's blade and stung his arm. Lightning lanced into him, but he seemed to ignore it. He grasped an armhole in Dara's armor and threw the slight elf from her feet. She slammed against a heavy table and rebounded. Her own leather breastplate dangled impotently from her body.

The coincidence was too great. Vinra couldn't have had the strength to rip even leather armor from the wearer's body with his bare hands. Before Nick tossed his breastplate away, he took the time to examine one of the broken buckles. The back of it had been filed nearly to the point of failure.

With a curse, Nick dropped his damaged gear and rushed to save Dara. He screamed a cry of rage and warning to distract Vinra from the lithe, unprotected elf, but no sound emerged. Vinra must have come into their rooms during the night. The assassin—no other word could describe him—had played them all for fools.

Raw anger overcame Nick as he charged forward, too late to stop Vinra's sword. How could he have been so stupid?

In that instant, Jasmine intervened, with a *sai* in each hand. Vinra batted the blades away with his own and thrust at Jasmine's heart.

But the monk was quick. The sword made but a shallow cut across the front of her shoulder as she spun away. She dropped to the floor and swept her heel at Vinra's feet.

The assassin leapt onto the sturdy table behind him, at once evading Jasmine's sweep and taking command of the high ground.

He turned then to parry Nick's swing. The fury Nick had built up behind the blow should have knocked Vinra from his feet, but the angle of the assassin's parry did little to impede Nick's momentum and his own weight carried him past. For a moment, Nick's back lay exposed.

Fortunately, Jasmine drew Vinra's attention. She faced him alone now and fought a purely defensive battle, using her *sais* to keep Vinra's sword at bay.

Dara backed away from the melee, her sword sheathed as she struggled to free herself from her tangled armor.

When she did, she tossed it into the stacks with a silent, disgusted oath and thrust her hand into a pouch at her belt. It came out empty. Frantically, she dug into the pouch again, searching for something that was no longer there. Finally, she drew her sword and charged back into the fight.

Nick drew a settling breath and put his rage on a tether. He wouldn't underestimate Vinra again. Stepping up to the table, he tightened his grip on his two-handed pommel and dealt himself back into the game.

Vinra's sword darted out of nowhere, a mere flash in the lamplight. Nick shifted desperately to block. He knocked the sword up, but not away. It pierced his shoulder and was gone, withdrawn to strike elsewhere.

Dara joined them. Three on one, now. Nick's swings were slowed by both old wounds and new, but his arms were still strong. He swung again and again. Vinra deflected strike after strike. They'd forced the assassin into a defensive posture, yet he managed to lash out every now and again.

Jasmine slipped a *sai* past Vinra's guard and plunged the point into the man's calf. He brushed it away and continued, seemingly unhindered by the wound.

Then Dara's sword dipped a little too far. Vinra drove his blade through the opening and deep into her chest. Her eyes snapped open and her whole body stiffened. The assassin twisted the sword as he wrenched it away and returned his attention to the others.

Jasmine's leg swung across the battlefield, inches above the table's surface, and swept Vinra's feet aside. His blade flew wide as he lost his balance and began to fall.

Nick hoisted his sword for a downward stroke that should have cut the man in half, but Vinra hit the table an instant before Nick's blade and twisted to move from its path.

He rolled to his feet.

The table splintered from the force of Nick's stroke and the two halves crashed to the floor.

Nick shoved the heavy obstacle away and pressed his advantage. Only then did he notice the profusion of blood on the floor and the deep rent his sword had bitten into Vinra's side. Tissues dangled from the wound.

The assassin staggered but continued to fight, his movements slowed. With one hand, he extracted an elixir from a pouch at his waist.

"Not this time," Nick mouthed as he lashed out at the vial. The blow shattered it in Vinra's hand and severed two of the assassin's fingers. Nick swung, a high, forceful strike.

Vinra's block lacked his former strength.

Nick shoved the blade aside and swung again.

The assassin reeled back against a table behind him.

Nick's next stroke sank into Vinra's shoulder and forced a display of pain into his face, the first Nick had seen since the battle began. His next swing knocked Vinra's sword from his hand and carved a path through his torso from his neck to his heart.

Blood splattered Nick's face.

Finally, his strength and anger spent, Nick released his sword and let it fall to the floor beside Vinra's tattered body.

CHAPTER 39

Z en cried out when the bloody blade emerged from Dara's back. He stepped forward, ready to drop the disguise he'd woven about himself, the layer of frost he'd coated his skin with to simulate the appearance of the moonglyph... but just then, the tide of the battle shifted in Nick's favor.

Nothing Zen could do now would help Dara anyway. If his lack of action had contributed to her death, the damage was already done. In the meantime, blood poured from Vinra's side and Nick's victory seemed all but certain. Zen would accomplish nothing by joining the fray now. Such an act would serve only to betray Gwyndarren and to provoke Nick's suspicion.

He stepped back, shored up the threads of the weave, and resumed his stricken posture. Better to let the disguise drop in concert with Vinra's death, when it could be sufficiently explained.

Finding no elixir in the pouches on Vinra's belt, Nick ran to the assassin's backpack and upended it onto the floor. Six vials tumbled silently out, four of them empty, along with the leftover hypnosis scroll Dara had been carrying since Gremauld's assassination, the scroll she'd apparently expected to find in her pouch during the battle.

He grabbed one of the vials, cursed Vinra again, and rushed to Dara's side. But it was too late. The girl's body lay peaceful in death, her punctured heart no longer beating. Not even Vinra's bottled magic could save her now.

Jasmine looked up from Beltrann's body and shook her head. Moistness filled Nick's eyes and his shoulders slumped.

Zen strode past with Vinra's sword in his hand, scattering the discarded vials with his feet. He retrieved Vinra's scabbard and sheathed the "ceremonial" weapon. A soft clatter broke the silence when he dropped it to the floor.

The reality of what had happened poured into Nick with the sound. He placed his hand on a table to hold himself upright. So much blood. So many bodies, all friends and confidants. He held the vial up and inspected its contents. "Some healer." In disgust, he let the bottle fall.

"His elixirs saved your life more than once," Jasmine said.

Nick flashed her a vile look. Who in the Abyss was she to defend Vinra? But the look she returned was neither contemptuous nor judgmental. She stated fact, nothing more.

"None of his magic was his own," Zen said. He presented the priest's dagger, an ornate piece with a night-black opal terminating the handle. "Did you notice that he always used this as the focal point of his darkness? I didn't. But now that I'm looking for it, its enchantment is obvious." He tucked the dagger into his belt and collected the roll of parchment from the clutter around Vinra's backpack. "Missing something?"

"He swiped Dara's scroll," Nick said. "Orc's blood. I'd kill the man if I hadn't already."

A few of the scholars emerged from hiding now that the fighting was over.

"Somebody should notify the council." Jasmine opened the door and spoke quietly with one of the sentries posted beyond.

The guard looked past her shoulder. His eyes widened when he saw the carnage. "Stay here," he told them, and then ran off down the hallway.

"What are we going to do about the Prophecy?" Jasmine asked when she returned.

"We're going to stop it." The intensity of Nick's conviction surprised even him. But after the deaths of his friends, he simply couldn't quit.

"Suppose there is no way to stop it?"

Zen looked back and forth between Nick and Jasmine as though waiting to see which way the coin would fall.

Nick's eyes went cold. "I don't believe that. I can't. Let me see the Codex."

After Jasmine handed it to him, he flipped through it to Mortaan's last prophecy and studied the lines. Mum had said the spacing would be inconsistent in the original, but the spacing here was clean and neat. He opened Jasmine's copy to the same page. The text matched exactly.

Zen folded several pages back to compare the text with one of the unevenly spaced prophecies. "It's Mortaan's own handwriting."

"But there's another version," Nick insisted. "One in which the Master is defeated. It's *that* version that's kept me going for the past four months."

"You had hoped it was based on the original," Jasmine said, with no question in her tone.

Nick scrubbed his brow with the heel of his palm. "Yes."

Zen put a hand on his shoulder. "That's just a fabler's legend. I'm sorry."

Nick brushed his hand away. "I don't care. I can't stomach the thought of the Master winning. I have to try to stop him." He slammed both books shut and thrust them at Jasmine. "I don't care what the Codex says. I choose to believe the legend."

The doors flew open and Trondorian soldiers flooded in from both ends of the library. Swordsmen arrayed themselves between Nick's company and the exits. Royal archers lined the railing on the upper level.

Nick startled at the sudden clamor, and then began scanning for Dalen among the men.

No one spoke.

When the soldiers parted, Balor Culhaven marched into the library, flanked by Dalen Frost and Pandalo Gundahar. All three wore medallions of Vexetan.

"That's them, all right." Dalen turned to the councilmen behind them. "They murdered the king."

The story continues in:

ASSASSINS' PREY
Age of Prophecy: Book II

ABOUT THE AUTHOR

Kirt Hickman was born in 1966 in Albuquerque, New Mexico. He earned a Bachelor's degree in electrical engineering in 1989 and a Master's degree in opto-electronics in 1991, both from the University of New Mexico. He began writing fiction in 2003. Kirt has also published the sci-fi thriller novels *Worlds Asunder* and *Venus Rain*, the writers' how-to *Revising Fiction: Making Sense of the Madness*, and the children's book *I Will Eat Anything*. Visit his website at www.kirthickman.com.

9 780979 633065